DEX HAVEN

KINGDOMS OF ELDORIA BOOK 2

Starlight
&
Luna Rising

Fated mates. Found family. And a
destiny they never saw coming.

For my one True Fated Mate-
I'm so lucky you found me,
and that your wolf blood
keeps me warm at night.

"The question isn't who is going to let me; it's who is going to stop me."
-Ayn Rand

Previously in Claiming Starlight
Kingdoms of Eldoria Book 1:

Olivia had gone back to Drakemoor Mountain to attempt to awaken the Dragonia after her first attempt ended with her being abducted by Eldric and taken to Magda in the Underworld.:

The next day, we made for the Drakemoore Mountain pass. I dressed in soft leather pants and a warm long knitted top and scarf. I wore tall boots and leather gloves. I remembered how cold it was the last time I made this trek.

A mixture of excitement and trepidation churned in my chest. The last time I'd been here, things had gone horribly wrong. But now, with Cade's steady presence beside me and our allies close behind, I felt a surge of confidence that I hadn't known I possessed.

The air grew cooler as we ascended, each breath carrying the crisp, bracing scent of pine and frost. The subtle change in the energy around us prickled along my skin, like a faint electric charge building in the atmosphere. It was as if the very mountains were alive, pulsing with an ancient power that called to something deep within me—a resonance I could feel in my bones.

"We're getting close," Cade murmured, his hand squeezing mine in reassurance. The warmth of his touch grounded me amidst the swirl of emotions. "Can you feel it?"

I nodded, my breath catching in my throat. "It's... overwhelming. Like a thousand voices whispering just out of earshot."

We rounded a bend in the path, and suddenly, the vista opened before us. I hadn't gotten to see this the last time. A vast plateau stretched out, surrounded by jagged peaks that seemed to pierce the sky. In the center of the plateau stood an enormous archway, its surface carved with intricate symbols and runes that glowed with a faint, ethereal light casting wavering patterns across the ground.

As we approached, the whispers in my mind grew louder, more insistent, each one like a ghostly breath against the shell of my ear. I could almost make out words now—a chorus of ancient voices calling out to me, urging me forward.

"This is it," I breathed, my heart pounding in my chest. "The entrance to Wyldhaven."

Cade nodded, his eyes scanning the area for any potential threats. "Remember what we discussed. Trust your instincts, Olivia. You were born for this."

Swallowing my nerves, I took a deep breath and stepped forward. The archway loomed before me, imposing and majestic, yet strangely welcoming. When I placed my hand on the cool, smooth stone, a shiver ran up my arm. The runes flared to life beneath my fingertips, pulsing with an intense blue light that seemed to seep into my very veins, igniting every nerve with a tingling energy.

The whispers in my mind swelled into a chorus of voices, a roar that threatened to overwhelm me. And then, in a single breath, everything fell silent.

I closed my eyes and reached out with my mind and magic as I'd been taught. In an instant, I felt myself transported—not physically, but in spirit—to another place.

Wyldhaven stretched out before me, an endless realm of mist and shadow, its landscape both beautiful and haunting. Massive forms shifted in the fog—dragons with scales that shimmered like jewels, wyverns with wings that seemed to span the sky, and creatures of myth and legend whose names had been lost to time. Their presence exuded a raw, primal power that sent a thrill of both fear and awe through me.

And then, I heard it—a voice like rolling thunder, yet as gentle as a whisper.

"Hello, Little StarHeart, we've been waiting for you.

CONTENTS

CHAPTER 1

Olivia

The wind whipped through my hair as I crested the summit of the Drakemoore Mountain pass, my heart pounding with anticipation. I gasped, taking in the sight before me— eight majestic creatures awaiting my arrival, their scales and feathers gleaming in the sunlight.

"We've been waiting for you, little StarHeart. I am Vaelith," a deep, resonant voice echoed in my mind. My gaze locked with the largest dragon, his silver scales shimmering like starlight catching the light in waves. *"They call me the ancient one."* He lumbered toward me on four massive legs.

"I'm... happy to meet you," I managed, my Texas drawl slipping out despite my best efforts. Dang it. I cleared my throat, trying to gather my composure. "Y'all are even more magnificent than I imagined. Is it alright if I talk to y'all out loud?"

A dark-scaled wyvern with a molten gold underbelly approached with a mischievous glint in his eye. *"Ain't you just the sweetest thing,"* he drawled, mimicking my accent. *"Don't you worry 'bout impressing us, darlin'. I'm Zarvyn, we're here for you. And yes, honey, we can hear you either way."* He stood tall on his two legs, his long tail swinging as he spoke.

Warmth crept into my cheeks, but I couldn't help smiling. His playful manner put me at ease even as I marveled at the

1

others. I was introduced to Eryndor, the emerald dragon, who regarded me with intelligent eyes that seemed to peer into my very soul. Beside him stood a wyvern, his obsidian scales gleaming dangerously, wings spread wide, his venomous tail twitching as if he was raring to go.

"Don't mind Skorn," a soothing female voice whispered in my mind. I turned, *"I'm Nyxara,"* her midnight blue scales almost iridescent in the light, amber eyes glowing with warmth. She seemed like the voice of calm for the wyvern. *"He's always itching for a fight."*

"Damn straight," growled Skorn, but there was a hint of affection in his tone. *"It's been too long since I gave a good beat down to a deserving son of a shadow beast."*

Movement on my left caught my attention. A charcoal gray wyvern with vibrant scarlet accents sauntered closer, head cocked to the side. *"I'm Drathom. And you must be our great savior, eh?"* he said, circling me with a critical eye. *"Bit scrawny, if you ask me."*

I bristled, my dander rising. "I may not look like much, but I've wrestled steers and stood up to bulls bigger than me, and that was before I had any idea about magic, or prophecies, or dragons! There's more fight in me than you'd think, buddy."

Drathom's eyes widened in surprise, then he threw back his head and gave what I assumed was a wyvern laugh. *"Oh, I like her,"* he chortled. *"She's got spirit."*

Giggling, I turned, still taking in the entire scene before me; the landscape was beautiful, my senses overwhelmed. Hills and mountains covered in lush greenery and flowers, the likes of which I'd never seen, dotted the plateaus. I was convinced this was a wonderland.

As the dragons bantered, my attention was drawn to two breathtaking creatures standing slightly apart—Pegasi. One stallion, a vision of pure white, his mane faintly aglow. Beside him stood a mare, her silver-gray coat shimmering, lavender eyes regarding me with gentle curiosity.

"Come closer, child," the mare nickered softly. *"I'm Thyra. Let me get a good look at you."*

I approached, marveled at their beauty. As I drew near, the stallion snorted and tossed his mane, sending sparks of light dancing through the air.

"Easy, my love," Thyra soothed. Turning back to me, her gaze was motherly. *"You've been through so much, haven't you? But you're safe now. We're here to help, Ariaxom and I."*

Tears pricked my eyes at her kindness. I reached out tentatively, and Thyra pressed her velvety muzzle into my palm. The simple gesture of acceptance nearly undid me.

"I don't understand," I whispered, looking around at the assembled Dragonia. "Why me? I'm nobody special."

Vaelith's voice rumbled through my mind once more. *"You are far more than you know, young one. The power that lies within you will shape the fate of Eldoria."*

I swallowed hard, fear and excitement warring within me. "I'll try with everything that is within me. What if I fail?"

"Then we fail together," the beautiful emerald green dragon, Eryndor, spoke with a deep yet gentle voice. *"But we will not let that happen. You are not alone in this fight, Olivia."*

As I looked at each of them—dragon, wyvern, and Pegasi alike—I felt a surge of belonging I'd never experienced before. For the first time in my life, I wasn't an outcast. I was part of something greater.

"Alright then," I said, squaring my shoulders and lifting my chin. "Where do we start?"

The dark-scaled dragon with his molten gold underbelly unfurled his wings and stepped forward. His voice was deep and rich, like warm honey. *"We start by standing united against the darkness that threatens our realm. Magda's creatures may be fierce, but they are no match for the combined might of the Dragonia and the chosen of Vesperia."*

My spine tingled with a shiver at the mere mention of Magda. Her reputation as the Goddess of the Underworld was well known, and I had felt the sting of her wrath firsthand. The prospect of confronting her minions sent a wave of fear through me. Yet, gazing into the determined eyes of these magnificent creatures, I felt a surge of courage beginning to swell within me.

"We've waited centuries for this moment," Nyxara added, her amber eyes glowing with an inner fire. *"To fight alongside the one who will bring balance back to Eldoria. Our loyalty to Goddess Vesperia has never wavered, and now we can finally prove our worth."*

I swallowed hard, overwhelmed by their faith in me. "I... I don't know what to say. Y'all are puttin' a lot of stock in someone who was doctorin' cows just a few weeks ago."

Skorn's obsidian-scales glistened in the sunlight as he let out a rumbling chuckle. *"Your humility speaks to your character, Olivia. But do not underestimate yourself. The Goddess chose you for a reason."*

I nodded, trying to push down the doubt that threatened to surface. "Well, I reckon we've got our work cut out for us. I can't tell you how much it means to have y'all on our side. I've been as nervous as a long-tailed cat in a room full of rockin' chairs until now."

Drathom tilted his wyvern head, his charcoal gray scales shimmering with hints of scarlet. *"I'm not familiar with that expression, but I sense it means you were feeling overwhelmed."*

I couldn't help but laugh then. "That's puttin' it mildly. But knowing we've got dragons, wyverns, and Pegasi on our side... well, that changes things considerably. And as far as not bein' familiar with the expression, y'all just joined Cade's club. He doesn't know what I'm talkin' about half the time, either. Oh, geez! How rude of me. Cade! Honey, come over here."

Cade, who had been watching from a short distance, taking it all in, approached. He had sent Kaelen and Amaya back to Vesparra, knowing we'd be here for a while. At my summons, he strode over and put his arm around my waist.

A smile the size of Texas split my face. "Honey, let me introduce you to the Dragonia of Eldoria. Y'all, this is King Cadence of Vesparra."

"We are honored to stand with you," Vaelith intoned solemnly. *"Our strength is yours to command in the battles to come."*

As I looked at each of them, my heart swelled with gratitude and determination. Turning to Cade, my voice filled with pride, "They said they are honored to stand with us."

Cade nodded to the group before him, "Thank you. I promise I'll do everything in my power to be worthy of your trust in this battle to save Eldoria from Magda's evil."

I grinned, marveled at this new connection. "This is incredible! It's like... like we're all part of one big family."

"That's precisely what we are." Eryndor's emerald scales glinted as he dipped his head. *"Bound by purpose and the Goddess's will."*

As we continued to share thoughts and feelings, and I interpreted for Cade, I felt a sense of unity wash over me. It was as if the jagged pieces of my past were being smoothed over and filled in by the strength and warmth of these magnificent creatures.

"Olivia," Vaelith's ancient voice cut through my reverie. *"One more thing, the Goddess has prepared for our arrival."*

Curious about what he meant, I raised an eyebrow. "Oh?"

Drathom stepped forward, his scarlet accents catching the light. *"Deep in the mountains behind Vesparra's castle, there are caves. They will serve as our home during this conflict."*

"The caves are vast," Skorn added, his obsidian scales gleaming, his wyvern tail swishing behind him. *"More than enough room for all of us, and close to both the temple and the castle."*

"That's amazing! I've seen the mountains but never thought about there being caves large enough to house creatures as large as y'all. Thank the Goddess she's one step ahead of us."

"*Indeed,*" Vaelith rumbled. "*Her foresight is unparalleled. It will allow us to respond swiftly when danger threatens.*"

As I stood there, surrounded by these majestic beings, I felt a surge of hope. Maybe, just maybe, we had a fighting chance against whatever Magda was about to throw our way. A wave of relief washed over me, settling deep in my bones. Knowing I could reach the Dragonia with just a thought made me feel safer than I had in years. It was like having an invisible tether connect us, ready to snap taut at a moment's notice.

"Y'all have no idea how much this means to me," my voice thick with emotion. "To have you so close, I can call on you in an instant... it's more than I ever hoped for."

Zarvyn's molten gold underbelly shimmered as he lowered his giant dragon head to my level. "*We are honored to stand with you, Olivia. Our bond will be our strength in the battles to come.*"

I reached out, placing my hand on his dark scales. The warmth that radiated from him was comforting, grounding. "I'm gonna do my best to be worthy of it all."

A gentle nudge against my back startled me, and I turned to find myself face-to-face with Ariaxom, the gorgeous white stallion.

"I don't know how much y'all know about me, but in the mortal realm, I was very much a horse woman. I doctored them, rode them, and loved them very much. It's wonderful to have beings so familiar on my side here. Please tell me the role y'all will play in this war we've got laid on our doorstep."

Ariaxom tossed his head, his voice proud and strong in my thoughts. "*We are the swiftest of the Dragonia. While our scaled brethren command the skies, we will be your eyes and ears on the ground and in the air. No enemy will escape our notice. And we bring our own special powers as well.*"

"*We will also be near to you when we arrive in Vesparra.*" Thyra added, her tone softening, "*We have special stables by the castle, so we'll be close at hand whenever you need us, day or night."*

I ran my hand along Thyra's silk smooth mane. "I can't believe all this is happening," I murmured. "It's like something out of a fairy tale."

Thyra nickered softly, nuzzling my cheek. *"This is no tale, Olivia. This is your destiny, and we are honored to be a part of it."*

As I stood there, surrounded by these magical beings, I felt the flicker of hope in my chest grow to a flame. Not just that, with every passing moment, my feeling of family continued to grow.

We decided we had tarried in the Drakemoore Mountains long enough. It was time to start this adventure in earnest.

Cade and I shadow misted our way back to Vesparra. We let everyone know we'd returned and were met with questions over our meal. Apparently, the Dragonia had done a bit of hunting for food on their journey. I wasn't entirely sure how that worked; I'd have to explore that later. But they were all ready to get started on some battle training upon their noisy arrival. The landing of several enormous beasts raised quite a ruckus.

The first order of business was to introduce our battle leaders to the Dragonia. Even though they couldn't communicate directly with each other, they would fight alongside one another. A sizeable crowd had gathered, standing in awe at the beautiful creatures before them. I stood at the feet of our new friends, dwarfed by their sheer size.

"YOU GOT THIS COUSIN!" I could always count on Miranda's encouragement. Her very loud and obnoxious, but wonderful encouragement.

The surrounding air crackled with energy, and I could feel the excitement radiating from the Dragonia and assembled warriors. Vaelith lowered his massive head to meet my gaze.

"We have waited eons for this moment, Olivia," he rumbled, his voice like thunder in my mind. *"To fight alongside the chosen of Vesperia, to defend Eldoria against the darkness... it is our*

greatest honor."

I swallowed hard, trying to find words that could match the gravity of the moment. "The honor is mine, Vaelith. I'll do my best not to let y'all down."

Zarvyn, the dark-scaled wyvern, snorted, sending a puff of smoke curling around his nostrils. *"You sell yourself short, little one. We can sense the power within you, waiting to be unleashed."*

"He's right," Eryndor chimed in, his emerald scales shimmering. *"But power alone won't be enough. We must prepare and train together."* The dragon moved with grace despite his size.

I nodded, my mind racing. "Alright, then. What do we need to do?"

Skorn, the obsidian wyvern, flicked his venomous tail. *"First, you must learn to ride. A dragon and its rider must move as one."*

"And don't forget us," Ariaxom whinnied. *"We Pegasi may not breathe fire, but our speed and agility can turn the tide of battle."*

I took a deep breath, trying to quell the butterflies in my stomach. "Okay, riding dragons and Pegasi. That's... that's a lot. What else?"

Nyxara's amber eyes glowed in the fading light. *"You must become comfortable fighting alongside us wyverns. Our venom and our strength will be crucial in close combat."*

"Yes, everyone will be in battle with y'all. Moving around you will be paramount. Avoiding accidental injuries must be a concern."

As we spoke, laying out plans and strategies, I felt a bit overwhelmed. This was so far beyond anything I'd ever imagined. Part of me longed for the simplicity of my old life, for the familiar smell of hay and horses.

But then I remembered the scars on my back from the years of abuse I'd suffered in foster care. I'd survived that. I'd overcome it. And now, I had a chance to make a real difference, to save an entire world.

I still marveled at the dragons as sunlight caught on their scales, creating a dazzling display of glittering colors. Their eyes seemed to hold a depth that went beyond their physical form, as they had lived for centuries and held within them the secrets of their ancient orders. They were living legends, each with their own unique markings and personalities, commanding awe and respect with every move. Their powerful wings shimmered in the sunlight, carrying them with effortless grace, and their eyes held the knowledge and wisdom of centuries. It was a sight that took my breath away and filled me with both fear and reverence.

The wyverns were no less awe-inspiring, whether with dark or lighter scales and beautiful underbellies. They assumed postures that were both regal and strangely avian. With only two legs, they folded their wings partially; the tips touching the ground for balance, creating an archway of leathery membrane above their back. Their powerful legs bent into a deep squat, allowing their haunches to lower, giving a stance reminiscent of a giant bird settled on its perch. Their tails, long and whip-like, coiled around them, either for additional balance or simply as a comfortable resting position. In this stance, they looked less like beasts of war and more like guardians of ancient lore, eyes alert even in while resting, scanning the horizon with unwavering vigilance.

I squared my shoulders, meeting each of the Dragonia's eyes. "Alright, y'all. Let's get to work. We've got a realm to save, and Magda isn't gonna wait around for us to be ready."

I looked to Cade and remembered an important thing: the prophecy mentioned my mate and me sharing power.

"Will Cade ride too? We share the Goddess Star mark. The prophecy mentioned that my One True Mate and I will share power."

Vaelith looked at me, wisdom gleaming in his ancient eyes. *"That, my little StarHeart, is strictly up to you. You alone know if he is worthy to share in your gift. If you will it to be so, then it will be so."*

"There is no better man in all the realms than Cadence Vesparra. He puts the well-being of his people and the people of Eldoria above himself. He loves the Goddess and does her will. I have never known a better man."

"Then let it be so."

Cade, who had gathered with the other kings and generals strategizing battle plans as I had been discussing much the same with the Dragonia, approached when I called. "Cade, can you come here, please?" He had an eager look on his face as he quickly covered the distance to us in the open field where we had gathered.

"Yes, my love." A chaste kiss on my lips set my heart racing. I heard more than one chuckle from the Dragonia behind me. "I've learned that my Wyldcaster gift is mine to share with my One True Mate if I choose to do so. You'd be riding dragons the same as me. I'd really like for you to do this with me. What do you say, Highness? You up for the challenge?"

CHAPTER 2

Cade

I stood there, staring at Olivia in awe as the meaning of her words sank in. She wanted me to ride with her, to share her Wyldcaster gift. My breath caught in my chest. This wasn't just any honor—it was *the* honor. To ride among the Dragonia, to soar beside her, bound not only by magic but by trust—Olivia was offering me something I hadn't dared dream of.

I swallowed hard, trying to find the right words. "You really want to share this with me?" I asked, my voice lower than usual.

She smiled, that radiant smile that made my heart twist and settle all at once. "There is no man in this realm who is worthier than you, my love."

I took a step closer, running a hand through my hair, still reeling from the weight of her offer. "Olivia... you do not know what this means to me."

The field around us buzzed with life. The Dragonia stretched their wings lazily, sunbeams catching on scales and feathers that shimmered in brilliant greens and golds. Wyverns huffed, flicking their tails, and the Pegasi nickered softly in the distance. It was like a world out of legend, one I'd never thought I'd be a part of—and she was handing me the key.

I watched her as she turned back to the Dragonia, a

lightness in her step I hadn't seen before. She was smiling, laughing—fully herself, in a way that made my chest ache with happiness. It was like watching her bloom into the woman she was always meant to be. Her joy was infectious, filling the air with a warmth I'd carry with me for the rest of my life.

And gods, seeing her like this—alive, confident, and fully in her element—made me love her even more. She wasn't just surviving anymore. She was thriving, standing among these magnificent creatures as if she'd belonged here all along.

"It would be my honor to ride with you," I finally said, my voice thick with emotion. "I'd follow you anywhere, Olivia."

Her eyes sparkled as she reached for my hand, lacing her fingers with mine. I could feel the pulse of magic between us, subtle and powerful, like a river ready to burst its banks. "Then let's make it happen," she whispered, a playful grin tugging at her lips.

For a moment, I couldn't breathe. She was everything. My mate. My heart. My forever. And now—soon—I'd fly beside her, through the skies and into battle, as it was always meant to be.

This wasn't just a gift. It was a promise.

And I intended to keep it.

Olivia

"Vaelith, Cade has agreed to honor me by accepting the gift of Wyldcaster magic. Do I just make a declaration, and he accepts it?"

"Yes, my little StarHeart. It must be a true and heartfelt declaration from you both. If either of you doubts, the bond will fail—and instead of a blessing, it will become a curse. So be certain your love for each other is pure before you proceed."

I turned to Cade. "He says we better be dang sure about the purity of our love, or we're screwed."

He grinned, that familiar warmth in his eyes. "I think we're good, baby girl."

"Alright, Iron Heart, here we go. Give me your hands." I took a deep breath, lost for a second in those ice-blue eyes of his. *God, I sure do love this man.* "As you are my mate, I want you to be my equal in magic. I give you the gift of Wyldcaster magic willingly, with the same trust and love that I had when I gave you my heart. I share it freely."

His voice was steady as he replied. "Starlight, being a Wyldcaster, isn't just about communicating with magnificent creatures. It's about responsibility, empathy, and connection. I endeavor to be worthy, always, of the trust you place in me, to reflect the character of the man you need me to be, and to always let you know how deeply I love you."

Zarvyn's voice rang out in our minds, boisterous and playful. *"Now, **that's** a love for the ages!"*

I turned to Cade, laughed. "Did you hear that?"

"I heard that!"

Vaelith's silver scales glimmered as he lowered his massive head to meet my gaze. His expression was serious as he began. *"Before we start your physical training, young one, we must arm you with knowledge. Magda's creatures are unlike anything you've faced in this, or any, realm."*

A shiver ran up my spine, and I struggled to keep my voice steady. "Tell us everything."

Zarvyn, his scales catching the fading sunlight, rumbled, *"The shadow beasts are her favored minions. They move like liquid darkness, their claws sharp enough to tear through dragon scales."*

"Lord have mercy," I muttered, glancing at Cade. "How do we fight somethin' like that?"

Eryndor's emerald scales shifted as he turned to me. *"With light, little one. Your elemental magic will be crucial. Water to slow them, earth to trap them, and ice to shatter their shadowy forms."*

I nodded, trying to imagine wielding that kind of power. My fingers tingled with the promise of magic I was only beginning to understand.

Skorn's obsidian scales gleamed as he added, *"And beware*

the void walkers. They can step between shadows, appearing anywhere darkness touches."

My heart raced, fear and determination wrestling inside me. "Alright, so how do we handle those nasty suckers?"

Nyxara's midnight-blue form seemed to blend into the encroaching twilight. *"We wyverns will be your best defense. Our venom disrupts their ability to shadow-walk."*

I glanced at Cade, grinning. "Y'all just watch out for him. That's one of his principal powers—besides all his cool vampirey stuff."

I took a deep breath, grounding myself. "Alright, let's get to it. No time like the present to learn how to ride a dragon, right?"

Vaelith lowered his wing, forming a makeshift ramp. *"Indeed, young one. Remember, we are bonded to you and your mate now. Trust in that connection."*

As I approached, my legs trembling slightly, I couldn't help but think of the abused horses I'd treated back in Texas. They'd flinch at a gentle touch, expecting pain. I knew that feeling all too well.

But as I placed my hand on Vaelith's scales, feeling the warmth and steady thrum of life beneath, something shifted. A connection—deep and primal—spoke of trust and strength.

I climbed onto his back, my heart pounding. "Alright, big fella. Let's show these monsters what happens when they mess with Texas... and Eldoria."

Cade climbed onto Zarvyn's back, a grin lighting his face. "Olivia, this is incredible. You okay?"

"Honey, I'm so much better than okay. So when we're up in the air, we'll need to go to that mind-talk too, right?"

"Yes, the wind will make regular communication impossible."

I shot him a playful look. *"Show-off."*

Drathom chimed in with a groan. *"I, for one, truly hope you keep any kinky talk to zero since we can all hear it. Please."*

Vaelith's deep, rumbling laugh vibrated through me as he spread his wings. *"Hold tight, little star. Your training begins now."*

As we took to the sky, the wind whipping through my hair, I felt a surge of exhilaration. For the first time in my life, I wasn't running from my past or hiding from my future. I was flying toward it, ready to face whatever came our way.

The thrill of flight quickly gave way to a mix of terror and awe as Vaelith soared higher, the ground falling away beneath us. My fingers dug into his scales, my breath coming in short gasps.

"Easy there, darlin'," I muttered, more to myself than the dragon. "Just like ridin' a horse. A really big, scaly horse that flies."

"Relax, Olivia." Vaelith's amused voice echoed in my mind. *"Feel the rhythm of my wings, the currents of the air. We are one now."*

"Shouldn't I have a saddle?" I muttered, glancing down at his massive form.

Closing my eyes, I focused on the sensations—the steady beat of Vaelith's wings, the way his muscles moved beneath me. Slowly, I began to relax, my body swaying in sync with his movements.

"That's it", Zarvyn called from below, Cade on his back, his dark scales glinting in the sunlight. *"You're a natural, little star!"*

I couldn't help but grin. *"Well, I'll be ding-danged. Guess all those years of barrel racing weren't for nothin' after all."*

As we swooped and dove, the other Dragonia joined us in the air. We flew close to Cade and Zarvyn, moving in formation. Eryndor's emerald scales flashed as he performed a graceful barrel roll, while Nyxara's midnight-blue form darted between clouds with impossible speed.

"Show-offs," I laughed, the sound carried away by the wind.

For hours, we practiced maneuvers, learning to move as

15

one. By the time we landed, my muscles ached, but a fierce joy burned in my chest. As I slid off Vaelith's back, legs wobbling, Skorn approached, his obsidian scales gleaming.

"You've done well today, Olivia," he said, his usually stern voice tinged with warmth. *"But remember, in battle, we must be more than friends. We must be a single, deadly force."*

I nodded, wiping sweat from my brow. "I hear ya. Back home, we'd say we need to be tighter than bark on a tree."

Drathom tilted his head, confusion evident in his glowing eyes. *"Bark on a... tree?"*

"It means *very* close," I explained, chuckled. "Sorry, sometimes my Texas comes out."

"We like your 'Texas'," Thyra said, her silvery coat shimmering as she trotted over. *"It's part of who you are, just as we are now."*

Her words warmed me, chasing away the lingering chill of old insecurities. Here, among these magical creatures, I felt accepted. Understood.

As the sun began to set, casting long shadows across the mountain pass, we gathered in a massive circle. The air hummed with energy, a sense of purpose settling over us like a cloak.

"Tomorrow," Ariaxom said, his white mane catching the fading light, *"we begin combat training. Are you ready, Olivia? Cade?"*

"You bet your bottom dollar I am," I replied, my voice strong and clear. *"Magda and her monsters are tough. We just have to be tougher."*

Cade chimed in, *"We'll work hard to be so."*

I looked around at the Dragonia, my new family. At Vaelith's ancient wisdom, Zarvyn's fierce loyalty, Eryndor's quiet strength. At Skorn's deadly grace, Nyxara's quick wit, Drathom's steady resolve. At Ariaxom and Thyra's unwavering support. Cade's unfailing love. And for once in my life, I felt... complete.

As night fell, we made our way to the caves, our hearts beating as one. Whatever challenges lay ahead, we'd face them together. And Vesperia help anyone who tried to stand in our way.

***

As I settled into our quarters in Vesparra's castle, my mind buzzed with the day's events. The exhilaration of meeting the Dragonia still coursed through me, but a nagging thought pressed at the edges of my consciousness. I couldn't shake the feeling that something was... stirring.

A soft knock at my door startled me from my reverie. "Come in," I called, surprised to see Kaelen's tall frame fill the doorway.

"Olivia," he said, his silver eyes troubled. "May I have a word?"

I nodded, gesturing for him to enter. "What's on your mind?"

Kaelen paced the room, his usual grace tempered by an uncharacteristic tension. "It's about Amaya," he said finally, his voice low and strained.

My heart skipped a beat. "What about her?"

He ran a hand through his mane of dark blonde hair. "I... I can't stop thinking about her. The moment I saw her after the two of you were rescued from the Underworld, I felt something shift inside me."

I frowned, trying to process his words. "What kind of shift?"

"Like recognizing a part of myself I didn't know was missing," he murmured, his gaze distant. "Olivia, I think... I think she might be my mate."

The words hung between us, heavy with implication. My mind raced, torn between joy at the possibility of Amaya finding her place here and concern over the complications this

17

could bring.

"Do you know if she felt something as well?"

Kaelen nodded, his jaw clenched. "There's no way she didn't. I didn't mention it to her, though. I know she's new to this world, even though she carries powerful magic. Believe me, I can feel that too. But how much does she really know of this world?"

He broke off, frustration evident in every line of his body. I saw the conflict raging within him—the primal urge to claim his mate warring with his sense of honor and duty.

"What are you going to do?" I asked, genuinely curious about how the powerful Alpha would handle this unexpected challenge.

"I honestly don't know. My instinct is to claim her, but I know I can't. Sleeping outside her door right now, just to be sure she's protected, is preferable, but I can't do that either. I just want to hold her and give her the care she's never had."

As he spoke, I pictured Amaya—my wild, creative sister—faced with this new reality. Would she embrace it? Fight it? The image of her standing toe-to-toe with Kaelen, all fire and defiance, almost made me smile despite the seriousness of the situation. The thought of her having this beautiful beast of a man on her side for the whole of her life filled me with a sense of peace, knowing I wouldn't have to worry about her.

"Just... be patient with her," I said finally. "Amaya's had to fight for everything in her life. I fear something within her broke when they took her to the Underworld and I honestly don't know how she'll react to the news of having a mate. But I'll do what I can to grease the wheels."

Kaelen's lips quirked in a small smile. "Now I see what Cade meant when he said he doesn't understand you half the time, but I'm certain that's helpful."

"It is. I just meant I'm gonna try to help move things along. She can be mule-headed and stubborn."

"I'm learning that—and wouldn't expect anything less

from your sister," he said, some of the tension easing from his shoulders. "Thank you, Olivia—for listening and offering to help."

As he left, I sank onto my bed, my mind whirling. The excitement of the Dragonia, the looming threat of Magda, and now this unexpected complication with Kaelen and Amaya... even in this magical realm, life was determined to keep me on my toes.

Cade walked in just as Kaelen walked out. "Entertaining other men in our bedchamber, my love?"

"All other men pale compared to you, Highness. Besides, that man has it bad for my baby sister. He's going to have his hands full with that one."

I watched as he slowly removed his clothing. "Well, I'm looking forward to quite literally having my hands filled with this one, even as we speak." He was in our bed in a heartbeat and swept me into his arms. Out of all the places in this realm, this was my favorite place to be.

CHAPTER 3

Amaya

The morning sunlight streamed through the gossamer curtains, casting a golden glow over Olivia's chambers. I hesitated at the threshold, my heart pounding as I took in the intimate setting before me. Olivia sat at a small table laden with pastries, fresh fruit, and steaming cups of tea. Her warm smile instantly put me at ease.

"Come in, sugar," Olivia called, beautiful and relaxed, totally comfortable in her new life. "I've been waitin' on you."

I stepped inside, drawn by the comforting aroma of cinnamon and vanilla. Max and Finn, her two large fluffy white dogs, ran to greet me.

"Hi boys! I haven't seen you in a few hours. I can tell you missed me!" Endless dog kisses were peppering my face.

Olivia put a stop to their playful greeting.

"Alright, that's enough, you two flirts. Go on now, shoo! Go find Seraphine. I think she has treats!"

At the word "treats," both dogs' ears perked up, and they flew out the open door and down the stairs, I assumed, looking for Sera.

I settled into the plush chair across from Olivia, still giggling at the encounter with her pups. I couldn't help but marvel at how at peace she looked, even in these luxurious surroundings. Her long, dark hair cascaded over her shoulders, and her deep purple eyes sparkled with affection.

"Thank you for inviting me. I've been dying to spend some time together. I just never know if it's appropriate anymore."

Olivia reached across the table, her hand gently covering mine. "Sweetheart, please don't ever feel that way. You're always welcome here. I was eager for us to have some time alone, time too."

I nodded, grateful to be with her after losing her in the mortal realm and then enduring our time in the Underworld. My world had been knocked off its axis more than once over the past few months, and I was still trying to get my bearings. As I sipped my tea, I felt some of the tension in my shoulders ease. Olivia had a way of making me feel safe, creating a bubble where the outside world couldn't touch us.

"Amaya," Olivia began, her voice tender. "I wanted to talk to you about Kaelen."

My breath caught in my throat, and I lowered my gaze to the intricate patterns on the china teacup. "Oh," I whispered, a mix of excitement and a bit of panic churning in my stomach.

"Honey, look at me," Olivia coaxed, and I reluctantly met her gaze. "I want you to know that whatever you're feeling, it's okay. Your emotions are valid, and you don't need to be ashamed of them."

I bit my lip, fighting back tears. "But I... I don't know what I'm feeling. It's all so confusing."

Olivia's eyes softened with compassion. "Of course it is, sugar. After everything you've been through, it's natural to feel overwhelmed. But I see the way you look at Kaelen, and the way he looks at you. There's something special there."

I felt the heat rise in my cheeks and couldn't help the small smile that tugged at my lips. "He's been so great to me," I admitted. "But I just feel so out of my depth, you know? He's a *king*, the Alpha of an entire kingdom. I'm just a girl from the mortal realm who didn't even know it *was* a mortal realm until a few weeks ago. What do I have to offer? Seriously? He's also a shifter. I'm not that either. His people would never accept me. I think he's only interested in me because I'm pretty. And we both know that kind of attraction gets old real quick. I don't offer enough past that."

Olivia squeezed my hand, her touch comforting me. "Amaya, listen to me. You are more than enough, just as you are. If you have feelings for Kaelen, whatever they may be, you need to trust them—and trust him. Don't let your fears hold you back from exploring something that could be beautiful."

I swallowed, nodding slowly. "Olivia, you know I don't have any experience with men. I've been on a random date here and there, but something always felt... 'wrong' about every guy I ever went out with. It felt like I was cheating on someone, which is ridiculous because I never had a genuine relationship. Talk about frustrating! I was awkward going on a date with Jerry from accounting. How could I navigate being with Kaelen, Alpha King of Therionis?"

Olivia's look of amusement suddenly became more serious. She leaned forward, her eyes intense. "Sweetpea, there's something I need to explain to you about Kaelen and what you're feeling. I know you're still new to magic, to this realm, and all that comes with it. Have you ever heard of Fated Mates?"

My brow furrowed. "I know you and Cade are fated, but I don't really know what that means."

She nodded, a soft smile playing on her lips. "It's a rare and powerful bond. Yes, Cade and I are Fated Mates. Ours was a bit different, though, because for our mate bond to sort of click into place, I had to actually fall in love with him first. But even before I did, it was like... my soul recognized its other half. And once I declared my love for him and the mate bond snapped into place, the connection was intense. For normal Fated Mates, it's more... instant."

I felt a flutter in my chest, thinking of the spark between

Kaelen and me the moment I saw him in that forest, right after Ollie and I came through the portal from the Underworld. He'd asked if I was hurt, and when I looked into his eyes, I'd felt it.

"Is *that* what this is?"

"I believe so, sugar. The bond Cade and I share... it's unlike anything I'd ever experienced. It's not just physical attraction —though, Lord knows, that's there too." She winked, and I couldn't help but giggle. "It's a deep, soul-level connection. We can sense each other's emotions and share strength. In battle, we move as one. It's an unexplainable connection that goes deeper than you can imagine. I can even hear his thoughts. Let me tell you, learning how to turn that little trick off has been *quite* a task."

My smile faded as doubt crept in. "But Olivia," I whispered, "what if it's not real? What if it's just... magic forcing us together? I'm attracted to Kaelen. I can't deny that—I mean, look at the man. But I'm scared. What if this bond takes away our choice? Our free will?"

Olivia's expression softened. "Oh, honey. I understand those fears, I truly do. The mate bond doesn't create love out of thin air. It's more like... a nudge. Fate knew you were truly meant to be together, so it pointed you toward someone who could be your perfect match. But it's still up to you to nurture that connection, to choose each other every day."

I wrapped my arms around myself, feeling vulnerable. "It's still hard to get past the doubts. I feel so young compared to him. I mean, seriously. What if I can't be what he needs?"

Olivia reached out, gently squeezing my hand. Her touch was warm, comforting. "Amaya, darlin', listen to me. There's no rush, no deadline. The bond doesn't demand instant perfection."

I met her gaze, her eyes filled with understanding. My voice quivered as I spoke. "I just don't want to screw something up. I don't want to embarrass you. You're the queen of Vesparra. I don't want your people to think your little sister is some kind of screw-up."

"Honey, this is something that cannot be messed up if you just listen to your heart." She laughed, adding, "Believe me, I'm still the biggest doof when it comes to stuff around here. Cade doesn't even understand what I'm sayin' half the time. You can't out-embarrass me, sister. Cade's the *king* here, and I have enough power to *level* this place. I'm as nervous as a hooker in church most of the time."

I couldn't hold in the big laugh that escaped me. "Really? You two seem so... in sync."

Olivia laughed, a rich delightful sound. "Oh brother, you should've seen us in the beginning. I felt as unworthy as can be."

"What changed?" I asked, leaning forward.

"Time," she said simply. "And trust. Cade... he showed me patience I never thought possible. He gave me space when I needed it, but he was always there when I reached out."

I felt a glimmer of hope. "And now?"

Olivia's eyes softened, a tender smile playing on her lips. "Now, I can't imagine my life without him. The bond we share... it's like coming home after a long, hard journey. It's safety, passion. He's my better days, the ones I always dreamed of."

As I listened, I couldn't help but picture Kaelen—his intense gaze, the way his presence made me feel both unsettled and strangely secure. He made me feel like I could let go of the control I always felt I had to grip so tightly. Could we have that kind of connection?

"I'm not saying it'll be easy," Olivia continued. "But, Maya, the possibility of what you and Kaelen could have... it's worth exploring. Don't let fear rob you of something beautiful."

I took a deep breath, feeling the weight of Olivia's words settle over me. My fingers traced the intricate patterns on the teacup, the warmth seeping into my skin.

"I'm just going to have to decide if it's genuine. That this 'mate bond' isn't just some joke of the universe, forcing two people together who have no business being a pair."

Olivia's eyes met mine, understanding radiating from them. I pressed on, the words tumbling out faster now.

"*I* want to choose Ollie. I want to fall in love because my heart decides it, not because some mystical force says I should. What if Kaelen only wants me because of this bond? What if I'm just... convenient? I know I sound so wishy-washy and immature. I'm annoying *myself*!"

My sister reached across the table, her hand covering mine. "Oh, sweetie," she said softly. "The mate bond isn't a cage. It's... it's more like an invitation."

I frowned, confused. "An invitation?"

Olivia nodded, her expression serious. "Think of it like this —the Goddess Vesperia has given you and Kaelen a unique opportunity. She's saying, 'Hey, you two will be really great together.' But it's still up to you to RSVP, so to speak."

I couldn't help but chuckle at her analogy, even as my heart raced with uncertainty.

"The bond doesn't guarantee love, Amaya," Olivia continued. "It's a potential for a deep, profound connection. But you still must nurture it, work at it. It's not some magical fix-all."

I bit my lip, considering her words. "So... we could still fail? Even with this 'divine matchmaking'?"

Olivia's laugh was tinged with a hint of sadness. "Sadly, yeah. Sometimes one or the other rejects the bond. It's apparently devastating for the one who's rejected."

If the mate bond wasn't infallible, then maybe... maybe there was room for real choice after all.

**

We'd changed into our leathers and walked in easy, companionable quiet to the training area.

A sharp whistle pierced the air, jolting me from my thoughts. I blinked, realizing we'd already reached the training grounds. The once-peaceful meadow now buzzed with nervous energy as warriors from all five kingdoms gathered, their faces grim with determination.

"All right, ladies!" General Nightstrom's booming voice carried across the field. "Let's see what you're made of!"

Olivia squeezed my hand, her eyes blazing with fierce protectiveness. "Ready, sis?"

I nodded, trying to quell the butterflies in my stomach. "As I'll ever be."

We jogged to join the others, the grass wet with dew. The Dragonia loomed at the far end of the field, their scales gleaming in the morning sun. My breath caught—I'd never seen anything so beautiful and terrifying.

"Today," the General continued, "we focus on evasion and counterattacks. Remember, these Underworld bastards are quick. You need to be quicker."

I glanced at Olivia, noting the set of her jaw. Her fierceness surprised me as she muttered, "Bring it on, y'all."

The training began in earnest. We were paired off, one person playing the "creature," the other defending. I faced a burly Aurelion warrior, his hands wreathed in flames.

"Don't hold back, little one," he growled, a hint of a smirk on his lips.

I felt a surge of indignation. *Little one?* I'd show him. Over the past days here, I'd been practicing with my magic. I didn't have to wait until I was 25 for it to come to me. When I breached Eldoria's barrier, the spell binding my power slipped away, and I'd felt magic fill every pore of my being. I didn't know what it was at first, but Kaelen had patiently been instructing me. I was ready for this.

As he lunged, I wove my magic, creating shimmering air currents that deflected his fiery assault. The flames licked harmlessly past me, singeing the grass.

"Not bad," he grunted, circling me warily.

I grinned, feeling my confidence grow. "You ain't seen nothin' yet."

We continued like this for what felt like hours, switching roles and facing new opponents. My muscles screamed, my clothes clung with sweat, but I refused to give in. With each round, I felt myself growing stronger, more in tune with my magic.

Across the field, I caught glimpses of Olivia. She was poetry in motion, her movements fluid and deadly. At one point, she effortlessly redirected a shadow shard from a Vesparran warrior, sending it harmlessly into the earth.

"Damn," I heard someone mutter. "No wonder she's the Chosen One."

Pride swelled in my chest. *That was my sister.*

As the sun climbed higher, General Nightstrom called for a brief break. I collapsed onto the grass next to Olivia, my chest heaving.

"You're doing great, Amaya," she said, passing me a waterskin.

I gulped greedily, relishing the cool liquid. "Thanks," I panted. "I'm feeling stronger every day. But, I still feel unsure sometimes, though."

Olivia's expression softened. "We all do, sweetie. But that's why we're here. To get ready, together."

I nodded, letting her words sink in. As I looked around at the diverse group of warriors, all united in purpose, I felt a hope rise in my spirit. It might not be an effortless task, but we stood a good chance against whatever the Underworld threw at us.

A bone-chilling screech pierced the air, sending shivers down my spine. I leaped to my feet, heart pounding, as a massive creature materialized at the edge of the training grounds. Its body was a twisted mass of shadows, writhing and pulsing with otherworldly energy. Razor-sharp claws glinted in the sunlight, and its eyes glowed with an eerie red light.

"Shadowraith," General Nightstrom's gravelly voice cut through the stunned silence. "One of Magda's nastiest creations. They feed on fear and can phase through solid objects."

I swallowed hard, my throat suddenly dry. "How do we fight something like that?"

"With this," Miranda's voice rang out as she stepped forward, a gleaming orb in her hand. She locked eyes with General Nightstrom, a silent understanding passing between them.

The General nodded, a hint of a smile on his usually stern face. "Show 'em how it's done, Majesty."

Miranda's lips curved into a determined grin. She raised the orb high, her voice ringing out clear and strong. "Mist of Thalassa, heed my call!"

The orb shattered, releasing a thick, swirling fog that engulfed the Shadowraith. The creature's screech turned to a confused howl as it thrashed blindly in the mist.

General Nightstrom didn't hesitate. He charged forward, his massive form a blur of motion. His sword, imbued with some kind of shimmering energy, sliced through the creature's shadowy form.

The Shadowraith's dying wail sent chills through my body, but I couldn't tear my eyes away. As the mist cleared, Miranda and the General stood side by side, both breathing heavily but wearing matching expressions of grim satisfaction.

"Holy shit," I whispered, equal parts terrified and awestruck.

Olivia squeezed my hand. "And that's just one of the creatures we might face," she murmured. "Magda's arsenal is vast and unpredictable. And we may not have those specific weapons at our disposal. We must learn to fight with what's available."

I watched as Miranda and General Nightstrom conferred quietly, their heads bent close together. Despite their vastly different appearances—her lithe grace contrasting with his imposing bulk—there was an undeniable synergy between them.

"They work well together," I observed.

Olivia nodded. "Miranda's intuition complements the General's tactical mind perfectly. It's why they often lead joint training exercises."

As if on cue, Miranda's voice rang out across the field. "All right, everyone! Let's run that drill again. This time, I want to see more coordination between elemental attacks and physical combat. Remember, these creatures don't fight fair—neither should we."

General Nightstrom's deep rumble followed. "And always keep your guard up. The real ones won't be giving you a second chance."

I took a deep breath, steeling myself for another round. As terrifying as that Shadowraith had been, a small part of me thrilled at the challenge. We were preparing for a war unlike anything Eldoria had ever seen, and I was right in the middle of it all.

"Ready?" Olivia asked, her eyes sparkling with a mix of determination and excitement that I was sure mirrored my own.

I nodded, calling my magic to my fingertips. "Let's do this."

CHAPTER 4

Olivia

The apartment door slammed shut behind us, our bodies thrumming with leftover magic and adrenaline from the day's grueling training. Cade's ice-blue eyes locked onto mine, darkening with desire, and my breath caught in my throat.

"Darlin'," I drawled, "I'm thinking we could use a shower."

A wolfish grin spread across Cade's face. "I couldn't agree more, my love."

His large hands found my hips, pulling me flush against his muscular frame. The scent of leather and pine enveloped me as his lips crashed into mine. I melted into the kiss, my fingers tangling in his jet-black hair.

We stumbled backward, shedding clothes like snakeskin. My blouse caught on a scar on my back, and I flinched. Cade's touch instantly softened, his eyes full of understanding and love.

"You're safe, Olivia," he murmured, gently freeing the fabric. "I've got you."

Warmth flooded my chest, chasing away the shadows of my past. I took his hand, marveling at how perfectly our fingers intertwined, and led him to the shower.

The warm water cascaded over us, washing away the day's sweat and tension. I closed my eyes, savoring the feeling of

Cade's muscular arms around me. His lips trailed along my neck, igniting a fire in my core.

"I love you," I whispered, my voice barely audible over the rush of water.

Cade's grip tightened. "And I you, more than words can express."

As we explored each other's bodies with eager hands, I couldn't help but marvel at how far we'd come. From strangers thrust together by fate to true mates, bound by blood and an unbreakable love.

The water ran over us, cleansing and renewing. In this moment, wrapped in Cade's embrace, I felt invincible—ready to face whatever challenges awaited us in the war that was undoubtedly on its way.

Amaya

Kaelen's hand rested on the small of my back as we walked, his touch both comforting and electrifying. The stone corridors of the castle seemed to close in around us, amplifying the tension crackling between our bodies.

"Here we are," he murmured, his deep voice sending shivers down my spine. "Your chambers, Amaya."

I turned to face him, my heart pounding. "Thank you, Kaelen. For... everything."

His silver eyes softened, a smile tugging at his lips. "I'll return shortly. There's something I want to show you."

As I slipped into my room, I couldn't help but wonder what he had planned. The anticipation made my skin tingle.

"Kaelen," I called out, surprising myself. He paused, looking back. "Be careful, okay?"

He nodded, his expression a mixture of tenderness and determination. "Always."

Once alone, I stripped off my training clothes and stepped into the shower. The hot water cascaded over me, soothing my aching muscles, but it did little to calm the storm of emotions within.

What am I doing? I thought, pressing my forehead against the cool tile. *Can I really trust this mate bond? Trust him?*

Unbidden, memories of Kaelen's gentle touches and fierce protectiveness flooded my mind. The way he looked at me, like I was the most precious thing in all of Eldoria.

"It's different this time," I whispered to myself, trying to believe it. "He's different."

As I rinsed the soap from my body, I realized my hands were trembling—not from fear, but from a potent mix of excitement and apprehension.

What if I'm not ready? The thought hit me like a punch to the gut. *What if I disappoint him?*

I closed my eyes, letting the water wash over my face. "Goddess Vesperia," I breathed, "give me strength."

A soft knock at the door startled me from my thoughts. My heart leaped into my throat as I heard Kaelen's deep, resonant voice. "Amaya? May I come in?"

I fumbled for a towel, wrapping it hastily around my body. "Just... just a minute!" I called out, my voice trembling slightly.

Taking a deep breath, I stepped out of the shower, water droplets trailing down my skin. I opened the door, and there he stood—all broad shoulders, leather, and piercing eyes. But it was what he held that caught my attention—a plush wolf, its fur a soft gray.

"I hope I'm not intruding," Kaelen said, his gaze softening as it met mine. He held out the stuffed animal. "I brought you something."

I blinked, caught off guard. "A... toy?"

He chuckled, the sound warming me from the inside out. "More than that. It's a symbol, Amaya. Of comfort, of safety." His voice lowered, filled with emotion. "A reminder that it's okay to seek solace in others. In me."

I reached out hesitantly, my fingers brushing against the

soft fur. "I don't understand," I whispered, even as a part of me ached to clutch the wolf to my chest.

Kaelen stepped closer, his presence enveloping me. "You've been alone for so long, fighting your own battles. But you don't have to anymore. This wolf... it's a promise. That I'll be here whenever you need me."

I stared at the plush animal, my vision blurred with unexpected tears. "Kaelen, I..."

His hand gently cupped my cheek, tilting my face up to meet his gaze. "You don't have to say anything, Amaya. Just know that I'm here whenever you're ready."

The sincerity in his eyes undid me. With trembling hands, I took the stuffed wolf, hugging it close. Its soft fur tickled my damp skin, and I breathed in its fresh, comforting scent.

"Thank you," I whispered, my voice thick with emotion.

Kaelen's smile was tender, his eyes shimmering with an intensity that made my breath catch. "May I?" he asked softly, his hand hovering near my waist.

I nodded, unable to form words. He drew me close, enveloping me in his warmth. I pressed my face against his chest, listening to the steady thrum of his heartbeat.

As I melted into Kaelen's embrace, a sense of peace washed over me. The plush wolf was nestled between us, a tangible reminder of his promise. For a moment, I allowed myself to believe that maybe it was possible, I could trust this feeling.

Kaelen's fingers trailed gently up and down my spine, leaving a trail of warmth in their wake. I shivered, suddenly very aware of my state of undress beneath the thin towel.

"You're trembling," he murmured, his breath warm against my ear. "Are you cold?"

I shook my head, not trusting my voice. How could I explain it wasn't the chill of the air making me quiver, but the heat of his touch?

Slowly, hesitantly, I lifted my head to meet his gaze. The intensity in his eyes made my breath catch. There I saw a desire that mirrored my own. But that familiar doubt stopped me. *Is this desire born of actual feeling, or is it forced by the mate bond?* I placed a hand on his chest and gave a small push.

Kaelen stepped back immediately, respecting my unspoken request for space. His eyes searched mine, concern etched across his features.

"Amaya?" he asked softly. "What's wrong?"

I clutched the plush wolf tighter, using it as a shield between us. "I... I'm not sure about this," I admitted, my voice barely above a whisper. "About us."

Pain flashed across Kaelen's face, quickly masked by understanding. He took another step back, giving me room to breathe.

"The mate bond," he said, realization dawning. "You're worried it's forcing these feelings."

I nodded, relief flooding through me that he understood without me having to explain further. "How can we know for sure?" I asked, hating the vulnerability in my voice. "How can we be certain this is real?"

Kaelen was quiet for a moment, his brow furrowed in thought. When he spoke, his voice was low and earnest.

"Amaya, the mate bond doesn't create feelings that aren't there. It simply... intensifies what already exists." He ran a hand through his hair, searching for the right words. "What I feel for you—it's not some magical compulsion. It's real, and it's mine."

I wanted to believe him, but doubt still gnawed at me. "How can you be so sure?"

His eyes softened as he gazed at me. "Because I've never felt this way about anyone before. The way my heart races when you're near, how I ache to protect you, to make you smile— that's all me, Amaya. The bond just helps me recognize it for what it is."

His words resonated within me, echoing truths. My heart stuttered at his words, aligning with my own tumultuous emotions.

"I... I think I understand," I said softly. "It's just... overwhelming. All of this is so new to me."

Kaelen nodded, a gentle smile tugging at his lips. "I know. And we can take this as slow as you need, Amaya. There's no rush."

Relief washed over me at his understanding. I hugged the plush wolf closer, drawing comfort from its softness. "Thank you," I whispered with a smile.

"Always," Kaelen replied, his voice warm. "Now, why don't you get dressed? I'll wait outside, and then maybe we could take a walk in the gardens. The night air might help clear your head."

I nodded, grateful for the suggestion. "I'd like that."

Olivia

The sun barely crested the horizon as Cade and I made our way to the training grounds. My muscles ached from yesterday's exertions, but a thrum of excitement coursed through my veins. Today, we trained with the Dragonia.

As we approached, I caught sight of Skorn, the massive wyvern, his scales shimmering like polished obsidian in the early morning light. My breath still caught in my throat at the sight.

"Holy crap," I whispered. "I'm still amazed at the size of that big ol' lizard."

Cade chuckled, his hand finding the small of my back. "I'm going to tell him you said that."

"You better not!"

General Nightstrom's booming voice cut through the air. "All right, maggots! Gather near your assigned Dragonia. Today, you'll learn to fight around them—and not get yourselves killed in the process!"

I scanned the grounds, searching for Vaelith. His massive

size and silver scales gleaming in the sun made the dragon easy to spot, and his piercing blue eyes met my gaze. As I approached, I couldn't help but marvel at his beauty.

"Howdy, looks like we're dance partners today."

The dragon's melodic voice echoed in my mind. *"Howdy, little StarHeart. Shall we show these earthbound creatures how we truly soar?"*

A grin spread across my face. "Darlin', you read my mind."

For the next few hours, Vaelith and I worked on coordinating our movements. It was exhilarating and terrifying all at once. Today's training differed from what we'd done two days ago. We had fitted the dragons with saddles that would let us wield our magic hands-free, without the fear of losing our seat. The training was intense as we learned to anticipate the dragon's every swooping dive and barrel roll.

During a brief water break, I noticed Miranda and General Nightstrom across the field. They moved in perfect sync, Miranda's water magic creating icy projectiles that the General shattered with precise strikes of his war hammer.

"Well, I'll be danged," I murmured, a smile tugging at my lips. "Looks like the Ice Queen's found her match."

Cade sidled up beside me, following my gaze. "You're doing, I assume?"

I shrugged, unable to keep the pride from my voice. "Maybe I gave 'em a little nudge. But that right there? That's all them."

As I watched Miranda laugh at something the General said, her eyes sparkling with genuine joy, a warmth spread through my chest. In this world of magic and danger, it was nice to see a bit of happiness bloom.

"All right, lovebirds!" Nightstrom's voice boomed across the field. "Break's over. Back to work!"

I turned to Vaelith, my body humming with renewed energy. "Ready to kick some booty, partner?"

The dragon's mental chuckle reverberated through me. *"Always, little StarHeart. Always."*

The training ground expanded as Farin's teams joined us, their presence adding an additional layer of intensity to the already charged atmosphere. I could feel the determination radiating from everyone, a shared purpose that bound us all together.

"All right, folks," Farin called out, his voice carrying across the field. "We're going to focus on Underworld creatures today. Nasty jerks, the bunch of 'em."

I leaned in, my curiosity piqued. "What kind of critters are we talkin' about?"

Farin stepped forward, his expression grim. "Shadow wraiths, hellhounds, and, if we're really unlucky, a few lesser demons."

"Well, that sounds just peachy," I muttered, feeling a shiver run down my spine.

Cade's hand found mine, giving it a reassuring squeeze. "We've got this, Starlight. Together."

For the next few hours, we strategized and practiced. I learned that my earth magic could trap shadow wraiths, while Cade's vampire speed made him ideal for taking down hellhounds. It was grueling work, but there was an undercurrent of excitement that kept us all going.

As the sun began to set, Farin called an end to the session. "Good work, everyone. We'll pick this up tomorrow."

CHAPTER 5

Olivia

Exhausted but satisfied, Cade and I made our way back to our apartment. The moment the door closed behind us, I felt the day's tension melt away.

"Lord, I'm beat," I sighed, my eyes closed. When I opened them, I found Cade watching me, concern etched on his face. But his gaze softened when those eyes locked onto mine, a heat in them that had nothing to do with the day's exertion. I pushed away from the door and crossed the room toward him until we were standing toe-to-toe; my hands rested gently on the crook of his arms. When I looked up at him, I still couldn't get over how effortlessly handsome he was.

"Let me help you with that, love," he said.

His hands found the hem of my shirt, slowly lifting it over my head. I returned the favor, my fingers tracing the hard planes of his chest as I unbuttoned his shirt.

"You know," I murmured, pressing a kiss to his collarbone, "I think I could get used to this kind of cool-down routine."

Cade's chuckle rumbled through his chest. "Oh, we're just fucking getting started, Starlight."

As our clothes hit the floor, I felt that familiar hum of our magical connection spark to life. It was more than just desire; it was a bone-deep need to be close, to reaffirm our bond after a day of facing the darkness that threatened our world.

We stumbled towards the bed, a tangle of limbs and heated kisses. As Cade lowered me onto the soft sheets, I couldn't help but marvel at how far we'd come. From strangers thrust into a world of magic and danger, to partners, lovers, true mates.

"What's going on in that beautiful head of yours?" Cade asked, brushing a strand of hair from my face.

I smiled up at him, feeling a wave of vulnerability wash over me. "Just thinkin' about how grateful I am to have you by my side through all this craziness."

His expression softened, and he leaned down to press a tender kiss to my lips. "There is nowhere else I'd rather be, my love."

I rolled him over onto his back. I never take charge, but I felt a surge of desire to do just that. He always took such good care of me, always meeting my needs. This time, I was going to knock his socks off first, if he had been wearing any socks, that is.

"What are you doing, Starlight?" he asked, his voice laced with intrigue.

"I'm taking care of you, Highness," I murmured against his lips before kissing him deeply. I pulled back and looked at his mesmerizingly gorgeous face. "You always take such good care of me, Cade. Let me take care of you tonight, please."

Cade

I reached up to trace her cheekbone gently, marveled at her very existence. I couldn't fathom living without her now, having found her after so much time searching, drifting alone in the darkness. This woman. She made every day of my life more than I deserved, and the way she was looking at me now, wanting to serve me, it was so much more than I ever dreamed of.

"I love you, baby. I'm yours," I told her as she started trailing kisses along my neck and chest, working her way down. She paused at my nipples to bite and lick, those amethyst eyes locking with mine. I'd propped my upper body on pillows so I could witness everything she did.

"Fuck, Starlight, you are so damn sexy. I love how your mouth feels on my body." I had my hands in her silky dark hair, pulling it back so I could see her stunning face as she worked her magic on me.

She continued to scoot down the bed and down my body. "Remember how you like for me to open myself to you, Highness?"

"I do, Starlight."

"I'd like for you to spread your legs apart, please. Then bend your knees and put your feet flat on the bed."

"As you wish, Majesty."

She fit perfectly between the barrier of my legs as she continued to slide down my chest, kissing as she went. She was nearing my lower stomach, where my cock lay, rock hard, and she kept kissing as she approached.

"Now, my love," she said quietly as she lightly circled my erection with her small hands, "I love this particular part of you. I find it most fascinating. Steel wrapped in velvet. I want to do to you what you do to me, but I think I need some instruction to do it just right."

She continued bringing her hands up and down my girth while she spoke; it was all I could do not to rock my hips in response to her touch.

"How 'bout you start to do what feels right and I'll guide you from there? The only thing I'd ask is that you keep your teeth out of the mix, at least for now." A smile split my face as she continued to look at me while stroking my length.

She was still all innocence and sunshine as she leaned down and carefully lapped at the crown of my cock, circling it with her sweet pink tongue. "Fuck, yes, Starlight, just like that. Lick and then suck on the crown just like that."

And damn if she didn't do exactly as I instructed.

"Now, baby, get it wet, all the way down. You can loosen

your hands for that. Lick down, then up. When you get to the top, let your saliva run from the top down the sides, then put my cock in your mouth and follow your hands as you run them down my length to my balls if you can. My length is going to be longer than your mouth can handle, sweetheart. Tighten your lips around me and move up and down, going deeper each time. Oh, goddess... yes..." I was leveraging my hips, using my feet on the bed to rock them up and down. "Shit, fuck, baby, that feels amazing. Now I'm going to go deeper; you might gag. It's okay if you do. Try to relax your throat, just think of it like you're trying to swallow me. Are you okay?"

Those godsdamn eyes, watering as they were, continued to hold mine, and she gave me an adorable little 'yes' with a nod of her head. And fuck, before I had a chance to go deeper, she reached under and started massaging my balls, too. "Fuck, Starlight, you're going to make me come if you keep that up." My hips bucked stronger, and I was hitting her throat more deeply than before. She pulled back, that girl; she was enjoying this as much as I was. Then she started circling again with her tongue and licked down to my balls. She sucked and licked them too, so sweet and easy. "Starlight, you amaze me. That feels unbelievable." She took one in her mouth while lightly tickling the other, then repeated the same steps with the other. I was about to lose my mind. I had the sheets gripped tightly in my hands as I struggled to keep from rocking.

Suddenly, she had my cock throat-deep again, and she'd found a way once more to swallow me down. And nothing had ever felt so fucking delicious. Up and down she took me as her saliva ran down her chin onto my groin. I had never seen her look sexier.

Then she gave me a little moan at the same time.

"Olivia, I'm going to come, angel. If you don't want me to come down your throat, you need to pull off of me." She sucked and took me even deeper; I swear I could see her throat bulge. One, two, three more pulls, and I exploded. My hips jerked several times. "FUCK STARLIGHT!! Gods, I love you."

She slowly continued to lick and clean my cock, then dragged her tongue back up my stomach to my neck, where she peppered me with tiny, sweet kisses, like she thought I was finished with her.

"Oh, sweetheart, you are fucking mistaken if you think we are done for the night." I flipped her onto her back and shoved my tongue into her mouth, kissing her like a man possessed. I could not get my fill of this woman. The mate bond was pulsing with love and desire like I'd never felt. I wouldn't have been surprised to see the star mark we both carried on our chests glowing with ethereal light; we were wound so tightly.

I reached my hand between us, and, of course, found her dripping wet. She moaned my name as I ran my fingers through her wetness, across her clit. "Always ready for me, always wanting what I can give you." I licked my fingers as she looked on, writhing on the bed with need.

"You need to come, baby?"

"Cade? So much! Please don't make me beg for it. I want to come, and I want you to bite me, too."

"My, my, so fucking demanding, aren't we, Olivia Ilyndor Vesparra?" I asked, a big grin on my face.

"Cadence!"

I was on my knees above her and entered her in seconds. Her surprised giggle was music to my ears. She threw her head back as I hammered my body into hers. I relished the feeling of hers rising to meet mine. The bond made lovemaking an intricate dance where we never had to learn the steps. Sympatico. I reached down between us and rubbed her clit just to heighten her feeling.

"Cade, that feels so good."

"Think you're going to come, Starlight? Because I want you to come before I bite you. Then you're going to come again. Do you understand, baby?"

"Yes, sir. I got it."

"Yes, you fucking got it." I circled her clit a tad bit faster, and she imploded. Her beautiful face was a work of art. Her body bowed and tensed as the feeling gripped her. I continued to rub, pulling every ounce out of her orgasm.

"You ready, Starlight?"

"So ready, Highness."

I sat on the bed, propped up against the headboard. My cock, anticipating what was to come, remained erect and ready. "Come here, Starlight."

She crawled over my lap and settled herself over my erection, sinking down perfectly. "Mmm, I love how you feel when I take you like this," her voice barely above a whisper.

"Me too, Starlight."

She pulled her long dark hair over her shoulder, and without hesitation, I sank my teeth into her neck, releasing my venom and pulling long drinks of her life-enhancing blood. Her body rocked back and forth on my shaft, and by the time I'd finished sealing her wound, we'd both come one last time.

I carried her to the washroom, and we took a steaming hot shower, washing and loving each other one last time before we sank between the sheets, spent, but oh so satisfied.

Olivia

The training grounds vibrated with raw power as I stood beside Cade, my heart racing with anticipation. Zarvyn, with his dark scales and gold underbelly glinting in the morning sun, let out a deafening roar that shook the very earth beneath our feet.

"Ready for this, darlin'?" I asked Cade, adrenaline coursing through my veins.

He flashed me a grin, his ice-blue eyes alight with excitement. "Born ready. Let's go play with some Dragonia!"

I nodded, pushing away the little doubts that always seemed to creep in. Cade believed in me, the Dragonia believed in me, and, at the end of the day, I believed in myself. We moved forward together, our steps in perfect sync as we approached our waiting Dragonia friends.

A wyvern swooped low overhead, its leathery wings stirring up dust and debris. I looked up to see the familiar midnight-blue scales and gold eyes belonging to Nyxara.

"Well, good mornin' to you too, Nyx," I called, ducking instinctively.

"Ha! Made you duck!" Her roaring voice entered my mind.

I shouted up at the beautiful wyvern. "You're a regular comedian, aren't you, girl?" She answered with a loud roar.

Cade watched our exchange, simply shaking his head.

I closed my eyes, reaching out with my Wyldcaster magic. The air around us hummed with life—the fierce determination of the dragons, the graceful strength of the Pegasi, the cunning of the wyverns. It was overwhelming and exhilarating.

This time I called to their minds, *"Morning crew!"*

My eyes met Cade's. "It feels incredible out here. The energy is almost electric!"

Ariaxom trotted over, his coat shimmering like moonlight. I reached out, running my hand along his silky mane. "Hey there, handsome," I murmured, feeling a connection spark between us. "Is everything going good for y'all?"

"Yes, little one, our accommodations are very nice. We are being well taken care of. But you, my dear, have a dragon to ride."

Cade mounted Zarvyn and extended his hand to me. "Come on, love. Time to take to the skies."

"We're riding double today?"

"There may be battles where only one of us can take riders. You need to know how to ride in tandem, little StarHeart. So don't gain any weight," the dragon teased with a snicker.

I reached for the rope attached to the saddle they'd fabricated, hauling myself up after Cade. I'd been learning to use my wind magic, so if I'd really wanted to show off, I could've just "flown" up.

As I swung into the saddle in front of Cade, he secured his arms around my waist.

Zarvyn spread his wings, muscles coiling beneath us. "Hold on tight," Cade warned, a hint of mischief in his voice.

We launched into the air, and for a moment, all my fears fell away. Up here, with Cade and these magnificent creatures, I felt invincible. As we soared through the clouds, practicing aerial maneuvers and magical attacks, I realized that this—this feeling of belonging, of purpose—was what I'd been searching for my entire life.

And as we prepared for the battles that lay ahead, I knew that with Cade by my side and this newfound family of magical beings, we'd lead this army to victory. And we'd do everything we could to keep everyone alive while we did it.

***

We'd taken our midday break for lunch and headed into the great hall. I walked with Miranda, nudging her playfully. "So, uh, you and Thorne seem to be awfully buddy-buddy out on the training field." I waggled my eyebrows, elbowing her in the side.

"Ollie, you really need to work on your subtlety."

I burst out laughing. "Since when have I *ever* been subtle?"

"Good point." She leaned in, lowering her voice. "He *is* something, isn't he?"

"That he is, sugar, that he is. I think I'm going to have to prepare Cade for losing his most trusted general once this war is over."

"Do you really think so?"

"Oh, my darlin' cousin. I see the way that man looks at you. And the way the two of you move together, it's like a symphony. You can't fake being that in sync. Have y'all spent any time together away from the training field?"

"Unfortunately, we haven't. He's always working. It's

like he refuses to stop planning, strategizing, meeting with commanders. Maybe he only sees me as a combat partner."

"No, girlfriend. Like I said, I see how he looks at you. It's way more than that. And I get it—he's leading the combined forces, so there's an enormous weight on his shoulders. But I'll speak to Cade. It's not healthy for Thorne to *never* take a break."

Miranda sighed, a wistful look crossing her face. "I appreciate that, Ollie. But I don't want you meddling. If something's meant to happen between Thorne and me, it will."

I rolled my eyes. "Sometimes fate needs a little nudge, sugar. But fine, I'll keep my nose out of it. For now." I was serious about that break, though. I knew battles were imminent, but not everyone had a partner like Cade, someone to help them unwind. Intense training and planning alone would eventually take its toll.

As we entered the great hall, the scent of roasted meat and fresh bread filled the air. My stomach growled in response, and we made our way to the long tables piled high with food. Cade was already there, deep in conversation with Thorne and a few other commanders.

I caught his eye and winked, earning a small smile, before he turned back to his discussion. As I loaded my plate, I couldn't help but overhear snippets of their conversation.

"... activity on the eastern border," Thorne said, his brow furrowed. "Scouts report strange movements near Shadowwood Forest."

Miranda raised her brows at me, and we sidled closer, sliding into the seats beside them. I couldn't resist and asked, "What kind of activity?"

Cade turned toward me, his expression grim. "There might be a small rift or breach. The scouts didn't stay long enough to get specifics, just that something feels... wrong."

Shadowwood Forest. A chill snaked down my spine. The forest had a reputation—dark, unpredictable, and far too easy to get lost in. If creatures from the underworld had come through a rift there, it wouldn't be easy to track them down.

"What are we dealing with, exactly?" Miranda asked, her tactical instincts already kicking in.

Thorne shook his head. "We don't know yet. We'll need to send a team to scout before we make a plan."

I looked at Cade, already knowing the answer. "I assume that means us?"

He gave a slow nod, his eyes flickering with pride—and worry. "With the Dragonia, we're the best shot at finding out what's going on. If we need to neutralize the threat, we can do that, too. If not, we'll get the intel and return."

"You think two dragons, or you wanna ride tandem? Maybe we could bring Drathom along. Wyvern support couldn't hurt."

"Maybe flying tandem is best for this mission. I'd kind of like Ariaxom along to be eyes in the sky, too. If we get into trouble, the Pegasi are the fastest way to get word back to Vesparra."

"Right away, Sire?" Thorne asked Cade.

Cade nodded. "Olivia and I will grab food, eat as we go, and get the Dragonia so they can be here for the briefing."

As we ate on the move, I couldn't help but feel a mix of excitement and trepidation. The Shadowwood was dangerous enough without the added threat of an enemy incursion, but this was what we had been training for. My mind was a whirl of battle plans, tangled up with my own personal battles I was trying to push aside. I was sure all kinds of mixed feelings were flowing through the bond.

There was no way Cade could miss it. "Penny for your thoughts, darling?"

I took a deep breath, then let out a small, bitter laugh as we walked. "I wanted to talk to you about our marking ceremony after the lunch break. But as usual..."

He stopped me halfway to the Dragonia's caves, placing his hands on my shoulders. "Starlight, you know there is nothing in the heavens or in this realm that could ever change my love for you. A ceremony won't make me love you more."

I stared at my feet, feeling a little foolish for bringing it up now. "I know there are bigger things to worry about. But... I thought we'd have done it by now." My voice cracked, betraying how much it mattered. "And I feel like such a brat for even wanting it when everything around us feels like it's crumbling."

I slowly raised my gaze to him. "Cade, I know you don't understand. I truly don't expect you to. I don't doubt you love me or that you're committed to me. It's just... it's just a silly traditional thing I grew up believing in and dreaming about for myself. We called it a wedding in the mortal realm. It's somethin' even a poor, unloved, and lonely girl in Texas dreamed about. And I feel like the most selfish, whiny butt for even feelin' sorry for myself because I can't have it now—and lord knows when we'll ever be able to." I was making myself more upset. "So, I gotta keep on livin' with a man who hasn't put a ring on it, cuz monsters are tryin' to kill everybody!"

His hands cupped my face, tilting it up, so I met his gaze. "We'll have it, Olivia. I swear. As soon as we take care of this, it'll be our priority."

I nodded, feeling both unreasonable and grateful. And that's when I noticed our audience. The Dragonia had gathered at the mouth of the cave, watching us with varying degrees of amusement and interest.

"We have company."

Cade looked over his shoulder. "Enjoying the show?"

Not surprisingly, Skorn, the wyvern, had to pipe up. *"No, please continue. I love whiny humans complaining about problems that aren't even problems. Boohoo, I have to save an entire realm because I have the most awesome magic in history. So I must wait to have a little ceremony, like that's a big problem. Maybe Vaelith can do the ceremony on the training field tomorrow."*

I spoke out loud, "Wow, Skorn. Point taken. Sorry, my *one*

little meltdown was so offensive to you. You don't have to be a dadgum butthead about it." I took a deep breath and addressed the group.

"Everyone—we have a potential breach in Shadowwood Forest. We need to go check it out. It'll be Cade and me tandem on Vaelith; I want Drathom coming as backup, and Ariaxom, I'd like you to be our eyes in the sky. We're heading to the castle for a briefing before we head out. Cade, you good?"

"Yes ma'am. I'm right behind you."

With that, we turned around and headed back to the castle. I felt both angry that my private conversation had been overheard and foolish because my outburst to Cade suddenly seemed petty and ridiculous.

CHAPTER 6

Olivia

As we walked from the caves, I felt the weight of responsibility settle over me again. There was no room for hesitation. If something had breached, we needed to find it and eliminate it before it could wreak havoc on the realm.

We reached the castle just as the commanders gathered, Kaelen standing at the forefront. He looked me over with that wolfish intensity, a knowing glance passing between us before he focused on the mission at hand.

"We're briefed on the situation," Kaelen said. "The rift was reported near the edge of Shadowwood Forest. Whatever came through won't stay hidden for long."

"Cade and I will fly tandem on Vaelith," I said, keeping my tone steady, masking the unease building inside me. "Ariaxom, we'll need you in the sky—if it's on the move, we can't let it slip past us. Drathom, back us up from the air. If we can drive it toward the clearing, you'll have a clean shot."

Cade gave a small nod, his hand brushing mine in a fleeting touch of reassurance. "We've got this."

"Don't forget to send word if things go sideways," Kaelen added, his expression tight. "We'll be ready to follow."

I looked to Amaya, who stood off to the side, tension radiating from her. "We'll be back soon. Hold things down here."

Her jaw clenched. "Just don't make me come rescue you."

I chuckled, though my heart wasn't in it. "Deal."

Just then, Grandpapa stepped through the crowd with a glowing crystal in his hand.

"This is the perfect time to test the crystal communications network we've been working on."

He handed me the small crystal and explained how to use it.

"To get a message back to us, just channel a bit of your energy into this communication stone and use this simple incantation:

Bridge the distance, our voices state,
To Vesparra in day or night,
Guide this stone with boundless light.

"That will trigger the corresponding stone that Kaelen will have in his keeping, and you'll be able to communicate directly with him."

"Grandpapa, I stand in awe of you." I kissed his cheek and slipped the stone into the pocket of my tunic.

With that, Cade and I made our way to Vaelith. His scales shimmered like molten silver in the torchlight as he stretched his wings in anticipation.

"Ready to fly, little StarHeart?" Vaelith's voice echoed in my mind, laced with excitement.

I climbed up the rope ladder onto the saddle attached to his back and settled in front of Cade. "Ready."

Skorn's voice came through my mind at that moment. *"Little one, I apologize for the cruel things that I said.. You deserve to have whatever ceremony you want. My attempt at humor was thoughtless. Now, go and beat the shit out of some son of a demon spawn for me. And stay safe."*

I quickly wiped a tear away. *"Accepted. And I will kill in your honor if the opportunity arises, sir."* A smile lingered on my face as we went toward the unknown.

Vaelith took several running steps, and leaped, carrying

us into the sky with a mighty beat of his wings. The ground fell away beneath us. Ariaxom shot ahead, his silvery wings blending into the twilight as Drathom followed from a distance. The air was sharp and cool against my skin, the landscape below a patchwork of trees and shadows.

The Shadowwood loomed in the distance, a dark mass that swallowed the horizon. As we approached, I scanned the forest floor, searching for any signs of movement. Vaelith's mind brushed against mine. *Something is here... it's waiting.*

"*There,*" Cade said, his voice low and tense, pointing toward a scorched clearing where the earth was torn open with deep gouges, as if something immense had clawed its way to the surface.

Vaelith let out a growl that reverberated through his massive frame as he tilted downward, his scales glinting in the dim light. I clung to Cade as we descended, the air thick with the scent of sulfur and charred earth. The moment Vaelith's claws scraped against the ground, a deep, guttural roar echoed from the shadows, making the trees shudder and my bones vibrate.

A hulking silhouette shifted at the edge of the clearing— a creature as dark as midnight, with flickers of molten fire licking along its skin and eyes that burned with malevolence. It moved like liquid darkness, each step scorching the ground beneath its feet.

"Stay close," Cade warned, his gaze unwavering as he dismounted and unsheathed his sword. Vaelith took a protective stance in front of us, his massive wings unfurling as he bared his teeth, a low, rumbling challenge spilling from his throat. Overhead, Drathom circled, hissing, as he trained his eyes on the beast below.

"*It's firebound,*" Vaelith rumbled, his voice like a landslide. "*Magic alone won't stop it—we need elemental force.*"

Cade's gaze shifted to me, calm but intense. "Water, Olivia. Draw as much as you can. It's our best chance."

I nodded, reaching out to the stream that twisted like a silver thread through the forest. I could feel the pulse of the water, cool and ancient, and I willed it to rise. Responding to my call, it surged toward me, gathering in a dense sphere above my outstretched hand.

The creature snarled and lunged, claws tearing into the earth. Cade moved in a blur, his sword slicing through the air to drive it back, while Vaelith snapped his jaws, fiery embers crackling between his teeth.

I hurled the water with all my might, the liquid crashing against the beast's molten hide. Steam exploded on impact, a furious hiss filling the clearing as the creature staggered, its skin smoking where the water struck.

"Again!" Cade's shout cut through the chaos, his voice steady amidst the fury.

With renewed focus, I drew more water, the stream twisting and surging as I launched wave after wave. The creature roared in defiance, each blast of water searing into its fiery core, weakening its movements until its fierce glow dimmed.

Just then, Drathom dove from above, talons outstretched as he raked across the beast's back, tearing through the seared flesh with a shriek of triumph. Vaelith lunged forward, his jaws closing around the creature's neck in a final, bone-crushing bite.

The beast let out one last, ear-splitting roar before collapsing to the ground in a heap of smoldering ash and twisted limbs, the fire in its eyes fading to embers.

Silence fell over the clearing, broken only by the hiss of steam and the labored breathing of our allies. Cade looked at me, a faint smile of relief on his face. "You were amazing, Olivia," he said softly, his hand resting briefly on my shoulder.

Vaelith's voice echoed in my mind, deep and proud. *"Well done, StarHeart. But the rift awaits. Let's seal this breach before it has a chance to spread."*

We sprinted toward the rift, a jagged tear in the very fabric of reality. It pulsed with a chaotic, sinister energy, each beat vibrating with the promise of darkness waiting to spill through. I raised my hands, feeling my magic surge to meet it, and poured everything I had into sealing the rupture. The tear shimmered, resisting, as if fighting me tooth and nail. But at last—with a final, deafening snap—it sealed shut, leaving an eerie silence in its wake.

I sagged against Cade, my breath coming in heavy bursts. "That... was intense," I panted, managing a weary grin. "But we did it."

He brushed a stray lock of hair from my face, his eyes warm yet serious. "Of course we did. But I'm sure this is just the beginning."

Vaelith rumbled with a low chuckle, folding his massive wings. *Not bad for mortals,* he said, his tone filled with dragon pride.

Ariaxom swooped down to join us, landing with a grace that only further fueled his smugness. *"I must admit, that was impressive. For humans,"* he added with a smirk, his eyes gleaming with that familiar Dragonia arrogance.

I rolled my eyes but couldn't help the grin that tugged at my lips. The Dragonia always had something to say.

Drathom landed beside us with a mighty thud, his dark scales glinting ominously in the moonlight. *"Next time, let's hope it's something with a bit more bite,"* he muttered, his eyes narrowing at the spot where the rift had been, as if daring it to reopen.

Cade laughed, pulling me closer. "I'd settle for boring missions any day," he murmured, though his gaze remained sharp, scanning the clearing as if already expecting the next breach.

"Y'all are nuts, if you call that boring." I said, shaking my head.

I leaned into Cade, exhaustion tugging at every muscle,

but beneath the weariness was a deep sense of pride—and a lingering edge of worry. This was the first rift, but more were sure to come, likely stronger, each one clawing its way into our world with relentless fury. We'd need every drop of magic, every ounce of strength we had to keep them at bay.

I took the communication stone from my pocket, thinking this was a good time to test it. Summoning a bit of my energy, I repeated the words Grandpapa had given me and waited. In just a few seconds, I heard Kaelen's voice.

"Olivia? Is everything alright?"

I could hardly believe how clearly his voice rang out. "We're fine! Heading back your way now! Will report when we arrive."

The relief was clear in Kaelen's response. "See you soon."

As we mounted Vaelith and lifted into the night sky, the weight of the coming battles settled over us like a shadow. But for now, we had each other, our laughter echoing through the starlit night.

And that would have to be enough.

We knew that starting tomorrow, we'd have to double our efforts on building command posts throughout the realm and increasing patrols.

As we soared back toward the castle, the adrenaline of battle slowly ebbed away, replaced by a bone-deep weariness. The cool night air whipped past us, carrying the scent of pine and damp earth. I leaned back against Cade, grateful for his solid presence.

"You're thinking too loudly," he murmured, his breath warm against my ear.

I sighed. "Just wondering how we're going to keep up if these breaches come with more frequency and in varied places."

His arms tightened around me. "We are going to have to figure out a more rigid patrol system. I think Farin has some sound plans in mind."

I thought about my step-grandfather and how very

grateful I was for him. "Thank the goddess for Grandpapa and his strategic mind. Between him and Miranda, we should be at least somewhat prepared to face the onslaught."

As the castle came into view, its spires reaching toward the star-strewn sky, I felt a sudden wave of exhaustion wash over me. The weight of our responsibilities, the constant vigilance required, and the sheer magnitude of what we faced threatened to overwhelm me for a moment.

Cade must have sensed my shift in mood through the bond. He pressed a gentle kiss to the top of my head. "One day at a time, Olivia. That's all we can do."

I nodded, drawing strength from his quiet confidence. As we approached the castle, I could see figures gathered in the courtyard, waiting for our return. Kaelen stood at the forefront, his posture tense until he caught sight of us. Even from this distance, I could see his shoulders relax slightly.

Vaelith landed with a graceful thud, his wings creating a gust of wind that ruffled the hair and clothes of those nearby. As we dismounted, Kaelen strode forward.

"Report?"

"Rift sealed, creature neutralized," I said, my voice steady despite my fatigue. "It was a firebound entity, just as dangerous as we feared. We took it down with a combination of water magic and brute force. But it being the first creature to make it through, I'd say we handled it perfectly. I'm not sure what other creatures we'll encounter or how soon it will be."

Kaelen nodded, his eyes scanning over us for any signs of injury. "Any injuries?"

"No, thank the Goddess," Cade replied. "But the forest took some damage. We'll need to send a team to assess and begin restoration efforts."

"Already on it," Amaya chimed in, stepping forward. "I've got a group ready to head out at first light."

I shot her a grateful smile. "Thanks, Amaya. We'll need to increase patrols in that area as well, just in case."

"Agreed," Kaelen said. "I'll speak with the captains about adjusting the rotation."

"We need to get Grandpapa's communication devices to the patrols and command centers. It worked like a dream!" I was so proud of him.

At the mention of his name, Farin stepped forward, his eyes twinkling despite the gravity of the situation. "Excellent news, my dear. I'll start mass-producing them immediately. We'll have every patrol and command post equipped within the week."

I felt a surge of pride and affection for my step-grandfather. His inventions could very well be the key to our survival in the coming days.

"Now," Kaelen said, his tone softening slightly, "you two should get some rest. We'll debrief fully in the morning."

I nodded, suddenly aware of just how exhausted I was. Cade's hand found mine, giving it a gentle squeeze.

"Come on," he murmured. "Let's get you to bed."

As we made our way through the castle halls, the weight of the day's events settled over me like a heavy cloak. The adrenaline had long since faded, leaving behind a bone-deep weariness that made each step feel like a monumental effort. After a hot bath and a meal in our room, I curled up in Cade's arms in our bed and had a wonderful, dreamless sleep.

CHAPTER 7

Amaya

I can't lie—I was proud of myself for contributing last night after Ollie and Cade returned with the Dragonia. They'd defeated the first creature we'd encountered from the Underworld, but that first rift and the battle had left significant scars on the land. I'd taken charge of setting things to rights.

The transition from a New York fashion designer to... whatever I was now... was staggering.

As I continued my task, a quiet sense of satisfaction settled over me. I may not have Olivia's commanding presence, but I'd held my own. I'd contributed. And in doing so, I'd discovered a strength within myself I'd never known existed.

When I led the team out to the Shadowwood to assess the damage, it felt right. My elemental magic was made for this, and I was eager to put it to work. I closed my eyes, feeling the pulse of magic thrumming through my veins. The earth beneath my feet called to me, a steady, grounding rhythm. With a deep breath, I reached out, willing a small mound of soil to rise.

"Come on," I muttered, my brow furrowing in concentration.

Slowly, the dirt began to swirl, lifting into the air. A grin spread across my face as I manipulated it, shaping it into intricate patterns.

"Not bad, Amaya," I whispered to myself, tucking a stray curl behind my ear.

Next, I turned my attention to the surrounding air. It whispered and danced, responding to my silent command. A gentle breeze caressed my skin, growing stronger as I focused my energy.

"This is... incredible," I breathed, marveled at how the elements bent to my will.

Finally, I reached out to the nearby stream. The water rippled, then rose in a graceful arc, twisting and turning as I directed it.

As I stood there, surrounded by the dance of earth, air, and water, a heady rush of power coursed through me. This newfound ability to shape the world around me was intoxicating.

But even as I reveled in my growing magical prowess, another thought intruded, sending a jolt of electricity through me.

Kaelen.

My hands faltered. The elements settled back into place as my concentration broke. I sighed, running a hand through my hair. I immediately went back to work and didn't stop until the job was done. But then, just as quickly, my thoughts drifted right back to *him.*

"Dammit," I muttered, frustration coloring my tone. "Why can't I stop thinking about him?"

The mate bond tugged at me, a constant reminder of our connection. It both thrilled and terrified me.

"It's not fair," I said to no one in particular, pacing along the riverbank. "I barely know him. How can I be destined for someone I just met?"

But even as the words left my mouth, I knew they weren't entirely true. In the short time I'd known Kaelen, I'd seen his strength, his loyalty, his fierce protectiveness. And gods help me, I *wanted* him.

"But is it real?" I wondered aloud, hugging myself tightly. "Or is it just this... this bond?"

The internal struggle raged on—desire warring with fear, longing with hesitation. I wanted to trust in the connection I felt with Kaelen, to let myself fall. But a lifetime of independence and self-reliance wasn't easily set aside.

"I'm not someone who doesn't know how to take care of herself," I said firmly, straightening my shoulders. "I don't need a mate to complete me."

Yet even as I spoke the words, I couldn't deny the way my heart raced at the thought of Kaelen's piercing silver eyes. The way his deep voice sent shivers down my spine. I thought of the weight of always having to carry everything alone. Since I was a child, I'd had to fend for myself. Poor Ollie wanted to be there for me so badly, and she did all she could, but how could she help when she was constantly being abused and separated from me? We were both robbed of the carefree lives children should experience.

On some level, I *wanted* to have someone else take care of everything for once. But not because something forced them to.

I groaned, flopping down onto the soft grass. "What am I going to do?"

The crunch of footsteps on gravel pulled me from my thoughts, and I looked up to see Kaelen approaching, his powerful frame silhouetted against the dimming sky. My heart leaped into my throat.

"Are you ready to go, Amaya?" His deep voice sent a shiver through me.

I stood, brushing grass from my clothes. "I've done all I need to do here. Not bad, huh?" I replied with a grin, though, for some silly reason, I suddenly felt awkward seeking his approval.

Kaelen's eyes searched my face. "You're incredible, Maya.

Are you sure you're fine to head back to Therionis with me? We don't have to go if you're not comfortable."

"No, I want to," I said quickly, surprising myself with the truth of it. "I just... it's a big step."

He nodded, understanding in his gaze. "It is. But I love the idea of it."

As we walked toward the portal, the air between us crackled with unspoken tension. I found myself hyper-aware of Kaelen's presence, the way his arm occasionally brushed mine, sending jolts of electricity through my body.

"I've packed some of your favorite snacks," Kaelen said, breaking the silence. "So you'd have them at my keep."

The thoughtfulness of the gesture caught me off guard. "You noticed what I like to eat?"

A small smile played at the corners of his mouth. "I notice everything about you, Amaya."

My cheeks flushed hot, and I looked away, unable to meet his intense gaze. We reached the shimmering portal, its surface rippling like liquid silver.

Kaelen held out his hand. "Together?"

I hesitated for a moment, then placed my hand in his. His warmth enveloped me, steadying my nerves. "Together," I agreed.

We stepped through the portal, the world dissolving around us in a kaleidoscope of color and light.

As the dizzying swirl faded, I gasped as Therionis materialized around us. A sea of emerald stretched as far as the eye could see, rolling hills blanketed in lush forests and verdant meadows. The air was thick with the scent of pine and wildflowers, a heady perfume that made my head spin.

"I love how beautiful it is here. I'd forgotten," I whispered, drinking in the sight.

Kaelen seemed to look on with pride as he gazed out over his kingdom. "Welcome home, Amaya."

Home. The word echoed in my mind, stirring something

deep within me. I'd only spent a few days here before, yet an inexplicable sense of belonging washed over me. My fingers itched to touch the grass, to feel the earth beneath my feet.

"I can't believe how much I missed this place," I admitted, surprised by the intensity of my emotions.

Kaelen's eyes softened as he looked at me. "Therionis has a way of calling to those who belong here."

I swallowed hard, unsure how to respond to the implication in his words. Before I could formulate a reply, movement in the distance caught my eye. A tall, lithe figure was striding toward us, her gait purposeful and predatory.

As she drew closer, I felt Kaelen tense beside me. The woman's beauty was undeniable—all sleek lines and dangerous curves, with hair like fiery sunlight and eyes the color of amber. But it was the cold calculation in those eyes that sent a shiver down my spine.

"Fiora," Kaelen said, his voice carefully neutral. "I wasn't expecting you."

Fiora's lips curved into a smile that didn't reach her eyes. "Kaelen, darling. You know I always like to greet you personally when you return." Her gaze slid to me, sharp and assessing. "And who might this be?"

I straightened my spine, refusing to be cowed. "I'm Amaya Ilyndor."

"Ah," Fiora purred, her tone dripping with false sweetness. "The mortal girl I've heard so much about."

Kaelen's hand found the small of my back, a gesture of support that didn't go unnoticed by Fiora. Her eyes narrowed almost imperceptibly.

"Amaya is my guest," Kaelen said firmly. "And an invaluable ally in our fight against Magda and the Underworld. And she's no more mortal than the rest of us."

Fiora's smile tightened. "Of course. How... fortunate for us all."

Caught between Kaelen's protective presence and Fiora's

thinly veiled hostility, I couldn't shake the feeling that I'd just stepped into a den of wolves—and I wasn't referring to the shifters. I wasn't entirely sure I knew how to navigate these treacherous waters.

Fiora's amber eyes locked onto mine, her gaze piercing. "I'm sure you'll find Therionis... quaint compared to your world. Do try not to get lost in our forests, dear. They can be quite dangerous for those unfamiliar with our ways."

The threat in her words was unmistakable. I swallowed hard, but met her gaze steadily. "I appreciate your concern, Fiora. But I'm a quick learner."

Kaelen's hand pressed more firmly against my back. "Amaya has proven herself more than capable," he said, his deep voice rumbling with a hint of warning. "Now, if you'll excuse us, we have matters to discuss."

As we walked away, I could feel Fiora's eyes boring into my back. My heart raced, but I forced myself to keep my head high.

Once we were out of earshot, Kaelen led me to a secluded glade. The tension in his shoulders eased slightly as he turned to face me. "I apologize for Fiora's behavior. She can be... protective of her position here."

I raised an eyebrow. "Her position? Or you?"

A flicker of something—regret? embarrassment? — crossed his face. "It's complicated. But that's not what we need to focus on right now." He gestured to a fallen log, and we sat down. "We need to discuss the patrols."

I knew we needed to discuss the patrols, but I wasn't letting this go. "Humor me. What exactly is her 'position'? And does she have... designs on you?"

His heavy sigh warned me I might not like what he had to say. "Fiora is from a prominent family in my pack. They fancied her as my Luna—my mate. They've been hopeful, especially since I hadn't connected with my Fated Mate—until now, of course. I've seen her socially, and yes, we were... involved, Amaya. I'm 82 years old. I've had a few relationships, but as you know, I've still waited for you." His voice softened. "I haven't been with Fiora in over a year, and it's been platonic since. But she keeps trying." He sighed, rubbing the back of his neck. "As for her position, she's my military liaison. A sort of secretary to the commanders. I believe she took the role just to be near me."

I let his words settle, feeling a slight blow to my ego but understanding the reality. Of course, he'd had beautiful women in his life. He was a powerful, gorgeous Alpha King; few men could be more desirable than that. I was grateful for his honesty.

I nodded, pushing the sting aside. "I understand, and I don't blame her." Taking a breath, I shifted gears. "So, the patrols. What's our strategy?"

The look he gave me was somewhere between confusion and relief. He gathered himself quickly, his brow furrowing in concentration as he explained. "Alright. Patrols. We'll need to establish a rotating schedule—start with the borders, then work our way inward."

"There's something else we need to address," I said, steeling myself. "The mate bond. How will it affect our ability to work together?"

Kaelen's eyes met mine, and for a moment, I felt like I was drowning in their depths. "The bond doesn't have to complicate things, Amaya. Unless we let it."

I swallowed hard. "And what if... what if I want it to?"

I tore my gaze from Kaelen's intense stare, my heart pounding. Before he could respond, a deep, melodic voice cut through the tension.

"Kaelen, if I may interrupt?"

Farin Thalassa, my grandfather, approached. His regal bearing commanded immediate respect. Relief washed over me—I was grateful for the distraction.

I jumped up, quickly giving him a hug and kissing his cheek. "Grandpapa, what a surprise!"

"Of course, Farin," Kaelen said, though a hint of frustration lingered in his voice. "What news?"

Grandpapa's dark eyes twinkled with wisdom as he addressed us. "I've taken the liberty of setting up three patrol command centers across Therionis: one near the northern border, another to the east, and a third here at the keep."

I couldn't help but be impressed. "That's incredibly thorough, Grandpapa. How did you manage it so quickly?"

He smiled, the corners of his eyes crinkling. "Years of experience, my dear. And a little help from our Vesparran allies."

Kaelen nodded approvingly. "Excellent work. This will streamline our defenses significantly."

As Grandpapa began detailing the specifics of each command center, I marveled at the respect he commanded. Even Kaelen, a king in his own right, listened intently to the older man's counsel.

Kaelen drew me back into the conversation. "We'd forgotten about Farin's crystal communication network."

It felt good to be part of the planning and protecting of the realm. I loved Kaelen respected my opinion and valued my input. "Oh, right! The crystal communications could create a linked system, allowing each center to monitor a wider area."

We discussed further how we could streamline communications and went into detailed discussions about troop positioning and logistics well into the evening. To my surprise, I enjoyed strategizing with Grandpapa and Kaelen as they each shared insights I hadn't considered. It sounded like our defense systems had finally started coming together. We'd need further meetings to get everything running at full capacity, but we were far closer than we'd been yesterday.

***

When I'd retreated to my chambers, it was well past dark. The day's events swirled in my mind like a tempest, refusing to settle. I absently tucked a wayward curl behind my ear, pacing the length of my room.

"What am I going to do?" I muttered, my fingers tracing the intricate patterns on a nearby tapestry. The silk was cool beneath my touch, grounding me in the present.

My thoughts drifted to Kaelen, his eyes seeming to pierce through my soul, even in memory. The way he'd looked at me during the strategy meeting—a mix of pride and something deeper, more primal...

I shook my head, trying to dispel the image. "It's just the mate bond," I whispered, but the words felt hollow.

A knock at the door startled me from my reverie. "Come in," I called, smoothing my dress nervously.

Fiora glided into the room, her presence as cold and imposing as ever. "I trust you're settling in well, Lady Amaya," she said, her tone dripping with false sweetness.

I forced a smile. "Yes, thank you. Everyone's been very welcoming."

Fiora's eyes narrowed. "Indeed. Kaelen seems particularly... attentive to your needs. Be careful, he's quite a heartbreaker. I'm more than familiar with his fine work." A cruel smile curved across her face.

The implication hung heavy in the air. Heat flushed my cheeks, a mix of anger and embarrassment rising within me. "Kaelen's been a gracious host; there is no question," I replied, struggling to keep my voice even.

Fiora's lip curled in a sneer. "Of course. Well, I'll leave you to your rest. We have a long day of patrols ahead of us tomorrow."

As the door clicked shut behind her, I sank onto the edge of my bed, my mind reeling. I couldn't help but wonder what exactly she was doing in the keep at this hour. I hadn't seen her at all the last time I was here—was she kept away on purpose then? Her thinly veiled hostility, Kaelen's intense gaze, my own confusing desires... it was all too much.

I closed my eyes, taking a deep breath. The scent of pine

and earth filled my lungs, reminding me of the power that now coursed through my veins. I was no longer just Amaya, the fashion designer from New York. I was Princess Amaya Ilyndor, daughter of a murdered king and queen, sister to the Chosen One of the Goddess Vesperia, wielder of earth, water, and air magic—and a key player in the defense of this realm.

"Enough," I said aloud, standing with newfound determination. "I can't keep running from this."

I strode to the window, gazing out at the moonlit forest. Somewhere out there, Kaelen was probably making his final rounds, ensuring the safety of his people.

"Tomorrow," I promised myself, my reflection resolute in the glass. "Tomorrow, I'll talk to Kaelen. We need to understand what this bond really means—what we truly feel for each other beyond the pull of fate."

As I prepared for bed, a sense of calm settled over me. Whatever came next, I would face it head-on. It was time to confront my feelings, to understand the depth of our connection. Only then could I find my place in this new world —and perhaps in Kaelen's arms.

CHAPTER 8

Olivia

With the departure of Amaya and Kaelen, Cade and I returned to our training sessions with the Dragonia. These majestic creatures were Eldoria's most formidable and enigmatic guardians. Our unique ability to communicate with them was a part of the gift given to us by the Goddess. It was truly one of her greatest blessings. I loved the time Cade and I spent training with these magnificent creatures and the relationships we had forged with them.

The sun bore down on our backs as we stood before the huge, emerald-scaled beast, Eryndor, his eyes, like pools of molten gold, bored into mine.

"You ready to go to work little StarHeart?"

"Apparently, I was literally *born* ready." I answered with a sideways grin.

He cut those golden eyes to Cade. *"The cheek on this girl, Cade. You ever going to tame her?"*

"Oh, no, sir. I like my Starlight with the wild streak she carries." Came his answer as he gave me a peck on the cheek.

I loved that I had been able to share my Wyldcaster abilities with him those weeks ago. It had become our greatest strength in our fight against the Underworld.

Vaelith lumbered towards us. *"Let's change things up a bit today. StarHeart, you haven't ridden Zarvyn yet. Why don't you give him a whirl?"*

"I think I can make that happen." I was already climbing up the rope ladder to the saddle that rested on his beautiful, dark scales.

"Cade, I've got you." Eryndor spoke to us in our minds as Cade make short work of mounting him.

As we soared through the crimson skies of Eldoria astride the dragons, I couldn't help but marvel at the surreal beauty unfolding before me. Below us, the heavily forested lands of Vesparra gave way to the lush, rolling meadows of land between the kingdoms of Eldoria. Forests, lakes, and mountains rose and gave way to rolling plains. The land was as varied as her people.

I urged Zarvyn to dive lower, feeling the wind whip through my hair and the power of his body rippling underneath me. Beside me, Cade gave a whoop of exhilaration, his unrestrained joy infectious as we raced the wind itself. I heard the rumble of the beast's laughter beneath me, and there was a kind of contentment that filled the empty corners of my heart.

In that moment, with the wind in our hair and our dragons soaring through the air, it felt as if the world was ours for the taking. The weight of our responsibilities as guardians of Eldoria seemed to lift, at least for a little while. We banked sharply, wingtips grazing, the crimson sky above us a canvas for our aerial ballet.

As we raced through the skies, something within me shifted—a newfound confidence in our abilities to protect this world we loved so fiercely. A warmth blossomed in my chest, not just from the adrenaline coursing through my veins, but also from the knowledge that Cade was beside me, his presence steady and sure.

I glanced over at him and was amazed at the look of contentment that rested on his face. He carried the weight of his kingdom on his shoulders every hour of the day. But in this moment, he seemed lighter somehow, and he was beautiful.

"I love you, Highness."

He looked over his shoulder and caught my eyes.

"I love you, Starlight."

Both dragons moaned in unison, grumbling at our words, then we all broke into laughter as we flew on.

"The southeastern command center is nearly complete," Cade was letting me know his observations. *"We should be able to extend our patrol range by next week."*

I leaned forward, signaling Zarvyn to draw closer to Eryndor. *"That's good news. Have we had any word from the northern outposts?"*

Cade's brow furrowed. *"Nothing concrete, but there are whispers of increased activity near the Shadowlands."*

My chest tightened. *"Rifts?"*

"Possibly. We can't afford to let our guard down."

I nodded, determination coursing through me. *"We won't. Whatever comes, we'll be ready."*

Cade's eyes met mine, filled with fierce love and resolve.

As we banked towards the east, I couldn't shake the feeling that this moment of peace was fleeting. But with Cade by my side and the strength of our bond, I knew we'd weather whatever storm was brewing on the horizon.

As Ilyndor came into view, my heart swelled with a mix of anticipation and anxiety. The sprawling village nestled among rolling hills and ancient forests was a sight both familiar and foreign. Zarvyn and Eryndor descended gracefully, their massive wings stirring up eddies of air as we touched down on the outskirts of the village.

I dismounted, my legs slightly wobbly from the long flight. As I tucked an errant strand of hair behind my ear, I caught sight of two figures approaching. My face broke into a genuine smile as I recognized Miranda and Thorne.

"Welcome home, Your Highness," Miranda called out, her

warm brown eyes sparkling with delight. She embraced me tightly, and I relaxed into her familiar presence.

"It's good to be back," I replied. "It's good to see you, *too,* Your Majesty. Being the Queen of Ilyndor looks good on you."

Thorne's imposing figure loomed behind Miranda, his face set in its usual stern expression. But as he clasped Cade's arm in greeting, I caught a glimmer of warmth in his eyes.

"The village has made significant progress," Thorne rumbled, his deep voice carrying a hint of pride. "We're eager to show you the developments."

As we set off, I couldn't help but be amazed at the changes. The last time I'd seen Ilyndor, it had been a shadow of its former self, ravaged by years of neglect and the damage of Cade's fury when I'd been kidnapped by Eldric. Now, signs of rebirth were everywhere.

"How are the villagers coping?" I asked, my gaze drawn to a group of children playing near a newly constructed well.

Miranda's expression softened. "It's been challenging, but their spirit is unbreakable. Every day brings new hope. They are so happy to be free of their previous cruel rulers—full of joy at having their magic returned to them."

We passed by homes in various stages of repair; the air filled with the sounds of hammering and the scent of fresh-cut wood. My chest tightened with a mixture of pride and sorrow. These were my people, resilient in the face of adversity, yet bearing scars that ran deep.

"The earth and air elements are thriving again," Cade observed, his hand resting comfortingly on the small of my back. "You can feel the balance returning."

I nodded, feeling the subtle shift in the surrounding energy. It was as if the land itself was healing, slowly but surely.

As we rounded a corner, I gasped. Before us stood a partially completed structure, its graceful arches and intricate stonework a testament to the skill of Ilyndor's craftsmen.

"Is that...?" I trailed off, overcome with emotion.

Thorne's usually gruff voice softened. "The new community hall. A place for gatherings, celebrations, and governance. A symbol of Ilyndor's rebirth."

Tears pricked at the corners of my eyes. This was more than just a building; it was a beacon of hope, a promise of the future we were fighting for.

"It's beautiful," I whispered, leaning into Cade's solid presence.

As we continued our tour, I felt a renewed sense of purpose coursing through me. The road ahead would be fraught with challenges, but seeing the resilience of my people, the strength of our allies, and feeling the unwavering support of my mate, I knew we would prevail.

Ilyndor was rising from the ashes, and with it, the promise of a brighter future for all Eldoria.

As we approached the newly constructed market square, I noticed a subtle shift in the dynamic between Miranda and Thorne. Their shoulders brushed as they walked side by side, and I caught Miranda stealing glances at the towering general when she thought no one was looking.

"The craftsmen have outdone themselves," Miranda said, her voice warm with pride. She gestured towards an intricately carved wooden stall. "Thorne, didn't you help design some of these?"

Thorne's cheeks flushed slightly, a rare sight on the usually stoic warrior. "I may have offered a suggestion or two," he growled, but I detected a hint of pleasure in his tone.

Their fingers brushed as they both reached to touch the smooth wood, and I saw Miranda's breath catch. Thorne's eyes softened as they met hers, a tender moment amidst the bustle of reconstruction.

I exchanged a knowing look with Cade, feeling a mixture of joy and melancholy. It was heartening to see new bonds forming, even as my thoughts drifted to Amaya and Kaelen.

As if summoned by my musings, a chill ran down my spine. The world seemed to tilt, and I gasped, clutching Cade's arm.

"What is it?" he asked, concern etching his features.

"I don't know," I whispered, my heart racing. "Something's wrong. We need to get to Therionis. Now."

We made our hasty goodbyes, the earlier warmth replaced by a growing sense of dread. We'd have to shadow mist because the distance was too great to fly on the Dragons and arrive in a timely way. They'd make their way back to Vesparra on their own.

***

The moment we shadow misted into Therionis, the air hit me thick and foul, like rot and sulfur. My heart pounded with a dark certainty I hadn't been able to shake. We were too late. *Something* had already come through.

Cade and I burst into a clearing at the edge of the forest, where Amaya and Kaelen were locked in battle. A hulking beast loomed before them, its body a nightmarish mass of sinewy shadows and spiked limbs that scraped the ground, leaving scorched marks wherever it touched. Its eyes blazed with a sickly, unnatural green light, and each step sent tremors through the earth. A rift like a jagged tear in reality pulsed behind it, oozing with darkness.

Amaya stood her ground, hands raised, magic crackling through her fingers, channeling water and air into a barrier that drove the creature back. Kaelen was in his wolf form, a streak of silver-gray fur darting under the creature's claws and slashing with powerful jaws. Together, they moved in a fierce, seamless rhythm. For a moment, I felt a flicker of pride for Amaya—she was holding her own, her magic surging in ways I'd never seen before.

As Cade and I rushed to help, I caught a flash of movement at the tree line. A woman with flaming red hair stood just beyond the battle, her expression sharp, eyes narrowed on

Amaya. Her lips curled into a sneer as she stepped forward, shifting in one smooth motion into a massive red wolf.

Before I could shout a warning, she launched herself at Amaya, her claws flashing in the dim light. I watched in horror as the wolf's massive paw raked across Amaya's shoulder, leaving a trail of deep, crimson wounds. Amaya staggered, gasping, clutching at her arm as blood seeped between her fingers. The red wolf's snarl twisted into something almost like a grin before she turned and melted back into the shadows of the forest, disappearing without a trace.

"Amaya!" I cried, starting forward, but Cade's hand gripped my arm, anchoring me as he nodded toward the creature.

"We have to finish this, *now*," he said, his voice tight with urgency.

I swallowed hard, forcing myself to refocus. Amaya hadn't fallen—she was back on her feet, her gaze fierce, despite the blood staining her clothes. I summoned my power, calling on the earth beneath me, pulling its strength into my bones as Cade and I closed ranks beside Kaelen.

The beast lashed out wildly, its claws just grazing Kaelen's side. Cade moved like lightning, his blade slicing clean through one of its spiked limbs, while Kaelen's powerful jaws tore into its exposed flank. Amaya, undeterred by her injury, wove threads of air and water that wrapped around the creature's head, blinding it, each jet of water sizzling as it touched the beast's fiery skin.

The creature staggered, hissing in rage, but it was weakening.

"Now!" Cade shouted.

I raised my hands and unleashed a surge of earth magic, binding its feet in solid rock. With a snarl, Kaelen delivered the final blow, his jaws crushing the beast's neck. It let out a death wail, disintegrating into a pile of ash and twisted bones.

As silence fell, the rift pulsed once, as if sensing its creation's defeat. I turned toward it, pouring every ounce of energy I had left into sealing the tear. The rift resisted, thrumming with a dark energy that seemed to claw back at me, but with one final surge of magic, I forced it shut.

I sank to my knees, drained, but forced myself up as Amaya stumbled toward us, clutching her shoulder.

"Who—who was that?" she gasped, her face pale as she looked toward the trees where the red wolf had vanished.

I clenched my fists, rage simmering under my exhaustion. Whoever she was, that red wolf hadn't come here to fight monsters.

"I'm not sure," I murmured.

Kaelen

The battle's aftermath was a blur of adrenaline and exhaustion. My hands shook as I tended to Amaya's wounds, my heart still racing from the fight. She winced as I cleaned the gash on her shoulder, her blue-green eyes flashing with a mix of pain and frustration.

"It's not that bad, Kaelen," Amaya snapped, trying to push my hands away.

I took a deep breath, forcing my voice to remain calm. "It's bad enough that it needs attention. Let me help you."

She glared at me, her blonde curls wild and tangled. "I'm not some damsel in distress. You got swiped by that creature, too."

"I know," I said softly, my fingers gentle as I applied a healing salve. "You were incredible out there. But even the strongest warriors need care sometimes."

Amaya's shoulders slumped, her defenses crumbling. "I just... I need to prove I'm worthy of being here. Of being your..."

She trailed off, but I knew what she meant. My mate. The word hung unspoken between us, heavy with promise and fear.

"You have nothing to prove," I murmured, my voice husky

with emotion. "You're already more than I could have ever hoped for."

For a moment, I thought I saw a flicker of vulnerability in her eyes. But then she squared her shoulders, wincing slightly at the movement.

"We should get back," she said, her voice clipped. "We don't want to leave Cade and Ollie waiting."

I nodded, helping her to her feet. As we made our way back to the others, I couldn't shake the feeling that there was more to her injury than she was letting on. But for now, all I could do was stay close and hope she'd let me in.

Olivia

As we prepared to shadow mist home, a chill ran down my spine. I turned to see the red-haired woman approaching, her eyes gleaming with barely concealed malice.

"Cade, who is that woman?"

I could tell by the look on his face that was a subject he wasn't excited to talk about.

"That is Fiora. She is a woman from Kaelen's past. He made the mistake of seeing her romantically for several months before he realized she was not the type of woman he wanted in his life. It's a difficult situation because she is part of one of the most powerful families in his kingdom. She was raised and groomed, hoping she'd be Kaelen's mate or Luna—what they call their queen. They didn't expect him to find his True Mate."

"Well, we need to talk about her. I saw her hurt Maya during the fight with that creature from the Underworld."

"Olivia, you cannot be serious. Leveling that type of accusation is dangerous. Are you positive about what you saw?"

I could not believe he just questioned me! He doubted me? There's no doubt he could feel the anger and hurt pouring through the bond. I turned away from him. Just as he'd put his hands on my shoulders to turn me back to him, the woman of the hour made her way over to us.

"Leaving so soon?" Fiora purred, her voice dripping with false sincerity. "I hope dear Amaya is faring well after today's... excitement."

I bristled, struggling to keep my outrage under control as I responded through gritted teeth, "Amaya is fine. She's fought beside your Alpha today and helped take down that creature from the Underworld. She is quite a warrior."

Fiora's lips curled into a smirk. "Oh, I'm sure she is. But one must wonder how long she can keep up with the demands of life in Therionis. It would be such a shame if she were to... fall short."

My fists clenched at my sides, anger bubbling up inside me. But before I could retort, Cade's steady hand on my shoulder stopped me.

"We appreciate your concern, Fiora," he said, his tone diplomatic but cold. "But I assure you, Amaya is more than capable. And I can further assure you, if I were to hear that anyone caused her any distress whatsoever, harmed her, in *any* way, they will *not* live to brag about it."

Fiora blanched for a moment, then quickly recovered and sauntered away. Her words echoed in my mind, planting seeds of doubt I desperately tried to ignore. I couldn't shake the image of Amaya, vulnerable and uncertain, facing challenges she might not be prepared for.

"Do you still doubt me?"

"I'm sorry Starlight. I didn't doubt you. I just wanted you to be careful, for Maya's sake. An accusation without absolute proof could hurt her standing in the pack. It's a different hierarchy than in Vesparra. They put pack above all. Amaya needs to help protect Kaelen from any factions that might come against him. They will need to tread lightly. I will speak to Kaelen before we leave."

CHAPTER 9

Cade

The shadows in Kaelen's study seemed to deepen as I delivered the news, my words lingering in the silence. "Olivia saw it happen, Kaelen. Fiora shifted during the battle... and she attacked Amaya."

Kaelen's silver eyes flashed with a dangerous light, his jaw clenching. The air between us was taut, crackling like the electricity that sometimes sparked at Olivia's fingertips during training.

"Where?" His voice was low and deadly, laced with barely contained fury.

I swallowed, feeling the weight of his gaze. "Her shoulder. You should check it, make sure it's not..." I trailed off, not wanting to voice the thought that it might be more than a physical wound.

Kaelen's fist came down hard on his desk, the wood groaning under the force. "That treacherous bitch," he snarled, his usual composure fracturing. "I'll tear her apart for this."

He paced the length of his office, his movements fluid and dangerous, like a caged predator ready to spring. The air around him shimmered with barely contained power, a sharp reminder of just how formidable—and relentless—Kaelen could be.

"I doctored that wound right after we took down the

creature," he said. "Maya didn't mention anything about where it came from."

"There's more." I hated to add fuel to the fire, but Kaelen needed to hear everything. "Fiora made a threat. Veiled, but unmistakable. She's not going to stop, Kaelen."

He stopped in his tracks, swinging his gaze to mine. Fury and an icy determination burned in his eyes, a combination that sent a chill down my spine. "She won't get the chance," he growled. "I'll end this before she can lay another finger on Amaya."

I nodded, feeling the same protective instinct surge in my chest. My thoughts shifted to Olivia, and a wave of gratitude washed over me that she had escaped the battle unscathed. "What's the plan?" I asked, already knowing that I'd stand beside him, whatever it entailed.

Kaelen's lips curled into a snarl, his elongated canines flashing in the dim light. "First, I check on Amaya. Then I hunt Fiora down and make her regret ever thinking she could touch my mate."

As he stormed toward the door, I couldn't help but think that Fiora had underestimated more than just Kaelen. She had underestimated the bond between him and Amaya—and in doing so, she might very well have sealed her own fate.

Amaya

I paced the length of my room, fingers absently tracing the intricate patterns etched into the cool stone walls of Therionis Castle. The air felt thick with tension, pressing in on me as my mind churned with a whirlwind of conflicting emotions. My shoulder still throbbed from where Fiora had clawed me, a stark reminder of the pain that simmered both within and without.

Suddenly, the door burst open, slamming against the wall with a resounding crack. Fiora strode in like she owned the place, her presence filling the room with a suffocating intensity. Her cold, predatory gaze locked onto mine as she prowled closer, her lips twisting in a smile that held no warmth. Instinctively, I took a step back, my heart hammering against my ribs.

"Well, well," Fiora purred, her voice a venomous whisper. "If it isn't our little pretender to the throne."

I squared my shoulders, forcing myself to meet her gaze, though every instinct screamed at me to look away. "You have no right to barge into my room without knocking. What do you want, Fiora?"

She laughed, the sound sharp and laced with cruelty. "Oh, darling. I want what's rightfully mine. The position of Luna, Kaelen's heart... all of it."

My stomach twisted, but I kept my voice steady. "Those choices belong to Kaelen. And he chose me. The mate bond—"

"The mate bond?" Fiora interrupted, her sneer deepening. "You think that bond makes you worthy? You're nothing but a weak, pathetic excuse for a Luna. You can't even control your magic properly."

"Just because I choose to not use my magic as a weapon against the people of this pack doesn't mean that I have no control over it."

Fiora's eyes glinted with a malicious glee as she stepped even closer. "Oh, sweet Amaya. Did you really think Kaelen could want someone like you? Someone so... weak?"

"You don't have any say in this," I whispered, but her words planted a sliver of doubt that wound its way into my heart.

She leaned in close, her breath hot against my ear. "Don't I?" Her voice was low, dripping with cruel satisfaction. "Then why did he catch me in the hallway earlier just so he could put his tongue in my mouth?"

The world tilted. I stumbled back, my legs hitting the edge of the bed. "No," I breathed, but the seed of uncertainty had already sprouted.

Fiora's laughter echoed off the walls as she sauntered

towards the door. "Face it, little girl. You're nothing but a temporary distraction. Kaelen will come back to me. He always does."

With one last mocking smile, she slipped out of the room, leaving me reeling. I sank onto the bed, my body trembling, unable to hold back the tears that blurred my vision. Fiora's words played on a relentless loop in my mind, each repetition chipping away at the fragile confidence I'd been holding onto.

I pressed my hands to my temples, struggling to sort truth from lies, to push back against the doubt taking hold in my heart. Yes, I was still new to this world, still learning. But what if Fiora was right? What if I truly wasn't worthy of being Luna?

The mate bond—something that had once felt like a gift —now felt like a weight, chaining me to a future I wasn't sure I could bear. Was I even deserving of Kaelen, of the responsibilities that came with this life? The room seemed to close in around me, my breath growing shallow. My tears fell unchecked, and I felt the depths of my isolation and uncertainty.

In this world that still didn't feel like home, I was caught between realms, with nowhere I truly belonged. And with that thought, a fresh ache pierced my heart.

A soft knock at the door jolted me from my spiral of despair. Hastily, I wiped my tears, my heart pounding. "Come in," I called, my voice barely above a whisper.

Olivia's familiar form slipped into the room, her eyes filled with concern. The sight of my sister sent a wave of relief crashing over me. She crossed the room in quick strides, her long brunette hair swaying with each step.

"Amaya, darlin'," her sweet voice washed over me, settling me. "I've been worried sick about you."

I tried to smile, but it felt more like a grimace. "I'm fine, Ollie. Really."

Her brow furrowed as she sat beside me on the bed. "Now, don't you try to pull the wool over my eyes. I can see clear as day things are goin' sideways."

Her warm hand found mine, squeezing gently. The tenderness of her touch nearly undid me.

"Has that Fiora been givin' you trouble?" she asked, her voice low and urgent.

I stiffened, Fiora's taunts flashing through my mind. "How did you—"

"I saw her," Olivia interrupted, her eyes flashing with anger. "During the battle. She shifted and attacked you, Amaya. I saw the whole thing."

My hand instinctively went to my shoulder, where the wound still throbbed. "You... you saw? That's what that was?"

Olivia nodded grimly. "That woman's got more venom than a rattlesnake. You need to tell Kaelen what's been goin' on."

I shook my head vigorously, panic rising in my chest. "No, I can't. What if... what if she's telling the truth? What if Kaelen really wants her instead of me?"

"Oh, honey," Olivia sighed, pulling me into a tight embrace. "That's just fear talking. You gotta trust your mate bond, and more importantly, you gotta trust your heart."

I buried my face in her shoulder, inhaling the comforting scent of home. "But what if my heart's wrong? What if I'm not cut out to be Luna?"

Olivia pulled back, her hands holding mine as she looked me square in the eye. "Now you listen here, Amaya Ilyndor. You are stronger than you know and twice as deservin' of love as that haint Fiora. Don't let her poison your mind with her lies."

I let her words sink in. She was right; I knew in my heart she was. But doubt was such a powerful enemy. "I'm scared, Ollie," I admitted, my voice barely audible.

"I know, sugar," she replied, her voice soft with understanding. "But bein' scared doesn't make you weak. It makes you human... or, well, you know what I mean."

Despite everything, a small laugh escaped me. Olivia

always knew how to make me smile, even in the darkest moments.

"Talk to Kaelen," she urged gently. "Give him a chance to explain. Your bond is stronger than Fiora's lies, I promise you that."

I nodded slowly, drawing strength from my sister's unwavering support. The path ahead still seemed daunting, but with Olivia by my side, I felt a flicker of hope reignite in my chest.

Olivia's eyes bore into mine, unwavering. "Listen here, darlin', that Fiora's about as trustworthy as a screen door on a submarine. She's lyin' through her teeth, mark my words."

Her words sparked a tiny flame of hope in my chest, a spark I clung to, desperate to believe. "You really think so?" I asked, my voice trembling slightly.

"I'd bet my last drop of blood on it," Olivia replied, tucking a stray lock of her dark hair behind her ear. "Kaelen loves you, Amaya. I've seen the way he looks at you—it's like you're his entire world."

My cheeks warmed, an uncomfortable mix of embarrassment and something softer, something dangerously hopeful. "But what if—"

"No 'what ifs'," Olivia cut me off gently but firmly. "You need to talk to him. Let him explain his side. No more runnin'. Trust in your bond, in your heart."

As her words sank in, I noticed Cade standing by the door, his eyes filled with concern. He nodded at Olivia, a silent signal it was time for them to go.

Olivia squeezed my hand. "We've gotta head back to Vesparra, sugar. But you remember what I said, ya hear?"

I nodded, suddenly not wanting them to leave. "I will. Thank you, Ollie."

Cade stepped forward, his presence a calming command. "Stay strong, Amaya. You're more capable than you realize."

They moved to the center of the room, wisps of shadow

mist beginning to swirl around their feet. Olivia blew me a kiss, her smile full of encouragement, while Cade's expression held a mix of determination and worry.

In a blink, they vanished, leaving behind only traces of dissipating shadow.

I sank onto my bed, their words echoing in my mind. Could I really trust my heart? Could I trust Kaelen? As I thought of him, those doubts dissipated. The Kaelen I knew was the most honorable man next to Cade I'd ever known. And I knew one thing for certain: I couldn't hide from this conversation any longer.

The door to my chambers burst open, startling me from my thoughts. Kaelen strode in, his eyes blazing with a mix of fury and concern that made my breath catch. His gaze swept the room before locking onto me, and in an instant, he was at my side.

"Amaya," he breathed, his voice laced with urgency. "You're hurt. Is it where I treated you earlier?"

I swallowed, my heart racing at his nearness. "Yes, it's... it's my shoulder," I managed, gesturing vaguely.

Without hesitation, Kaelen's hands moved to my robe. "May I?" he asked, his tone softening even as his jaw remained tense.

I nodded, words lost, as he gently slipped the fabric aside and guided me to turn slightly, revealing my shoulder blade. His fingers, calloused yet impossibly gentle, traced the angry red marks Fiora's claws had left.

"That bitch," he growled, the sound rumbling through his chest like thunder. "I'll tear her apart for this."

As he examined the wound, I shivered, and not from the pain. "It's not that bad," I whispered, trying to calm the storm I saw building in his eyes.

Kaelen's gaze snapped to mine, fierce and protective. "Not that bad? Amaya, she attacked you. *My mate. My love.*" The last words came out in a possessive growl that sent a thrill down my spine.

He turned away, rummaging through a nearby cabinet and returning with a jar of salve. As he applied it to my shoulder, his touch was so gentle it nearly brought tears to my eyes.

"Why didn't you tell me?" he asked, his voice a mix of hurt and restrained anger.

I bit my lip, the conflict within swirling like a storm. "I... I didn't want to cause trouble. And part of me wasn't sure you'd believe me over her."

Kaelen's hands stilled, and he cupped my face with his free hand, compelling me to meet his gaze. "Amaya, listen to me. You are my mate, my priority. I will always believe you, always protect you. Do you understand?"

I gazed into the depths of his silver eyes, and felt an overwhelming surge of emotions, unnamed yet powerful. In that moment, with his hands soothing my skin and his words resonating in my ears, I wanted nothing more than to believe him, to trust in us.

I nodded, my throat tight with emotion. "I understand now," I whispered, barely trusting my voice. "She said you'd been intimate since we'd been back. That she was who you wanted. I knew it couldn't be true. I knew you'd never lie to me. But the doubts..." A tear escaped, trailing down my cheek.

"I hope you'll never doubt me again."

Kaelen's thumb brushed my cheek, and I leaned into his touch, craving the comfort it offered. As he finished tending to my wound, I found myself studying him intently; the furrow of concentration between his brows, the set of his jaw, the way his muscles tensed with each careful movement—it all spoke of a devotion I'd never experienced before.

"You really do care, don't you?" The words slipped out before I could stop them.

Kaelen's eyes met mine, a mix of surprise and something deeper swirling in their silver depths. "Of course I do, Amaya. How could you doubt that?"

I swallowed hard, feeling my walls crumble. "I thought... maybe it was just the mate bond. That you felt obligated."

He set the jar of ointment down and wiped his hand on a nearby towel. He cupped my face again, his touch achingly tender. "The bond may have brought us together, but my feelings for you go far beyond that. You're strong, brave, and beautiful—inside and out. How could I not care for you?"

My heart raced, and I realized with startling clarity that I loved this man. Not because of fate or magic, but because of who he was. The thought both terrified and exhilarated me.

"Kaelen, I..." I hesitated, then steeled myself. "I won't let Fiora come between us anymore. I choose you—bond or no bond. I love you."

His eyes widened, a smile spreading across his face that made my breath catch. "Amaya," he breathed, leaning in close. "You do not know how long I've waited to hear that."

As his lips met mine, I felt a surge of strength I'd never known. No more doubts, no more fears. Whatever challenges lay ahead, we'd face them together.

Kaelen's lips moved against mine with a tenderness that soon gave way to hunger. His hands slid down my sides, igniting a trail of heat that made me shiver. I pressed closer, my fingers tangling in his mane-like hair, savoring the solid warmth of his body against mine.

"Amaya," he murmured, his voice a low rumble that sent tremors through me. His eyes seemed to darken with desire, yet there was a question in them, a hesitation.

I knew what I wanted. What we both needed.

"Mark me," I whispered, tilting my head to expose my neck. "Make me yours, Kaelen."

His breath hitched, and I felt him tense against me. "Are you sure?" he asked, his voice strained. "Once it's done, there's no going back. I don't want you to feel—"

A myriad of emotions flashed across his face—surprise, joy, and a fierce possessiveness that sent my heart racing.

"Gods, Amaya," he breathed, pressing his forehead to mine. "I love you too. More than I ever thought possible."

He stood from the bed, and it was clear he'd already showered and prepared for bed, wearing only dark cotton pants and a loose dark t-shirt. He swiftly removed them, and before me stood a vision, a god incarnate. His muscled chest and abs, complemented by long golden locks flowing down his back, made him look like he belonged on the cover of a romance novel. I'd never seen a more beautiful man. He approached me slowly as I lay on my bed, and with gentle hands, he untied the white cotton robe I was wearing.

"Can you sit up for me, my Luna?" he asked.

I complied, and he slid the robe off my shoulders, pulling it from beneath me and tossed it aside. Completely exposed to him, I felt no shame, no embarrassment.

A growl rumbled in his throat as his eyes devoured every inch of my body.

"I swear to the Goddess, I've never seen a more perfect female in my entire existence."

"I've never been with a man before, Kaelen. But I trust you to take care of me."

He leaned over me, claiming my mouth in a ravishing kiss. His tongue explored every crevice of my mouth as I opened freely to him. My hands tangled in his long, wavy locks, pulling him closer, desperate for more of his touch. He pulled back slightly, his silver eyes locked on mine.

"Thank you for this gift, my mate. I'm going to do such delightful things to you, Luna. If there's anything you don't like, please tell me, otherwise, I don't plan on stopping. This will include you taking my knot, Maya. *That* I cannot stop. Tell me you understand."

Thankfully, I had read a couple of books on shifter history, so I was familiar with all the aspects of their mating, so this information was not a surprise or unwelcomed. I held his gaze, my voice steady. "I understand, my Alpha."

His tongue traced a path down my neck to my breasts. His growls filled the room. Those sounds vibrated through me, igniting a tingling sensation in places I'd never felt before. It was as if his growls called out to me, and I responded with sounds of my own, primal and raw. I thought to quiet them, feeling a flush of self-consciousness.

"Don't you dare go quiet on me, Maya. I want to hear every sound you make. My Luna is calling to me, and I will answer."

"Alpha." His journey continued down my body, his lips and tongue leaving a trail of heat, his growls a constant melody. He reached my most intimate parts, a place no man had ever seen or touched.

"And no male has ever been here before?" His fingers dipped inside my wet opening as he asked.

"No, Alpha," I whispered, as my body writhed to a pleasure so intense it bordered on overwhelming.

"I'm going to stretch you a little, my sweet Luna. You are so tight; my cock is going to fill this opening completely. I'm adding another finger, love."

I felt the additional pressure as he opened his fingers inside me. My gasps and moans mingled with his growls, echoing through the room.

"You are the most exquisite woman in this realm, Luna."

Kaelen

I was losing my godsdamned mind. I'd never seen a female more fascinating than my Luna. The realization that she was finally mine both exhilarated me and challenged my control.

"Maya, I'm going to taste you, my love. You are going to enjoy this immensely."

I scooted down the bed, withdrawing my fingers from her tight opening. Never breaking her gaze, I licked them clean, savoring her essence. The look on her sweet face was priceless. "Don't look so surprised, my mate. You are delicious."

I placed my hands on her upper thighs, holding her open for me, then I went face-first into her tight, wet opening. My tongue delved as far as it could go, as her back bowed up from the bed.

"Oh, Alpha, ahh, mmm."

I hummed back to her as I devoured her juices like a man dying of thirst, then licked my way up to her clit and circled it with my tongue.

"Kaelen! Mmm, yes, there, please, stay there!"

I stayed there, relentless in my attention until her body surrendered to the pleasure and shook with her release. Her cries of 'Alpha' were the sweetest music to my ears.

"Luna, it makes me extremely happy to hear you call me your Alpha." I kissed my way up her stomach, pausing at her perfect, round breasts to suck and kiss several times before reaching her mouth.

"I love you, Amaya. Now, I'm going to mark you as my mate forever. Are you ready?"

"Yes, Alpha. I'm absolutely ready."

"I need you to turn over to your hands and knees, baby. Put some pillows under your tummy to make it more comfortable."

She did as I asked, then lowered her head to her arms, raising her perfect ass high in the air. Her back arched as I stroked down her spine, finding her round and firm cheeks. Someday I'd sink my teeth into them. I ran my fingers between them down to her beautiful opening, still dripping with arousal for me.

"I love how you are so ready to take my cock. So proud to call you my Luna. You are perfect for me and for our pack. The way you fought today was a thing of beauty. You are fierce and magnificent; and defended our people with courage and strength."

I lined my rock-hard erection up with her entrance and slowly pushed in. "You okay, sweetheart? I know I'm large, and your pussy is so deliciously tight."

"I'm good, Alpha. You can push in more. I need it."

I pushed in a little more until I felt the barrier of her innocence.

"Luna, this will hurt, but then it will feel so good, I swear it."

"PLEASE, Alpha!"

That's all I needed to hear. I drove into her, breaking past her maidenhood. She gave a little gasp, which quickly turned into whimpers and sounds of a woman loving what her mate had to give her. I grasped her hips and continued my sweet assault.

"You feel so good, Luna. I've felt nothing close to how spectacular your body feels connected to mine. You fit perfectly, sweetheart."

I was getting close. My erection was swelling even larger with my knot.

"Are you still ok, my love?"

"Yes, Alpha. I feel... so... full."

"That's my knot expanding sweetheart. You were made to take it Luna. It will feel too large, but it was made for you, love."

I felt my canine teeth elongate, and I leaned over her back, pulling her up slightly and moving her hair aside. "Are you ready to take my mark also, Luna?"

"Yes, Alpha. Please, mark me. I'm yours, today and always."

"My mate," I growled, "My love."

As my knot continued to swell, I bit down, her blood filling my mouth. My climax exploded. At the same moment, I felt her tighten around my knot as she came with an incredible release.

"ALPHA! Mmmm yes... I love you."

The mate bond instantly snapped into place, sending a chain reaction throughout the pack. They knew their Alpha had found his Fated Mate, and we had completed the bond. They now had a Luna. My knot eased as we laid connected in each other's arms.

I nuzzled against Amaya's neck, inhaling her intoxicating scent, now mixed with my own. The mate bond hummed between us, a tangible connection that filled me with a sense of completion I'd never known before.

"How do you feel, Luna?" I murmured, pressing a gentle kiss to her shoulder.

She turned her head to meet my gaze, her eyes shining with a mix of love and wonder. "I feel... whole," she whispered. "Like a part of me I didn't even know was missing has finally clicked into place."

I smiled, running my fingers through her silky hair. "That's the completed mate bond."

She snuggled closer, her body molding perfectly against mine. "I can feel you," she said softly. "Not just physically, but... here." She placed her small hand over her heart.

"I've waited a lifetime for you, Luna. I know the road ahead won't be easy, but together, we can weather any storm."

CHAPTER 10

Olivia

I blinked awake, a soft sense of contentment washed over me like a warm Texas breeze. Well, butter my butt and call me a biscuit—I actually felt at peace for once. A small laugh escaped my lips as I stretched languidly in the plush bed, relishing the rare sensation of waking up without a knot in my stomach.

My eyes traced the intricate patterns carved into the ceiling, marveling at the craftsmanship. This was a far cry from the water-stained plaster of my old foster home. A bittersweet pang of nostalgia tugged at me, but I shoved it aside. No use dwelling on the past when the present was so dadgum good.

A soft knock at the door interrupted my musings. "Come in," I called, sitting up and running a hand through my tangled mess of dark hair.

Margaret bustled in, her arms laden with fabric that shimmered in the morning light. "Good morning, my lady," she chirped, laying out a stunning dress on the bed. "I hope you slept well?"

"Like a baby, Margaret," I replied with a grin. "And how many times do I have to tell you to call me Olivia?"

She tutted, helping me to my feet. "At least once more, my lady. Now, let's get you dressed for the day."

As Margaret helped me into the dress, I adored the way

the fabric felt against my skin—soft, rich, like something spun straight out of a dream. A far cry from the scratchy hand-me-downs I'd grown up wearing.

"I swear, Margaret, sometimes I feel like I'm living in a dream," I murmured as she laced up the back. "All this finery...it's more than I ever thought I'd have."

Margaret's hands stilled for a moment. "You deserve every bit of it, Olivia," she said softly. "And so much more."

A lump rose in my throat, and I blinked back the sudden dampness in my eyes. "Now don't go buttering me up too much," I laughed, trying to lighten the mood. "If you keep this up, I might just melt right out of this pretty dress."

Margaret laughed, giving the laces one last tug. "There," she said, stepped back and admired her handiwork. "You look absolutely radiant."

I turned to the mirror, and for a moment, I hardly recognized the woman staring back at me. The dress hugged my curves in all the right places, its deep purple hue setting off the unusual color of my eyes. I saw a flash of the scared, scarred girl I used to be, but she faded quickly, replaced by the strong, confident woman I had become.

"Well, this is just gorgeous," I whispered, smoothing my hands over the soft fabric. "Guess I clean up pretty good after all."

***

I stepped into the dining hall, my heart swelling at the sight before me. The Circle gathered around the massive oak table, their laughter and chatter filling the air like a warm embrace. Sunlight streamed through the stained-glass windows, casting a kaleidoscope of colors across their faces. It wasn't the ornate tapestries or the gleaming silverware that caught my eye, but the genuine smiles and easy camaraderie of these people who'd become my family.

"Well, if it's not the belle of the ball," Seraphine called out, raising her glass in my direction. "Come on in, Highness. We saved you a seat."

A grin tugged at my lips as I made my way to the empty chair beside Cade. "Y'all are gonna give me a big head with all this sweet talk," I muttered, settling into my seat.

Under the table, Cade's hand found mine, giving it a gentle squeeze. "Good morning, my love," he murmured, his eyes twinkling with a warmth reserved only for me.

"Mornin' handsome," I replied, my stomach doing a little flip. Even after all this time, he still had that effect on me.

As we dug into the spread before us, I just loved how natural it all felt. The banter, the laughter, the sense of belonging—it was everything I'd ever dreamed of and more.

Suddenly, Cade cleared his throat, a hint of nervousness breaking through his usually confident demeanor. "I have an announcement to make," he said, his voice carrying across the table.

The chatter died down, and all eyes turned to him. My heart raced, a mix of anticipation and excitement swelling inside me.

"Olivia and I have decided to move forward with our marking ceremony," Cade continued, his grip on my hand tightening. "We believe it's time to fully embrace our destiny and strengthen our bond."

A rush of emotions swept over me—joy, excitement, and love overflowing for this man. Knowing he was doing this because I'd asked meant the world. "Thank you, Cade. This means everything to me." I hesitated for a second, practicality fighting with the happiness in my heart. "Are you sure we should do this now, with everything else going on?"

His eyes met mine, a smile tugging at the corners of his mouth. "There's nothing I want more, my love. Are *you* ready?"

I took a steadying breath, feeling the gravity of the moment sink in. "Honey, I am past ready," I replied, my voice clear and strong. "I'll proudly wear your mark, Highness."

I gave him a wink, trying to lighten the emotion swelling between us.

The table erupted in congratulations, but all I could focus on was Cade's face—the love and pride shining in his eyes. We'd faced so much together already; this was the next step in truly binding our lives. And that, more than any ceremony or magic, was what truly mattered.

As the excitement over Cade's announcement settled, I took a moment to really look around the table. My heart swelled at the sight of this newfound family. Miranda caught my eye, her warm, brown gaze filled with happiness for me. Next to her, Thorne's usually stoic face softened as he gave me a slight nod of approval.

"My gravy, I don't think I've seen a more beautiful family this side of the mortal realm," I drawled, unable to contain my grin. "We are the epitome of what family's supposed to be."

Gaylene let out a sweet laugh, her eyes twinkling. "Oh, Olivia, you do have a way with words, don't you?"

Darius chimed in, his deep voice rumbling with amusement. "I must admit, your Texas colloquialisms add a certain... flavor to our gatherings."

I laughed, letting the warmth and joy of this moment sink into my bones.

"The only way it could be more perfect is if my sister was here."

No sooner had the words left my mouth than Kaelen and Amaya strolled into the dining hall.

"Did I hear someone say she wanted her sister?"

I turned, jumping out of my chair to embrace Amaya in a crushing hug.

"Cade and I are getting married! Or uh... marked... or whatever the frick-a-frack you wanna call it!"

Amaya's laughter filled the room, the most beautiful sound in the world to me, especially after all she'd been through lately.

"I'm so happy for you, Ollie!"

She pulled back, and that's when I noticed the new marking on her neck. She followed my gaze, a soft blush spreading across her cheeks.

"And I have equally wonderful news to share!"

Kaelen stepped up beside her, his massive frame towering over her. He placed a gentle kiss on her forehead, a warm smile lighting his face as Amaya looked at me, then around the table.

"Over the past several days, after lots of talking and, well, a fair amount of soul-searching on my part," — she laughed — "I realized that not only is Kaelen my Fated Mate, but I truly love this incredible man. And with all the chaos going on, I decided I didn't want to wait any longer. I told him I wanted his mark." She paused, smiling as she glanced around the table. "As some of you probably noticed, we've had our own private mating ceremony."

A beautiful blush deepened her glow, making her look even more radiant.

"Oh, baby girl, I'm so happy for you. Cade, aren't we thrilled for them?"

Cade had already made his way to my side and was pulling Kaelen into a hearty bear hug.

"Brother, welcome officially to the family," he said, his voice thick with emotion.

Cade already loved Kaelen like a brother, but now their relationship as in-laws, or whatever they'd call it here in Eldoria, connected them even more deeply.

Amaya and Kaelen took the empty seats at the table, and we talked about her new role as Luna of Therionis, teasing Kaelen about just how lucky he was to have her. I knew she'd take to her position like a champ.

Tears pricked at the corners of my eyes. "I'm just so happy for you both. I knew it wouldn't take long. It's tough when everything comes at you all at once, but you've come so far, so fast."

Miranda raised her glass. "To Amaya and Kaelen," she toasted. "May your bond bring strength to both your hearts and to Therionis."

We all raised our glasses, the clink of crystal echoing through the room, followed by a chorus of congratulations. As I sipped my drink, I couldn't help but reflect on how far we'd come. From scared, lonely girls to women finding our power and place in this magical world.

Who'd have thought, I mused, *that a couple of Texas foster kids would end up here, surrounded by so much love and acceptance?* I caught Amaya's eye and winked. "I know our parents would be so proud if they could see us now."

As the celebratory mood lingered, Cade cleared his throat, his expression turning serious. "I'm curious," he said, his deep voice cutting through the chatter. "Have you decided what punishment Fiora will face?"

We took a moment to explain the treachery Fiora had unleashed on Amaya, her ambush and venomous threats fresh in our minds.

The atmosphere shifted, a chill settling over the room like a sudden frost. I felt my spine stiffen, remembering the pain that the witch had inflicted.

"Banishment?" Thorne suggested, his usually jovial face hardening.

I couldn't help but pipe up. "Seems awful lenient for someone who tried to rip my sister's arm off."

Cade's lips twitched, suppressing a smile at my colorful description. "It's not a decision to be made lightly," he said. "But you must consider all options."

Darius leaned forward, his golden eyes gleaming. "Whatever is decided, it must send a clear message. You can't appear weak."

I nodded, my voice thoughtful. "But Kaelen must be prudent as well. Fiora's family is prominent, and they could raise a stink over it. Last thing we need is some kind of coup for

Kaelen to face."

"Can we table this for now?" Miranda interjected gently. "Kaelen and Cade will probably come to a suitable solution later. For now, we have happier matters to discuss." She turned to Cade and me, a knowing smile on her face. "Like a certain marking ceremony."

My heart skipped a beat, and a flush crept up my neck. Cade's hand found mine under the table, giving it a reassuring squeeze.

"Indeed," Cade said, his voice warm with affection. "It's time to officially welcome Olivia into the Vesparran line."

Gaylene clapped her hands, her face lighting up. "Oh, how wonderful! We'll blend the traditional Vesparran rituals with the mortal ring ceremony Cade mentioned you wanted, Olivia."

I blinked, suddenly feeling overwhelmed. "Yes, I definitely made a bit of a fuss about him putting a ring on it." I giggled.

Laughter erupted around the table, easing the tension left by the Fiora discussion.

Cade chuckled as he lifted my left hand. "I remember something about a vein running from this finger going straight to the heart?" His finger trailed softly up my arm.

I swatted his arm playfully, my cheeks burning. "Easy there, Highness. Let's focus on the ceremony, for now."

As the others began discussing details—everything from ancient blood rites to cake flavors—I found myself swept up in a whirlwind of emotions. Part of me was thrilled at the prospect of officially joining Cade's family, while another part quaked at the enormity of it all.

"My stars, we're doin' this," I whispered. "I'm so happy right now, I don't know what to do with myself."

"Four days," Cade announced, his voice clear and resolute. "We'll hold the ceremony in four days. That should give us enough time to prepare and ensure every precaution is in place."

My heart skipped a beat. "Four days? If we're inviting the entire kingdom, can we get everything ready that fast?"

Miranda took my hand, smiling. "Olivia, remember—we have magic. Trust me, we can get it done."

Kaelen nodded, his eyes gleaming with a mix of excitement and concern. "It's soon, yes, but we can't risk waiting too long. The threat of new rifts is always present, and we need to solidify your position within the Vesparran clan as soon as possible."

I swallowed hard, a knot of anxiety forming in my stomach. "And what if something goes wrong? What if a rift opens right in the middle of the ceremony?"

Seraphine reached across the table, squeezing my hand reassuringly. "That's why we're taking every precaution, sister. We'll have wards in place and the strongest mages from every kingdom on guard."

"Besides," Thorne added with a wink, "if anything tries to crash the party, they'll have to get through us first. Plus, I doubt the Dragonia would stand for anything trying to hurt their Chosen One."

I took a deep breath, drawing strength from their unwavering support. "Alright then," I said, a smile spreading across my face. "Let's do this."

As the conversation shifted to preparations, I felt the undercurrent of tension among us. For all our bravado, we knew the risks we were taking.

Before I could dwell on it further, Cade stood, his expression serious. "Now that we've settled on the ceremony, we need to discuss the creature we encountered in Therionis. To the war room, everyone."

The mood shifted palpably as we moved from the warm, sunlit breakfast room to the dimly lit, stone-walled war room. Gone were the smiles and laughter, replaced by grim determination.

I took my seat at the large circular table. It's funny, just weeks ago, I was diagnosing cattle ailments and patching up show horses. Now, I was in a war council, preparing to face threats beyond my wildest imagination.

Well, sugar, I thought to myself; *you wanted adventure. Looks like you've found it in spades.*

I leaned forward, my gaze fixed on the detailed renderings at the table's center. The grotesque creature we'd faced in Therionis was depicted from several angles: twisted limbs, gnashing teeth, skin that seemed to writhe. Just looking at it made my skin crawl.

"Alright, y'all," I said, "let's catalog this sucker and note how we kicked its hiney."

Miranda shot me an amused glance. "Colorful as always, cousin. But you're right. We need everyone to understand what we're up against—and the best ways to defeat it."

Cade pointed to key areas on the drawings of the creature. "We've identified several weak points," he explained. "The joints where its limbs connect are particularly vulnerable."

"Like the soft underbelly of an armadillo," I replied, my mind racing. "Hit 'em where they're softest. And having teams that wield different types of magic is a good bet for any creatures. With this one, Amaya deployed water. I trapped it in stone using earth magic, Cade used rune-infused steel, and Kaelen finished it off in wolf form, tearing out its throat."

This had truly been a multi-kingdom effort.

As we cataloged details and strategized, I found myself fully engaged. My experiences on different ranches, handling ornery livestock and weathering unpredictable storms, had honed my problem-solving skills in ways I hadn't anticipated.

"What about getting this information to the command centers?" I asked.

Thorne nodded approvingly. "Excellent point, Olivia. We'll send the catalog of creature information to all command centers as soon as it's available."

I grinned, feeling a surge of pride. Having a foundation

of knowledge for every threat we might face would make dispatching them faster—and safer.

As we continued discussing tactics, I felt a growing sense of purpose. This wasn't just about my safety anymore; it was about safeguarding an entire realm, a world I'd only recently claimed as my own.

Cade spoke up, his tone firm. "We need to get Ignis and Farin more involved. Farin's been invaluable with tech and logistics, but we need more manpower now. I propose we move operations to the Crystal Citadel. It'll serve as a centralized hub for planning and coordination."

Everyone nodded in agreement. The kings and queen would bring their generals to coordinate strategies, discuss troop formations, and prepare defenses there.

As the meeting concluded, a sense of readiness settled over me. We had a plan, we had each other, and by the Goddess, we had the will to see it through.

Walking out of the war room, I caught my reflection in a polished shield hanging on the wall. The woman staring back at me wasn't just Olivia, the large animal vet anymore. She was Olivia Ilyndor Vesparra, protector of Eldoria, ready to face whatever came her way.

Bring it on, I thought, a fierce smile curving my lips. *We're ready for you.*

CHAPTER 11

Olivia

I stood on the battlements of Vesparra's towering citadel, the earlier bravado I'd displayed now crumbling like sand through an hourglass. The wind whipped my dark hair around my face as I gazed out at the horizon, my heart heavy with regret.

"Dadgum it, Ollie," I muttered to myself. "You just had to go and tempt fate, didn't you?"

My cocky words from earlier echoed in my mind: "Bring it on. We're ready for you." Now, as the sky darkened with an ominous hue and the air crackled with malevolent energy, the true weight of an impending battle settled upon me.

But, as my stomach roiled with worry—something else stirred within me—a fierce, unwavering resolve. This was my home, my people. I'd be danged if I let some hell spawn take it without a fight.

"We can handle this," I whispered, clenching my fists. "Eldoria will not fall. Not on my watch."

As if in response to my declaration, the world fell into turmoil. The communication crystal I always carried buzzed to life, and I heard Miranda's voice.

"Olivia, are you there?"

"I'm here, Miranda, go ahead!"

"It looks like we've got a rift opening outside the walls of Ilyndor, just past the forests. It's big. We're going to need help here."

"We've got you, girl. Let me round up the Dragonia, and we're on our way."

"It looks like you have a bit of time, but not much."

I heard the panic in her voice.

"Hang in there. Help is on the way."

As I headed downstairs, the crystal buzzed again.

"Cade? Olivia? Anyone there?"

It was Grandpapa.

"It's Olivia, sir. I'm here."

"It's good to hear your voice. We have a rift trying to open outside the walls of Thalassa, close to the beach."

What in the world was going on?

"There's one opening outside Ilyndor as well. I'm about to head that way. I'll send Cade with a dragon your direction. Hang in there. He'll be there soon."

"Thank you, granddaughter."

"Sweet baby Jesus," I breathed, as I ran the rest of the way down the stairs.

"CADE! We have trouble!"

He met me at the foot of the stairs.

"What is it? What's wrong?"

"All hell has broken loose. I got a message from Miranda that a rift is opening in the forest outside of Ilyndor. I told her we'd be on our way to help. Then, as I was coming down the stairs, I got a message from Grandpapa. Another rift is opening in Thalassa by the beach." I took a deep breath. "We're gonna have to split up and go to each location without each other."

Cade put his hands on my shoulders and looked me in the eye. "We've got this. We'll go and kill these assholes, and then we'll meet back at home. Then I'm going to fuck you *so* hard."

I smirked, a mix of resolve and anticipation in my voice.

"I'm gonna hold you to that, Highness."

Dressed in our leather battle gear, we ran out to the courtyard. I whistled for Ariaxom and Thyra. They were there in seconds.

"We've got rifts opening on opposite sides of the realm. Splitting up is the only thing we can do."

I closed my eyes and called for Vaelith and the entire Dragonia crew as we walked out to the clearing beyond the castle walls.

"What awaits us, little StarHeart?" Vaelith's words cascaded into my mind.

"I'm afraid it's something big. They're opening rifts outside of Ilyndor and Thalassa. We're splitting up. Eryndor, Vaelith, and Skorn, y'all are with me. Zarvyn, Nyxara, and Drathom, y'all are with Cade. Thyra, I'd like you to come with me. Ariaxom, that leaves you with Cade. Everybody good?"

The affirmations echoed in my mind.

Cade walked up to me and wrapped his arms around me, squeezing me tight. "I love you, Starlight. Go and kick some ass, my beautiful warrior."

"I love you, Iron Heart. Stay alive. I mean it Cade. Stay. Alive." I kissed him like my life depended on it.

We mounted up and off we flew.

As we soared towards the southeast, I caught sight of Cade mounting Zarvyn, the dragon's dark scales shimmering with an otherworldly gleam. Drathom, Nyx, and Ariaxom flanked them, their powerful forms a stark contrast against the rugged landscape of Vesparra.

Cade's voice echoed in my mind, our mate bond thrumming with intensity. *"Stay safe, Olivia. I'll see you when this is over."*

I sent back a wave of affection tinged with determination. *"You better, cowboy. Don't do anything stupid out there."*

My mind was a mix of trepidation and resolve as we covered the distance from Vesparra to Ilyndor. As we neared the forest outside the castle walls, it was just in time to see a rift larger than the two I'd already encountered ripping the earth open. We dove to a landing to assess the situation. I slid off Vaelith's back, trying to get the lay of the land.

"Vaelith, let me know if dragon ice is appropriate to kill any of these mofos, okay? And Eryndor, give us cover from the air."

Several voices of agreement rang out. *"You got it, little StarHeart."*

"We're with you, little one."

"Be careful, Olivia."

From the gaping maw of the rift, nightmarish creatures poured forth. Writhing tentacles, razor-sharp claws, and rows upon rows of gnashing teeth emerged from the swirling darkness. The beasts that crawled and slithered into our world defied description, their forms a twisted mockery of natural life.

"Olivia!" Miranda's voice cut through my shock. She appeared at my side, her dark curls wild and her eyes filled with fear. "It's worse than we imagined." She ran over to Thorn and took a battle stance. Alongside them, several of their troops took up defensive postures.

I took a deep breath, steeling myself. "Let's fight, cousin. We've got to give 'em everything we've got." She and Thorn worked in tandem, destroying the uglies coming up through the ground with a mix of Miranda's water magic—ice spears, and fantastic whirlpool chakrams with spinning water blades that sliced and diced through these beasts like they were made of butter.

As fast as Miranda shot her water weapons, Thorn had his air magic to whip them, adding pressure to spin them into vortexes, increasing their damage. Other creatures coming through were met with his vortex hammers that created continuous shockwave blasts until there was nothing left but masses of goo on the ground.

Their troops deployed various forms of magic and

weaponry, holding back the creatures, but not working quite fast enough.

Then, as if on cue, an ear-splitting shriek pierced the air. I looked up to see a massive, bat-like creature soaring towards us, its leathery wings blocking out what little light remained in the sky.

"Incoming!" I shouted, summoning my magic. Purple energy crackled around my hands as I prepared to face the onslaught.

The battle for Eldoria raged, and I'd be dadgummed if I'd let my realm fall without giving it my all. I felt nothing but burning determination. These monsters would feel the full force of my magic.

"Alright, you ugly butt face," I growled, a fierce grin spreading across my face. "Come at me."

I sprang into action, my hands moving swiftly as I armed myself for the battle ahead. The familiar weight of runestones filled my pockets, their etched surfaces pulsing with latent power. I grabbed a handful of mist orbs, securing them to my belt with practiced ease. Their cool, water-filled surfaces reminded me of the countless times we'd drilled strategies.

In this moment, every Western movie I'd ever watched flooded my brain, and I became the hero of them all.

"Y'all better watch out," I muttered, channeling my elemental magic into my fingertips. Purple sparks danced across my skin, a testament to the raw power I commanded. "This looks like a pretty day for makin' things right."

Despite the chaos erupting around us, a surge of confidence washed over me. I may not have Cade by my side, but I was far from helpless. Training and my own innate abilities had prepared me for this moment.

I threw the first orb at the bat-like creature, using a good dose of wind magic to propel it. It burst into a thick, blinding fog, causing the creature to spin erratically, its wings flailing, clawed tips grasping for purchase. I shot a blast of fire towards it, and it was quickly engulfed, turning to a pile of ash on the ground. One down.

"Incoming!" Skorn's warning pierced my mind.

The sky darkened as a horde of winged monstrosities poured from the freshly opened rift. Their putrid stench reached us even at this distance.

"Holy crap," I muttered, channeling magic into my palms. "Looks like they sent the whole gang."

I quickly mounted the saddle on Vaelith's back and took to the sky next to Skorn. *"Indeed. Shall we greet them properly, young one?"*

A feral grin spread across my face. *"By all means. Let's take these suckers out."*

We dove into the fray, Eryndor firing flames from his giant maw, my elemental magic crackling around us. I hurled fireballs at the nearest creatures, their flesh sizzling on impact. Vaelith's icy breath froze another group solid, their frozen forms shattering as they hit the ground.

"Behind you!" Thyra's warning came just in time.

I spun, narrowly avoiding razor-sharp claws. With a flick of my wrist, I summoned a water whip, slicing through the beast's wing. It plummeted, screeching.

"Nice moves, Majesty," Skorn cackled, dive-bombing a cluster of enemies.

The battle raged on, a symphony of magic, claws, and otherworldly shrieks. I lost track of time, focused solely on the rhythm of combat. Each spell, each dodge, each counterattack flowed seamlessly into the next.

Miranda, Thorne, and their troops were waging a fierce battle on the ground, taking out lumbering creatures left and right. They were a magnificent team, fighting in complete synchronicity.

As I incinerated another wave of creatures, a stray thought of Cade crossed my mind. I hoped he was faring as well as we were.

"Focus, Olivia," I chided myself. "He can handle himself."

I reached for a mist orb, hurling it into a dense cluster of enemies. The resulting explosion of thick fog bought us a moment's reprieve.

"How many more of these mofos are there?" I panted, wiping sweat from my brow.

Vaelith's rumbling voice carried a note of concern. *"They seem endless. We must find a way to close the rift."*

I nodded, gritting my teeth. *"Then that's what we'll do. Any ideas on how to get closer without becoming demon chow?"*

Thyra's melodic laugh rang out. *"Oh honey, that's what we're here for. Leave the distraction to us."*

As my companions drew the bulk of the horde away, I urged Vaelith towards the pulsing tear in reality. The malevolent energy emanating from it made my skin crawl.

"Here goes nothing," I muttered, channeling every ounce of power I could muster. "Let's seal this sucker shut."

I raised my hands, feeling the combined magic of Eldoria's kingdoms surge through me. The air crackled with energy, my hair lifting in an unseen breeze. Just as I was about to unleash the spell, a searing pain ripped through my chest, stealing my breath.

"Cade," I gasped, nearly falling from Vaelith's back.

The agony wasn't mine, but his. Our mate bond flared to life, flooding me with his pain and fear. My vision blurred, the battlefield before me replaced by flashes of Cade's perspective —blood, so much blood, and a monstrous creature looming over him.

"No!" I screamed, torn between two realities.

Vaelith's concerned rumble brought me back. *"Olivia, what's wrong?"*

I struggled to form words, my heart racing. *"It's Cade. He's... he's badly hurt. I can feel it."*

Panic clawed at my throat. How could I be here when Cade needed me? But the rift still yawned before us, spewing more horrors with each passing second.

"I can't... I must..." I choked out, torn between duty and desperation.

Skorn's gravelly voice cut through my turmoil. *"You must finish this, Olivia. For all of us."*

He was right, damn him. I clenched my fists, forcing myself to focus. "Hold on, Cade," I whispered. "I'm coming."

As I reached for my magic again, something shifted within me. The pain of our bond, my fear for Cade, my determination to save him—it all coalesced into a new, fierce power. It burned through me, wild and untamed, demanding release.

I gasped, feeling it build to a crescendo.

Without conscious thought, I thrust my hands toward the rift. Raw, primal energy erupted from my palms—a swirling vortex of elements I'd never wielded before. Fire and ice, earth and air, blood and shadow—all merged into a force of pure creation and destruction.

The rift shuddered, its edges curling inward. Creatures caught in the maelstrom disintegrated, their unholy shrieks cut short. The very fabric of reality seemed to bend to my will.

As the last of the rift sealed shut, the new power receded, leaving me drained but exhilarated. I turned to my stunned companions, my eyes wide with wonder. I slid off Vaelith's back, stumbling a bit. I was drained.

The last of the underworld creatures crumbled to ash, their unearthly shrieks fading into the wind. My chest heaved as I struggled to catch my breath, the taste of victory bitter on my tongue. Cade's pain still pulsed through our bond, a constant reminder of the urgency that gripped my heart.

I grabbed Miranda's shoulders a bit too tightly. "Miranda, I need to get to Cade. I think he's..."

"I know, Ollie," Miranda cut me off, her tone gentle but firm. "Trust me."

I forced myself to release her; and nodded. "Sorry, I just—"

"He'll be okay," she assured me, backing up and squeezing

my hands. "Go. I've got this."

Without another word, I sprinted towards the shimmering portal that would take me to Thalassa. My heart pounded in my ears, drowning out everything but the urgent need to reach Cade.

As I plunged into the swirling vortex, the familiar disorientation hit me like a punch to the gut. Colors blurred, reality twisted, and for a terrifying moment, I felt like I was being torn apart.

"Come on," I growled, fighting against the portal's chaotic energy. "Work with me here!"

I focused on Cade, on the pull of our bond. His presence was a beacon, guiding me through the tempest. With each second that passed, his life force seemed to dim, slipping further away.

"Don't you dare die on me, Cadence Vesparra," I snarled, pushing harder against the portal's resistance. "I swear to the Goddess, if you leave me now—"

The portal suddenly spat me out, and I stumbled onto soft sand. The salty breeze of Thalassa hit my face, but I had no time to appreciate its beauty. My eyes frantically scanned the horizon, searching for any sign of the battle.

"Where are you?" I whispered, my voice breaking. "Cade, please..."

The scene before me stole the breath from my lungs. Thalassa's pristine beaches were marred with blood and chaos. Bodies of fallen warriors and grotesque Underworld creatures littered the sand, the once-lush gardens trampled and burning. The air crackled with residual magic, heavy with the stench of death and destruction.

My heart threatened to burst from my chest as I spotted a cluster of people near the water's edge. Time seemed to slow as I raced towards them, my legs feeling like lead with each step.

"No, no, no," I chanted, the words a desperate prayer.

As I drew closer, the crowd parted, revealing the broken form of my mate. Cade lay motionless on the blood-soaked sand, his jet-black hair matted with crimson, his muscular body battered beyond recognition.

"Cade!" I cried out, falling to my knees beside him. My hands hovered over his body, afraid to touch him, to confirm the horrifying reality before me.

His ice-blue eyes, usually so full of strength and wisdom, fluttered open weakly. "Olivia," he whispered, his voice barely audible. "You... shouldn't be here. It's not safe."

A hysterical laugh bubbled up in my throat. "Dadgum it, Cade. Even now, you're trying to protect me?"

I cradled his face gently, my tears falling onto his cheeks.

"Don't you dare leave me," I commanded, my voice thick with emotion. "You hear me? We've got too much left to do, you stubborn man."

Cade's lips twitched in a faint, bloody smile. "Always... so bossy."

With those words, his body went limp once again.

"Why is he lying here on the beach? He needs to be inside. Why haven't you taken him inside? Where is the King? Where's my grandfather?"

"He's too weak to move," a voice behind me said softly. I turned to see Grandpapa approaching, his face etched with worry. "We feared jostling him would only make things worse."

I nodded, understanding but frustrated. My eyes scanned Cade's broken body, cataloging every wound, every drop of blood. The damage was catastrophic. No ordinary healing could fix this.

"What happened?" I choked out, my fingers gently stroking Cade's cheek.

Grandpapa's voice was heavy with regret. "The rift... it was unlike anything we've ever seen. The creatures that came through... Cade fought like a man possessed Olivia. He saved countless lives. But then..."

His voice trailed off, and I knew. Cade had sacrificed

himself to save others. Of course he had. My brave, foolish mate. I had to do something. Why would the Goddess allow this? What could she be trying to show me through this? That I still trusted her? That I can trust the All Father to take care of everything when my mate is lying here dying? What?

Then I heard her voice, as I had so many times before. *"Olivia. Do you trust me? Have I ever truly let you down? Can you trust me now?"*

CHAPTER 12

Olivia

The sand beneath my knees was cold and damp, grains clinging to my skin as I hunched over Cade's broken body. My hands trembled, longing to touch him, still too afraid of hurting him. Moonlight spilled across his pale face, highlighting the angry red gashes that crisscrossed his chest, raw and glistening like open wounds.

"Please..." I whispered, my voice cracking with desperation. "Please don't leave me."

Tears blurred my vision as despair clawed at my heart. The Goddess's words echoed faintly in my mind, a fragile whisper of hope, but how could I believe when Cade lay so still, his chest rising in shallow, uneven breaths?

A breeze stirred, cool and laced with salt and something ancient, a sensation that prickled across my skin. I looked up to see a magnificent white stallion stepping through the mist. His mane glowed faintly in the moonlight, his presence both otherworldly and comforting.

"Lady Olivia," Ariaxom's deep voice resonated in my mind, steady yet soothing. *"I've come to assist."*

Relief flooded me, quelling the panic threatening to pull me under. "Ariaxom," I breathed, hope flickering to life. "Can you help him?"

The Pegasus dipped his head, compassion shining in his

deep brown eyes. A subtle shimmer of magic radiated from his body, its warmth brushing over Cade's wounds.

"His injuries are grave," Ariaxom intoned, his voice calm but resolute. *"But there is still hope."*

Lowering his majestic head, Ariaxom unfurled his wings, their span wide and powerful as they folded protectively over Cade. With a deep, resonant breath, he seemed to pull energy from the very ocean itself. A soft, silvery light rippled along his mane and feathers, ebbing and flowing like the tides.

"Hold on, my friend," Ariaxom murmured, the words resonating in my mind as though the ocean itself had spoken.

"What can I do?" I asked, my voice trembling as I searched for a way to help.

Ariaxom's gaze met mine, ancient wisdom reflected in his kind eyes. *"Your presence alone strengthens him, Lady Olivia. Your bond with King Cadence is powerful—it draws him back toward life."*

He bent closer to Cade, the surrounding light intensifying. The air seemed to hum with a sacred energy, the rhythm of waves crashing on a distant shore echoing faintly in my ears. Ariaxom's wings pulsed with light, waves of silver rippling outward and enveloping Cade.

My fingers tightened around Cade's limp hand, willing him to feel my touch. "Please... stay with me," I whispered, my voice breaking.

The majestic Pegasus lowered his head, his countenance now glowing with an ethereal light. *"Our magic intertwines with the life force of the injured. It's a delicate balance - we can mend flesh and bone, but the will to live must come from within."*

"Goddess, please," I whispered, my eyes fixed on Cade's face. "Give him strength."

As Ariaxom began the healing process, I gasped. The surrounding air shimmered, taking on an opalescent quality. Tendrils of silvery light emerged from him, weaving themselves around Cade's battered body. The magic pulsed with a rhythm that matched my racing heartbeat.

He extended his wings, guiding the seawater with a gentle but purposeful pull. The water seemed to respond, rising to hover in glistening streams around Cade's body. Slowly, Ariaxom channeled the power of healing into the water, creating threads of light that wound through Cade's broken bones, knitting them with delicate but unyielding energy.

With each wave, Cade's battered form seemed to draw in the sea's vitality. His cuts closed as the salt water coursed over them, carrying away blood and mending the tissue beneath. His ribs, once fractured, slowly aligned, held steady by the soft glow of the water magic that Ariaxom directed with precision and care.

The silver glow faded as Ariaxom's wings folded tightly to his sides. He stepped back, his movements graceful but deliberate. He lowered his head to nudge Cade's shoulder.

Cade stirred, a faint groan escaping his lips. His chest rose in a deeper breath, the tension in his features easing ever so slightly.

"*Rest now,*" Ariaxom whispered, brushing his muzzle against Cade's shoulder. "*I'll take you to a place where you can heal.*"

"*He is stable enough to move,*" Ariaxom announced, his tone tinged with quiet triumph. "*But he will need further care once he is inside.*"

Tears streamed down my face as I leaned over Cade, brushing his damp hair back from his forehead. His eyelids fluttered weakly, a flicker of awareness sparking in his eyes.

"Olivia," he rasped, his voice barely audible.

"I'm here," I whispered, choking on a sob. "I'm here, Cade."

"*Lady Olivia,*" Ariaxom interjected gently, his gaze unwavering. "*We must act swiftly. I will carry him.*"

I nodded, scrambling to my feet as Ariaxom crouched, allowing me to help maneuver Cade onto his broad back. The Pegasus rose smoothly, his strength a miracle in itself.

As we began the journey back to the castle, I placed a hand on Cade's chest, feeling the faint but steady rhythm of his heartbeat beneath my palm. Relief flooded through me, mingling with determination.

Cade was alive—and I would move heaven and earth to make sure he stayed that way. The glow around them faded to a gentle warmth, enough to keep Cade sustained for the journey to the castle.

***

We brought Cade back to our old room. With Kaelen's help, I carefully bathed him and dressed him in loose linen pants. His body, though visibly mending, was still pale and fragile. Kaelen's usual unshakable demeanor was strained—he looked almost as wrecked as I felt.

"Goddess, help me, Kaelen," I said, my voice breaking. "If he doesn't wake up and talk to me soon, I'll go batshit crazy."

Kaelen placed a reassured hand on my shoulder. "He'll wake up, Olivia. I've never known a man stronger than Cade. Nothing in this realm or any other could keep him from you. Just give him time. And not to be unkind, but... you could use some time to get yourself together too."

For the first time, I glanced down at myself. Dirt, blood, and grime covered me from head to toe. My hair hung in a tangled mess. I looked like I'd been rode hard and put up wet.

"Oh stars," I muttered. "You're right. Can you sit with him while I grab a quick shower?"

Kaelen gave me a soft smile. "It's always an honor to tend to my brother."

His words struck something deep inside me. Tears welled in my eyes as I threw my arms around his neck. "Kaelen, I don't know what I'd do if I lost him. I can't go on without him. I felt it when he went down—I swear, it felt like a part of me had died. And I couldn't go to him. I had to keep fighting those monsters, but all I wanted was to be by his side. What if he'd died, and I couldn't have said goodbye? I'd never have forgiven myself."

Kaelen pulled back enough to look me in the eye, his expression resolute. "You must stop thinking about what could have been, Olivia. You were here. You fought for him— and I know your presence helped save him. He's going to be alright. We just need to let his body heal. It's going to take time, but Cade's strong, stronger than you or I even know."

He paused, his lips curving into a small grin. "Now, go get cleaned up. You don't want to look like this when he wakes up, do you?"

Despite myself, I laughed softly. "No, I don't suppose I do." I glanced back at Cade, my heart twisting. "I'll be quick."

***

As the hours ticked by, my anxiety grew sharper, gnawing at the edges of my resolve. Cade lay motionless, his face eerily serene, as if lost in a dream I couldn't reach. I clung to his hand, my thumb tracing absent patterns across his skin, the warmth of his touch the only thing tethering me to hope.

"Remember when we first met?" I murmured, leaning close. My voice was soft, trembling with the weight of memory. "You walked right into my dream, bold as could be, and I was done for. You didn't know that, did you? I thought you were the most beautiful man I'd ever seen."

I choked on a bittersweet laugh, my fingers tightening around his. "We've come so far, Cade. Fought battles I didn't think I'd survive. You've been my anchor through all of it. And I am not about to let you slip away now. You hear me? You're too dadgum stubborn for that."

My voice cracked on the last word, and I leaned forward, resting my head on the edge of the bed. I was still holding his hand, our fingers intertwined like lifelines.

"I love you," I whispered, my lips brushing his knuckles. "And I swear by the Goddess, if you don't wake up soon, I'll find you. Wherever you are, I'll drag you back myself. That's a promise, Cade."

The words hung in the air, fierce and raw, a vow whispered to the man who had become my entire world.

***

I'd left a healer with Cade and made my way to the war room, my steps heavy with exhaustion and worry. The weight of the oak doors groaned as I pushed them open, and the murmur of hushed voices spilled into the corridor like a tide of tension. Inside, the air was thick, almost oppressive, as though the room itself carried the burden of what had transpired.

Leaders from four kingdoms stood around a massive table carved with intricate runes, their faces drawn, shadows flickering across them in the dim light of the wall sconces. Farin's deep, melodic voice carried above the murmur, steady and unshaken.

"The rifts may not be as manageable as we'd hoped," he said, gesturing to a map sprawled across the table. Red and black markers dotted the surface like scars. "We can't afford to be caught off guard again."

I slid into place between Amaya and Miranda, their warm arms immediately intertwined with mine in silent support. Across the table, Kaelen's eyes met mine, his gaze momentarily softening with sympathy before returning to its sharp, commanding intensity.

"How's Cade?" Miranda whispered, her voice low.

"Still unconscious," I replied, swallowing the tightness in my throat. "But stable."

Ignis, his fiery hair glowing like embers in the low light of the room, slammed his fist on the table. The sound echoed through the room like a thunderclap. "We need an action plan! We cannot keep fighting defensively. The next breach could destroy a city!"

"And we'll have one," Kaelen growled, his voice low and rumbling, like the promise of a storm. "But reckless moves will only leave us more vulnerable. We need coordination, not chaos."

I nodded, finding my voice amidst the turmoil. "He's right. We can't afford to throw ideas at the wall and hope something sticks. If we do this, it must be airtight."

Farin leaned forward, his dark eyes alight with thought. "What we need is diversity—teams that blend magics and abilities from all our kingdoms."

"Exactly," I said, warming to the idea. "Mist Orbs from Thalassa for concealment, paired with Vesparra's Shadow Shards for stealth strikes. Ilyndor's Elemental Wards for defense while Aurelion's Flare Arrows finishes the fight. Each kingdom brings something unique—together, we can cover every angle."

"It's not just about the tools," Kaelen interjected, his gaze sweeping the table. "We need fighters of every kind—mages, shifters, vampires — working as one."

As the discussion swirled, I could almost see it: patrols of mixed warriors, their strengths balancing each other, their movements seamless. A tapestry of abilities standing vigilant against the looming threat. My heart raced, torn between hope and the fear of what we might face next.

"The command centers," Farin mused, stroking his beard thoughtfully. "We must fortify the command centers and keep them manned around the clock,"

"Agreed," I said, my mind churning with ideas. "And the patrols—they can't just be from one kingdom. We need all of them working together, training together. Familiarity breeds trust, and trust will win battles."

Miranda nodded, her expression one of fierce determination. "Unity," she said, her voice carrying across the room. "That's how we'll survive this."

Kaelen's gaze lingered on me, his silver eyes steady. "Then it's settled. We'll create cross-realm patrols and arm them with everything we have. This isn't just a battle for kingdoms anymore. It's a battle for survival."

A hush fell over the room as his words sank in. The weight of what lay ahead loomed heavy, but in the sconce lights, I saw a glimmer of something else: resolve. We weren't just preparing for war. We were preparing to win.

"It can't just be us," Miranda said softly, her eyes meeting mine. "The royals, I mean. We can't shoulder this burden alone."

A heavy silence fell over the room as the enormity of our task pressed down on us. My thoughts flickered to Cade, lying unconscious just rooms away, and to all the lives already lost in this war against the rifts.

"No," I said, my voice firmer than I felt. "It must be all of us. Every kingdom, every mage, every shifter, every soldier capable of wielding magic must stand together. This is our realm, and we'll defend it together."

I paused, meeting the eyes of everyone around the table. "The royals will continue to bring firepower, yes. But the Dragonia? They're our trump card—reserved for the battles that demand overwhelming force. For the creatures that refuse to fall."

The weight of my words settled over the room, heavy but galvanizing. Murmurs of agreement rippled around the table, the tension easing as resolve took its place.

I clenched my fists, drawing strength from the surrounding faces. "This won't be easy. We've got a long, hard fight ahead of us. But for the first time since the rifts appeared..." My voice softened, steady with conviction. "I feel hope."

Magda

"How did that insipid little bitch close both rifts so completely?!"

Magda was storming across the grounds of the Underworld on a mission to exact retribution for this failure.

120

Her inability to cross the barrier into Eldoria was becoming an obsession that teetered on the brink of madness.

Magda's rage echoed through the cavernous halls, her voice carrying a bitter chill that made even the most hardened demons flinch. Her spiked, crimson heels clicked against the obsidian floors as she stalked towards the Chamber of Shadows, where her most trusted advisors awaited.

"My lady," a hooded figure materialized from the darkness, his voice a raspy whisper. "Perhaps we underestimated the strength of their combined magic."

Magda whirled on him, her eyes flashing with murderous intent. "Underestimated?" she hissed. "I do not underestimate Vexus. I conquer. I destroy. And yet here I stand, trapped in this realm while that bumbling girl and her merry band of fools survive to fight yet another day."

She lashed out, her hand connecting with Vexus's face, sending him sprawling across the floor. Dark ichor oozed from the gash her nails left behind.

"I want solutions, not excuses," Magda snarled. "Find me a way through that barrier, or I'll feed you to the hellhounds piece by piece."

Vexus scrambled to his feet, bowing low. "Of course, my lady. We've been experimenting with new methods of corrupting the natural rifts. If we can destabilize them from this side..."

"Enough!" Magda cut him off. "I've heard your theories before. What I need are results."

She swept into the Chamber of Shadows, where a circle of hooded figures awaited her. The air crackled with dark energy, shadows writhing at the edges of the room.

"Tell me, what damage was done when both rifts shut closed today. Something tells me that this news will not sit well with me."

"Well, Goddess, when The Chosen managed to close both rifts simultaneously, there was a considerable disturbance.

She somehow disrupted the magic that you had been using to create the rifts. I'm afraid the spells you had been using will no longer work."

This revelation sent Magda into an even greater rage. Her eyes flashed with an infernal light, her teeth bared in a snarl of pure fury. The shadows in the chamber writhed and twisted, responding to her anger.

"Useless!" she shrieked, her voice reverberating off the obsidian walls. "All of you, utterly useless!"

With a wave of her hand, dark tendrils of magic lashed out, wrapping around the throat of the demon who had spoken. He clawed desperately at the shadowy bonds as they lifted him off the ground.

"My lady," another figure stepped forward, his voice trembling. "Perhaps if we could study the residual energy from the closed rifts, we might find a—"

"Silence!" Magda roared, flinging the choking demon across the room. He hit the wall with a sickening crunch and slid to the floor.

"My lady," Vexus dared to speak, "we dealt a decisive blow today. King Cadence was left a bloody heap on the beach as the rift closed. He might have been mortally wounded."

Her evil laughter filled the hall.

"Unless someone separated his head from his body, he is still alive. But I'm happy to hear that he endured pain, at least."

Her pacing continued without ceasing.

"None of this could have happened if it weren't for her. That little traitor. Rotting in a cell in the dungeon isn't punishment enough. I want my pound of flesh. Bring Princess Callie up here. I want her punished properly for causing me all this inconvenience. And send Eldric to me as well. It's time he took his place beside me. He can start by teaching his cousin the consequences of crossing the Goddess of the Underworld."

CHAPTER 13

Olivia

I gripped Cade's hand tightly, my eyes locked on his pale face. The steady rise and fall of his chest was the only movement in the dimly lit room—a cruel mockery of peaceful sleep. Each breath he took was a lifeline, a fragile thread tethering him to this world. My heart ached with every shallow inhale, each one a reminder of how close I'd come to losing him.

"Come back to me, Cade," I whispered, my voice breaking on the words. "I can't do this without you."

Memories surged through me—his crooked smile, the warmth of his arms wrapped around me, the way his ice-blue eyes sparkled when he teased me. They felt so vivid, so real, that the stillness of his face now was a knife to my chest. I squeezed my eyes shut, willing away the tears threatening to fall.

My thumb traced the lines of his palm, every curve, every callus etched into my memory. "I need you, Cade. More than I've ever needed anyone. You make me stronger... braver. Without you, I'm..." My voice faltered, unable to finish the thought.

The weight of it all—the looming war, the rifts tearing apart our world, the constant danger—bore down on me, and I pressed his hand to my cheek, seeking comfort in his touch.

"Please," I murmured, my voice barely a breath. "Please come back to me. I love you."

And then, his fingers twitched.

Hope surged through me, wild and fierce. I gasped, leaning forward. "Cade? Cade, can you hear me?"

He didn't respond, but I swore I felt the faintest squeeze. My heart galloped as I rested my head beside his hand on the bed, my fingers entwined with his.

"You remember the first time you kissed me?" I said softly, the memory warming the chill that had settled in my chest. "That was my first kiss. You were my first everything. My first kiss, the first man to ever see me with no clothes..." A soft laugh bubbled up, surprising even me. "The first man to touch all my lady parts," I added with a chuckle. "Oh, my stars, I'm losing my mind. Cade, do you see what you're doing to me? I'm going nuts without you."

"I can see that."

The voice was hoarse, barely above a whisper, but it was unmistakably Cade's.

I shot up so fast, my chair almost toppled backward. "Cade?!"

His eyes, heavy-lidded and groggy, blinked up at me. The sight of them after three agonizing days hit me like a punch to the chest. Tears sprang to my eyes as I leaned over him, cupping his face in my hands.

"Hi, handsome," I whispered, my voice trembling with joy. "You've been gone way too long, you know that?" I pressed a flurry of tiny kisses across his face, unable to contain the wellspring of emotion that threatened to drown me. "Are you thirsty? Let me get you some water."

I turned to the nightstand, fumbling with the pitcher and glass, my hands shaking as I poured.

"Olivia," he rasped, his voice rough from disuse. "Slow down."

I froze mid-pour, clutching the glass. His eyes held mine,

steady despite the weakness in his voice. "You're such a love," he managed, the words rough but laced with warmth. "Yes, please, I'll take some water."

Blinking back tears, I hurried back to him. "Lean up just a little," I said, grabbing an extra pillow to prop him up. "Let me help you get comfortable."

Once he was settled, I held the glass to his lips, watching as he took slow, measured sips. The simple act of seeing him drink, of hearing his raspy breathing grow steadier, loosened the tight coil of fear in my chest.

"How long have I been out?" he asked, his voice still faint but more present than before.

"Three freakin' days," I said, my voice breaking again. "I thought I'd lost you, baby."

"I heard."

My brow furrowed. "What do you mean, you heard?"

He paused, his gaze distant, as if searching for the right words. "I mean, I heard you," he said softly. "I heard conversations... Kaelen, the others. But mostly, I heard you crying." His voice faltered, and his eyes filled with something I hadn't seen in them before: guilt. "My heart was breaking for you. I wanted so badly to hold you, to tell you everything was okay, but I couldn't move. I couldn't reach you."

My breath caught in my throat as I cupped his face again, my thumbs brushing over the stubble on his cheeks. "You're here now," I whispered, the tears I'd been holding back spilling over. "That's all that matters."

He closed his eyes, leaning into my touch. "I'm here, Starlight. I'm not going anywhere."

"So you heard every single rant I went on while I sat next to you, huh?" I teased, leaning closer to Cade.

"Oh yes. Every one of them." His voice was still hoarse, but carried a hint of humor. "Some were... quite enlightening."

Heat crept up my neck. "Especially the ones where I discussed what I wanted to do to you if you were awake?"

Cade's lips twitched into a weak smile. "Let's just say, they were... motivating."

I laughed softly, brushing a lock of hair from his forehead. "I thought if I got a good enough fantasy going, you'd wake up." I sat back, suddenly serious. "Do you need to get out of bed? Should I call Grandpapa to help?"

He nodded slightly. "That's probably a good idea."

I sent Cressida to fetch him, but of course, she brought half the realm along for the occasion. Grandpapa, Kaelen, Amaya, Seraphine, and Thorne all filed into the room, their faces alight with relief and curiosity.

"Well, I'm glad I thought to put a robe on my mate." I joked as the room filled with bodies. "Since apparently, this is now a public event."

Seraphine all but barreled through everyone to reach Cade. She kneeled beside him, her hands cupping his face, her tears streaming freely.

"Brother, don't you ever scare me like that again," she choked out, her voice trembling. "I mean it."

Cade's lips curved into a faint smile. "I'll do my best to stay alive next time, promise." He gently pulled her hands from his face, squeezing them in reassurance.

Kaelen stepped in, helping Cade to the washroom and then back to the living area. Every movement seemed to cost Cade effort, his body still frail, but he was determined to sit upright in an armchair. The sight of him there, weak but smiling, brought a lump to my throat.

I had Cressida bring a tray of hearty soup and bread, and Cade ate slowly, each bite seeming to restore a flicker of strength. The room, as always, turned to business, the conversation shifting to strategies for war, rift detection, and our ultimate goal of facing Magda.

As Cade sipped from his water, I voiced the thought that had been bothering me. "So Magda still hasn't come through herself. The rifts have been plenty big enough for her scrawny butt to get through. There must be something stopping her —a barrier or... something. Until she can cross over, it seems like she's content to send her army of killer creepies to wreak havoc."

"She's doing a fine job of that," Miranda said dryly, leaning back in her chair. "The chaos she's caused already is enough to weaken morale if we're not careful."

I turned to Miranda, a new thought sparking. "How did you realize the rift was about to open? It was outside the castle walls, right?"

She nodded. "I felt it—a sort of tremor. Something in the air felt... off. When I checked the trees, I noticed they were shaking, but there wasn't any wind. Then I saw the faint shimmer, and I knew it was a rift."

I turned to Farin. "What about you, Grandpapa?"

He stroked his beard thoughtfully. "Similar. It's hard to put into words, but I felt it in my body, like the earth itself was shifting. I knew it was something significant."

"If we could somehow harness that feeling," I mused, "and use it for early detection..."

Grandpapa's eyes lit with that familiar spark of innovation. "I'm already working on something. It's not quite ready, but soon."

I shook my head and smiled despite the tension. "Grandpapa, I don't know what we'd do without you."

"Hopefully," he said with a small grin, "you'll never have to find out."

Cade looked like he was fading fast. The energy it had taken to sit up and greet everyone was draining from him. His pallor, though better than before, was still concerning. Enough was enough.

"Well, y'all," I said, clapping my hands and offering a smile to soften the blow, "it's been lovely to celebrate Cade's miraculous awakening, but he's fading. Time for the patient to get some rest."

"Now, Starlight, I think I can make that—"

"We'll see y'all tomorrow!" I cut him off, ushering everyone toward the door like I was herding cattle.

Amaya stopped to hug me on her way out, her arms squeezing me tight. "We're heading back home," she said, her tone laced with apology. "We still have Fiora business to deal with."

I cupped her face, forcing her to look at me. "Of course, baby girl. You go do Luna stuff. Kick some booty. We'll be fine here. I love y'all bunches."

"I love you too, Ollie." Her voice was soft but steady.

I shut the door behind the last of them and leaned against it for a moment, letting the quiet seep back into the room. Then I turned to Cade, whose tired eyes sparkled with amusement.

"Let's go, Highness," I said, crossing to him. "You need to rest if you want to get back to one hundred percent."

"You're right," he admitted, his lips twitching in that way that made my stomach flip. "But don't get used to being the boss."

I grinned. "Oh, don't you worry. If it gets you back on your feet, I'll boss you from here to Vesparra and back."

"And speaking of that," I added, more softly now, "you haven't fed in a few days. Would that help your recovery?" His brows arched, and I rolled my eyes. "And wipe that look off your face. I'm not talkin' about sexy time, you hound dog."

The sound of his laughter washed over me, warm and familiar. Relief spread through me like sunlight breaking through clouds. But then, without warning, it all hit me— how close I'd come to losing him, the horror of seeing him broken and bloodied on that beach. Tears welled up, hot and unstoppable, spilling down my cheeks before I could hold them back.

"Starlight," Cade said, his voice gentle as he opened his arms to me. "Sweetheart, come here. What's wrong?"

I crossed the room in two shaky steps and melted into his embrace. It was the first time I'd felt truly whole since I'd arrived in Thalassa. But the dam had burst, and the sobs came hard and fast. My words tumbled out between hiccupping gasps.

"Y-y-you w-were so st-still," I stammered, clutching his shirt. "B-barely breathing. Th-there was s-so much blood. I was s-so afraid to touch you. I didn't want to hurt you." My voice cracked, raw with anguish. "I didn't want you to leave me, Cade. I c-couldn't stand the thought of being alone again. Without y-you." I gasped. "I c-can't live without you."

"Starlight, honey," he murmured, his voice a comfort to my frayed nerves. He tilted my chin up, forcing me to meet his eyes, his thumbs brushing away the tears streaking my face. "I'm right here. I'm never leaving you."

I tried to nod, but my throat felt too tight. He cupped my face with such tenderness, his eyes steady and sure. "There is nothing in this realm or any other that could take me from you. Do you hear me?"

I stared at him, my breath hitching, and finally nodded. Slowly, the storm inside me settled, my sobs tapering into quiet sniffles.

"Now," Cade said gently, "I'm going to lie down before I fall down. And yes, my love, I think feeding would help if you're up for it."

I got him settled back into bed, propping him against the pillows until he looked more comfortable. He was still pale, his exhaustion etched into every line of his face, but he offered me a faint, teasing smile.

I slipped out of my dress and into a simple nightgown, crawling onto the bed beside him. The feel of his presence beside me filled a part of my heart I hadn't realized was still aching.

"Do you want my wrist or my neck?" I asked softly, brushing his hair back from his face. "Whatever's easiest for you."

"Woman," he drawled, his voice low and rough, "I always want to feed from your gorgeous neck. Crawl up here, please."

I crawled up next to him, turned my back, and twisted so we were chest to chest. My neck was level with his luscious mouth.

"I think I've made this as easy for you as possible, cowboy."

"Indeed, you have Starlight. You are so beautiful."

He laid sweet kisses along the column of my neck. I tilted my head toward my shoulder, giving him all the access he needed. After a few more kisses, I felt the brush of his fangs, then the bite. The sensation of my blood filling his mouth was followed immediately by the euphoria of his venom. My rapturous moans filled the room as he drank. This bite differed from those during intimacy; it felt primal, raw. I channeled the feeling back through our bond and was gifted with Cade's own euphoric groans mixed with a growl.

After a few moments, he released his bite and licked the wounds closed. I was left limp from the intense high. I pulled up, turned, and cuddled into his side.

"Feel better?"

"Like a new man, Starlight. Like a brand-new man."

CHAPTER 14

Fiora

I traced my fingers along Zane's muscular chest, feeling the heat of his skin beneath my touch. The moonlight filtered through the sheer curtains, casting ethereal shadows across our entwined bodies. I gazed up at him, my eyes wide with adoration.

"Can you imagine it, Zane? Us ruling Therionis together?" I purred, nuzzling into the crook of his neck. "I'd be the perfect Luna for you."

Zane's arm tightened around me, but I sensed a flicker of hesitation in his amber eyes. "Fiora, you know Kaelen has chosen Amaya as his mate."

I kept my expression serene, suppressing the scowl that threatened to surface, and kept my voice soft, persuasive. "But is she truly fit to be Luna? Think about it, my love. She's an outsider, unfamiliar with our customs and traditions. She's not even a shifter. We are a kingdom of shifters."

My words seemed to plant a seed of doubt in Zane's mind, the gears turning behind his furrowed brow. Encouraged, I pressed on, my tone dripping with honey-coated venom.

"Amaya may have magic, but does she understand the intricacies of pack politics? The delicate balance we must maintain with the other kingdoms?" I sighed dramatically, my fingers trailing softly down his arm. "Our people need a strong, experienced Luna by their Alpha's side."

Zane's jaw clenched, his gaze distant as he considered my words. I knew I had him right where I wanted him. Sitting up, I straddled his hips, drawing his focus to me.

"You've seen how she struggles with even the simplest pack dynamics," I whispered, leaning in close, my breath warm against his ear. "How can she possibly lead us through these turbulent times?"

A low growl rumbled in Zane's chest, his hands gripping my waist with a possessive intensity. "You're right," he murmured, his voice thick with conviction. "Therionis deserves better."

Inwardly, I rejoiced. My carefully woven web of manipulation was working perfectly. I cupped Zane's face, staring into his green eyes with an intensity that bordered on obsession.

"You could give them better, Zane," I breathed. "With me by your side, we could make Therionis stronger than ever before."

As Zane pulled me down for a passionate kiss, I allowed myself a small, triumphant smile. I had planted the seeds of doubt, and soon, they would bloom into the downfall of Kaelen and his precious Amaya.

I smoothed the high collar of my dress, ensuring every strand of hair was in place, every detail immaculate. Presentation mattered, especially now. As I swept into the grand dining room of my family's estate, the air shifted, charged with anticipation. They knew I had news. They just didn't know how explosive it would be.

"My dear family," I began, my voice a symphony of feigned distress, carefully measured to hook their attention, "You will not believe what I witnessed."

The clatter of forks against porcelain filled the room as all eyes turned to me. My cousin Lyra, so annoyingly naïve, froze mid-bite, her curiosity practically dripping from her widened eyes. I took a moment, savoring the suspense, letting their impatience ripple through the air. Then, with a dramatic sigh, I let the words fall like stones into water.

"Amaya, our supposed Luna, attacked another pack member in a fit of magical rage," I declared, my voice trembling as if the memory itself pained me. "She nearly killed the poor girl over nothing more than some kind of misunderstanding."

Gasps erupted around the table, sharp and delicious. My cousin Lyra's eyes darted between me and the others. "But... but how? I've never seen her be anything but kind! Gentle, even!"

I shook my head slowly, the picture of solemnity. "It seems her power is too great for her to control," I said, allowing my voice to quaver. "And that makes her a danger—to all of us."

"This is outrageous!" Uncle Davin thundered, his fist crashing against the table. The force rattled the silverware, a mirror of his growing fury. "Kaelen allows this... this *witch* to threaten our people?"

Inside, I glowed with satisfaction, though my expression remained carefully mournful. "I fear he can't see beyond the mate bond," I murmured, lowering my gaze as though I bore the weight of such a revelation. "He refuses to see the threat she poses—not to himself, not to us, and not to the kingdom."

The room erupted into angry voices, their righteous indignation spiraling exactly as I'd intended. I sat back slightly, letting the waves of outrage build, feeding on their fear and disgust. It was almost too easy.

"We can't let this stand!" my sister Aria's voice rang out, worried but resolute. "What can we do? How do we stop this?"

Perfect.

I straightened in my seat, my eyes hardening just enough to convey quiet authority. "We must stand united," I said, allowing a note of resolve to edge my voice. "For the safety of our people, we have no choice. We must force Kaelen and Amaya to see reason—or they will face the consequences of their blindness.

The fire of righteous indignation blazed to life in their eyes. My family was a sea of nodding heads, their minds already spinning with ways to enact this newfound mission of justice. They didn't need to know the truth. They didn't need to know this was nothing more than a web of lies. All they needed was the conviction I'd gifted them and their own self-righteousness.

As murmurs of agreement and plans of action swirled around me, I allowed myself the faintest of smiles. *Kaelen, you blind fool,* I thought as my fingers traced the edge of my coffee cup. *You do not know the storm that's about to crash down upon you and your precious little Luna.*

Amaya

The council chamber was heavy with tension, the kind that tried to steal the air from your lungs. Kaelen entered behind me, his presence like a storm cloud rolling in, silent but charged. His eyes swept the room as he strode to the head of the table. He moved with a commanding grace, but I caught the faintest ripple of tension in his jaw. Whatever was coming, he knew it wouldn't be easy.

Zorion, his Beta, stood at his right hand, his posture rigid with readiness. Around the table, the council members shifted uneasily in their seats, their furtive glances betraying a shared sense of unease. My pulse thrummed in my ears as I took a seat to Kaelen's left. Whatever this was, it would not be good.

Kaelen didn't waste time. "Let us begin," he said, his voice a steady rumble that demanded attention.

But before he could say another word, Elder Marcus, Zane's father, rose from his chair, his weathered face set with grim determination as he locked eyes with Kaelen.

"Kaelen Therionis," he began, his voice sharp and cutting, "I stand before this council to proclaim my son Zane's challenge for the position of Alpha."

For a moment, the air seemed to freeze. Then, like a dam

breaking, chaos erupted.

"What?!" Councilwoman Bartima exclaimed, her shock evident in her wide eyes.

"This is unprecedented!" Elder Marius barked, his chair scraping loudly as he shot to his feet. "On what grounds?"

I turned to Kaelen, searching for any crack in his composure. His jaw tightened slightly, but his expression remained cool and unyielding. This was a man who had faced worse storms and emerged victorious.

Elder Marcus raised his voice, cutting through the rising din. "The grounds," he said, each word deliberately, "are that his mate has compromised the current Alpha's judgment. We believe he can no longer lead our pack effectively."

Kaelen's fingers flexed subtly on the table, a sign only those who knew him well would catch. "And in what way do you claim my mate has compromised me?" he asked, his voice calm but laced with steel.

The council chamber buzzed with murmurs.

"... the human girl..."

"... too much power..."

"... danger to us all..."

Fiora's father, Ronan, stood next, his expression smug. "It has come to my attention," he said, his voice oily and condescending, "that your mate lost control of her magic in a fit of anger and injured a member of our pack. And you, Alpha, did nothing."

The room went still. My chest tightened as the accusation landed. My pulse roared in my ears. This was it—the moment everything would change. I forced my expression into neutrality, though fury and indignation churned within me. The claim was absurd, and I opened my mouth to defend myself, but Kaelen raised a hand, silencing me with a small shake of his head.

He stood slowly, every movement deliberate, and addressed the room. "The only person who has attacked anyone in anger recently is your daughter, Ronan," Kaelen said, his voice like a growl of thunder. "While we were battling the creature that breached the rift outside our kingdom, Amaya risked her life for *your* lives—to keep you safe. And it was *Fiora*, in her wolf form, who swiped Amaya's shoulder, laying it open in the heat of battle."

Gasps rippled around the room, and Kaelen's silver gaze pinned Ronan in place. "Her sister, The Chosen, saw Fiora shift and attack Amaya. *That's* the only attack that has occurred, and the only failure I've committed as Alpha is not yet addressing Fiora's punishment."

Ronan's lips thinned, his eyes narrowing. "Did *you* see this attack, Alpha?" His tone was almost mocking, dripping with thinly veiled disrespect.

Kaelen didn't flinch. "Are you questioning the word of The Chosen?"

"I'm simply saying she's an outsider," Ronan said, shrugging in mock innocence. "She doesn't know our people. It's possible she could be mistaken."

A low, warning growl rumbled in Kaelen's chest. His power radiated through the room, making the air feel charged. "It's clear," he said, his voice deadly calm, "that you, and perhaps others, question my ability to rule this kingdom. I hear your challenge," Kaelen said, his eyes flashing with a dangerous light, "and I accept it."

The finality of those words sent a chill down my spine. As the council erupted into fresh debate, I couldn't help but wonder: what would this mean for our pack? For Therionis? And most of all, for the fragile peace we'd fought so hard to maintain in Eldoria?

I watched as Kaelen's eyes swept the room, taking in every face, every reaction. His composure was unshakeable, but I could sense the gears turning behind that stoic facade. He wasn't just listening; he was strategizing, calculating every potential outcome of this challenge.

"Before we proceed further," Kaelen's deep voice resonated through the chamber, silencing the whispers, "I'd like to address the council on a matter of utmost importance to our realm's security."

Elder Marcus' brow furrowed. "Alpha, with all due respect —"

"The safety of Eldoria takes precedence over internal politics. I am still Alpha of this pack and King of Therionis. You *will* respect me," Kaelen cut him off, his tone brooking no argument. "We face threats that cannot wait for the resolution of this challenge."

I felt a surge of admiration. Even now, with his leadership contested, Kaelen's first thought was for protecting his people.

He strode to the center of the room, commanding attention without effort. "We must have an immediate increase in military patrols across Eldoria. Just four days ago, there were two very large rifts that opened on opposite ends of the realm — one outside of Ilyndor and one in Thalassa. King Vesparra nearly lost his life. It took magic from several kingdoms, plus the Dragonia to defeat the creatures coming up through the rifts. If Queen Olivia hadn't been able to close both rifts, we'd all likely not even be standing here today."

A collective shudder ran through the room. I felt my skin prickle at the implication.

"We cannot afford to be caught unprepared," Kaelen continued, his voice gaining intensity. "We've ascertained that it will take teams of soldiers from each kingdom with a variety of magical weapons to make a force effective enough to fight Magda's monsters. Beta Zorion will oversee the implementation."

As he outlined the details of his plan, I couldn't help but be impressed at his foresight. He'd clearly been working on this strategy for some time, anticipating threats before they fully materialized.

"And what of our resources this will require?" Elder

Marius questioned, though his tone was more curious than confrontational.

Kaelen nodded, as if he'd expected the query. "I've reallocated funds from non-essential projects. Our defenses will be bolstered without additional strain on our people."

The council members exchanged glances, a mix of approval and lingering tension clear in their expressions. Even those who had seemed ready to support the challenge couldn't deny the wisdom of Kaelen's proposal.

As I watched him command the room, effortlessly shifting the focus from the challenge to the safety of the realm, I felt a surge of loyalty. This was why Kaelen was our Alpha. Not just his strength or his lineage, but his unwavering commitment to our people's well-being.

Yet, as the meeting continued, a small voice in the back of my mind whispered doubts. Would this be enough to quell the dissent? Or was the challenge just the beginning of a larger upheaval that threatened to tear our pack apart? We adjourned the meeting, deciding the challenge would take place in five days.

I felt the blood drain from my face as Kaelen's words echoed in my mind. A challenge for Alpha. My hands trembled as I gripped the edge of the ornate wooden table, my knuckles turning white.

"How could this happen?" I whispered, more to myself than anyone else. The weight of responsibility crashed down on me, threatening to suffocate me.

My magic stirred restlessly within me, responding to my turbulent emotions. A small gust of wind rustled the papers on the table, and I forced myself to take a deep breath, trying to calm the storm brewing inside me.

"This is my fault," I said, my voice barely audible. "If I hadn't come here, if I wasn't—"

Before I could finish, Kaelen was at my side, his large hand enveloping mine. The warmth of his touch sent a shiver down my spine, momentarily cutting through my anguish.

"Amaya," he said, his deep voice soft yet firm. "Look at me."

I raised my eyes to meet his piercing gaze. The intensity I found there made my breath catch in my throat.

"This is not your fault," Kaelen stated, his tone brooking no argument. "The challenge was inevitable. There are always those who seek power, who wish to test the strength of their Alpha."

He cupped my face gently, his thumb stroking my cheek. "You are not responsible for the ambitions of others. You are my mate, my Luna, and together we will face this and any other challenge that comes our way."

I leaned into his touch, drawing strength from his unwavering conviction. "But what if—"

"No," Kaelen interrupted, pulling me closer. "There are no 'what ifs'. I chose you, Amaya. The Goddess chose you for me. Our bond is unbreakable, and it strengthens us."

As he spoke, I felt the truth of his words resonate through our bond. The turmoil inside me subsided, replaced by a growing sense of determination.

"We're in this together," I said, my voice stronger now. "Whatever comes, we face it as one."

Kaelen's lips curved into a smile, pride shining in his eyes. "That's my brave Luna," he murmured, pressing a kiss to my forehead.

In that moment, surrounded by Kaelen's strength and love, I felt the last of my doubts melt away. We might face challenges, but we would face them together. And together, we were unstoppable.

CHAPTER 15

Amaya

A commotion outside drew my attention, breaking through the tension that lingered in the air. I glanced at Kaelen, his brow furrowed in concentration as he listened, head tilted slightly.

"What is it?" I asked, anxiety creeping into my voice despite the calm expression he wore.

His eyes softened, a faint smile tugging at his lips. "Come see for yourself," he said, taking my hand.

Curiosity prickled at me as we made our way downstairs. The murmurs grew louder, accompanied by the tantalizing scent of roasted meats, fresh bread, and sweet desserts. When we stepped onto the porch of the pack house, the sight before me took my breath away.

The clearing was alive with pack members, a vibrant sea of faces filled with determination and warmth. Each one carried something—a steaming dish, a basket of bread, a jug of cider. The scents mingled in the crisp air, wrapping around me like a comforting embrace.

"What's all this?" I whispered, my voice catching in my throat.

An older woman with silver-streaked hair stepped forward, her warm brown eyes locking onto mine. Her hands cradled a pot, steam curling from beneath its lid. "We heard about the challenge, Luna," she said, her voice steady and sure. "We wanted you to know where we stand."

She handed me the pot, and the savory aroma of venison stew wafted up, rich and earthy. The weight of it in my hands felt heavier than the iron pot itself. It was more than food—it was solidarity.

"I... I don't know what to say," I stammered, tears pricking at the corners of my eyes.

Kaelen stepped closer, taking the pot from my hands. His smile was tender, a reminder of his steady presence. "You don't need to say anything," he murmured. "Just feel."

I closed my eyes, and the pack bond thrummed through me like a living thing. Waves of energy, love, and unwavering loyalty surged from every direction, wrapping me in their collective strength. It was overwhelming, a tide of emotion that nearly swept me off my feet.

"Luna Amaya!" a childish voice piped up.

I opened my eyes to see a little girl no older than seven, holding up a plate of misshapen cookies. Her cheeks were flushed pink, her eyes shining with pride.

"I made these for you myself!" she declared.

I kneeled, taking the plate with both hands as if it were a priceless treasure. "Thank you, sweetheart. They look absolutely delicious."

The surrounding crowd chuckled softly, the warmth of their smiles infectious. As I stood, I met more gazes—some familiar, others new—all reflecting the same message: *We stand with you.*

"I never thought..." I began, my voice thick with emotion. "Not being from here, I mean..."

A gruff voice cut through the murmurs. "You're exactly what we need," an older man said, his weathered face breaking into a small, approving smile. "You bring new blood, new ideas. And you make our Alpha happy. That's more than enough for us."

Kaelen's chest rumbled behind me, a sound of quiet pride. His voice brushed against my ear as he whispered, "See? They see you as I do."

The gratitude swelling in my chest was almost painful in its intensity. These people—*my* people now—had stood with us. Faced with uncertainty and division, they had gathered, not just with food but with unwavering support.

I turned to the crowd, my voice steady despite the lump in my throat. "Thank you. All of you. I promise I'll do everything in my power to be worthy of your trust."

A wave of cheers swept through the clearing as pack members began setting up tables and laying out the feast. The air filled with laughter and conversation, the tension from earlier replaced by a sense of unity and hope.

We dined on delicious food and shared conversations about the past and the future. I had a sense that even though the path forward would be rocky; we had people who'd fight for and with us.

Kaelen's hand slid into mine, his fingers lacing with my own. "Come," he murmured, his breath brushing the shell of my ear. "We need some time alone."

I glanced up at him, warmth pooling in my chest, and nodded. He led me away from the bustling activity, his grip firm but gentle. We slipped back into the pack house, the sounds of the celebration fading as we ascended the stairs to our private quarters.

The door clicked shut behind us, sealing us in the quiet sanctuary of our room. Kaelen turned to me and pulled me into his arms. The world outside faded away as I melted into his embrace, the scent of pine and earth wrapping around me. A low hum of contentment escaped my lips, almost like a purr.

"Amaya," he murmured, his voice a low rumble that sent shivers down my spine. "How are you feeling?"

I pulled back slightly, meeting Kaelen's intense gaze. "Overwhelmed," I admitted, my voice barely above a whisper.

"But... grateful. I never expected..."

"To be accepted?" Kaelen finished, his hand gently brushing a stray curl from my face. The warmth of his touch sent shivers down my spine, settling me in a way nothing else could.

"Yeah," I sighed, a soft laugh escaping. "I keep waiting for the other shoe to drop. Like someone's going to realize I'm just faking my way through this."

Kaelen's expression hardened—not with anger, but with resolve.

"My love, you're not faking anything. You're exactly what this pack needs. You're exactly what I need."

My heart soared at his words, loving the feeling of belonging. "It's a funny feeling to know that I've found a home. I'd always hoped I'd find a place where I would be loved and accepted. But I never thought it would actually happen. Maybe that's why I get scared sometimes that I might not measure up —that I won't be able to carry the weight of being Luna."

Kaelen tipped my chin up, his eyes fierce as they met mine. "Then let me carry it with you. Your strength isn't yours alone anymore—it's ours."

I pressed my forehead to his chest, feeling his steady heartbeat against my skin. "I'm scared, Kaelen," I whispered, letting the confession tumble out. "This challenge... What does it really entail?"

His arms tightened around me, the motion equal parts reassurance and hesitation. "It's a fight," he said finally, his voice heavy. "In the arena. We'll fight until only one of us is left standing," he declared, his voice thick with emotion.

My breath caught. "Do you mean...?"

"Yes, love," he said softly. "It's to the death or if the winner feels merciful, he can choose to allow the loser to live."

The weight of his words pressed down on me, and for a moment, I couldn't speak. When I finally looked up, his gaze burned with determination. "But don't you dare worry," he continued, his voice firm. "I will win. I promise you, I'll be the one walking back to you when it's over."

Something inside me cracked, giving way to a torrent of emotions. I tilted my head up and kissed him, pouring everything I couldn't say—my fears, my hope, my love—into that moment. His lips met mine with equal intensity, grounding me even as the world spun.

When we broke apart, my breath came faster, my heart pounding in my chest. "We'll survive this," I said, my voice steady despite the chaos inside me. "For Therionis. For the pack. For us."

Kaelen's lips curved into a small, proud smile as he took my hands. "That's my Luna." He paused, his thumb brushing over my knuckles. "What do you see for us, Amaya? For our future?"

I closed my eyes, inhaling the earthy scent of the forest outside. "I see a Therionis where everyone—shifter, mage, anyone—feels safe. Where we build a kingdom that protects its people and thrives on the strength of its magic. Where the forests stretch wide and strong, untouched by darkness."

"And?" he prompted, his voice soft but insistent.

"And," I continued, opening my eyes to meet his, "we lead by example. Together. We show them that strength isn't about fear or control. It's about trust, respect, love."

Kaelen leaned in, resting his forehead against mine. "Together," he murmured.

"Always," I whispered, the word carrying a promise I intended to keep.

Without another word, Kaelen wrapped me in his arms, cradling me against his chest. His gaze burned into mine, stripping away every barrier I thought I'd built. Then he reached for the buttons on my dress, his massive hands moving with surprising care. I stood still, my breaths growing shallow as each undone button exposed more skin.

The intensity in his gaze softened as he leaned in, his lips brushing mine. "You're everything, Amaya," he whispered, the words a vow.

As his hands found my waist, he unbuckled the belt I wore. It fell to the floor; the buckle clattering as it did. In this moment, there was no fear, no doubt—only us. His hands reached up to push the dress from my shoulders, leaving it in a puddle of fabric on the floor. I was left standing in a pink lace bra and matching panties.

"You are by far the most exquisite female my eyes have ever seen, my Luna, beyond compare."

His large hands grasped my face, and he kissed me like a starving man, as if I were his last meal.

"Maya, I want to take away all of your worries and concerns. I want to give you a moment of peace where you don't have to think about the future, or what tasks need your attention. You've been carrying that weight for far too long. Let me give you some freedom, baby."

Between spoken words, kisses peppered my mouth.

"That sounds... wonderful. I'd love that."

"That's why I gave you the stuffed wolf. I see how you cling to it when you sleep."

He was gazing into my eyes as he held my face in his hands. I suddenly felt shy about how much I loved hugging the toy when I slept or napped.

"Don't do that, sweetheart. Don't feel shy or silly about that. It's natural to want a place, to feel carefree. I want to be that place for you when I can. I know it's only in certain times, but it makes me happy. That is what being your Alpha means to me. It's something very different from what I am to the pack."

When he said that, my stomach did a little flip, and it felt good—right.

"That's not weird?"

"Of course not, baby. It's just between us. It just means that I'm the one who provides love and comfort and takes care of all your needs. You can let go sometimes and leave everything to me. Does that sound good?"

I thought for just a moment, then nodded.

"I need your words, sweet girl."

"Yes, Alpha."

It was like I had turned a switch on in Kaelen. He picked me up and laid me on the bed, his movements swift and sure. In less than a minute, I was out of my bra and panties. And in the next, he was out of his clothes and lying next to me, his hands caressing every inch of my body.

"I want you to straddle me, Luna." His voice was commanding, yet laced with desire. "I know you've never done that, but I want to feel you take me as deep as you can."

His command was like a switch for me too; I wanted to please him so much. I straddled his waist and slid back, my heat rubbing against his length. He was so long and wide. I held myself up with one knee to the side and took him in my hand, holding his eyes the entire time. The love and lust pouring through our bond intoxicated me. I stroked the head of his erection through my wetness a few times, my arousal so great that I practically poured down his length. Then I eased him into my opening, slowly lowering myself down, inch by glorious inch.

"Your tight heat is strangling my cock, Luna, and it feels so fucking good. Keep going, baby girl."

"Yes, Alpha," was all I could manage as I kept lowering myself until he was fully inside me. I had never felt so full. Leaning forward, I placed my palms on his chest and rocked my hips.

"You are a miracle, my Luna," he growled.

"Mmm, Alpha, it feels... deep, sooo deep, good."

He began to move into me from below. Then he pulled me down and took one of my breasts into his mouth, sucking and biting. I was getting so close.

His hands grabbed my face, and his tongue was suddenly exploring my mouth. I couldn't get enough. I licked his mouth, kissed his face, neck, and licked down his cheek as he rammed into me from below. Then, without warning, he flipped us, and I was on my back with Kaelen now slamming into me from above.

"Maya, you are the fucking Luna of Therionis. There is NO OTHER who will take your place." Each word was driven home with a thrust of his hips, as though he could brand the truth into me forever. I felt his knot expand, filling me until I thought I could take no more of him; the feeling was overwhelming.

"Alpha! I'm getting so close! It's so good!"

He reached down and rubbed my clit with his thumb, and that's all it took for me to explode into what felt like a million pieces. My growling moans filled the room, my body wracked with shudders with my release.

Kaelen's body tensed and shook with the force of his climax, rattling the bed frame beneath us. As he caught his breath, he leaned down and brushed his lips against mine in a gentle, loving kiss. I could feel his knot still tightly lodged inside me, holding us together as the waves of pleasure and emotion coursed through our bond. My heart overflowed with love and devotion for my mate, and I knew he felt the same for me.

"I love you, my Alpha."

"You are forever mine, my Luna."

The future of Therionis stretched out before us, full of uncertainty but also brimming with hope. And I knew, deep in my bones, that we would meet it head-on, united, determined, and unbreakable.

CHAPTER 16

Callie

The cold stone floor bit into my aching flesh as I lay motionless, each breath a battle against the pain that was my constant companion. Magda's guards had shown no mercy the last time, their fists and boots leaving a canvas of bruises across my skin. Amazingly, the ribs, which I know for a fact, were broken yesterday, seem to be fine today. Injuries must heal faster here than in the mortal realm. I closed my eyes, searching for a glimmer of hope in the darkness that threatened to consume me.

"Olivia... Amaya... It was worth it." I whispered, my voice barely audible even to my own ears. The thought of their escape brought a small smile to my cracked lips, despite the price I was now paying for my part in it. I guess it had been a few weeks since I'd sprung them from this hell. Time had no meaning where I was.

A distant scream echoed through the dungeon, sending a shiver down my spine. The oppressive atmosphere of the Underworld pressed down on me. The damp air clung to my skin like a second layer of grime. I forced my eyes open, taking in the bleak surroundings of my cell.

Dim light flickered from torches mounted here and there, casting eerie shadows that danced across the mold-covered walls. The darkness seemed alive, writhing and pulsing with malevolent energy. I couldn't help but wonder if this was how my birth parents had felt when they tried to escape this hellish realm.

"Some royal heritage," I muttered bitterly, thinking of the revelation that I was born to Underworld royalty. "Fat lot of good it's doing me now."

My mind raced with thoughts of survival. I analyzed my situation as I would a challenging business deal back in the mortal realm. But this was no negotiation over farm equipment; this was life and death.

"Come on, Callie," I urged myself, gritting my teeth as I pushed myself into a sitting position. "You've dealt with tougher customers than these demon bastards."

The movement sent fresh waves of pain through my body, but I refused to let it show. Years of working in a man's world had taught me to mask my vulnerabilities, to project confidence even when I felt anything but. Of course, I could always use my beauty to an advantage there. Not here. She'd done her best to take that away from me too, even all but shaving my beautiful golden curls from my head. Not gonna lie. That hurt almost as much as the physical torture she'd inflicted.

"Magda thinks she can break me?" I asked aloud, my voice growing stronger with each word. "She does not know who she's dealing with." I gave a bitter laugh. That's mighty big talk for a girl locked in a cage.

Another scream pierced the air, closer this time. I tensed, wondering if it was my turn to face whatever horrors awaited beyond my cell door. The thought of Magda's cruel smile made my blood boil, but I pushed the anger down, channeling it into determination even if it was mixed with fear.

"I *will* survive this," I vowed, my eyes fixed on the shadows beyond the bars. "And when I do, I'll make sure Magda pays for every bruise, every scream, every moment of suffering she's inflicted."

As I sat there, surrounded by the suffocating despair of the Underworld dungeon, I clung to the fragile threads of my life in the mortal realm. The love of my adoptive parents. The laughter I'd shared with Olivia. The simple joy of a sunny summer day. These memories were my lifeline—the lights that would guide me through this nightmare.

"You want a show, Magda?" I whispered, the faintest hint of my usual sass creeping into my voice. "Well, honey, I'll give you one hell of a performance."

The words were mostly bravado, but down here, bravado was all I had.

A metallic clang echoed through the air, sharp and menacing. Footsteps, deliberate and heavy, grew louder with each second, the sound reverberating off the damp stone walls. My heart raced, each beat a wild staccato as I struggled to push myself off the cold floor.

I sent up a silent prayer, though I knew it was likely useless. *Goddess, if you can hear me through all this hellfire and brimstone, I could really use some strength right about now.*

The cell door creaked open, revealing two hulking demon guards. Their grotesque faces twisted into cruel leers, glowing eyes burning with malicious intent.

"Well, aren't you two a sight for sore eyes?" I quipped, trying to summon the fire that used to come so easily to me. "Let me guess, you're here to escort me to the spa?"

The larger of the two snarled, his clawed hand darting out to grab my arm. "Silence, worm. Your smart mouth won't save you now."

I bit back a cry of pain as his claws dug into my skin, bruising the already tender flesh. "Easy on the merchandise, big guy. I bruise like a peach."

They yanked me forward, dragging me into a dimly lit corridor that reeked of sulfur and decay. My mind raced, scrambling for anything—*anything*—that could turn this situation around.

"So, boys," I said, forcing a lightness into my tone, "any chance you'd consider a bribe? I can get you a great deal on combine harvesters."

The smaller guard let out a gravelly snort, a sound that grated like nails on slate. "Your pathetic attempts at humor won't work here, traitor."

Traitor.

The word cut deeper than I expected, sharper than their claws. I was Callie Langston, damn it. Daughter of James and Marie Langston. Top sales rep at Hughes Ag Equipment. I wouldn't let them reduce me to some *Underworld cast-off*, even if that's exactly what I'd become.

"You know," I grunted, stumbling as they yanked me around a corner, "I'm thinking customer service isn't your strong suit."

Their laughter echoed off the walls, dark and mocking, twisting around me like a noose. My legs trembled, exhaustion and fear threatening to pull me under, but I forced myself to keep moving.

You're Callie Langston. I repeated the mantra in my mind like a shield. *You've gotten through worse. You'll get through this too.*

But deep down, I wasn't so sure.

As we traversed the winding corridors, my mind clung to memories of happier times like a lifeline. Dad's face beaming with pride when I closed my first big sale. Mom's warm hugs, her cinnamon-scented embrace warding off chilly mornings. Olivia's laughter ringing through the kitchen during our late-night gossip sessions.

A pang of longing pierced through me, sharp and bittersweet.

"Keep it together, Callie," I whispered under my breath, forcing my voice to stay steady. "You've got this."

The smaller guard sneered, his twisted grin almost gleeful. "Talking to yourself already? Pathetic."

I mustered a weak smirk, a flicker of defiance igniting in my chest. "Just practicing my acceptance speech for 'Underworld Prisoner of the Year.' I hear the competition's stiff."

The guard's hand shot out, delivering a sharp slap across my face. My head snapped to the side, and the coppery taste of blood spread across my tongue. I bit back a wince, refusing to give him the satisfaction of seeing me falter. Instead, I focused on the rhythm of my steps, each one a small victory.

Finally, we stopped before a set of towering obsidian doors, their dark surface pulsing faintly as though alive.

The larger guard smirked as he shoved me forward. "Ready for your big debut, traitor?"

I squared my shoulders despite the screaming protest of my bruised ribs. "Can't wait," I muttered, stepping through the doors as they creaked open.

The eerie crimson glow bathed the cavernous great hall beyond, casting jagged shadows that seemed to twist and writhe like living things. At the far end, seated on a throne of jagged black stone, was Magda. Her beauty was as terrifying as it was mesmerizing—an unnatural perfection that felt like a warning. Beside her stood Eldric, his sharp features cold and unreadable.

"Well, well," Magda purred, her voice curling through the room like smoke. Her dark eyes glinted with sadistic delight. "If it isn't our little troublemaker."

I forced myself to meet her gaze, straightening my spine despite the pain. "Magda," I said evenly, letting sarcasm edge my tone. "Love what you've done with the place. The 'eternal damnation' vibe really ties the room together."

From the corner of my eye, I caught Eldric's lips twitch, a flicker of amusement he quickly masked with icy disdain.

"You should show more respect, Callie," he said, his voice cutting through the tension like a blade. "Your fate hangs by a thread."

I turned my gaze to him, the cousin I hadn't known I had. "Respect is earned, Eldric," I shot back, my voice unwavering. "Not demanded."

Magda's laughter rang out, sharp and mocking, reverberating off the obsidian walls. "Oh, I'm going to enjoy breaking you, little one."

Her crimson lips curled into a sneer as she descended the dais, her stilettos clicking with each deliberate step. "You thought you were so clever, didn't you?" she taunted, her voice laced with venom. "Helping your precious Olivia and that brat Amaya escape."

My heart thundered in my chest, but I forced my expression to remain steady. *Don't give her the satisfaction, Callie. Hold your ground.*

"Cat got your tongue?" Magda's nails traced along my jawline, sharp enough to draw thin lines of blood. Her smile was all cruelty, a predator savoring its prey. "Or perhaps you've finally realized the gravity of your petty rebellion?"

Summoning every ounce of courage I had left, I met her blazing eyes head-on. "I'd do it again in a heartbeat."

Her lip curled into a cruel sneer, making the cavernous hall feel smaller, the shadows closing in like sentinels. "You insolent little—" Magda's voice sliced the air like a blade as she whirled away, the ends of her black gown snapped like a whip behind her. "Do you even comprehend what you've done? The chaos you've unleashed?"

The air thickened, the temperature dropping sharply as her voice rose. Waves of malevolent energy pulsed outward, making my skin crawl. Still, I stood firm, even as my knees wavered beneath the crushing weight of her fury.

"My carefully laid plans, my rifts—" Her words dripped venom, each syllable a lash. "That meddling Olivia has thwarted them all! Eldoria should already be mine, reduced to ash and shadows, a masterpiece molded by my will!"

Her rage was a physical force, suffocating and heavy. Yet

despite it, a flicker of pride sparked inside me. Go, Olivia, I thought, clinging to that sliver of triumph like a lifeline.

Magda's head snapped toward me, her hellfire eyes burning. "And you—stand there like the smug little brat you are—should grovel for my mercy. I should flay the skin from your bones for your insolence!"

Fear surged like an icy wave, threatening to drown me, but I swallowed it down, forcing my voice to steady. "Threats won't change anything, Magda. Eldoria will never be yours."

Her laughter was sharp and hollow, slicing through the tension. "You pathetic fool. That's where you're wrong. Eldoria will fall—perhaps not today, but soon enough. And when it does, you'll wish for death long before I'm finished with you."

A chill crawled up my spine, but I met her blazing eyes, refusing to waver. "I'm not sorry, you know?" A faint, humorless smirk tugged at my lips. "If anything, I'm proud. Olivia and Amaya are free, and now they have time to figure out how to stop you. You don't scare me."

Magda's lips curled as she smiled, a dagger hidden in velvet. "Oh, sweet Callie," she purred, the mockery in her tone like a coiled serpent. She began circling me, her stiletto heels echoing against the cold stone floor, a deliberate, menacing rhythm. "You cling to your pitiful defiance like a drowning rat clawing at a splinter of wood. It means nothing. You mean nothing."

Her words twisted like barbs, probing at insecurities I didn't want to acknowledge. But I lifted my chin higher. "You're wrong about that," I shot back, my voice sharper than I felt. "You know I'm not nothing—otherwise, you wouldn't waste your breath."

Magda froze mid-step, her expression shifting from mocking to calculating, her eyes narrowing as though seeing something new in me. "Oh, my dear," she said, her voice a dangerous caress, smooth as silk. "Do you even know what you are?"

The question caught me off guard, the weight of it sinking into my chest like a stone. My throat went dry. "What I am?" I repeated, hating the quiver of hesitation in my voice.

Magda's laugh rang out, sharp and cutting, like a blade dragging across a stone. She leaned closer, her eyes alight with cruel delight. "You don't, do you?" she sneered, as though I were the punchline to some inside joke. "It's laughable. All this time, and you've never once questioned why you lack the markings of your kind. No wings. No claws. No talons or fangs. You're not like your cousin Eldric, that delicious little half-breed offspring of an Eldorian elemental and the Underworld."

She paused, her gaze narrowing as if savoring the words she would unleash next. "You, my dear Callie, are something else entirely."

"What do you mean?" My voice came out sharp, but my chest tightened with unease. I forced myself to stand tall, though her words clawed at my resolve.

Magda tilted her head, her breath icy against my cheek as she leaned in. "Oh, darling. You're a full-blooded child of the Underworld. Royalty, no less. But not once have you stopped to ask yourself what that makes you."

The hall seemed to close in, the air suffocating and heavy. My fists clenched, nails digging into my palms, but I refused to flinch. Her words burrowed deep, planting seeds of doubt I didn't want to acknowledge. She was right—I didn't know. I'd never dared to think about it.

Magda's eyes gleamed with wicked satisfaction, her smile sharp as a dagger. "Shall I enlighten you, little one? Or would you prefer to stumble in ignorance a bit longer?" She paused, her voice softening mockingly. "No, that won't do. You've meddled in my plans far too much to be allowed such favor."

The weight of her words pressed down, but I fought the panic rising in my chest. "Say whatever you're going to say, Magda," I bit out, my voice steadier than I felt. "I'm not afraid."

Her laugh echoed, a sound so full of malice it made the

shadows in the hall seem alive. "Oh, but you will be," she purred, circling me now. "Because once you understand what you are, you'll see how pathetically futile your rebellion truly is."

A part of me wanted to snap back, to deflect her venom with my own, but another part—a darker, quieter part— needed to know. The question she'd planted was one I couldn't take back.

"You are a *revenant*, Callie," she said finally, her voice smooth as silk, cutting as a blade. She let the word hang in the air, heavy with meaning. "A rare gift of the Underworld, born of death and imbued with its power. The very essence of destruction flows through your veins. You could raise armies of the fallen, sow chaos with a mere thought, rip the balance of the realms apart... if only you had the will."

Her words hit me like a blow, stealing the air from my lungs. My stomach churned, and my voice came out in a rasped whisper. "You're lying."

Magda's grin widened, her eyes glittering with mockery. "Am I?" she asked, each word dripping with condescension. "Have you never wondered why your wounds heal faster than they should? Why death skirts around you no matter how many times you fling yourself into danger?"

I swallowed hard, memories rushing back in an unwelcome tide. Bruises that faded overnight. The knife wound from Magda's guards that had closed within minutes. The icy sensation that surged through my veins whenever I felt trapped, desperate.

"No," I whispered, my voice trembling as I shook my head, willing her words to vanish. "I'm nothing like you."

Her laughter burst forth again, a symphony of malice that seemed to echo endlessly. "Oh, sweet Callie," she drawled, her voice both mocking and triumphant. "You're not just like me— you're worse. I only destroy what stands in my way. But you? If you ever unlock your potential, you could unmake everything.

Eldoria, the Underworld, even the fragile balance, holding them together."

I staggered back, my breaths coming in shallow gasps as the enormity of her words threatened to crush me. "You're wrong. I'm not a monster."

Magda stepped closer, she smiled cold and sadistic. "Oh, but you are. And that, my dear, is the very thing that will make you magnificent."

"Devils," Magda cooed, stepping closer, her voice low and menacing, "don't get to choose what they are. You are what the Underworld made you—a tool, a weapon. You've just been too naïve to see it."

Her words stabbed deep, cutting at fears I dared not name. The weight of her accusation pressed against my chest like a stone. But then, from somewhere deep within, a flicker stirred —a spark of defiance, fragile but burning brighter with every breath I took.

"If that's true," I said, forcing steel into my voice, "then why haven't I used this power yet? Why haven't I become the monster you say I am?"

Magda's expression faltered, just for a heartbeat. The smug confidence in her eyes flickered, replaced by a shadow of something else—uncertainty? Frustration? It was gone so quickly I almost doubted I'd seen it.

"Because you're weak," she spat, her tone venomous. "Your mortal sympathies, your pathetic loyalties, have kept you blind to your own nature. But don't worry, little revenant. I'll carve that weakness out of you, piece by piece, until all that remains is your true self. And then, you'll kneel before me."

I straightened, my mind reeling, but my resolve unshaken. "You can beat me, imprison me, try to break me. But you'll never have me, Magda. I'd rather die than kneel to you."

Her eyes flared with hellfire, the glow illuminating the cruel lines of her face. The temperature in the room plummeted, frost creeping along the edges of the stone floor.

The guards at the walls shifted uneasily, their breath visible in the icy air.

Magda tilted her head, her voice dropping to a deadly whisper. "Oh, my dear," she said, every word a knife's edge, "I don't need your cooperation. Only your power."

She flicked her wrist, a languid gesture that summoned the guards flanking the room. Their hulking forms advanced toward me, their eyes glinting with malevolence.

"Take her back to her cell," Magda commanded. "She'll need to be... softened before we begin."

Strong hands gripped my arms, dragging me toward the towering doors. My muscles screamed in protest, but I kept my head high, forcing myself not to flinch under Magda's gaze.

Her words echoed in my mind, each one heavier than the last. A revenant. A weapon of death and destruction. Was that truly all I was? A tool forged for chaos?

But as the guards hauled me away, another thought surfaced—quiet but insistent, defying the darkness.

A weapon can choose where it points.

And I would be damned if I let Magda choose for me.

CHAPTER 17

Cade

I stood at the entrance of the open-air cathedral, my heart pounding like a war drum. Towering obsidian columns stretched toward the heavens, their black surfaces gleaming under Vesparra's enchanted skies. Below, the polished stone floor shimmered like liquid night, each step reflected back at me—a silent reminder of the gravity of this moment.

Then I saw her.

Olivia moved toward me, her dark hair cascading like a waterfall of midnight, her deep purple eyes locked onto mine. My breath hitched. She wasn't just beautiful; she was radiant. Confidence and vulnerability radiated from her in equal measure, an unshakable grace that rooted me in place.

"By the Goddess," I whispered, awe slipping past my lips unbidden.

Her smile bloomed, shy yet radiant. "Howdy, stranger," she said, her Texan accent a playful contrast to the solemnity of the setting. "I can't believe we're finally doin' this."

I chuckled, her warmth easing the tightness in my chest. As she reached me, I took her hand, marveling at how perfectly it fit in mine. The simple gesture steadied me, a physical reminder of the bond we shared.

"Ready?" I asked, my voice low and filled with emotion.

Olivia nodded, her eyes glistening with unshed tears. "I'm so ready, baby."

Together, we turned toward the center of the cathedral where the priestess awaited. Our footsteps echoed softly against the stone, each step carrying us closer to our shared destiny. The weight of my crown as King of Vesparra pressed down on me, but Olivia's presence was a balm, her hand in mine an anchor.

All around us, our people watched. Vampires, elementals, and shifters from every corner of Eldoria had gathered, their eyes filled with hope and expectation. Their energy hummed in the air, mingling with the cathedral's magic—a palpable reminder of the responsibility we bore.

"Are you okay?" Olivia whispered, her grip tightening slightly.

I glanced at her, a soft smile tugging at my lips. "Just thinking about how far we've come," I murmured. "From Texas to Eldoria, from strangers to... this."

Her gaze softened, a flicker of understanding shining in her eyes. "We've got this, Cade," she said firmly. "Together."

As we reached the center of the cathedral, my heart swelled with pride. Olivia, with her fierce heart and indomitable spirit, had become more than my mate. She was my partner in every way, my equal. Together, we had faced monsters, both literal and figurative, and emerged stronger.

The priestess raised her hands, her voice resonating through the sacred space as she began the ceremony. I took a steadying breath, feeling the pulse of Vesparra's ancient magic thrumming through my veins.

Whatever challenges lay ahead, I knew one thing with absolute certainty: with Olivia by my side, we could face anything.

The priestess's voice cut through the air, deep and resonant, carrying the weight of centuries of tradition. "Goddess Vesperia, Creator of our Realm, we call upon you to witness this union."

A shiver rippled through me as the magic in the cathedral intensified, wrapping around us like an unseen mantle. It wasn't just power—it was a living, breathing presence, ancient and all-encompassing. My eyes met Olivia's, and I saw the same awe mirrored there.

"By the power of the Five Kingdoms," the priestess continued, her words reverberating off the gleaming obsidian floor, "we seek your blessing on this bond."

The vampiric blood magic within me stirred, awakening in response to the ceremony's energy. Beside me, Olivia's grip on my hand tightened. Her Wyldcaster magic, wild and untamed, reached out instinctively, twining with my own. It felt as if our very souls were being drawn closer, the boundaries between us dissolving.

"Cade," Olivia whispered, her voice trembling with awe. "I can feel it. It's like... like the entire realm is holding its breath."

I nodded, my chest tightening with the enormity of her words. The air felt alive, thrumming with a power older than the stars themselves. The priestess gestured for us to approach, her expression solemn, her gaze heavy with ancient purpose.

"You now stand at the threshold of the Veshara," she intoned, her voice resonant and commanding, "a covenant that intertwines your hearts, your powers, and your destinies under the watchful gaze of Vesperia. Step forward."

Each step toward her felt monumental, the polished obsidian beneath our feet gleaming with reflected light. The ceremonial dagger lay in the priestess's outstretched hands, its blade catching the flickering starlight filtering through the cathedral's open dome. I took it first, the cool metal grounding me as I felt its weight in my palm.

"Steady," I murmured, my gaze locking with Olivia's. Her eyes, though shining with determination, flickered briefly with apprehension. "I've got you."

With a swift motion, I drew the blade across my palm. The sharp sting was fleeting, and the blood welled instantly, warm against my skin. I passed the dagger to Olivia, who held it with quiet determination. I watched as she drew the blade with precision, her breath steady, her expression fierce. The priestess took the blade and Olivia's palm gripped mine.

As our blood dripped into the carved obsidian trough, the air around us thickened. It felt charged, alive, as though the cathedral itself held its breath. Crimson streaks flowed down the dark stone, the contrast striking and visceral.

"To Vesperia," I whispered, my voice hushed with awe. The runes etched into the floor shimmered faintly, then erupted into brilliant light. Brilliant light raced outward in intricate patterns, forming a radiant circle that encased us. Shadows at the cathedral's edges swayed and shifted, retreating in reverence to the divine glow.

The energy surged, electric and powerful, coursing through every fiber of my being. I could feel Olivia's presence —her magic intertwining with mine in ways that defied explanation. It wasn't just harmony; it was fusion, two forces becoming one.

"Cade," Olivia breathed, her voice barely audible over the hum of magic. Her eyes were wide, reflecting the light as though she herself were aglow. "It's beautiful."

I turned to her, and for a moment, the world narrowed to just us. Her dark hair shimmered like liquid night, her expression a mix of awe and something deeper—something sacred. "You're beautiful," I murmured, my voice rough with emotion.

The light pulsed again, brighter this time, as though the magic itself celebrated our union. I squeezed Olivia's hand, anchoring myself in her strength.

The priestess stepped forward, her robes trailing like liquid shadow. She reached out with a black cloth, wiping our palms with deliberate care. The sting of the cuts vanished instantly as the blood flow ceased.

"The Goddess Vesperia blesses this union," she proclaimed, her voice ringing through the cathedral. "The Veshara has begun its weaving. You may now recite the Vesparran vows to seal your souls."

Taking a deep breath, I turned to face Olivia fully. The weight of the moment settled over me, a mantle of responsibility and love I embraced wholeheartedly. As King of Vesparra, and the Goddess's Favored Son, I had spoken many oaths. But none had ever felt as significant as this. We felt it was important to use the ancient language of Vesparra for this part of the ceremony.

I was humbled to give my vows to Olivia. *"Renyr aesca, senar'thal esca venor. Vel'sari thal'essa, en'mar vi cales vanar. Avena vesparra, cara'thien valesa si."* I then gave the translation. "My star, my soul is bound to yours. Your light is my guide, your love, my strength. Before Vesparra, I vow to honor and cherish you."

I was so proud of how hard Olivia had worked to learn her vows. Our ancient tongue was hard to learn.

Her amethyst eyes held mine as she spoke. *"Renyr aesca, thal'mari en'rion. Vel'sari caer'thar, en'mar si venar vestra. Avena vesparra, cara'thien cales vi."* A tear escaped her eye as she recited the translation, "My star, you are my heart's sanctuary. Your touch is my haven, your bond is my destiny. Before Vesparra, I vow to love and protect you."

Her voice, strong yet tender, filled the cathedral. As she continued, I felt each word resonate within me, a promise etched into the fabric of my being. Our vows intertwined, a harmonious duet that echoed off the obsidian columns and soared towards the open sky above.

I couldn't tear my gaze from her. The way the starlight danced across her skin, the gentle curve of her lips as she spoke, the strength in her eyes that belied the scars of her past —it all overwhelmed me. This was my mate, my queen, my everything.

As our vows concluded, I felt a shift within me. It was as if the very essence of Eldoria had recognized our bond, sealing it with an unbreakable force. The truth of our words settled deep in my soul, a warmth that spread from my core to the tips of my fingers.

The priestess stepped forward once more, this time bearing a small, ornate box. "The rings," she announced, her voice reverent.

When she opened it, the Vesparran rings gleamed with an almost ethereal light. Forged from the rarest metals of our land, they pulsed faintly, as if infused with the essence of our bond.

With hands that trembled slightly — from emotion, not fear — I took Olivia's ring. The metal was cool against my skin, but I could feel the latent power within it. I gently took Olivia's left hand in mine, marveling at how perfectly it fit.

"With this ring," my voice low and deliberate, "I bind myself to you. A love with no beginning and no end, as unbroken as the circle it represents. You are mine, Olivia, and I am yours—forever, in this life and every one after."

As I slid the ring onto her finger, the air seemed to pulse, the glow of the runes brightening in acknowledgment. Magic flared, wrapping around us like an invisible thread.

Olivia's lips trembled as she took my ring. Her touch was featherlight, but the weight of her love was palpable as she cradled my hand.

"Cade," she whispered, her voice rich with emotion. "With this ring, I promise you my heart, my soul, and all that I am. Through every trial and triumph, I'm yours, my love. Forever and always."

As she slipped the ring onto my finger, the magic surged again, a wave of warmth that stole my breath. The runes on the floor glowed brilliantly, casting the cathedral in radiant starlight. I felt our connection solidify, a bond not just of love but of power and purpose.

The priestess stepped forward once more, her voice ringing out over the hum of magic. "The Veshara has woven your souls together forever with the blessings of the Goddess Vesperia."

The priestess's voice rang out, formal and steady, grounding us both. "Are you ready for the marking ritual?"

I nodded, swallowing against the tightness in my throat. "We are."

Her hands lifted in a graceful gesture, and I felt the familiar tingle of my blood magic stirring to life. Olivia loosened the belt on her flowing dress, allowing her to bare her left shoulder. The scars on her back, a roadmap of her past sufferings, were no longer hidden.

I placed my hand on her shoulder, my touch feather-light. Her skin was warm, her presence anchoring me in the moment.

"This might sting a bit, sweetheart," I murmured, my voice soft.

Olivia's lips curved in a confident, teasing smile. "Don't you worry about me, Highness. I've got this."

I chanted, ancient words flowing from my lips like a song only my soul remembered. The magic responded instantly, weaving through my veins, pulsing in rhythm with my heartbeat. As I traced the sigil on her shoulder, my magic took form, shimmering faintly like starlight etched into her skin. Vines and stars took shape, weaving a pattern of beauty and strength.

The moment felt timeless, perfect. Every step of my life had brought me here, to her.

I covered her shoulder to shield her sigil and turned, letting Olivia take her turn.

Her eyes, shimmering with love and determination, locked onto mine. She raised her hand and rested it over my heart. A jolt of energy surged through me at her touch, warm and electrifying.

"My turn, darlin'," she said with a smile that held more strength than I'd ever seen.

I unbuttoned my shirt and slipped it down to reveal my left shoulder. Her fingers brushed my skin, her touch light yet charged with power.

The air around us shifted as Olivia called upon her magic. I felt it bloom like the first light of dawn, gentle but unyielding. The surrounding atmosphere shimmered. The elements—earth, air, fire, and water—blending into a unique current that was purely hers.

Her fingers moved with practiced ease as she traced the sigil on my shoulder. Each stroke of her magic sent sparks dancing through my body, igniting something primal and eternal.

"You're so deeply inside of me," I whispered, the awe in my voice undeniable. "I can feel you, Olivia—not just your touch, but... everything."

She smiled through the tears glistening in her eyes. "I know, my love. It's like our souls are dancin', isn't it?" Her sigil was uniquely my Starlight. It included some of the same vines and stars as mine, but also an intricate heart rising from the center.

Her words filled the sacred space, and as she completed the sigil, a wave of emotion crashed over me. Love, hope, fear, and joy—each emotion a thread woven into the tapestry of us.

"Look," Olivia breathed, turning to reveal the sigil on her back to me. Then we stood back-to-back as our sigils reached for each other.

The marks on our shoulders glowed, softly at first, then brighter, pulsing in perfect synchronization with our heartbeats. As we watched, the light from each sigil stretched outward, tendrils of radiance reached for one another. When they met, the lines fused and ascended, forming the unmistakable shape of the Goddess Mark above us—a radiant symbol glowing for all to see.

The power of our bond surged, rippling outward in waves I swore I could see sweeping across Eldoria. The air hummed, crackling with energy and promise, as though the realm itself celebrated with us.

"Can you feel it?" I asked, my voice barely a whisper.

Olivia nodded, her wide eyes reflecting the brilliance of the mark. "It's like the entire realm is singin', Cade. Everything's... alive."

I pulled her into my arms, overwhelmed by the depth of our connection and the unmistakable blessing of the Goddess. Her body fit against mine as though it had always belonged there.

"This is it, my love," I said, my voice thick with emotion. "This is our forever."

The priestess stepped forward, her voice clear and commanding. "By the grace of Goddess Vesperia, I pronounce you united in sacred bond!"

The gathered witnesses erupted into cheers, their joy reverberating through the cathedral like a wave of pure energy. I kissed Olivia, my lips lingering on hers as the world seemed to hold its breath. This was our beginning, our destiny, and with every fiber of my being, I knew we were ready for whatever lay ahead.

The crowd's deafening applause washed over us, a tidal wave of shared jubilation. I turned to face our people, my heart swelling with pride and joy. Olivia's hand found mine, her fingers threading perfectly between my own as we stood united before the multitude.

"Well, I'll be ding dang," Olivia whispered, her voice warm with humor. "We really did it, didn't we?"

I chuckled softly, squeezing her hand. "We certainly did, my love."

As my gaze swept over the sea of faces—Vesparrans, Thalassans, Ilyndorians, Therionians, and even Ignis and a few

Aurelions, all united in celebration—I felt a surge of hope. This wasn't just about us; it was a symbol of the unity we'd fought so hard to achieve. For the first time in years, the fractured kingdoms of Eldoria stood as one.

Then a hush fell over the crowd. The air thickened, humming with an ancient, primal energy that prickled against my skin. I felt it before I saw it—a power older than the kingdoms themselves. The Dragonia were approaching.

"Oh my stars," Olivia breathed, a smile splitting her face.

The majestic creatures moved with an otherworldly grace, their scales shimmering like living gemstones in the cathedral's radiant light. Vaelith, the massive, silver-scaled dragon whose very presence seemed to bend the air around him, approached. As he stepped forward and bowed his colossal head, humility washed over me like a tide.

"*Cadence Vesparra*," Vaelith's voice resonated in my mind, rich and timeless. "*Olivia Ilyndor Vesparra. We offer our blessing upon your union.*"

I bowed deeply to my friend. "Thank you Vaelith. We're honored you are all here as witnesses."

The Dragonia's shining blue eyes fixed upon us, brimming with millennia of wisdom. Under his gaze, I felt the bond between Olivia and me deepen, as though the blessing itself fortified our love.

"*Your union bridges more than just two hearts,*" Vaelith continued. "*It is a beacon of hope for all Eldoria.*"

Beside me, Olivia, completely at ease with her dragon friend, was beaming. "We're glad you came, big guy," she quipped, her lips quirking into a grin.

I bit back a laugh, marveling at her ability to bring lightness even to such a monumental moment. It was one of the countless reasons I loved her.

The dragon, amused, dipped his head again. Then, with a graceful sweep of their wings, the gathered Dragonia unleashed a dazzling display of elemental magic. Fire, water, air, earth, and shadow wove together in a symphony of light, illuminating the cathedral in breathtaking hues. The magic rippled outward, filling the air with a crackling energy that seemed to bind every soul present into a single, unified whole.

As the display faded, leaving a shimmering afterglow, I turned to Olivia, my heart brimming with love. "Whatever challenges lay ahead," I said, my voice low but sure, "we'll face them together."

She smiled up at me, her hand tightening around mine. "Not just us, Cade. All Eldoria. Together."

The surrounding celebration swelled once more, laughter, music, and jubilant voices filling the air. I looked down at Olivia, her eyes sparkled with a joy that took my breath away.

"Well, Highness," she teased with a wink, "looks like we did it."

I chuckled, my chest warm with affection. "Indeed, we have. How does it feel to be the Queen of Vesparra, Starlight?"

She wrinkled her nose adorably. "Honestly? A little terrifying. But these days, I think I can handle just about anything."

Unable to resist, I pulled her close, savoring the feel of her against me. "Let's steal a moment away from all this," I whispered, nodding toward a secluded alcove.

Once hidden from prying eyes, I cupped Olivia's face in my hands, tracing the curve of her cheek with my thumb. "You are everything to me," I murmured, my voice thick with emotion. "My queen, my love, my destiny."

Her eyes glistened, her voice trembling with vulnerability. "I never thought I'd have this," she whispered. "Genuine love, a family, a purpose. You've given me all of that, Cade."

I kissed her, pouring every ounce of my devotion into the connection. When we finally parted, breathless, I rested my forehead against hers. "We've given it to each other. And together, we'll give hope to all Eldoria."

The celebration buzzed faintly in the background, but for

now, in this perfect moment, it was just us. Two souls bound by love, ready to face whatever the future held.

CHAPTER 18

Amaya

My heart was still overflowing the morning after Ollie's and Cade's marking ceremony. After all the heartache my sister had endured in her life while in the mortal realm, it was only fitting that she got her happily ever after. I could not have chosen a better mate for her. If ever there was a Prince Charming for her, Cade was it.

Every element of the ritual pulsed with magic, light, and love, and I couldn't help but feel a small stirring of jealousy rise in my heart. I wanted that for Kaelen and me. Did that make me an awful person? The prospect of bringing shame to him, of being less than what I needed to be, still haunted my thoughts. I didn't possess the raw shifter power that coursed through Kaelen's veins. How could I ever be worthy of such a sacred ritual?

My chest tightened as I imagined Kaelen's silver eyes, usually so full of warmth when they gazed upon me, filled with disappointment instead. Would he realize I was unworthy of being his Luna? That I couldn't give him the strong shifter heirs the Therionis kingdom deserved?

I shook my head, trying to dispel the dark thoughts. Kaelen had chosen me, hadn't he? But doubt gnawed at my insides like a hungry beast. I had to know for certain.

Taking a deep breath, I steeled myself and headed toward

Kaelen's study. The corridors of the keep were illuminated by flickering torchlight, with windows at the ends of each hall casting a faint, silvery glow. Intricate tapestries lined the walls every few steps, each depicting scenes of battles and victories that had shaped the Therionis kingdom. When I reached Kaelen's study, I paused to admire the heavy wooden door, its surface adorned with masterful carvings of wolves and other animals that populated their kingdom—a striking tribute to the skill and artistry of his people.

"Come in, Amaya," Kaelen's deep voice called from within, sending a shiver down my spine. Of course, he'd sensed my presence.

The sunlight flooded the room, giving an extra glow to Kaelen's chiseled features. I could see some subtle lines of tension around his mouth. It was clear the weight of being the Alpha of his pack came with a host of worries. I still couldn't help but admire his blonde mane of hair that looked almost silver in the morning light. Sometimes I was almost struck dumb by his otherworldly good looks and commanding presence.

"What troubles you, my love?" he asked, crossing the room in two long strides. His large hands cupped my face, thumbs brushing away tears I hadn't realized I'd shed.

"I... I want..." The words caught in my throat. Swallowing hard, I tried again. "Kaelen, I want us to have a marking ceremony. Like Olivia and Cade."

His eyes softened, a small smile playing at the corners of his lips. "Is that what's been weighing on your heart, little one?"

I nodded, unable to meet his gaze. "But I'm not a shifter. I'm not physically strong like you. How can I be a proper Luna for your people? I don't want to make a mockery of your tradition."

Kaelen's grip on my face tightened slightly, forcing me to look up at him. The intensity in his eyes took my breath away.

"Amaya Ilyndor," he growled, his voice low and fierce, "You are my Fated Mate. The other half of my soul. Your ability to shift is not a measure of your worth, neither is the strength of your magic—which is incredibly powerful, by the way."

"But—" I protested, only to be silenced by his finger on my lips.

"No buts," he said firmly. "We will have our marking ceremony, I promise you. After the challenge battle, when our position is secure, I will claim you publicly for all to see."

Hope bloomed in my chest, fragile but undeniable. "You truly want to claim me? Even though I'm... different?"

Kaelen's laugh rumbled deep in his chest. "Oh, my little mate, I have already claimed you," he said, his voice low and resonant. "When I bit you that first night you gave yourself to me, that was the mark of my claiming. The ritual in front of the pack will only serve as a proclamation to everyone that you are my chosen, the true Luna of Therionis." He spoke the words as he pulled me close, his hands firm yet gentle. "But I want you to know, right here and now—your differences from everyone else make no difference to me. Your compassion, quick wit, bravery, and unwavering loyalty—these are the qualities that make a true Luna. The pack sees it, even if you don't yet."

I melted into his embrace, the warmth of his body centering me as I breathed in his familiar scent of pine and leather. For a moment, I let myself believe in his words, in the future he painted for us. But deep down, a small, insistent voice, I couldn't quite silence, whispered doubts. *You don't belong here. You'll never truly fit into this world of primal magic and ancient rituals.*

It would take time, but I resolved to silence that voice. I would find the strength to become what Kaelen believed I already was.

As if sensing the flicker of uncertainty still lingering within me, Kaelen tilted my chin, his eyes blazing with an intensity that made my knees weak. "I will spend every day proving to you how worthy you are, Amaya," he vowed, his voice rough with emotion. "And even though I've already marked you as mine, when we complete our public marking, there will be no doubt in anyone's mind—least of all yours—that you were born to be my Luna."

Before I could respond, his lips claimed mine in a kiss so searing it left me breathless. For that moment, every insecurity, every doubt, faded away like smoke in the wind. In Kaelen's arms, I felt strong, worthy. For now, that was enough.

***

The moon, nearly full, hung low in the sky, casting an ethereal silver glow over the forest clearing. The air hummed with energy as the pack gathered in the clearing, their excitement palpable in the crisp night. I watched from the edge, my heart aching with a mixture of longing and envy as I observed their easy camaraderie. The way they moved, their connection to one another, seemed to pulse in rhythm with the moon itself.

"What are they doing?" I whispered, pressing closer to Kaelen's warm, solid frame.

His arm tightened around me, his presence a comfort. "It's a blessing ritual," he explained, his deep voice rumbling through me. "The moon amplifies our connection to our inner beasts, to the magic that flows through our veins. Days before the full moon, we gather like this to give thanks to the Goddess."

I swallowed hard, the sharp awareness of what didn't flow through me cutting deep. "And I can't... I mean, I'm not..."

Kaelen turned to face me, his eyes catching the moonlight, making them even more luminous. "Amaya," he whispered, cupping my face in his large hands. "You may not shift with the moon, but your magic is no less potent. Your connection to the earth, to the very air we breathe—it's different, yes, but just as vital."

I knew my magic mattered. My royal lineage assured I possessed immense power, but that wasn't the issue. My magic wasn't *their* magic. It didn't feel like enough. "But how can I be a proper Luna if I can't even take part in these rituals?"

"By creating new ones," Kaelen said, his voice firm but kind. "Our union will unite two worlds, two types of magic. That's an opportunity, not a limitation."

His words warmed me, but as my gaze returned to the pack, I couldn't shake the feeling of being an outsider. The challenge battle loomed closer, and with it, the true test of whether we'd still be a part of this pack.

"Kaelen," I began hesitantly, "the battle... I'm scared. Not just for you, but for what it means for us, for the pack."

His expression softened, and he pulled me closer. "I know, my love. But I need you to trust in me, in us. Your support gives me strength like nothing else."

A flicker of determination flared within me, chasing away my doubts. I squared my shoulders. "Then you'll have it. Every ounce. I may not be able to shift, but I'll find a way to help. To prove myself."

Kaelen's eyes darkened, flashing with pride and something deeper, more primal. "You have nothing to prove, Amaya. But I love your fire." He leaned in, his lips brushing my ear, sending a shiver down my spine. "After this battle, we'll have our own ritual. One that binds us in ways no one can question."

I appreciated the way Kaelen loved and accepted me. But he shouldn't have to reassure me every second of every day. I determined then and there that I had to get over this insecurity. My time in the Underworld seemed to have stolen my grit. This girl, who was worried all the time, wasn't the Maya I used to be. I didn't like who I'd become, and it was time to reach down inside to find the woman who made it alone in New York City. I was better than this. Kaelen saw it. It was time I saw it, too.

The pack's chanting swelled, their voices blending in a

cadence that reverberated through the clearing. I let myself sink into Kaelen's embrace, drawing strength from his unwavering belief in me. Whatever challenges lay ahead, I vowed to face them at his side. Together.

***

The market bustled with activity, a cacophony of voices and scents assaulting my senses. I wove through the crowd, my fingers trailing over vibrant fabrics and gleaming trinkets. Despite the festive atmosphere, tension vibrated beneath the surface. Whispers of the upcoming challenge battle followed me like shadows.

A flash of crimson caught my eye—Fiora, the person who had caused the upheaval in our lives. Her lips curled into a sneer as she approached, flanked by two burly shifters.

"Well, if it isn't Kaelen's little human pet," she purred, venom dripping from every word. "Shouldn't you be locked away in the keep? It's dangerous for fragile things like you out here."

I felt my magic stir, responding to the surge of anger. "I'm exactly where I belong, Fiora," I replied, keeping my voice steady. "Perhaps you should worry less about me and more about your boyfriend's impending defeat."

Fiora's eyes flashed dangerously. "You insolent little—" She lunged forward, claws extending.

Instinct took over. I threw up my hands, air and earth magic swirling together. A wall of vines erupted from the ground, tangling around Fiora's legs and arms. Her companions growled, advancing.

"I wouldn't," I warned, electricity crackling between my fingertips. My heart raced, but a newfound confidence steadied my voice. "I may not have claws, but I'm far from defenseless."

"What's going on here?" A deep voice cut through the tension. Zorion, Kaelen's beta, pushed through the gathering crowd. His dark eyes assessed the situation quickly.

Fiora snarled, still struggling against my magical restraints. "This human witch attacked me! She has no right —"

"I saw everything," Zorion interrupted, his tone leaving no room for argument. "Luna Amaya defended herself against unprovoked aggression." He turned to me, a hint of approval in his gaze. "Impressive control, Luna."

Relief washed over me, but I maintained my stance. "Thank you, Zorion. I'd appreciate your help in resolving this... misunderstanding."

Zorion nodded, addressing the onlookers. "This altercation is over. Return to your business." To Fiora, he added, "I suggest you and your companions leave. Now."

As the crowd dispersed, I released my hold on the vines. Fiora stumbled back, hatred burning in her eyes. "This isn't over," she hissed before stalking away.

Zorion placed a reassuring hand on my shoulder. "You handled that well, Amaya. Kaelen will be proud."

I exhaled shakily; the adrenaline fading. "I just... reacted. I didn't want to hurt anyone."

"That restraint speaks volumes," Zorion said. "It's a quality that will make you an excellent Luna."

His words settled something within me. I felt my confidence surge.

CHAPTER 19

Amaya

The day of the challenge battle dawned with a palpable electricity in the air. I stood at the window of our chambers, watching as a steady stream of carriages and riders poured into the Therionis grounds. My stomach churned with a mixture of anticipation and dread, each moment stretching endlessly before me.

"Amaya?" Kaelen's deep voice rumbled behind me, steady and reassuring. "It's time."

I turned to face him, momentarily stunned by his presence. His eyes burned with a fierce determination that both thrilled and terrified me. His dark blonde hair fell in waves around his shoulders, and the way he carried himself —confident, powerful—made my chest tighten with love and fear.

"I'm ready," I lied, my voice barely more than a whisper.

I clutched the plush wolf Kaelen had given me one last time, the softness of its fur a meager comfort against the chaos swirling inside me.

As we made our way toward the arena, the crowd parted for us like waves retreating from the shore. Their faces, a mixture of curiosity and apprehension, blurred as I focused on putting one foot in front of the other.

Suddenly, a familiar voice cut through the din. "Amaya!"

My heart leaped as I turned to see Olivia weaving through the throng, Cade towering behind her like a protective shadow. Relief surged through me, and I broke away from Kaelen, throwing myself into her arms.

"You came," I breathed, my voice breaking as tears pricked at the corners of my eyes.

Olivia held me tightly, her presence a haven for my worried heart. "Of course we did. We wouldn't miss this for the world."

Cade's imposing figure loomed beside us, scanning the crowd with the vigilance of a warrior. "Let's get you to the royalty box," he said, his tone leaving no room for argument.

As we entered the arena, the roar of the crowd hit me like a physical force, the noise reverberating through my body. Excitement and tension crackled in the air, a living thing that wrapped itself around us. I clung to Olivia's hand as we ascended to the royalty box.

"How are you holding up, darlin'?" Olivia murmured, her eyes searching mine with sisterly concern.

I swallowed hard, forcing down the lump in my throat. "Terrified," I admitted, my voice barely audible over the din. "But having you here... it helps more than you know."

A flash of movement caught my eye. Miranda glided toward us, her dark curls bouncing with each step, Thorne at her side. Her smile was warm and genuine, but the concern in her eyes was unmistakable.

"Amaya, sweetheart," she said, pulling me into an embrace. "I'm so glad to see you. Are you ready for this?"

I nodded, though my voice failed me. Miranda squeezed my hand, her touch grounding me in the moment.

Grandpapa wasn't far behind. His towering presence radiated calm, and when he leaned down to press a kiss to my forehead, I felt a small piece of my tension unravel.

"Hello, child," he said, his deep voice steady and comforting. "I see we've all gathered here to watch your man show this kingdom who the true Alpha and King is."

His serene smile and peaceful manner eased the storm in my chest.

"I'm so glad you're here," I murmured, standing on my toes to kiss his cheek.

As we took our seats, I scanned the arena below. The sand of the battle circle gleamed golden in the morning light, surrounded by towering stone walls etched with ancient runes. The air was electric, alive with the thrumming pulse of magic and the anticipation of hundreds of onlookers.

"It's magnificent," I whispered, awe momentarily eclipsing my fear.

Kaelen leaned close, his breath warm against my ear. "Remember," he murmured, his voice low and intimate, "no matter what happens down there, you are my strength. My mate. My Luna."

I turned to him, committing every detail of his face to memory—the unwavering resolve in his eyes, the slight curve of his lips as he gazed at me. My heart ached with love, fierce and unyielding.

"I love you," I said, my voice trembling with intensity.

A horn blared, cutting through the noise and silencing the crowd. My heart thundered in my chest as the announcer's voice boomed across the arena, signaling the start of the challenge battle.

"Citizens! We gather today to witness a challenge for the rightful title of Alpha and King of Therionis!"

The announcer's voice echoed across the massive arena, his words met with a rumble of anticipation from the crowd. Hundreds of shifters filled the stands, their roars and cheers creating a cacophony that rattled my bones.

I gripped the arms of my chair, my knuckles white as I tried to steady my breathing. This wasn't just a fight—it was a battle for everything we'd built, for the future of Therionis. For Kaelen.

Olivia slipped her hand into mine, her warmth a minor

comfort. On my other side, Cade radiated calm strength, but I caught the flicker of tension in his sharp gaze. Miranda's reassuring smile from the row ahead gave me a sliver of steadiness, and Grandpapa's unyielding presence at my back was a silent promise: I wasn't alone.

But none of it eased the anxiety twisting in my gut.

The low growl of the crowd hushed as Zane appeared, his sleek panther form prowling onto the arena floor. Midnight-black fur rippled over muscles honed by years of combat. His tail flicked back and forth, his golden eyes sweeping the arena like a predator surveying his prey. When his gaze landed on our box, a slow, menacing snarl curled his lips.

"Goddess," I breathed, dread coiling in my chest. "He's enormous."

"Kaelen's stronger," Olivia murmured, though her voice betrayed her uncertainty.

As if summoned by her words, Kaelen strode into the arena. His eyes locked onto mine, just for a heartbeat, but it was enough to steady me. Without breaking stride, he shifted. Almost instantaneously, bones cracked and stretched, muscles ripped under his skin as fur erupted in waves of shimmering brown and gold. In mere moments, his wolf stood where the man had been, massive and awe-inspiring. He was a force of nature, his dark gold and brown fur catching the sunlight like liquid fire.

"By the Creator," Cade muttered beside me. "He looks even bigger than I remembered."

Kaelen's dire wolf let out a low growl, the sound reverberating through the arena as he met Zane's gaze. The two Alpha beasts began to circle, their movements slow and deliberate, every step charged with power. Zane's claws scraped deep furrows into the earth, while Kaelen's lips peeled back in a snarl that revealed fangs gleaming like polished ivory.

"Come on, love," I whispered under my breath, my heart pounding. "You've got this."

The first clash came without warning. They collided in a blur of fur and fury, the sound of their impact like thunder shaking the earth. Zane's claws raked Kaelen's shoulder, drawing blood, but Kaelen responded with a bone-crushing bite that sent the panther skidding across the dirt.

The crowd roared as they fought, the air thick with the metallic tang of blood and the raw energy of battle. Kaelen seemed to gain the upper hand, his sheer size and strength pinning Zane to the ground. But as he lunged for a decisive blow, something shifted.

A faint shimmer, like a heatwave, flickered around Zane's body. His movements grew faster, more precise, as though an unseen force were guiding him. Kaelen hesitated, shaking his head as if disoriented.

"Wait," I said, leaning forward. "Something's not right—"

Zane surged upward, his claws tearing into Kaelen's side. My mate's pained howl ripped through the air, and I clutched the edge of my seat, helpless. He stumbled, his powerful frame swaying as Zane pressed the attack.

"He's cheating!" I cried, rising halfway out of my chair. "There's magic—he's using magic!"

Cade's hand closed over my arm, his face grim. "We can't interfere. If we do, Kaelen loses the right to the title."

I wanted to scream, to tear through the rules that bound us to this deadly spectacle. "But he'll die! I won't just sit here and watch—"

"There," Olivia hissed, pointing. Her voice was tight with barely contained fury. "Do you see it? Near the arena's edge. That cloaked figure. I can feel the magic radiating from him."

My gaze followed her finger, locking onto a shadowy figure standing just beyond the combat zone. Rage surged through me, cold and searing all at once. My mate's life was on the line, and this coward was tipping the scales with cheap tricks.

Kaelen faltered again, blood streaking his golden fur. Zane's panther form moved with unnatural speed, his claws a blur as he aimed for Kaelen's throat.

"No," I whispered, my chest tightening. Not like this.

A calm determination settled over me, sharper than fear. I met Olivia's gaze, her amethyst eyes blazing with the same resolve. "I have an idea," I said, my voice steady despite the chaos.

Together, we worked quickly, our magic weaving an invisible web. Olivia channeled her energy into the air around the cloaked figure, while I anchored it with earth magic, forming an unbreakable barrier.

"Now," I murmured, my fingers twitching as I unleashed the spell.

The net of energy slammed into the cloaked figure, their magic dissipating in a burst of light. The shimmering haze around Zane vanished instantly, leaving him vulnerable. In the arena, Kaelen's silver eyes cleared, the fog of confusion lifting as he regained his footing.

"That's it," I breathed, relief and triumph surging through me. "Fight back, my love."

As if hearing my thoughts, Kaelen lunged forward with renewed strength. With a feral snarl, he lunged at Zane, his massive jaws closing around the panther's shoulder. The force of the attack sent Zane crashing to the ground, his yelp of pain echoing through the arena.

The crowd erupted as Kaelen dominated the fight, his powerful form pinning Zane beneath him. The panther thrashed and clawed, but Kaelen's teeth found his neck, holding him in a grip that left no room for doubt. Zane stilled, his golden eyes wide with submission.

He suddenly he shifted back into his human form. "I yield," he choked out. "I yield!"

The referee's voice rang out, clear and resolute. "The challenge is over! Kaelen Therionis remains Alpha King!"

Kaelen released Zane, throwing back his head in a victorious howl that reverberated through the arena. The sound sent chills down my spine, a primal declaration of strength and triumph.

The crowd erupted into a cacophony of cheers, their voices swelling into a unified chant:

"Kae-len! Kae-len! Kae-len!"

I sagged against Olivia, my body trembling with the overwhelming relief that flooded through me. "He did it," I whispered, barely able to believe it. "He really did it."

Cade grinned with approval as he clapped a hand on my shoulder. "He did it with your help. That was some quick thinking, Amaya."

In the center of the arena, Kaelen shifted back into his human form, his powerful frame radiating raw energy even as Zorion handed him a robe. My breath hitched as his eyes locked onto mine, the love and pride in his gaze unmistakable.

"My Luna," he mouthed, and in that instant, every lingering doubt I'd harbored about my place in this world melted away. I belonged here—with him, with this pack, with our people.

As one, we rose to join our Alpha, the bond between us a living, breathing thing, ready to face whatever challenges lay ahead—together.

But the euphoria of victory was fleeting. A tense hush fell over the arena as two brawny pack members dragged Fiora into the clearing, her face twisted with defiance and barely contained rage. The crowd's energy shifted, anticipation thick in the air.

Kaelen's presence was suddenly beside me, his warmth a steadying force against the chill of what was to come.

"By the power of the Goddess Vesperia, you will speak only truth," intoned an elder, pressing a glowing runestone to Fiora's forehead.

Fiora's eyes widened as the magic surged through her. Her body stiffened, her expression contorting with pain. "I... I arranged for Zane to cheat," she spat, each word clawing its way out of her throat. "I wanted Kaelen to fall, to prove he was weak."

Gasps rippled through the crowd like a shockwave. Angry murmurs followed, voices rising in disbelief and condemnation. My gaze flickered to Fiora's family—her mother's face crumpled with shame, while her father's jaw was set in a rigid clench, his eyes blazing with restrained fury.

"Why?" Kaelen's voice was low and dangerous, a growl laced with fury.

I shivered, grateful the anger wasn't directed at me.

Fiora's laugh rang hollow, tinged with bitterness. "Because you chose her," she hissed, her venomous gaze locking onto me. "A human. You made her Luna when it should have been me!"

"The Goddess chose Amaya for me," Kaelen said, his tone cutting through the crowd's whispers like a blade. His voice rang with an authority that sent a hush rippling through the onlookers. "And you never understood. Amaya is not human, Fiora. While not of shifter blood, she was born in this realm, of Eldorian royalty no less. She is more worthy to stand as Luna of Therionis than you could ever be simply by her status of birth. Your actions have not only dishonored yourself but endangered our entire pack."

My chest swelled with pride at Kaelen's words. His unyielding support wrapped around me, shielding me from Fiora's hate.

The elder stepped forward, his face grim, his voice heavy with judgment. "Fiora of Therionis, for your treachery against your Alpha and your people, you are hereby banished from our lands and sentenced to live the rest of your days in the Badlands."

A collective gasp rose from the crowd, the weight of the punishment settling over them.

Fiora's father stepped forward, his expression raw with pain. "We... we renounce her. She is no longer of our blood."

Fiora's composure shattered as the guards dragged her away, her anguished screams echoing through the arena.

I turned into Kaelen's chest, burying my face against the comforting solidity of him. His arms wrapped around me, holding me close. The steady rhythm of his heartbeat beneath my ear was a comfort.

"It's over, little one," he murmured, his voice soft yet resolute. "We're safe now."

***

The next hours passed in a blur of celebration and preparation. Kaelen's injuries, though painful, healed swiftly thanks to his shifter nature. I spent every spare moment by his side, tending to his wounds and savoring the quiet moments we shared amidst the chaos.

"Are you nervous?" I asked that evening, curled up beside him in our bed. The marking ceremony was only days away, and while excitement coursed through me, a flutter of anxiety danced in my stomach.

Kaelen chuckled, the sound low and warm, pulling me closer against him. "Nervous? No. Impatient? Absolutely." His fingers traced lazily teased patterns along my skin, sending delicious shivers through me. "I've waited a lifetime for you, Amaya. I can't wait to make you mine in every way."

Heat blossomed in my cheeks, and desire coiled low in my belly. "I'm already yours," I whispered, my voice soft but certain.

His eyes darkened, a predatory gleam flickering within them. A low growl rumbled deep in his chest as he tipped my chin up, forcing me to meet his gaze. "And I'm yours, little one. Forever."

The intensity of his words settled over me like a warm blanket, easing away the tension of the day. As I drifted off to sleep in Kaelen's powerful arms, his steady heartbeat beneath my ear, I couldn't help but smile. Whatever challenges we faced, whatever uncertainties still lingered, one truth stood unshaken—our love was stronger than any magic.

That night I dreamed of a beautiful snow-white wolf.

Callie

Nauseating darkness enveloped me, a suffocating weight that threatened to steal my last breath. I wanted to scream as I dug my nails into my palms, each prick of pain a stark reminder of my imprisonment in this godforsaken realm. The cold, damp stone beneath me chilled me to the core without mercy as I struggled to maintain my composure, knowing that escape from this hellish place was impossible.

"You can't escape what you are, little revenant." Magda's voice slithered through the shadows like silk. "Embrace your true nature. Join me, and we'll bring Eldoria to its knees."

I refused to answer, clenching my teeth so tightly I feared they might crack. The faint echo of dripping water somewhere in the distance was the only sound that filled the space between us, apart from the steady drumbeat of my racing heart. Magda didn't need light to see me trembling. Her predatory presence was palpable, her smile audible in each word.

"You still think you're her, don't you?" she continued, her tone taking on a mocking lilt. "Callie... the girl who loved sunlight, who believed in heroes and happy endings. That girl is gone. She died the moment you woke up in the ash."

I shut my eyes tightly, willing away the memories that clawed at me—memories of fire licking at my skin, of soot filling my lungs as I collapsed on the burning ground when I landed here. Her words cut through me like jagged glass because, deep down, I feared they were true. But if I let myself believe her—if I surrendered to that gnawing doubt—then I would be lost. No. Not yet. Not now.

"You're wrong," I spat, my voice wavering like a fragile thread. "I'm still me."

Magda's laugh was low and venomous, echoing through the cavern like a serpent coiling tighter around its prey. "Oh, little one, denial is such a sweet habit for the broken," she purred. "But I've seen what lies in your heart now... The hunger, the rage. It will devour you from the inside, whether or not you admit it."

I turned my face away even though I could see nothing but darkness, refusing to give her the satisfaction of seeing the wet shine in my eyes. Her words burrowed into my chest like worms into rotting wood, but I didn't dare let them take root.

"Leave me alone," I whispered, though it sounded pitiful even to my own ears.

"You will give in, Callie, and become what you were born to be. The person standing by my side when I destroy Eldoria will be you."

"Never," I hissed, surprised by the venom in my voice. "I won't betray Olivia or Eldoria."

Magda's laughter echoed off the stone walls, sharp and cruel. "Such loyalty! And for what? You're nothing but a corpse given false life. Do you really think they'll accept you once they know the truth?"

Beneath the fear, a spark of defiance flickered. I thought of Olivia, of the five kingdoms of Eldoria that depended on us. Her words sliced through me, prodding at my deepest fears. What if she was right? Would Olivia recoil in horror if she discovered what I truly was? I shook my head, banishing the doubt. No. Olivia's heart was too pure, too good to abandon me. I thought of Cade, her mate. He was much like me.

"You're wrong," I said, my voice hardening like steel. "Olivia would never turn her back on me. Unlike you, she understands the meaning of love and friendship."

Magda's eyes flashed dangerously in the dim light. "Love? Friendship? Such quaint notions. Power is the only currency that matters, you foolish girl."

I met her gaze, unwavering. "Then you'll always be poor,

Magda. No matter how much power you accumulate, you'll never know true happiness."

For a fleeting moment, I thought I glimpsed something in Magda's eyes—pain? Regret?—but it was gone as swiftly as it came, replaced by icy fury.

"We'll see how long you cling to those pretty ideals," she hissed. "I have eternity to break you, little revenant. And break you I shall."

As Magda's footsteps receded into the darkness, I slumped against the wall, exhaustion seeping into my bones. How long could I resist her relentless psychological assault? The fear gnawed at me, an unwelcome companion in this realm of nightmares.

But beneath the fear, a spark of defiance flickered. I thought of Olivia and the five kingdoms of Eldoria that depended on us. I may be imprisoned in the Underworld, my very identity in question, but I would not let Magda win.

"I am Callie Langston," I reminded myself again. "Friend of Olivia, the protector of Eldoria. And I will not break."

I heard the heavy tread of footsteps approaching, and my heart sank. Eldric. His towering form filled the doorway, those piercing green eyes scanning the room before settling on me. I steeled myself for another round of torment.

But something was different this time. Eldric's shoulders slumped, the usual arrogance in his posture replaced by... hesitation? Guilt? It was hard to tell in the flickering shadows.

"Callie," he said, his voice low and strained, "I need you to cooperate today. Please."

I snorted. "Why start now? I thought you enjoyed our little sessions."

Eldric flinched, and for a moment, I saw raw pain flash across his face. "I never enjoyed—" He cut himself off, running a hand through his reddish-brown curls. "Magda's losing patience. If I can't make progress soon..."

"What, she'll put you in time-out?" I sneered, even as a part of me registered the genuine fear in his eyes.

"Something like that," Eldric muttered. He took a step closer, and I instinctively shrank back. But instead of grabbing me, he crouched down, meeting my gaze. "Look, I know you have no reason to trust me. But I'm trying to help you here."

I laughed bitterly. "Help me? That's rich coming from the one who's been torturing me for weeks."

Eldric's face twisted with shame. "I know. And I can't undo that. But things are changing. The rifts—" He glanced over his shoulder nervously. "Magda wants them opened within the week. If that happens, Eldoria will fall."

My blood ran cold. A week? It was too soon. Olivia and the others couldn't possibly be ready. I searched Eldric's face, looking for any sign of deception. But all I saw was exhaustion and a desperate plea for... redemption?

"Why are you telling me this?" I whispered.

Eldric's hand twitched, as if he wanted to offer comfort, but restrained himself. "Because I can't do this anymore. I've done terrible things, Callie. But I want to make it right."

I wanted to believe him. Goddess help me, I did. But trust was a luxury I couldn't afford down here.

"Pretty words," I said, keeping my voice hard. "But actions speak louder."

Eldric nodded, a sad smile tugging at his lips. "Fair enough." He stood, retrieving a small vial from his pocket. "Here. It's not much, but it should ease some of the pain."

I eyed the vial suspiciously. "How do I know it's not poison?"

"You don't," Eldric admitted. "But think about it—if Magda wanted you dead, you'd be dead already."

He had a point. Slowly, I reached out and took the vial, our fingers brushing for a moment. A feeling of... family... passed between us, and Eldric jerked his hand back as if burned.

"I'll do what I can to buy us more time," he murmured, already backing towards the door. "Just... hold on, okay?"

As Eldric disappeared into the shadows, I uncorked the vial and sniffed cautiously. The familiar scent of healing herbs wafted up, sparking a faint glimmer of hope in my chest. Maybe, just maybe, my cousin could be an ally in this hellish place.

I clutched the vial to my chest, my mind racing. Eldric's actions didn't align with the cruel, power-hungry man I'd come to know. The subtle kindness in his eyes, the hesitation in his touch—it all hinted at something more. But could I trust it? Could I trust him?

Magda's venomous voice still echoed in my head, a constant reminder of the danger that surrounded me. I uncorked the vial again, inhaling deeply. The soothing scent of lavender and chamomile mingled with something earthier— valerian root, perhaps?

"What's your game, Eldric?" I muttered, rolling the vial between my palms. The cool glass was a stark contrast to the oppressive heat of the Underworld.

As if summoned by my thoughts, Magda's cackling laughter echoed through the cavernous space. I tensed, every muscle in my body coiled tight as a spring. But her voice faded, growing distant. She was leaving.

Suddenly, Eldric materialized from the shadows, his green eyes wild with urgency. "Callie," he whispered, crouching beside me. "We have little time."

I jerked back instinctively, but his next words froze me in place.

"I have a plan to get us out of here."

"Us?" I echoed, suspicion warring with hope.

Eldric nodded, his voice low and intense. "When Magda opens the rifts, there will be chaos. It's our chance to escape."

I narrowed my eyes. "And why should I trust you?"

"Because I'm your only option," he said bluntly. "And because... I can't be part of this anymore. What Magda's planning—it's too much. Even for me."

The raw honesty in his voice caught me off guard. I studied his face, searching for any hint of deception. "What changed?"

Eldric's gaze dropped. "You did," he admitted softly. "Your loyalty, your strength—it made me question everything. And... I felt something inside me, telling me there was peace waiting for me in Eldoria. Goddess knows I don't deserve it, and it may be a fabrication of my mind, but it's got to be better than this hell."

My heart thundered in my chest, hope and fear battling for dominance. "If you're lying to me, Eldric..."

"I'm not," he interrupted, his eyes meeting mine with fierce intensity. "I swear it on my life."

I took a deep breath, weighing my options. The smart move would be to reject his offer, to play it safe. But something in my gut told me to take the risk.

"Okay," I whispered, hardly believing the words coming out of my mouth. "I'm in. What's the plan?"

CHAPTER 20

Amaya

I awoke with a gasp, my body aching as if I'd run for miles. Sunlight streamed through the curtains, casting a warm glow across the unfamiliar room. For a moment, I'd forgotten where I was - not in my cramped New York apartment, but in the grand keep of Therionis.

As I stretched, a sharp twinge let me know I must have slept with tension from yesterday's events. My muscles protested, and I winced, rubbing my arms. Fragments of a dream flitted through my mind like leaves caught in a breeze —a white wolf, running free through the forest bathed in silver moonlight. The image filled me with an odd, bittersweet longing.

"It felt so real," I murmured, closing my eyes to recapture the fleeting vision.

In my mind's eye, the white wolf reappeared, its fur shimmering like snow kissed by moonlight. But this time, it wasn't alone. Beside it ran a larger wolf, darker and commanding, its presence radiating power. They moved together, their strides perfectly synchronized as they navigated the shadowy woods.

My breath caught. A warmth bloomed in my chest, spreading outward. "Kaelen," I whispered, the realization sending a shiver down my spine. The larger wolf was him—

there was no mistaking the resemblance to his dire wolf form.

Slowly, I sat up, groaning as my stiff body protested. "Why do I feel like I've been hit by a Mack truck?" I muttered, brushing my hair from my face. Despite the discomfort, hope bubbled up inside me, fragile yet insistent. The dream had left behind a lingering sense of joy, an inexplicable certainty that I wasn't as lost as I thought.

"Is this what it means to have a mate?" I wondered aloud, heat rising to my cheeks. Or was I just imagining things, grasping at symbols in my dreams to make sense of this new life?

But the memory of the two wolves—their connection, their unity—chased away my doubts. Beneath the fear and uncertainty I'd carried since arriving in Therionis, a spark of belonging ignited. The thought was exhilarating.

"Maybe I'm not as out of place here as I thought," I whispered, the corners of my mouth curving into a hesitant smile. For the first time in what felt like forever, the future didn't seem like an insurmountable wall—it felt like a door waiting to be opened.

Reaching for the plush wolf Kaelen had given me, I pulled it close, its soft fur brushing against my skin. I buried my face in it, inhaling the faint scent of pine and earth that still clung to it. The smell was so uniquely Kaelen, it grounded me in this strange, shifting reality.

"I'm glad you're here, little guy." I whispered to the toy, feeling silly but comforted all the same. My eyelids grew heavy once more as the soft morning light bathed the room, and I drifted off again, the plush wolf cradled tightly in my arms.

A gentle touch on my shoulder stirred me from sleep. I blinked groggily, my vision focusing on Kaelen gazing down at me, filled with concern.

"Amaya," he whispered, his deep voice wrapping around me like a warm blanket. "How are you feeling?"

I struggled to sit up, wincing as soreness rippled through

my body. "Like A herd of your pack members have trampled me," I admitted with a weak laugh. "But the dream I had... was beautiful, Kaelen."

His brow furrowed, his interest piqued. "You had a dream? Tell me about it."

I described the white wolf, its shimmering fur glowing in the moonlight, and the larger, darker wolf that had run beside it. As I spoke, I found myself leaning toward Kaelen, drawn to his warmth and the steady strength he radiated.

"It felt so real," I whispered, my voice barely audible. "Like a promise of something... more."

Kaelen's hand found mine, his touch as gentle as it was electric. "Dreams can be powerful things in our world, Amaya. Especially between mates."

My breath caught, my heart racing as his words sank in. "What does it mean?"

He hesitated, the slightest flicker of something unreadable passing through his eyes. "It means you're becoming attuned —to this world, to me, to our bond." His voice softened. "But for now, you need to rest. Let your body and magic heal."

I nodded, exhaustion creeping over me once more. But as Kaelen rose to leave, I reached out, my fingers curling around his hand. "Stay?" I asked, hating the vulnerability in my voice but needing him there.

Kaelen's expression softened, and he crouched beside me, his thumb brushing over my knuckles. "Of course, little wolf. I'm not going anywhere."

As my eyes drifted closed, the last thing I saw was Kaelen sitting by my side, his protective gaze steady and unwavering. Wrapped in the comfort of his presence, I let myself slip into the embrace of sleep, knowing that whatever changes were coming, I wouldn't face them alone.

Kaelen

I watched as Amaya's eyes fluttered closed, her breathing evening out into the soft rhythm of sleep. Her golden hair shimmered in the sunlight spilling into the room, a radiant contrast to the turmoil stirring in my chest. The white wolf in her dream... could it truly mean what I dared to hope?

Leaning down, I pressed a gentle kiss to her forehead, her skin warm—too warm for a one of her elemental order. "Rest, my little mate," I whispered, my voice rough with emotion. "I'll find answers for you."

I rose from the bed, my gaze lingering on her peaceful form before I strode purposefully from the room. The corridors of the keep blurred as I made my way to Zorion's quarters, my thoughts a maelstrom of possibilities and uncertainties.

"Zorion!" I rapped sharply on the door. "I need you. Now."

Moments later, my Beta appeared, his dark eyes sharp despite the early hour. "What is it, Alpha?"

Pushing past him into the room, I ran a hand through my hair, trying to steady my racing thoughts. "It's Amaya. She had a dream—a white wolf running beside what she described as my dire wolf form."

Zorion's brows shot up, his usual calm shaken. "You don't think...?"

"I do," I growled, pacing the length of the room. "Her skin is feverish, her body aches. All signs point to a potential shift."

"But she's not from a shifter lineage," Zorion argued, though doubt flickered in his eyes. "There's no precedent for—"

"No *known* precedent," I interrupted, my voice taut with urgency. "But the legends... the old stories of Fated Mates... what if they're more than just myths?"

Zorion's gaze darkened, his expression unreadable. "You believe she might transform? That she could become one of us?"

My fists clenched at my sides as I fought to contain the storm brewing within me. "I don't know. But I'll do whatever it takes to find out."

Zorion exhaled slowly, his shoulders tensing. "What do you propose?"

I met his gaze, determination burning in my chest. "We seek out the one being who might have the answers we need. It's time to visit the sage of Mt. Theron."

Zorion stiffened. "Zephyrus? But he's—"

"Eccentric? Unpredictable? Yes," I said, a grim smile tugging at my lips. "But he's also our best chance of understanding what's happening to Amaya. We leave after lunch."

Zorion nodded, the weight of the decision settling between us. "You know the risks. The path through Mt. Theron isn't just dangerous—it's treacherous. And Zephyrus... his temper is as legendary as his knowledge."

I let out a low, humorless chuckle. "When has anything worth doing ever been easy?"

Zorion's lips twitched in a reluctant smirk. "Fair point. But this is a man who turned an entire caravan into toads because they interrupted his tea."

The image of Zephyrus, wild-eyed and muttering incantations, briefly surfaced in my mind. I pushed it aside, focusing on the importance of our mission. "If there's even a chance he can help us understand what's happening to Amaya, then we have no choice."

My voice trailed off as I thought of her, sleeping fitfully in our bed, her body preparing for a transformation she couldn't possibly comprehend. A fierce protectiveness gripped my chest, tightening like an iron vice.

"I know," Zorion said softly, his usual stoicism giving way to a rare gentleness. "We'll face whatever comes. But Alpha, we need to do this quickly. The full moon is just days away."

I nodded, my resolve hardening. "Then prepare to leave. Pack light but bring extra provisions. And Zorion..."

"Yes?"

"Bring the Runestones of Resonance. If Zephyrus proves... uncooperative, we may need to make a quick exit."

Zorion's brows shot up, but he nodded without hesitation. As I turned to leave, I stopped with a last instruction.

"And for the love of the Goddess, don't mention toads to Amaya. The last thing we need is for her to worry about that on top of everything else."

A grin broke across Zorion's face, a flash of humor that briefly lightened the tension in the room. "Understood, my king. No amphibian talk. Got it."

As the door clicked shut behind me, the weight of our impending journey settled over me like a heavy shroud. The enormity of what lay ahead loomed large, but beneath the worry and uncertainty, a spark of hope flickered. If the old legends were true—if Amaya could truly become one of us—the implications were nothing short of staggering.

I closed my eyes, letting my thoughts drift to her. I pictured her running beside me in wolf form, her fur as white and luminous as moonlight, her presence strong and unshakable. The image filled me with a fierce determination.

"Hold on, my love," I whispered as I made my way to tell her of my departure, my voice thick with emotion. "We're going to figure this out. I promise."

Amaya

I smoothed my hands over the shimmering fabric, savoring the cool silk against my skin. The deep sapphire blue caught the light, tiny crystals winking like stars scattered across a midnight sky. For the first time in what felt like forever, I felt... peaceful.

"What do you think about adding a cascade of silver leaves along the neckline, Amaya?" Lyra, the dressmaker, held up a delicate string of metallic embellishments, her eyes bright with excitement.

I grinned, my fingers already itching to sketch the

design. "It's perfect. Like moonlight trickling through forest branches."

Lyra nodded with a satisfied hum, pinning the embellishments in place. I closed my eyes, momentarily losing myself in the creative process. It was almost like being back in my New York studio, before everything went to hell. Before Magda. Before the chaos. Before...

The creak of the den door pulled me from my thoughts. Kaelen's towering form filled the doorway, his eyes locking onto mine with that magnetic intensity that always made my heart skip. But this time, something in his expression made me pause.

"Amaya," he said, his voice a low rumble that vibrated through my chest. "I hope I'm not interrupting."

I shook my head, my smile faltering slightly. "Not at all. We were just finishing up. Is everything okay?"

His jaw tightened, almost imperceptibly. To anyone else, he would have seemed his usual composed self, but I'd learned to read the small shifts in his demeanor. Something was off.

"Everything's fine," he said, a little too quickly. "I just wanted to let you know I'll be heading out on some pack business this afternoon. It shouldn't take more than a day or two."

A knot formed in my stomach. "Pack business? Is it... is it about Magda?"

He shook his head, his expression softening. "No, nothing like that. Just routine matters that need my attention."

I nodded, trying to push aside the nagging feeling that he wasn't telling me everything. "When do you leave?"

"After lunch," he said, his gaze steady, though his shoulders carried a weight he wasn't sharing. "I thought we could eat together before I go."

"That sounds good," I said, forcing a smile. As Lyra packed up her tools and slipped out of the room, I turned back to him. "Are you sure everything's alright? You seem... tense."

Kaelen crossed the room and pulled me into his arms. His warmth surrounded me, his scent enveloping me in his presence. I leaned into him, hoping to ease the tightness in my chest.

"I'm fine," he murmured into my hair. His lips brushed my temple, sending a shiver through me. "Just a lot on my mind. But nothing for you to worry about, I promise."

I wanted to believe him. I *needed* to believe him. His hand pressed firmly against my back as we made our way to the dining hall, his touch steadying me. But the unease lingered, twisting in my gut.

As I stole a glance at Kaelen's profile—strong, resolute, and just the slightest bit distant—I couldn't shake the feeling that something big was coming. Something that would change everything.

The dining hall was quiet, except for the soft clink of silverware against plates and the occasional crackle from the hearth. I pushed my food around, my appetite disappearing as my eyes lingered on Kaelen. Across the table, he seemed lost in thought, his brow furrowed as he chewed absently.

"You're going to wear a groove in your forehead if you keep that up," I teased, my voice light, though I felt anything but.

Kaelen's eyes snapped to mine, a small, somber smile tugging at the corner of his lips. "Sorry, little one. I didn't mean to be such poor company."

I reached across the table, my fingers brushing his. The warmth of his skin steadied me. "You don't have to apologize. I just wish..." I hesitated, choosing my words carefully. "I wish you could tell me what's really going on."

He sighed, turning his hand to capture mine fully. "I know," he said, his tone low and heavy. "And I will. I promise. As soon as I have answers."

"Answers to what?" I asked, unable to keep the edge of frustration from my voice. The distance he was placing between us, even unintentionally, was bothering me.

Kaelen's thumb traced slow, soothing circles on my palm, calming me as he always did. "To questions I'm not even sure how to ask yet," he admitted. "But I swear to you, Amaya, I'll be back before the ceremony. Nothing could keep me from that."

That gave me at least some reassurance as I swallowed the lump forming in my throat. "I trust you," I whispered, and despite everything—the secrecy, the uncertainty—I meant it. I trusted this man with every bit of my soul.

"I know," Kaelen said, his voice soft and steady. "And that means everything to me."

We finished our meal in a companionable silence. My eyes couldn't help but notice how his gaze kept drifting toward the window, as if he was eager to get on the road ahead. Whatever "pack business" awaited him, it was expedient that they get to it. And though part of me wanted to demand answers, to beg him not to go, I knew I couldn't.

Later, in our chambers, I watched Kaelen rush around with sharp, purposeful movements. His hands moved almost absentmindedly, tossing clothes and supplies into a well-worn leather pack. His brow remained furrowed, his thoughts clearly elsewhere.

"Are you *sure* you don't need help?" I asked, hugging the stuffed wolf to my chest, its softness a minor comfort against the tension building in the room.

Kaelen paused, his eyes softening as they met mine. The storm in his expression cleared, if only for a moment. "I've got this, love," he said, his voice gentle. "You should be resting."

I bit my lip, resisting the urge to remind him—yet again—that I wasn't fragile, but I didn't want our last conversation before he left to be me acting like a brat. Instead, I asked, "At least tell me what you're taking. I want to know you'll be safe out there."

He nodded, gesturing to the pack. "Dried meat, hard cheese, water skins. Some healing herbs, just in case."

"In case of what?" The question slipped out before I could

stop it, my worry cracking through my composure.

Kaelen's jaw tightened, and for a moment, his gaze darted to the window, distant and thoughtful. "It's just a precaution," he said carefully. "The journey to—" He stopped himself, catching the slip, then softened his tone. "—where we're going can be unpredictable."

A knock at the door interrupted us, sparing Kaelen from more questions. Zorion's deep voice rumbled through the wood. "Alpha, the horses are ready."

"Be right there," Kaelen called, his tone steady despite the turmoil in his eyes. He turned back to me, his expression raw with emotions he couldn't seem to put into words. "Amaya, I —"

I stepped forward, closing the distance between us, and pressed my finger to his lips. "Don't," I whispered, my voice trembling. "Don't say goodbye. Just... come back to me. Promise me that."

He exhaled shakily, then pulled me into his arms, his embrace fierce and protective. "Always," he murmured against my hair, his voice low and fervent. "You're my heart, Amaya. My home."

I breathed him in, inhaling his scent. When he finally released me, it felt like a piece of me went with him, leaving an ache that burrowed deep.

"I love you," I said, my throat thick with unshed tears.

His silver eyes softened as he cupped my face in his powerful hands. His thumb brushed my cheek, his touch reverent. "And I love you. More than I ever thought possible."

His lips found mine, the kiss deep and desperate, laden with all the words he couldn't say aloud. It wasn't just a kiss— it was a promise, a plea, and a vow wrapped into one searing moment.

When we broke apart, I was breathless, my hands clutching his tunic as though letting go would break me. I forced myself to step back, meeting his gaze. "Go, my Alpha," I whispered, my voice trembling but resolute. "The sooner you leave, the sooner you'll come back. And the sooner we'll make our commitment before the Goddess and our people."

Kaelen nodded, his jaw tight as he slung his pack over one shoulder. At the door, he hesitated, his hand resting on the frame. He looked back at me, his eyes filled with a fierce determination that sent a jolt straight to my heart.

"I will return to you, my Luna," he vowed, his voice steady as a promise etched in stone. "I swear it on my life."

And then he was gone, the door closing softly behind him, leaving only the lingering warmth of his touch and the faint scent of him in the air. I stood motionless, hugging the stuffed wolf to my chest as if it could fill the hollow ache his absence left behind.

I rushed to the keep's highest tower. From there, I watched Kaelen and Zorion ride into the forest, their figures shrinking against the sprawling green of Therionis. My heart clenched, torn between pride in his strength and the gnawing worry that I couldn't shake.

"You better come back in one piece, you stubborn wolf," I muttered, gripping the cool stone of the parapet.

As if he'd heard me, Kaelen turned in his saddle. Even at this distance, his eyes found mine, a connection that sent a shiver through me. He raised a hand in farewell, his touch a phantom memory that ghosted across my skin.

I stayed at the parapet long after they disappeared into the tree line, my gaze fixed on where I'd last seen him. The wind carried echoes of Zorion's booming laugh back to me, and despite myself, I grinned, thinking of the two friends sharing a moment of levity on whatever quest they were on.

Kaelen

"I swear by the Goddess Kaelen," Zorion said with an exaggerated sigh, "if you don't stop fretting, I'll shift and bite your royal ass."

I huffed, indignation flaring. "I do not fret, Beta. I... strategize."

"Strategize my tail," he retorted, shaking his head. "You're wound tighter than a shadow shard before it cracks. What's got you so on edge about this Zephyrus character, anyway?"

I rolled my shoulders, trying to ease the tension coiling there. "It's not Zephyrus that worries me. It's..." My gaze flicked back toward the castle, hoping to catch one last glimpse of Amaya, even though I knew we were far past seeing distance.

Zorion's teasing demeanor softened, his dark eyes understanding. "She'll be fine, my friend. Amaya's tougher than she looks."

"I know," I said quietly, nodding more to myself than to him. "But if what we suspect is true... if she's truly about to shift... I should be there. What if she needs me?"

"She's going to be fine," Zorion said firmly, his tone brooking no argument. "We need answers. And for that, we need the cantankerous old bastard on that blasted mountain. Besides, I'm more worried about coming back with a permanent tail attached than Amaya not handling what's coming her way."

My laugh echoed through the forest, breaking the tension. "You're right." My mind wandered briefly to my Luna, her unwavering determination and sharp wit. She never ceased to amaze me with her ability to adapt, no matter the odds. She'd made friends with several of the women in the pack, and I know they'd help her if anything arose.

"Let's pick up the pace," I said, determination threading through my voice. "The sooner we reach Mt. Theron, the sooner we can return."

CHAPTER 21

Olivia

The roar of wind whipped my hair as I soared through the crisp mountain air, my thighs gripping the saddle on the back of Vaelith, our largest dragon. His silver scales reflected the glow of the sun like prisms. Below me, the rocky terrain of Vesparra stretched out in a patchwork of gray and green.

"Alright, Vaelith," I called out, patting his neck. *"Let's do a little crop dustin'!"*

I leaned forward, guiding the massive creature into a steep dive. My stomach lurched, but exhilaration coursed through my veins. At the last second, I pulled up, skimming just above the treetops.

"Little StarHeart, I'm forever baffled by your terminology, but I love it when we ride together."

"Nicely done, love!" Cade's deep voice echoed in my mind. He flew beside me on Eryndor, his midnight-black hair streaming behind him. *"Now, let's try that pincer formation we discussed."*

I grinned, relishing the challenge. *"You heard the man, Vaelith. Time to make the king eat our dust!"*

With a series of hand signals, I directed the other Dragonia to flank us. We climbed higher, then split into two groups, diving towards an imaginary target from opposite directions.

"Yeehaw!" I couldn't help the twang that slipped into my

exclamation. *"Y'all are doin' amazing!"*

As we regrouped, hovering in a loose circle, Cade flew closer. His eyes sparkled with pride and something deeper, more primal. *"You're a natural, Olivia. The way you connect with them... it's breathtaking."*

I felt heat rise to my cheeks, and not just from the wind. *"Well, I've got a pretty outstanding teacher,"* I teased, throwing him a wink.

Before Cade could respond, a sharp tingle in the pocket of my tunic caught my attention. The crystal network — someone was trying to contact me.

I grabbed the crystal and held it in both of my hands. Amaya's voice filled the air, tinged with worry. "Ollie? Are you there? I... I need to see you. Can I come visit?"

I looked over, meeting Cade's concerned gaze. *"It's Amaya,"* I explained quickly. *"She'd like to come for a visit."*

Turning my attention back to the crystal, "Of course, sweetie. Come now, we'll be waitin' for you."

As the connection ended, I couldn't shake the knot of worry forming in my gut. What could have my usually bubbly sister sounding so anxious?

"Alright, folks," I called out to our Dragonia squadron. *"Looks like we're cutting this training session short. Let's head back to the castle."*

***

I paced the grand entryway of Vesparra Castle, my nerves jangling with each click of my boots on the polished stone floor. Cade's steady presence behind me was both comforting and maddening—I wanted to melt into his arms, but I couldn't shake the restless energy coursing through me.

The massive oak doors finally creaked open, and there she was. My little sister, my sunshine girl. But the Amaya who walked in was a far cry from her usual effervescent self.

"Amaya," I breathed, rushing forward to envelop her in a hug. As I pulled back, I studied her face. Dark circles shadowed her usually bright blue-green eyes, and her mass of blonde curls hung limp around her shoulders. "Sweetie, what's wrong?"

Amaya attempted a smile, but it didn't reach her eyes. "I'm okay, Ollie. Just... not feeling great."

I exchanged a glance with Cade, seeing my concern mirrored in his gaze. He stepped forward, his imposing frame softening as he addressed my sister with a brotherly kiss on her forehead. "It's good to see you, Amaya. Why don't we move this to somewhere more comfortable?"

As we settled into the cozy sitting room, I couldn't help but notice how Amaya perched on the edge of her seat, her posture taut as a bowstring. My heart ached, remembering a much younger Amaya, tense and watchful in our foster home.

"Spill it, sis," I said gently. "What's going on?"

Amaya twisted her hands in her lap. "I've just been feeling... off. For a couple of days now. It's probably nothing, but—" She broke off, biting her lip.

"But?" I prompted.

"Kaelen and Zorion had to leave on some urgent business," she continued, her voice small. "They didn't want to go, but... I don't know. I just felt so alone, and I was already feeling sick—"

I leaned forward, taking her trembling hands in mine. "Hey, you're not alone. You've got us, always."

Cade's deep voice rumbled from beside me. "Have you been experiencing any specific symptoms, Amaya?"

She shrugged, looking miserable. "Fatigue, mostly. And these weird... I don't know, tingling sensations? Like my skin doesn't fit right anymore."

I frowned, a nagging worry gnawing at the back of my mind. "And you said this started after Kaelen and Zorion left?"

Amaya nodded. "Well, actually, right before. I started feeling bad that morning. I told Kaelen about it. Gods, I probably sound like such a baby. I'm sorry for barging in on you guys like this. It's just that our mating ceremony is tomorrow night. I don't want to be sick for that."

"Don't you dare apologize," I said fiercely. "You're family, Amaya. We're here for you, no matter what."

As I pulled her into another hug, I caught Cade's eye over her shoulder. The concern etched on his face told me he was thinking the same thing I was—whatever was happening to my little sister; it was far from ordinary.

Seraphine joined Amaya and me for lunch while Cade took care of kingdom business. Sera had an equally worried countenance when she saw Amaya. After lunch, we headed to the library where we played a few board games to pass the time until I thought Amaya would pass out from exhaustion. Cade stopped by to ask me to go with him to check on a few things, and I asked if she'd let Seraphine take her to her room to get her get some rest. She was more than happy to take me up on that offer.

I watched Cade's broad shoulders as he strode purposefully down the torch-lit corridor, his jet-black hair swaying with each step. The worry etched on his face mirrored my own as we approached Ilyria's chambers.

"What do you think is happening to her?" I whispered, my voice barely audible over the crackling flames.

Cade's eyes met mine, a storm of emotions swirling within them. "I'm not sure, but Ilyria might have some answers."

He rapped his knuckles against the heavy wooden door, and we heard Ilyria's cracked voice call out, "Enter, Your Majesty."

As we stepped inside, the scent of herbs and incense washed over us. Ilyria sat hunched over an ancient tome, her wrinkled hands tracing the yellowed pages.

"Ilyria," Cade began, his tone betraying a hint of urgency, "we need your insight. It's about Amaya."

The old mage's dark eyes flickered with interest. "Ah,

the young one. I sensed a disturbance in her aura. Tell me everything."

As Cade recounted Amaya's symptoms, I found myself pacing, my mind racing with possibilities. What if something was seriously wrong with my sister?

Ilyria listened intently, her brow furrowing deeper with each detail. When Cade finished, she leaned back, a knowing glint in her eye.

"Your Majesty," she said, her voice barely above a whisper, "I believe young Amaya may be on the cusp of a profound transformation."

My heart leaped into my throat. "What kind of transformation?"

Ilyria's gaze shifted to me, her expression softening. "There is an ancient legend, my dear. It speaks of shifters who find their Fated Mates, among other magical orders. When such a bond is formed and the shifter marks their mate, it is said that the mate can be... turned."

"Turned?" Cade echoed, his voice thick with disbelief. "You mean Amaya could become a shifter?"

I felt my knees go weak, and Cade's powerful arm wrapped around my waist, steadying me.

Ilyria nodded slowly. "It is an incredibly rare occurrence, but not unheard of. The symptoms you describe align with the legends."

My mind reeled with the implications. "But Kaelen hasn't marked her yet, has he?"

Cade's eyes caught mine, a flicker of realization in them.

"He did, my love. He claimed her with his bite the first night she told him she wanted to be his in every way. Remember, they announced it the morning I announced the date of our marking ceremony? It wasn't in a formal mating ritual like they will have under the full moon tomorrow night, but it was official in the eyes of the Goddess."

"Oh, that counts," Ilyria mused. "And the bond between

Fated Mates is powerful magic indeed, official ritual or not. It's possible it was enough to trigger the change."

As we left Ilyria's chambers, my thoughts were a tangled mess. Cade's hand found mine, his touch grounding me.

"I can't believe I forgot about him claiming her. I'm a terrible sister."

"You're a perfect sister. Much has happened since that day, Starlight."

"What are we gonna to do?" I asked, my voice barely above a whisper.

Cade's eyes met mine, determination blazing within them. "We support her, no matter what happens. But Olivia, we can't tell her about this yet. Not until we're certain."

I nodded, understanding his caution. "You're right. I don't want to get her hopes up if we're wrong."

"We'll be there for her," Cade promised, pulling me close. "Whatever comes, we'll face it together."

As we made our way back to Amaya, I felt a mix of anticipation and fear coursing through me. She decided to portal back to Therionis after dinner since her ceremony was tomorrow, and she had a long list of preparations. I told her I'd be there first thing in the morning to help her with all that I could. My little sister's world might be about to change forever, and I swore to myself that I'd be there to guide her through every step of the journey.

***

I collapsed onto our bed, the weight of the day finally catching up to me. Cade followed, his muscular arms encircling my waist as he pulled me against his chest. The warmth of his body seeped into mine, easing my frayed nerves.

"You okay, darling?" he murmured, his lips brushing against my ear.

"After the day I've had? You could always make it better,

Highness."

"Starlight... take your clothes off."

Oh, how I loved it when Cade took over and I no longer had to think about anything.

"Yes, Highness."

I slipped off the satin gown and matching panties I had on. On my knees, naked before him, I was instantly dripping with anticipation. Cade had removed his loose pajama pants and was on his knees before me. His length was hard and proud in his hand.

"What you do to me, Starlight, at a moment's notice, still amazes me."

I looked down as he stroked his hand up and down his erection. I licked my lips in anticipation of a taste.

"You look like you want to devour me whole, Starlight. If you're a very, very good girl, I may let you."

He maneuvered around the bed until he was lying on his back, his head on the pillow.

"Now, Starlight, I need you to come all the way up here by my head, please."

I crawled up the bed as he asked until I was even with his beautiful face.

"Face the headboard. Grab ahold of it with both hands and lift your right leg over my face until that fucking gorgeous pussy is even with my mouth, sweetheart."

Oh stars! He wanted me to straddle his face! I hesitated just a moment.

"Olivia, your king has given you an order, and yet, there you sit. Do I need to repeat my instructions?"

"N-no, Highness. I just... ok, I'm doin' it." I followed his instructions explicitly. His hands reached up and took hold of my hips, steadying me as I settled my most private parts right over his glorious tongue. He began to lick, and my hips rocked to the rhythm he'd established.

"Mmmm." I was lost to the sensations.

I held tight to the headboard with both hands now as his masterful tongue stiffened and slipped deep inside me, lapping at me like a man dying of thirst.

"Cade, please." I begged for release now.

He flattened that magical, fantastic tongue against my tiny bundle of nerves while tossing his head side to side. I was sure I would rip the headboard completely off the bed.

"Oh baby, right there, right there, yes, mmm." My body shook and quaked with the rush of my release as I gushed all over Cade's mouth. I felt way too good to be mortified that I'd just bathed his face in my wetness. He continued to lick and suck as my body jerked and spasmed in the most delicious aftershocks.

I pushed myself down his body until my mouth was even with his, and I devoured him with open-mouthed kisses. My tongue explored every inch of his mouth. I tasted myself as I licked, sucked, and kissed his mouth and face. I worked my way down to his neck, giving the same treatment, tasting and exploring the body I knew so well yet could never get enough of.

He flipped me onto my back and entered me with one smooth thrust. His size filled me so completely that I let out a gasp. "I love you, Cade," I grunted.

"You are a fucking wonder, Starlight."

He was relentless, and I loved every single time he pounded into my core. I loved I couldn't tell where he began and I ended. We were, in every way, one.

He leaned over me as his body pistoned in and out, and with one swift movement, his fangs distended. I offered my neck to him, and he bit down, sure and true, causing me to come harder than I had earlier; the force causing black spots to form in front of my eyes. But I held on because there was nothing more fascinating than watching Cadence Vesparra lose control when he came. And oh, what a sight it was.

Exhaustion took me. My last memory was of Cade gently

cleaning me with a warm, damp cloth, the feeling of being cherished filling my heart.

CHAPTER 22

Kaelen

The jagged peak of Mount Theron loomed before us, its snow-capped summit hidden behind wisps of cloud. I exhaled, my breath misting in the frigid air as Zorion and I nudged our horses up the steep, rocky path.

"We've got to be getting close," I growled, my muscles tense with urgency. The fate of my mate—of Amaya—hung in the balance.

Zorion nodded grimly, his dark eyes scanning our surroundings. "We should see his hut soon. But this mountain has claimed many lives. We must tread carefully."

I clenched my jaw, fighting the urge to shift and bound up the treacherous slope on four legs. But we needed to keep our provisions close, so we had to proceed with caution.

"Tell me again what you know of this Zephyrus," I said, as my horse leaped over a narrow crevasse.

Zorion's brow furrowed as he followed. "Little is certain. He's said to be as old as the mountain itself, with knowledge of magics long forgotten. But his aid comes at a price."

A chill that had nothing to do with the biting wind ran down my spine. What price would I pay to ensure Amaya's safety? To my shame, I knew the answer—any price at all.

We climbed in silence after that, the only sounds being

our horses' labored breathing and the crunch of gravel beneath their hooves. My thoughts turned to Amaya, so young and vulnerable, unaware of the power that slumbered within her. I longed to shelter her, to give her the carefree moments she'd long been denied.

At last, we crested a ridge and beheld a crude dwelling hewn into the very rock of the mountain. Before it stood a figure, tall and lean, with hair as white as the surrounding snow.

Zephyrus.

He turned to face us, moving with agonizing slowness. His eyes, a startling shade of turquoise, swept over us with ancient wisdom—and unmistakable mischief as we dismounted.

"Ah," he said, his voice as dry and rasping as wind over stone. "The wolf-king comes at last, seeking answers." A smile played at the corners of his mouth. "But are you prepared for the questions, I wonder? For every trial overcome, another awaits—each more difficult than the last."

I squared my shoulders, meeting his gaze. "Whatever the cost, whatever the danger, I will face it. For her."

Zephyrus's smile widened, revealing teeth unnaturally sharp. "We shall see, young king. We shall see."

His eyes gleamed with an otherworldly light as he raised a gnarled finger. "Your first test, wolf-king. Bring me a moonbeam."

I blinked, frustration rising in my chest. "A moonbeam? But it's daylight, and even if it weren't—how does one capture light?"

My mind raced, searching for hidden meanings. Was this some metaphor? A trick? I clenched my fists, acutely aware that each passing moment brought us closer to the full moon—closer to Amaya's transformation.

Zorion cleared his throat beside me. "My king," he murmured, his deep voice tinged with excitement. "The Luna Lyra flower."

Of course. I could have kissed my Beta at that moment. "The moonbeam flower," I breathed, recalling the delicate white blossoms that shimmered like captured moonlight. "It grows only on this mountain."

Without waiting for confirmation, I set off, scrambling over lichen-covered rocks and through patches of stubborn snow. The crisp air burned my lungs as I searched, desperation fueling every step.

There—nestled in a crevice, protected from the harshest winds. A cluster of Luna Lyra, their petals gleaming even in the weak sunlight. I plucked one carefully, cradling it as I made my way back to Zephyrus.

The ancient being's eyes widened fractionally as I presented the blossom. "Well done," he rasped, a hint of approval in his tone. "But cleverness alone will not suffice. Are you prepared for the next riddle?"

I nodded, steeling myself. "Whatever it takes."

Zephyrus's lips curled into a smile that sent a chill down my spine. "Very well. Answer me this: I am not alive, but I grow; I don't have lungs, but I need air; I don't have a mouth, but water kills me. What am I?"

I frowned, turning the words over in my mind. Beside me, Zorion shifted uncomfortably, clearly out of his element with these word games. But this... this I could handle.

The answer hit me like a bolt of lightning. "Fire," I said, unable to keep the satisfaction from my voice. "You're describing fire."

Zephyrus inclined his head, those unnerving eyes never leaving mine. "Correct again, wolf-king. But do not grow too confident. The hardest riddle is yet to come, and it may cost you more than you're willing to pay."

His eyes narrowed, a sly glint dancing in their depths. "For your final riddle, Kaelen Therionis, answer me this: What is built on trust, broken by doubt, and mended by love?"

My brow furrowed as I contemplated the riddle. Trust.

Doubt. Love. The words echoed in my mind, stirring something deep within me. I closed my eyes, allowing my thoughts to drift to Amaya. Her blue-green eyes filled with both fierce determination and vulnerability. The way her blonde curls caught the sunlight. The tender moments we'd shared, and the walls she'd built around her heart.

"A bond," I breathed, opening my eyes to meet Zephyrus's gaze. "The answer is a bond."

As I spoke, I felt a warmth in my chest, an echo of the connection I shared with Amaya. Despite her initial resistance, despite her fears, our bond was genuine. It was fragile, yes, but also unbreakable in its own way.

"Elaborate," Zephyrus commanded, his voice low and intense.

I took a deep breath. "A bond, like the one between mates, is built on trust. Doubt or fear can shatter it, but true love... true love can mend even the deepest cracks."

Zephyrus regarded me for a long moment, his ancient face unreadable. Then, slowly, he nodded. "You speak from the heart, wolf-king. Perhaps there is hope for you yet."

The old man's demeanor shifted, the mischievous glint in his eyes fading to something more somber. "Now, we must discuss matters of grave importance. The transformation your mate faces is no small thing."

I felt my muscles tense, anxiety coiling in my gut. "So it's true? The transformation?"

Zephyrus sighed, his ancient visage suddenly bearing the weight of countless years. "The legend of the Fated Transformation is older than the mountains themselves," he began. "Long ago, when the Goddess Vesperia wove the first threads of the world, she created bonds so strong that not even death could sever them. But for a rare few—those whose souls were destined to ignite the balance of power—she granted a gift like no other. Only a Fated Mate of pure elemental blood can receive this gift. The claiming bite from her mate unlocks a dormant part of her soul." Zephyrus's expression turned somber, his tone a blend of reverence and warning.

He tapped his staff against the ground, a spark of ancient magic lighting his turquoise eyes. "The claiming bite you gave her awakened the dormant power in her blood—a gift tied to her elemental heritage and your bond as Fated Mates. But the transformation is incomplete."

Kaelen's heart pounded, his mind racing.

"The power lies dormant," the sage continued, "building within her. Feverish skin, aching bones, restlessness—those are the signs. Her soul is preparing for the shift, and the full moon is the key that unlocks it. But it's not just the moon, Alpha. It's your public claiming, the moment you stand together before your pack and the Goddess. That combination of moonlight and magic will spark her transformation."

Zorion let out a low whistle. "And if it doesn't? What happens then?"

Zephyrus's lips curled into a grim smile. "If the transformation fails, she'll remain as she is, and the wolf inside her will slumber forever. But if she succeeds—if she's strong enough to endure it—she won't just shift. She'll become something new. A hybrid—a creature of immense power, both wolf and elemental, unlike anything this realm has seen in centuries. She will retain her magic, Alpha, but she'll gain the strength of the beast."

Kaelen's chest tightened as the sage leveled him with a piercing stare.

"But be warned," Zephyrus growled, his voice dropping. "The shift isn't just physical. It will test her mind and spirit. She'll be caught between the wildness of her beast and the essence of her magic. If she isn't strong enough to reconcile the two, it could destroy her—or drive her mad."

I swallowed hard, my throat suddenly dry. "And what will she awaken into?"

Zephyrus's lips thinned. "That, wolf-king, is the question

that should keep you up at night."

As he spoke, I couldn't help but picture Amaya—her blonde curls wild in the wind, those blue-green eyes flashing with a mixture of vulnerability and strength. The thought of her changing, of losing any part of who she was, sent a chill down my spine.

"There are risks," Zephyrus continued, his words cutting through my thoughts like a knife. "The transformation isn't guaranteed to succeed. And even if it does, Amaya will face a battle within herself."

"What kind of battle?" I demanded, my voice rougher than I intended.

"A war between her human nature and her newly awakened powers. Between the woman you know and the creature she might become." Zephyrus's eyes narrowed. "If she can't find balance, if she can't reconcile these two halves of herself... the consequences could be dire."

My chest tightened, anxiety clawing at my insides. I wanted to roar, to challenge fate itself. Instead, I forced myself to ask, "What consequences?"

Zephyrus's voice dropped to a whisper. "Madness. Loss of self. Or worse—she could become a danger to everyone around her, including you."

The weight of his words crashed over me like a tidal wave. I thought of Amaya's smile, her gentle touch, the way she looked at me with a mixture of longing and fear. The idea of losing her to this transformation, of watching her struggle against herself, was almost too much to bear.

"Is there nothing I can do?" I asked, hating the desperation in my voice.

"I need to be there for her," I said, my voice low and determined. "I need to help her through this."

Zephyrus shook his head, his expression softening. "Your role is limited, Alpha King. You can offer support, love, and strength, but the journey is Amaya's alone."

I clenched my fists, frustration bubbling up inside me. "There must be something more I can do!"

"Listen well, Kaelen," Zephyrus said, his tone suddenly stern. "Amaya must find her own balance between her beast and her magic. You cannot fight this battle for her, no matter how much you wish to."

I closed my eyes, trying to calm the storm of emotions within me. When I opened them, I met Zephyrus's gaze with renewed determination. "I understand. I'll be there for her, in whatever way she needs me."

Zephyrus nodded approvingly. "That, young king, may be the most important thing you can do."

"We need to go," I said, my voice rougher than usual. "Amaya needs to know what's coming."

Zephyrus stood slowly, his joints creaking like ancient tree branches. A mischievous glint appeared in his eyes. "Before you dash off like love-struck puppies," he chuckled, "remember this: sometimes the most powerful magic comes from a well-timed joke."

I blinked, caught off guard. "What?"

The old man's wrinkled face split into a grin. "Laughter, my boy. It can break tension like nothing else. Don't forget to breathe, to smile. Your mate will need that strength as much as any other."

Despite everything, I felt a smile tugging at my lips. "I'll keep that in mind."

"Good," Zephyrus nodded. "Now go. And may the Goddess watch over you both."

We didn't need to be told twice. Zorion and I burst out of the dwelling, the crisp mountain air filling our lungs as we began our descent. Our horses' hooves were nimble, though the path was treacherous, loose stones skittering as they moved with sure-footed grace.

"We're cutting it close," Zorion growled beside me.

I nodded, my mind racing. "The ceremony... we need to

prepare Amaya, but we can't overwhelm her." The image of her face, those eyes that held so much power and vulnerability, flashed through my mind. "She needs to know the risks, but also the potential."

We leaped over a narrow ravine, the wind whipping through our hair. "Do you think she's ready for this?" Zorion asked, his voice tight with concern.

I hesitated, my heart clenching. "She has to be," I finally said. "But Goddess help me, I wish I could take this burden from her."

The mountain path twisted sharply, and we slowed our pace to navigate a particularly treacherous section. "You heard Zephyrus," Zorion reminded me. "Your support is crucial. Don't underestimate that."

I nodded, grateful for his steadfast presence. As we continued our frantic descent, I couldn't shake the image of Amaya, caught between two worlds, struggling to find her balance. "I'll be there for her," I vowed, as much to myself as to Zorion. "Whatever happens, we'll face it together."

As the base of Mt. Theron loomed closer, my resolve solidified like steel in my veins. The surrounding forest blurred, a tapestry of greens and browns, but my focus remained razor sharp.

"Kaelen." Zorion's voice cut through my thoughts. "What's your plan when we reach Amaya?"

I swallowed hard, the weight of responsibility settling heavy on my shoulders. "I'll tell her everything. No secrets, no sugar-coating. She deserves the truth."

My mind raced with images of Amaya—her fierce independence, her creative spirit, the way her eyes sparkled when she laughed. Gods, how I longed to shield her from this. But I knew better. She was stronger than that, stronger than even she realized.

"And if she balks?" Zorion pressed, his tone gentle but probing.

I clenched my jaw. "Then I'll remind her of who she is. Not just my mate, but a force of nature in her own right. This ceremony... it's not about me claiming her. It's about her claiming her own power."

The trees began to thin, signaling our approach to the mountain's base. My heart thundered in my chest, a mix of anticipation and dread.

"I'm terrified," I admitted, my voice barely above a whisper. "Terrified of losing her, of her suffering. But I'm also filled with hope. Amaya has always been extraordinary. This transformation... it could be the key to unlocking her full potential."

Zorion reassured me. "Then let that hope guide you, my friend. Amaya will need your strength tonight."

I nodded, drawing in a deep breath as we broke through the tree line. The sprawling expanse of Therionis spread before us, and somewhere within, Amaya waited. My mate. My heart. The future of our kingdom.

"Whatever comes," I murmured, steeling myself for the challenge ahead, "I'll stand by her side. Through fire and shadow, through triumph and tragedy. We'll face it together."

CHAPTER 23

Amaya

Olivia was helping me prepare for the mating ceremony that was only a couple of hours away.

"I hope Kaelen makes it back in time. I cannot imagine the humiliation I'll face if I have to walk out alone and make apologies for his absence."

"Maya, now don't be silly. Wild horses could not keep that man from bein' here for you. Trust me, sweet girl. Come hell or high water, Kaelen will be here in plenty of time for your ceremony."

She stood behind me as I sat in front of a large, framed mirror, weaving shimmering white flowers through my golden curls. Her voice cracked with emotion as she spoke again.

"I've never seen you look so radiant, my itty-bitty girl."

"Aww, you haven't called me that in years, Ollie. And don't cry, you're gonna make me cry." I laughed, though my voice wavered as tears threatened to spill.

All at once, a ruckus erupted downstairs, shattering the peaceful moment. My heart jumped into my throat, and I whirled toward the door as Kaelen's unmistakable voice bellowed.

"Where is Amaya?" he demanded, his deep tone

reverberating through the stone halls.

Cade's steady voice followed, calm yet firm. "Brother, she's making ready for your mating ceremony. Let me take you to her."

Their footsteps echoed, growing louder as they approached the room where Olivia and I had been perfecting my appearance.

I moved to the room's large window, pulling the shutters open just in time to see Kaelen striding through the hallway. He moved with fluid grace, every step imbued with an Alpha's power and purpose. His mane of blonde hair flowed behind him with each stride, and his eyes burned with intensity. Guards and servants scattered like leaves, scrambling to clear his path.

Despite my nerves, my breath caught at the sight of him. Even now, with tension etched into every line of his body, he was breathtaking.

I turned away, forcing myself to focus on the present. "Come on," I murmured, tugging Olivia with me to the center of the room. My pulse thundered in my ears.

Olivia's steady presence was a lifeline as we retreated from the window. She reached out, adjusting the folds of my ceremonial gown with the same care she always showed.

"Kaelen wouldn't be storming in like this without good reason," she said quietly, her words meant to soothe.

"I know," I replied, though my voice wavered. Anxiety buzzed beneath my skin like a living thing.

My gaze drifted to the silver mirror once more, where a stranger stared back at me. My hair shimmered with the flowers Olivia had threaded through it, the cascading waves glimmered like captured moonlight. The gown, a masterpiece of deep sapphire silk adorned with delicate embroidery, hugged my frame like a second skin. My skin glowed, my eyes shone—but inside, I felt like a little girl playing dress-up in a queen's robes.

"You look beautiful, Amaya," Olivia said gently, her hands coming to rest on my shoulders.

I met her gaze in the mirror, managing a shaky smile. "Thank you. I just wish I felt as confident as I look."

"It's normal to be nervous," she assured me, smoothing a loose curl back into place. Her eyes brimmed with affection and pride. "This ceremony is a big step."

I nodded, trying to will away the swirling chaos of emotions inside me—excitement and dread, hope and fear. This wasn't just about me or even Kaelen. This was about stepping into a role I hoped I was ready for.

As if sensing my turmoil, Olivia squeezed my shoulders, reassuring me with her calm. "Remember, no matter what happens today, we're in this together. You're not alone anymore. *We're* no longer alone."

Her words settled over me like a soothing balm, their weight bringing a much needed reassurance.

I closed my eyes, drawing strength from her presence. The years of surviving on my own, of bracing for rejection and abandonment, had left scars I still carried. But now, standing on the threshold of this new chapter, I let myself believe I didn't have to carry the weight alone.

When I opened my eyes, I saw something different in my reflection. A spark of determination. A flicker of strength.

I wasn't just Kaelen's mate. I was a queen in the making.

Whatever challenges lay ahead, I would face them. For my sister, for my people, and for myself.

The chamber doors burst open, and Kaelen's commanding presence filled the room; Cade was hot on his heels. My breath caught as his eyes locked onto mine, a storm of emotions swirling in their depths—urgency, reassurance, and something deeper I couldn't quite name.

Olivia looked from Kaelen to me, her knowing smirk softening the moment. "Cade, I think there are some things we need to attend to downstairs."

Cade grinned, clearly catching onto her ploy. "Yes, my love. I believe there are a few matters that need our attention. Kaelen, Amaya, if you'll excuse us." He tipped his head with exaggerated formality before slipping through the door, his arm draped protectively around Olivia's waist.

The room felt smaller with Kaelen standing still in its center, his focus entirely on me. His chest rose and fell with restrained urgency, and the energy radiating from him sent a ripple of nervous anticipation through my stomach.

"Amaya," he said, his deep voice wrapping around my name like a promise. "You look exquisite. Your beauty rivals the Goddess herself." He wrapped me in his arms.

He then stepped back, as though steadying himself, before continuing. "I have news from the sage."

I swallowed hard, my fingers twisting nervously in the folds of my gown. I was thoroughly confused. "Wait, what sage? Who is *he*, and what news did he have?"

He took my hands in his. His grip was firm, his touch sure—a stark contrast to the look of worry etched on his face..

"Oh, right, sorry," he said, with a slight shake of his head. "That's where Zorion and I have been. I suspected something that needed to be verified before our mating ceremony. There was only one person I knew of who I could trust to give me the information I needed."

"Kaelen, please, take a breath. It's okay. We have a few minutes. You're not making any sense."

He exhaled slowly, the tension in his shoulders easing slightly. "We traveled up Mt. Theron to see the sage, Zephyrus," he explained, his deep voice steady with a weight of certainty. "I needed answers, Amaya. There's a legend—one that I suspected might hold the truth about what's happening to you."

"Now, I'm getting a little nervous. *What's* happening to me?" I repeated, my pulse quickening. "A legend of what, exactly?"

Kaelen led me to the loveseat in the corner of the room. His hands wrapping securely around mine as though he were anchoring himself to me. Then he continued, "A legend of true mates from different magical orders," he said, the intensity in his silver gaze rooting me in place.

My breath hitched as a mix of hope and disbelief swirled in my chest. "Okay... what does this legend say about them?"

His grip on my hands tightened ever so slightly. "It says," he began, his words deliberate, "the Goddess Vesperia gifted some with bonds so strong that even death couldn't break them. These souls are destined to bring balance to the realms, bridging two worlds of magic. But," Kaelen continued, his voice dipping lower, "only a fated mate whose elemental blood is pure can receive this gift. When I bit you the night I claimed you, it triggered your transformation. That's why you've been feeling feverish and unsettled. It awakened something dormant within you—something waiting for this moment. The transformation won't be completed until I claim you before the pack and the Goddess under the full moon tonight."

The room spun slightly, my thoughts tangling like a whirlwind of disbelief and wonder. "So, you're saying that not only will I... shift into a wolf," I paused, trying to wrap my mind around the enormity of it, "but I'll also keep my magic?"

Kaelen nodded, his expression resolute. "You won't just keep it," he said, his tone edged with awe. "You'll amplify it. You'll become something entirely new—a hybrid with the strength and instincts of a shifter and the raw elemental magic of a mage. It's something that hasn't existed in millennia, Amaya."

"Holy shit," I whispered, my heart pounding in my chest.

Kaelen's expression softened, but the worry in his eyes remained. "But that's not all, sweetheart."

"Of course it isn't," I muttered, pinching the bridge of my nose.

The tension in his broad shoulders was clear. "This

transformation isn't just physical. It will be a battle for your mind as well."

My stomach twisted at his words. "What do you mean, a battle for my mind?"

Kaelen's jaw tightened, and he took a steadying breath before continuing. "The beast will want to take complete control. It will be wild, untamed, and it won't recognize reason or restraint. You must fight with all your power and love to overcome it. Once you win the battle, you will master your wolf and live in harmony with her for the rest of your life. But if you lose..." He hesitated, the weight of his next words hanging heavily in the air.

"If I lose?" I prompted, my voice barely above a whisper.

Kaelen's voice dropped, raw and laced with pain. "If you lose, it will be a horror for you and everyone near you. To quote the sage, 'a thing of nightmares.'"

"Oh, come on, Kaelen!" I threw up my hands in frustration, my emotions boiling over. "Can't anything ever be easy?"

"Few things worth having rarely are, my love," he said gently. "But I believe in you."

I stared at him, my chest heaving with a mix of fear and determination. "Well, there is one thing I know that's true."

"And that is?"

"I will not live my life without you." My voice rang with conviction, every word a promise. "And so there is no choice but to go forward. I will happily face this challenge, and I will defeat it. We will stand united and come out as one. By midnight tonight, we will run through the forest—me as a beautiful white wolf and you, your gorgeous dire wolf, together."

Kaelen's lips curved into a slow smile, pride and love shining in his eyes. "That's my Luna."

I stood, brushing my hands down the folds of my gown. "But before we get to the midnight run, we better fill Olivia and Cade in. Something tells me she is going to have her Texan on full display before I calm her down."

Kaelen chuckled, the sound deep and rich. "I wouldn't expect anything less from your sister. Let's prepare, my love. Tonight, everything changes."

I waited for Kaelen to shower and quickly change into his wedding vestments. Then we stepped out of the chamber into a whirlwind of activity. The keep of Therionis hummed with life, the quiet intensity of our private moment now replaced by an explosion of movement and sound. Servants hurried past with arms laden with flowers and ceremonial cloths, their footsteps echoing faintly against the stone walls. The air was alive with excitement and nervous energy, a collective buzz that seemed to vibrate through the very ground beneath us.

The ceremony would take place in the outdoor cathedral, with the festivities spilling seamlessly into the surrounding forest. I marveled at the transformation as we moved through the bustling courtyard. "It's like the whole indoors has moved outside," I murmured, taking in the delicate decor and elegantly arranged tablescapes nestled amongst the trees. The scent of pine mingled with wildflowers, a heady reminder of the beauty that had first captivated me upon arriving in Therionis.

Spotting Olivia in the crowd, I caught her eye and gestured for her to join us.

"We need a moment alone," I said softly when she approached. "You'd better bring Cade too."

Kaelen and I explained the situation as best we could. Cade listened intently, his expression grim yet resolute, while Olivia's emotions flickered across her face like an open book. At one point, I had to physically stop her from taking a run at Kaelen—her Texan fire flaring to life at the idea of anything threatening me.

"Ollie," I said, placing a hand on her arm, "I don't want to have to leg wrestle you over my mate. Calm down."

She huffed but relented, her lips twitching into a reluctant smile. By the time we emerged from the quiet room where we'd sought privacy, the tension between us had eased. While a faint undercurrent of worry lingered for what lay ahead, the shared laughter and camaraderie had lightened our moods. Faith in the Goddess's guidance bolstered us, leaving no room for doubt.

And amidst this band of merry revelers, it was impossible to remain somber for long.

Kaelen chuckled, the low, rich sound rumbled through his chest and sent shivers down my spine. "We Shifters do love a party—especially when it's for something this momentous."

The energy around us was infectious as we weaved our way through the crowds. Snippets of conversation floated in the air, mingling with bursts of laughter and the occasional clink of glasses. The variety of accents hinted at the vast diversity of the gathered guests, representatives from every corner of Eldoria.

"Look," Kaelen murmured, leaning close as he nodded toward a nearby group.

I followed his gaze, my breath catching when my eyes landed on two familiar figures—Miranda Thalassa and Thorne Nightstrom. Miranda was a vision of elegance, her dark curls cascading like silk down her back as she laughed at something Thorne had said. The imposing general, known for his stoic demeanor, appeared uncharacteristically at ease. A subtle smile softened his sharp features as he looked down at her, his storm-gray eyes warm in a way I'd never seen before.

"They make quite the pair, don't they?" I observed, captivated by the unspoken connection crackling between them.

Kaelen's hand tightened slightly around mine, a quiet affirmation of his agreement. "Indeed. Though I fear their positions may complicate things."

I frowned, considering the truth in his words. "A queen and a general from different kingdoms... that can't be easy."

"No," Kaelen said, his tone weighted with understanding. "But if there's one thing I've learned, it's that genuine connections—genuine bonds—have a way of overcoming even the most daunting obstacles."

A hush fell over the crowd as Farin Thalassa entered, his towering frame and regal bearing instantly drawing every eye in the crowd. The deep blue robes he wore shimmered like sunlight playing on water, a subtle nod to his lineage. My breath hitched as I took in the quiet authority he exuded, every step deliberate, every movement graceful. His warm brown eyes swept over the gathering, radiating a calm assurance that seemed to settle even the most restless spirits.

"Farin," Kaelen called, his face lighting up with a rare, genuine smile. The two men clasped forearms in a gesture that spoke of unshakable trust, their brotherhood evident in the firm embrace.

"Brother," Farin replied, his rich, melodic voice cutting through the silence with ease. "I trust all is in order for the ceremony?"

I didn't wait for Kaelen's reply. "Grandpapa!" I cried, running into Farin's arms. His laughter rumbled deep in his chest as he wrapped me in a warm, steady embrace. He pressed a kiss to my forehead, and instantly, the swirling nerves in my chest eased.

There wasn't a more calming presence in all the realm, and I marveled at how effortlessly his arrival seemed to bring tranquility to the bustling preparations around us.

"Amaya," he said softly, holding me at arm's length to study me. His eyes crinkled at the corners as his gaze swept over me, pride shining in his expression. "What a beautiful mate you are for Kaelen. You look as radiant as the moon tonight."

I blinked back the prick of tears, smiling up at him. "I'm so glad you're here, Grandpapa."

Olivia stepped forward then, her face glowing with affection. Farin's eyes lit up with delight as he reached for her hands, taking them gently in his own.

"My dear," he murmured, his voice full of warmth and reverence, "you look radiant."

Olivia blushed under his gaze, her smiled soft and genuine. "Thank you, Grandpapa. We don't see you nearly enough."

Farin chuckled, the sound rich and soothing. "You're right, child. It's been far too long. But tonight, let us make up for lost time."

His presence, as steady and enduring as the tides, gave my soul a much needed assurance. As we stood there, surrounded by the bustling preparations and the hum of excitement, I couldn't help but feel that with Farin here, everything was exactly as it should be.

As they spoke, their conversation warm and effortless, I marveled at the gentle strength that radiated from my grandfather. How could someone so steadfast, so wise, have ever been tied to someone as treacherous as my grandmother? The thought stirred a flicker of sadness within me, but I pushed it aside. Whatever the circumstances, my grandfather's heart had never darkened, his light untouched by her shadow.

Before I could dwell further, a sudden burst of vibrant energy rippled through the air, pulling me from my thoughts. The lively chatter of the crowd stilled as the sea of guests parted once more, heads turning toward the source of the commotion.

"Amaya! Olivia!" Seraphine's silver hair streamed behind her as she rushed forward, her eyes sparkling with excitement. "Oh, look at you both! Absolutely stunning!"

Before I could respond, she swept us into a whirlwind embrace, her laughter ringing like a bell. Her energy was so infectious, I couldn't help but laugh with her, some of my earlier tension slipping away.

"Seraphine," I grinned as she released us, "I swear you bring the party with you wherever you go."

She winked, her navy eyes gleaming with mischief. "Someone has to keep things lively around here. This lot gets far too serious for my taste. Now, spill everything! How are you feeling? Are you ready for this grand adventure?"

Her rapid-fire questions and effervescent energy instantly brought joy to my soul. As she chattered, her vibrant presence filled the space with warmth, and I realized just how much I'd come to depend on this patchwork family of ours.

Over her shoulder, Kaelen caught my eye. His gaze softened, the love and pride there enough to make my heart skip a beat. In that moment, surrounded by this mismatched yet perfect group of people, I felt an unexpected surge of optimism.

"You know what?" I said, my fingers curling around Seraphine's hand as I smiled at her and then Kaelen. "I think I am ready. Whatever comes next, we'll face it together."

The warm atmosphere suddenly chilled as King Ignis emerged from the tree line, his stiff posture and tight-lipped expression starkly contrasting Seraphine's exuberance. The sunlight glinted off his crimson and gold ceremonial armor, giving him an imposing, almost otherworldly presence. His sharp eyes scanned the crowd, lingering briefly on each face before settling on Kaelen. A knot formed in my stomach as I watched his measured approach.

"Alpha," Ignis greeted, his voice low and tightly controlled. "Everything looks... impressive. It's fortunate that things with Magda have quieted, at least for now, to allow this opportunity for you and your Luna."

Kaelen nodded, his silver eyes meeting Ignis's fiery gaze with a calm intensity. "Thank you, Ignis. It's good to see you here. Are things in Aurelion progressing well? Your troops— are they battle-ready?"

A shadow flickered across Ignis's face, his jaw tightening almost imperceptibly. "We're prepared," he replied, his words clipped. "Troops stand ready to join the allied forces should another rift open. Goddess forbid it happens soon, but we'll be ready when it does."

Sensing the tension building between the two men, I stepped forward, forcing a smile to my lips. "King Ignis," I said, keeping my tone warm but steady. "It means a great deal to us that you're here."

His gaze flicked to me, sharp and assessing, before softening just enough to reveal the internal conflict simmering beneath his stoic exterior. "Luna Amaya," he said, inclining his head with deliberate politeness. "You look... radiant. It will be an honor to witness this ceremony and offer Aurelion's fire in unity with the other kingdoms."

"Thank you, Your Majesty," I replied, inclining my head. "Your presence, and Aurelion's support, means everything. A united front is precisely what we need in these times." I kept my voice steady, though I was keenly aware of his reservations about crossing magical bloodlines. That he was here at all was a testament to the importance of our shared cause.

At my side, Olivia slipped her hand into mine and gave it a reassuring squeeze. Her silent solidarity grounded me as the moment passed and the bustle of the crowd resumed.

Kaelen turned back to me, his expression unreadable but his touch steady as he placed a hand at the small of my back. Together, we watched as Ignis moved toward the gathering guests, his powerful form cutting a path through the throng.

"That went well," Olivia whispered, her Texan drawl laced with dry humor. I shot her a look, and she grinned, ever the steady source of levity in tense moments.

"Well," Seraphine chirped, her voice a little too bright as she tried to dispel the lingering tension, "shall we go over the procession order one more time? I'd hate to trip over my own feet and ruin all this finery!"

Her animated gestures and detailed descriptions of the ceremony's choreography drew a few chuckles from the nearby attendants. But as she continued, my thoughts drifted, spiraling into the worries I'd been trying so hard to suppress.

How many others felt like Ignis? How many of the guests here saw this union as a threat rather than a blessing? Would they ever fully accept me as Luna, or would my differences always set me apart?

"Amaya," Kaelen's deep, soothing voice cut through the noise in my mind. I looked up to find him standing beside me, concern etched into the strong lines of his face. "Are you alright?"

I forced a small smile, willing the knot in my chest to loosen. "Just nervous, I suppose. It's a lot to contemplate."

Kaelen nodded, his eyes understanding. "Remember," he said softly, his voice like a soothing balm, "we face this together. You are my kick-ass Luna, and you can take on anything that comes your way."

I couldn't help but grin at his words. As I leaned into the comforting strength of his presence, my gaze wandered across the throng of people. Ignis stood at a distance, his sharp features unreadable. For a fleeting moment, I thought I saw something flicker across his face—resignation, maybe jealousy —before he turned and disappeared into the crowd.

"Together," I whispered, as much to reassure myself as to affirm Kaelen's words. "No matter what comes next."

Taking a deep breath, I let the whirlwind of emotions settle. The bustling preparations around us faded into the background as I closed my eyes, mooring myself in the moment.

"I never dreamed this day would come," I murmured, the words tumbling out before I could stop them.

Kaelen tilted his head, his warm, steady presence anchoring me. "What's on your mind, little one?"

I opened my eyes, meeting his gaze. The intensity of his eyes both steadied and unraveled me. "Freedom," I whispered. "Belonging. For so long, they were just... fantasies. Impossible dreams I'd conjure up on endless nights in New York, alone and aching for something I couldn't name. I used to imagine a place where I would be loved and accepted. And now…"

"And now?" Kaelen prompted gently, his large hand resting reassuringly on the small of my back.

A shaky laugh escaped my lips. "Now that it's real—now that I have you and this pack—it feels like more than I deserve. But it also comes with a price. Doesn't anything worth having?"

Kaelen's eyes softened, his expression filled with quiet strength. "I'd pay any price if it meant being right here, with you."

I felt the tears threaten to fall, but I blinked them away, my heart swelling with gratitude. "I'm thankful to the Goddess that she blessed me with this unimaginable gift," I said, my voice thick with emotion. "She's literally given me everything I've ever wanted."

Kaelen pulled me closer, his lips brushing against my temple. "And you've given me everything I've ever needed."

In that moment, the storm inside me quieted, leaving only a sense of peace and resolve.

CHAPTER 24

Amaya

I stood at the edge of the natural amphitheater, my hand entwined with Kaelen's, feeling the warmth of his skin against mine. My heart raced, a mix of excitement and nerves coursing through my veins. I took a deep breath, inhaling the scent of pine and wildflowers that filled the air.

Kaelen's eyes met mine, a soft smile playing on his lips. "It's time, my love," he spoke, his deep voice sending a shiver down my spine.

I nodded, unable to find my voice. The weight of what we were about to do pressed down on me, both thrilling and terrifying.

As we took our first step forward, the crowd stood in hushed anticipation, their faces a blur of excitement and wonder. The colors of their clothes blended like a vibrant tapestry, their eyes reflecting the soft glow of the path ahead. Trees stretched towards the sky, their verdant leaves rustling in the wind. The path before us glowed with an otherworldly light, illuminating our way to the Heartstone.

"They're all watching us," I whispered, feeling the eyes of hundreds upon us.

Kaelen squeezed my hand reassuringly. "They're here to support us, to witness our union."

We moved slowly, deliberately, each step bringing us closer

to our destiny. The moss beneath our feet pulsed with a soft, ethereal light, as if the very earth was blessing our journey.

As we passed, I heard the murmurs of the pack and our allies. "Blessing upon you," one voice whispered. "May the Goddess smile upon your union," said another.

I felt a lump form in my throat, overwhelmed by the love and support surrounding us. For so long, I had been alone, fighting for survival. Now, I was part of something greater, about to bind myself to the man I loved and the pack that had become my family.

Kaelen's thumb traced circles on the back of my hand, a tender gesture that kept me focused on the moment. I looked up at him, astounded at the strength and grace he exuded. He looked so handsome, his cloak of fur draped regally over his broad shoulders. The moonstone circlet rested on his brow, catching the light like liquid silver. His blonde hair caught the moonlight, giving it a light all its own.

"I can still hardly believe this is happening," I confessed, my voice barely above a whisper.

Kaelen's eyes softened. "You deserve this and so much more, Amaya. I promise to spend the rest of our lives showing you just how cherished you are."

As we neared the Heartstone, its pulsing energy seemed to reach out to us, calling us forward. The significance of what we were about to do hit me anew. This wasn't just a ceremony; it was the beginning of our forever. Just months ago, I never could have imagined this would be my destiny.

The high priestess was a figure of ethereal beauty. She was like a divine statue brought to life, her silver robes flowing like a waterfall in the moonlight. As her arms rose, the air itself seemed to quiet, and the crowd held their breath in anticipation. And as her voice echoed through the night, it was as if her words were ancient magic, coursing through our veins and connecting us to something greater.

"Goddess Vesperia, Creator of our Realm, we call upon

you," she intoned, her words echoing through the forest.

I felt a surge of energy, like static electricity dancing across my skin. The surrounding air seemed to thicken, charged with an otherworldly power. My breath caught in my throat as I sensed the divine presence of Vesperia herself.

Kaelen's hand tightened around mine. I glanced up to see his eyes wide with awe, his jaw set in reverence. He felt it too, this connection to something greater than ourselves.

As the priestess's chant grew in intensity, I saw wisps of light gathering around us, swirling and pulsing in time with the Heartstone. It was beautiful and terrifying all at once.

"Are you ready?" Kaelen whispered, his gaze never leaving mine.

I swallowed hard and nodded. This was everything I'd ever wanted, yet feared I didn't deserve. "I... I am," I stammered.

Kaelen's expression softened. He turned to face me fully, taking both my hands in his. "Amaya Ilyndor," he began, his deep voice steady and filled with emotion. "From the moment I first saw you, I knew you were my Fated Mate. But you've become so much more than that."

My heart raced as he continued, "You are my partner, my equal, my heart. I vow to protect you, to cherish you, to stand by your side through whatever challenges we may face. I promise to be your shelter in the storm, your strength when you falter, and your biggest supporter in all your dreams."

Tears welled in my eyes as the weight of his words sank in. This wasn't just duty or fate. This was a choice, a commitment born of love.

"Our path may not always be easy," Kaelen said, his voice thick with emotion, "but I swear to you, on my life and on my crown, that I will never stop fighting for us, for our pack, and for the future we'll build together."

As he finished, I felt a warmth bloom in my chest, a sense of belonging I'd never known before. This was home. This was where I was meant to be.

I took a deep breath, steadying myself as I met Kaelen's intense silver gaze. My voice rang out clear and strong, belying the butterflies in my stomach.

"Kaelen Therionis," I began, "I stand before you not just as your Fated Mate, but as a woman who chooses you with everything I am." I squeezed his hands, drawing strength from his touch. "I vow to be your partner in all things, to face our challenges head-on, and to celebrate our triumphs together."

My voice wavered slightly as I continued, "I promise to be your anchor when the world storms around us, to support you in your duties as Alpha, and to remind you of the man you are behind the title." A tear slipped down my cheek, but I didn't falter. "I vow to love you fiercely, to challenge you when needed, and to stand by your side, come what may."

Kaelen's eyes shimmered with emotion, and I felt a surge of love so powerful it nearly took my breath away. "Fate may have initiated our bond," I said softly, "but our love is a choice I make gladly, every day. I promise to nurture it, to cherish it, and to let it guide us as we build our future together."

As I finished, the high priestess stepped forward, holding a shimmering cord woven from strands of Kaelen's fur and threads that pulsed with elemental magic. "Join hands," she instructed, her voice reverberating through the clearing.

Kaelen's large, warm hand enveloped mine, and I couldn't help but be amazed at the contrast—his strength, my delicacy, yet both equally vital to our union. The priestess wound the cord around our joined hands, each loop symbolizing a facet of our bond.

"With this cord," she intoned, "we bind your fates, your hearts, and your souls." The magic in the threads hummed against my skin, sending shivers down my spine. "As your hands are bound, so too are your destinies intertwined."

I looked up at Kaelen, seeing a mix of awe and love reflected in his eyes. This was it—the moment that would change everything. As the final loop was secured, I felt a surge of power rush through me, our connection stronger than ever before.

The binding cord began to glow, threads of silver and gold unraveling into glimmering filaments. They lifted from our wrists in slow, fluid swirls, transforming before our eyes. Stardust. Tiny sparks of light drifted upward, weightless and free, like a thousand tiny stars returning to the sky.

A soft gasp rippled through the crowd. The priestess's smile widened, serene and certain.

"The Goddess is pleased," she declared, her voice carrying the weight of prophecy. "Her light rises with you, and her favor rests upon your bond."

My heart swelled with the weight of it all—Kaelen's steady gaze, the warmth of his hands still clasped in mine, and the knowledge that something far greater than us had blessed this moment. The air shimmered with magic, and I could feel it— the universe had shifted.

Then his grip tightened. His eyes seemed to darken, turning from reverence to something far more primal.

"Amaya," he murmured, his deep voice sending shivers down my spine. "It's time for me to mark you. This time, the marking is more than just a bite. It's a fusion of our souls, a testament to our eternal bond."

I nodded, steeling myself. "I'm ready."

He lowered his head, his breath hot against my neck. I felt the scrape of his teeth, and then — Pain. Sharp and searing. It bloomed where his fangs pierced my skin. I gasped, my fingers digging into his shoulders. But as quickly as it came, the pain transmuted into something else entirely. A rush of warmth flooded through me, carrying with it flashes of Kaelen's memories, his emotions, his very essence.

"Oh," I breathed, overwhelmed by the intensity of our connection.

As Kaelen withdrew, I felt a spark of magic ignite between us, a visible manifestation of our bond. He pressed his forehead to mine, his eyes shining with love and wonder.

"My mate," he growled softly. "My everything."

Before I could respond, movement at the edge of the clearing caught my attention. Four figures approached, each radiating an aura of magical power.

"All the kingdoms of Eldoria give their blessings," Kaelen explained, his arm wrapping protectively around my waist.

The first to step forward was Grandpapa. "I bless your union with the adaptability of water and the strength of ice." He raised his hands, and a gentle mist enveloped us, leaving behind a cool, invigorating sensation.

Next came a Miranda. "May your bond be as unshakeable as the mountains and as nurturing as fertile soil." She touched the ground, and I felt a subtle vibration beneath my feet, as if the very earth was embracing us.

Ignis was next. "Let passion and warmth always kindle between you." With a gesture, he conjured a ring of harmless flames around us, their heat a comforting caress.

Cade came next, adding a drop of his blood to the Heartstone. "Let this blood represent life and unity for you and the realm."

As the royals retreated, I turned to Kaelen, overwhelmed by the beauty and power of the blessings we'd received. "Is it always like this?" I asked, my voice hushed with awe.

He smiled, a rare, unguarded expression that made my heart skip. "No, my love. This is something truly special—just like you."

I felt a shift in the air, a tingling sensation that made the hair on the back of my neck stand up. Olivia stepped forward, her dark tresses flowing around her like a living cloak. Her deep purple eyes seemed to glow with an otherworldly light as she approached us.

"Goddess, hear me," Olivia's voice rang out, clear and strong despite the informal drawl that usually colored her speech. Her hands emitted a soft, pulsing radiance. "I invoke your blessing upon this union."

As she spoke, I felt a warmth envelop me, like being wrapped in a cocoon of pure light. Kaelen's hand tightened around mine, and I knew he felt it too.

"By Your grace, Vesperia," Olivia continued, her voice gaining power, "protect these two souls. Guide them through the trials that await."

The light emanating from Olivia's hands intensified, bathing us in its glow. I gasped as I felt a presence - vast, ancient, and benevolent—brush against my consciousness.

"Is this... Her?" I whispered to Kaelen, my voice trembling.

He nodded, his eyes wide with reverence. "The Goddess herself," he murmured.

As the divine presence retreated, leaving behind a lingering sense of peace and protection, Kaelen straightened. His posture shifted, and I recognized the Alpha asserting himself.

"It's time," he said, his deep voice carrying easily through the amphitheater.

Kaelen threw his head back and let out a howl that seemed to shake the very trees. The sound reverberated through my body, awakening something primal within me. Around us, the pack joined in, regardless of the animal, big cat, fowl, and otherwise, their voices melding into a haunting chorus that spoke of unity, strength, and wild freedom.

I joined in, my voice blending seamlessly with the cries of the pack. In that moment, I felt more connected to Kaelen, to the pack, to this world than I ever had before. We were one—bound by love, by magic, by destiny.

As the howl faded, Kaelen turned to me, his eyes shining with pride and love. "Welcome home, my mate," he said, his voice husky with emotion.

I smiled back, feeling the weight of our new status settle upon me. No longer just Amaya, but the Alpha's mate, Luna, protector of the pack. It was daunting, exhilarating, and completely right.

I swallowed hard, my heart pounding as Kaelen guided me towards a small altar of rough-hewn stone. Atop it sat an ornate silver chalice, its surface etched with ancient runes that seemed to shimmer in the moonlight.

"One last thing." Kaelen's voice was low, meant only for my ears.

I nodded, unable to find my voice. The significance of what we were about to do weighed heavily on me.

Kaelen lifted the chalice, his movements fluid and reverent. "With this offering, we bind ourselves not just to each other, but to the land and our people," he explained, his eyes locked on mine.

I watched, transfixed, as he brought the rim of the chalice to his hand. Without hesitation, he drew a small ceremonial dagger across his skin. Blood welled up, dark and rich, dripping into the chalice.

"Your turn, love," he murmured, offering me the dagger.

My hands trembled as I took it. "I've never..." I whispered, fear and anticipation warring within me.

Kaelen's free hand cupped my cheek, his touch anchoring me. "I'm here, always."

Taking a deep breath, I pressed the blade to my hand. The sting was sharp but brief. I watched, mesmerized, as my blood joined Kaelen's in the chalice.

"Earth of Therionis," Kaelen intoned, his voice carrying across the amphitheater. "We offer our lifeblood, a symbol of our dedication to this land and its people."

Together, we tipped the chalice, letting our mingled blood spill onto the forest floor. The earth seemed to drink it in eagerly, and for a moment, I swore I felt a pulse of energy beneath my feet.

"It's done," I breathed, a sense of awe washing over me.

Kaelen nodded, his eyes shining with pride and love. "We are one with the land now, as we are one with each other."

The high priestess stepped forward, her arms raised to the star-studded sky. "Great Goddess Vesperia," she called out, her voice resonating with power, "we ask for your final blessing upon this union."

A hush fell over the gathering as the priestess chanted in an ancient tongue. The surrounding air seemed to thicken, charged with an otherworldly energy that made the hairs on my arms stand on end.

Suddenly, a warm breeze swept through the amphitheater, carrying with it the scent of wildflowers and pine. Tiny motes of light, like fireflies made of stardust, swirled around Kaelen and me.

"Ooh," I gasped, watching in wonder as the lights danced across our skin.

Kaelen's grip on my hand tightened. "It feels extraordinary." He whispered, his voice filled with awe.

I nodded, unable to speak. The magic in the air was palpable, wrapping around us like a warm embrace. It felt like coming home, like finding a piece of myself I never knew was missing.

As the lights faded, and the breeze died down, the high priestess lowered her arms. "It is done," she declared. "May your union be blessed, your love eternal, and your reign long and prosperous."

I turned to Kaelen, my heart so full it felt like it might burst. "I love you," I said, my voice barely above a whisper.

He pulled me close, his forehead resting against mine. "This is just the beginning, my love," he murmured. "Our greatest adventure starts now."

As we stood there, surrounded by our pack and blessed by the Goddess herself, I felt a surge of hope and excitement for the future. Whatever challenges lay ahead, we would face them together - as mates, as partners, as one.

The forest exploded into a cacophony of joyous howls and cheers. I laughed as Kaelen swept me off my feet, spinning me in a circle before setting me down amidst the sea of well-wishers. The scent of roasting meat and sweet honey cakes filled the air, mingling with the earthy aroma of the forest.

"Come, my Luna," Kaelen said, his silver eyes twinkling. "Let's celebrate."

We made our way through the crowd, accepting hugs and congratulations. The pack had transformed the clearing into a festive wonderland. Lanterns hung from tree branches, casting a warm glow over everything. Tables groaned under the weight of food and drink, while a group of musicians struck up a lively tune.

"May I have this dance?" Kaelen asked, offering his hand with a playful bow.

I grinned, taking it. "I thought you'd never ask."

As we twirled across the forest floor, I caught glimpses of our friends and family. Olivia danced with Cade, her face flushed with laughter.

"Are you happy?" Kaelen murmured in my ear.

I pulled back to look at him, struck once again by the intensity of his gaze. "More than I ever thought possible," I admitted. "But as well... anxious."

His brow furrowed. "About what, little wolf?"

"The transformation," I whispered, glancing at the sky. The moon was climbing higher, a constant reminder of what was to come. "I know I'm strong enough... I guess it's just the unknown. What if it's too hard?"

Kaelen's arms tightened around me. "You're more powerful than you know, Amaya. And I'll be with you every step of the way."

I nodded, trying to draw strength from his confidence. As the night wore on, I found myself watching the moon's progress, ready to get to it. Finally, as it neared its zenith, Kaelen appeared at my side.

"It's time," he said softly.

My heart thundered in my chest as we made our way to

the ancient cathedral. Our closest friends and family followed, their earlier jubilation replaced by a solemn anticipation. The stone walls of the cathedral loomed before us, etched with runes that seemed to pulse with an inner light.

The bioluminescent glow of the flowers had dimmed, replaced by a shimmering barrier of light created by the Dragonia. Their presence was both awe-inspiring and reassuring, their immense forms gleaming like living gemstones under the moonlight.

Vaelith, the leader of the Dragonia, stepped forward, his voice low and resonant as he addressed Olivia. *"We will shield this place while she fights for control. The Goddess wills it."*

Olivia turned to me, her expression soft but determined. "The Goddess's blessing is with you, Amaya. She sent the Dragonia to protect this space and give you the privacy you need to go through your transformation. They'll stay until you've shown your wolf who's boss, my itty bitty girl."

Tears pricked my eyes, and I pulled Olivia into a fierce hug. "Thank you, Ollie, for letting me know—and for just being you."

She sniffled, patting my back with a lighthearted grin despite the gravity of the moment. "You've got this, sweet girl. Show that beast who's in charge."

Kaelen's warm hand found mine as I turned to face him. "Ready or not, it's time, little wolf," he said, his eyes searching mine for any hesitation.

I took a deep breath, trying to steady my racing heart. "I guess I'm ready, then."

Together, we stepped into the cathedral. The cool stone floor beneath my bare feet was a stark contrast to the fire building inside me, and I welcomed its reassuring presence as panic clawed at my edges.

I had exchanged my ceremonial gown for a simple, loose robe—anything else would have been pointless now.

The air inside the cathedral was alive, thrumming with

ancient, untamed magic that seemed to pulse with the rhythm of my heartbeat.

"Breathe, little wolf," Kaelen whispered, his hand steady on the small of my back.

I obeyed, drawing in a shaky breath as I tilted my face toward the glass dome above. Moonlight streamed through, cool and silver, bathing the space in a holy radiance. As the light touched my skin, a jolt of raw energy surged through me, sharp and electric.

I gasped, clutching Kaelen's arm for support. The transformation was beginning.

"It's starting," I breathed, fear and exhilaration warring within me.

The first wave of pain hit like a freight train, and I stumbled. Kaelen caught me effortlessly, lowering us both to the ground with infinite care. "I'm here," he murmured, his voice steady and sure. "Let it come."

A guttural groan escaped me as my bones began to shift, the sensation foreign and excruciating. Memories surged behind my eyes, sharp and unwanted. The cell. The suffocating darkness. Olivia's screams.

"No," I whimpered, shaking my head violently, trying to banish the images.

Kaelen's voice cut through the haze, rich and commanding. "Stay with me, Amaya. You're safe. You're loved."

I clung to his words like a lifeline as another spasm tore through me. My skin felt too tight, my muscles igniting with searing heat as they twisted and reformed. Through the fog of agony, I caught fleeting glimpses of the others—Olivia's face was taut with worry, the high priestess's serene expression glowing in the moonlight, and the Dragonia's barrier shimmering faintly in the background.

"I can't," I gasped, my breath hitching as tears streamed down my face. "It hurts too much."

Kaelen cupped my cheek, his touch centering me, his eyes

fierce with determination. "You can," he said, his voice low but unwavering. "You've survived worse, my love. This pain will pass, and you'll emerge stronger. You were born for this."

I nodded weakly, his words igniting a flicker of hope within me. Another wave of pain slammed into me, and suddenly, memories rose unbidden—Olivia in the foster home, small and scared, while I stood helpless. My body convulsed as the scene morphed into the sting of cruel taunts from bullies, their laughter echoing in my ears.

My wolf's voice growled through my mind, mocking me. *"Pathetic. You'll shift and stay a wolf forever. You're too weak to control me."*

"No!" I screamed back, both aloud and in my mind. "You cannot beat me!"

The searing pain intensified, my bones breaking and reforming, every nerve alive with fire. A scream ripped from my throat as fur sprouted across my skin. My senses exploded —colors burning brighter, scents flooding my awareness in dizzying waves. I was changing, no longer fighting the inevitable.

This time, I embraced it.

"LISTEN TO ME, WOLF!" My voice echoed in the space between us, a battle cry in my mind. *"You are subject to ME! This is MY body, my soul. I'll share it with you. We'll run together, free and strong, but you will NEVER take control from me. I will decide when we shift. I am the Alpha here."*

The wolf stilled, her growls softening into a low, rumbling hum. Then, I felt it—a bowing of her will to mine. Respect. Submission. A surge of love and pride radiated from her, wrapping around me like a warm embrace.

Relief flooded through me, and with it, a fierce, primal joy. I had done it. I had claimed my wolf, not as an enemy to defeat but as a partner, a piece of me to cherish.

Kaelen's voice reached me, filled with awe. "Amaya... you did it."

I lifted my head, feeling the power of my new form coursing through every fiber of my being. I wasn't just Amaya anymore. I was more. Stronger. Whole.

And I was ready.

Kaelen's dire wolf appeared before me, his massive form radiating strength and reassurance. His familiar scent—pine, earth — wrapped around me like a comforting blanket, settling me in this new reality.

"You did it," his voice echoed warmly in my mind, a steady presence that soothed the last remnants of doubt. "Look at yourself, my beautiful mate."

I turned, catching sight of my reflection in the polished surface of a ceremonial stone. A great white wolf stared back at me, her fur shimmering like freshly fallen snow under the moonlight. Her luminous blue-green eyes, so familiar yet transformed, glowed with power and pride.

My wolf.

For the first time in years, I felt whole. Complete. The cracks and fractures that had splintered my soul seemed to mend in that instant, a sensation as wondrous as it was overwhelming.

"You are beautiful, wolf," I whispered in my mind, unsure if it was for her or for myself.

She preened under the compliment, a playful puff of pride rising from her. Her joy became mine, and I threw my head back, unleashing a howl that carried every ounce of triumph, relief, and sheer exhilaration I felt.

The pack answered, their voices blending with mine in a symphony of celebration. Each note wrapped around me like an embrace, solidifying the bond I now shared with them. I wasn't just accepted—I was one of them.

Kaelen's wolf stepped closer, his eyes glowing with unrestrained admiration. He brushed his muzzle against mine, a gesture both tender and reverent.

In that moment, surrounded by my new family, wrapped

in Kaelen's unwavering love, I knew I had found my true home. The fragmented pieces of my life—past pain, fleeting hope, and relentless perseverance—had come together in this single, perfect moment.

A memory surfaced, bright and vivid: my dream of our wolves running side by side through the forest, free and unstoppable.

It wasn't just a dream; I realized. *It was a promise.*

Excitement surged through me, an irrepressible urge to move, to run. I took a few tentative steps on my new legs, marveling at the effortless grace of my movements. With a mischievous growl, I nipped at Kaelen's flank, daring him to follow.

His wolf let out a playful bark, his body tensing in anticipation.

And then I sprang forward, bursting out of the cathedral and into the forest. The wind rushed past me, the scents of pine and earth filling my heightened senses. Each stride felt like freedom incarnate, my heart pounding with exhilaration as my white paws blurred against the forest floor.

Kaelen was right behind me, his powerful form a golden blur as he kept pace. Together, we raced beneath the moonlit canopy, our howls echoing through the trees—a celebration of love, unity, and the boundless joy of finding where we belonged.

CHAPTER 25

Kaelen

The first rays of morning light filtered through the trees, casting a golden glow upon our naked forms intertwined on the forest floor. I blinked awake slowly, my body still thrumming with the intimacy Amaya and I had shared all night after shifting back to our human forms from our wolves. Fatigue weighed heavy on my limbs, but it was a blissful sort of exhaustion, born from love and a primal connection.

As I gazed down at Amaya's sleeping face nestled against my chest, a fierce protectiveness surged through me, warring with the deep yearning she always stirred in my soul. Her blonde curls fanned out like silk threads, her rose-petal lips slightly parted. I ached to wake her with gentle kisses, to lose myself once more in her intoxicating scent and touch.

But I also knew I had a duty to keep her safe, especially now when she was so vulnerable in sleep's embrace. Our people would begin stirring in these early morning hours, and while shifters were notorious for our lack of modesty, Amaya was still new to our world. I doubted she'd appreciate being paraded before our pack in such a state of undress. I needed to get her back to the secure walls of our keep where she could rest and prepare for the day.

With the utmost care, I gathered Amaya's delicate form into my arms, cradling her against my bare chest as if she were the most precious treasure in Therionis. She sighed softly and nuzzled closer, but did not wake.

"I've got you, my heart, my Luna," I murmured, pressing a reverent kiss to her brow. "No one will cast their eyes upon you until you are comfortable with the idea, as long as I draw breath."

As much as I wanted to linger in our quiet forest haven, I knew we were vulnerable every moment, not knowing when Magda would strike again. I hated we couldn't rest easy until she was defeated. With one last look at the beauty of nature that had sheltered our intimacy throughout the night, I began the short trek home, my sleeping mate held securely in the protective circle of my arms, ready to face whatever challenges the day held.

The cool morning air caressed my bare skin as I carried Amaya through the tranquil forest, my body heat keeping her warm as I traversed the well-worn path. Shafts of golden sunlight pierced the canopy of leaves in various sizes, creating a mesmerizing dance of light and shadow across the moss and stones I traveled. The soft rustle of leaves underfoot and the gentle sway of branches overhead created a soothing symphony that added to the profound peace I felt in this moment. I had long dreamed of finding my Fated Mate and had all but given up hope of her existence when Amaya all but fell into my life.

I gave a small whisper of thanks to Vesperia. "Thank you, Goddess."

As we journeyed toward the keep, the forest stirred to life around us, a symphony of sounds and movements that mirrored the vibrant pulse of our people. Birds trilled their morning greetings, their melodies weaving through the trees, while squirrels darted across the underbrush in playful abandon. In the distance, the faint scent of a grazing deer herd drifted on the breeze, a reminder of the abundance and balance within our lands. Pride swelled in my chest. This was our kingdom, thriving under our leadership, a sanctuary for all who called it home.

Amaya's soft, steady breathing brushed against my neck, a gentle whisper that grounded me in the moment. Her warmth nestled against me, her trust implicit even in sleep. I held her a little closer, my heart swelling knowing that she was mine —my Fated Mate, my Luna. The bond we shared vibrated like a living thing between us, a connection forged by the Goddess herself. It transcended words and touch, uniting our very souls in an unbreakable harmony.

As the keep came into view, its weathered stone walls rising proudly from the forest like a sentinel, a renewed sense of purpose settled over me. Each step I took was deliberate, carrying us closer to the sanctuary of our quarters, that sacred place meant for only us. The sentries on duty straightened as I approached, their heads bowing in deference. Their gazes reflected respect and admiration—not just for their Alpha, but for the Luna cradled in my arms.

Inside our chambers, the familiar scents of home wrapped around us. I crossed to the bed, gently laying Amaya down on the plush furs that adorned it. She stirred slightly but didn't wake, her golden curls creating a halo across the dark pelts. The soft light filtering through the windows kissed her skin, adding a light and glow to her beautiful form. I stood there for a moment, entranced by her beauty and the sheer weight of my love for her.

With a tender touch, I brushed my fingers against her cheek, reluctant to break the quiet reverence of the moment. Finally, I turned toward the adjoining bathing chamber, intent on preparing a soothing bath for my mate. The forest floor had left its mark on both of us, and the thought of washing away the dirt and sweat while caring for her brought a smile to my lips.

As I worked, filling the basin with warm water, my thoughts drifted. I imagined the life we would build together, one of peace after the battles with Magda and her minions were finally won. But I pushed those distant worries aside. For now, this morning was ours—a brief, perfect reprieve from the chaos of the world. Here, in the sanctuary of our chambers, surrounded by the soft light of dawn and the promise of a shared future, I allowed myself to dream of eternity with the woman who had become my entire world.

The water cascaded over my hands as I filled the oversized marble tub, steam curling upward in delicate tendrils. The scents of lavender and chamomile mingled with the warm air, their calming presence a silent promise of comfort. Each movement was deliberate, a physical manifestation of the love and care I held for Amaya. I poured fragrant oils into the water, watching them swirl in mesmerizing patterns across the surface, the ripples echoing the quiet peace settling over my soul.

Amaya's face drifted to the forefront of my thoughts, as it often did. My mate—strong, resilient, breathtakingly beautiful inside and out. She'd faced trials that would have broken most, yet she stood unwavering, a beacon of hope and determination. That inner light captivated me, pulling me toward her as surely as the moon guides the tides. I knew, with every fiber of my being, that together we would build a life forged in love, trust, and the indestructible bond of true mates.

Lost in my thoughts, the soft padding of footsteps behind me almost escaped my notice. I turned, and there she stood in the doorway, a vision that almost stole the breath from my lungs. Amaya's golden hair fell in loose waves around her shoulders, her eyes heavy with sleep but alight with affection. She wore a shy smile, one that made my chest tighten with a deep and unshakable love.

"Kaelen," she murmured, her voice rough with sleep but filled with affection. "You didn't have to do all this for me."

I crossed the distance between us in two quick strides, my hands finding her waist and pulling her close. She fit against me perfectly, two halves of the same whole.

"It's my pleasure, sweet girl," I said, my voice low. "Though I'll admit, you're pretty gorgeous, even covered in dirt, leaves, and all."

Her gaze dropped to her body, and her laughter bubbled up, light and adorable. "Oh, my stars! I'm a mess!" She shook her head, her grin contagious. "Well, I guess it's a good thing you want to pamper me, then. But first..."

She reached up, her fingers tracing the contours of my face with deliberate tenderness. Her touch was electric, leaving warmth in its wake as if she were etching her love directly onto my skin. I closed my eyes, surrendering to the moment.

In that instant, the world beyond these walls ceased to exist. There were only us—two souls bound by a force older than time itself. As her fingers explored, mapping every line and angle of my face, I felt the weight of our connection, the deep and abiding truth that we were meant for this, for each other.

Her voice, barely a whisper, broke the silence. "You're everything to me, Kaelen. You know that, don't you?"

Our lips met in a searing kiss, a collision of passion and desire that threatened to consume us both. I poured every ounce of my love, my devotion, into that kiss, my hands exploring the soft, delicate curves of her body, committing every inch of her to memory. Amaya responded with equal fervor, her fingers tangling in my hair as she pulled me impossibly closer, our bodies molding together, evidence of two becoming one.

With a strength that felt effortless, I lifted her into my arms, never breaking the connection between us. The fragrant steam from the waiting tub swirled around us as I gently lowered her into the warm water. Her contented sighs were my reward, sending a surge of satisfaction through me.

"This feels amazing," she murmured, her eyes fluttering closed as she sank into the soothing embrace of the bath.

"Is your body sore, my Luna?" I asked, a touch of concern coloring my voice.

She tilted her head, considering the question before breaking into a soft chuckle. "You know, it actually isn't." Her smile turned mischievous. "How is that even possible? After everything my body went through last night... I mean, seriously. My bones were literally breaking as I shifted! Not to mention all the ways you twisted and turned me all night long... Not that I'm complaining. Twist me and turn me anytime you want to!"

Her giggles filled the room, and I couldn't stop the grin that spread across my face. She was utterly enchanting, and I was utterly captivated.

"That, my exquisite Luna, is one of the many gifts of being a shifter." I knelt by the tub, my gaze locked on her glowing face. "I wasn't entirely certain how much of shifter magic you'd inherit as a hybrid, but it seems accelerated healing is definitely part of your magical arsenal."

She leaned her head back against the edge of the tub, her laughter softening into a warm smile. "Well, that's good to know. But..." Her eyes flicked up to meet mine, a shy yet playful look in their depths. "I was really enjoying the way you were pampering me, so I'm not ready for you to stop just yet."

A low chuckle rumbled in my chest. "I could spend my life with my hands on you, my love. It would never be enough."

I grabbed a soft cloth, pouring a generous amount of lavender-scented soap onto it before gently lathering her skin. The scent filled the air, blending with the steam in a way that felt like pure serenity.

"This soap," I explained as I ran the cloth over her shoulders, "is made by one of our fox families. They have a gift for creating things like this—beautiful, soothing, and entirely unique to Therionis."

"It smells heavenly, Kaelen," she murmured, leaning forward as I worked the cloth down her back, washing away the remnants of dirt and leaves from the forest. "I can't wait to meet them and learn about how they make it. Ahh, that feels wonderful."

I moved to her arms, washing them with the same care, watching as the water lapped softly against her glowing skin.

"Your turn to scoot back, baby," I said, my voice low and warm as I stripped away what little barrier still separated us. "Let me join you."

She did as I asked and moved to the back of the large marble tub so I could sit across from her. I took her foot in my hand and washed up her calf to her thigh, my eyes never leaving hers, as I massaged her muscles along the way.

"You could always get a job as a massage therapist if you ever lose a challenge for Alpha, you know," she quipped.

"Well, I'd likely be dead, so it would be difficult."

She suddenly sat up, sloshing water over the side of the tub.

"Never say that! Not even joking! My heart cannot stand the thought of it." Her eyes were suddenly shiny with unshed tears.

"Come here, sweetheart. I was only joking."

I pulled her to me, so she straddled my lap. Cupping her face in my hands, I wiped a tear with my thumb. "I'm sorry to upset you. But baby, I'm right here. No worries." I kissed her lips. "I'm not going anywhere." Another kiss. "You're stuck with me." Kiss. "Forever."

Amaya kissed me back with an intensity that spoke of desperation. Her tongue filled my mouth and her fingers tangled in my hair. Her body moved against mine. I lifted her, turned, and sat her on the wide ledge of the bathtub.

"Sit right there, Luna." Her feet were still in the tub on either side of me as I faced her. "Now, put your feet on my shoulders."

"Your shoulders?"

"Don't make your Alpha tell you twice, Luna." She

immediately put her feet upon my shoulders, opening herself up to me.

"There is not a more beautiful bare pussy in this realm, sweetheart. I am going to lap every drop of your wetness until you're whimpering your release. Does that sound like something you'd like, Luna?"

"Oh, Goddess, yes, Alpha."

I took my hands and pulled her ass toward me as she gripped the sides of the tub. With the first swipe of my tongue through her wetness, my wolf gave a soft, guttural growl. Much to my delight, Maya's wolf answered with a beautiful growl of her own. I lapped and sucked, then, making my tongue as stiff as possible, I used it to enter her gorgeous opening. I thrust it in and out, as deep as I could, over and over until Maya's head fell back, lost in the feeling. When I withdrew, her whine told me of her displeasure, but only for a moment until my fingers replaced my tongue. I sank my index and middle fingers in and out of her until her moans filled the room. Then I leaned down, licked and then sucked her clit while pumping my fingers in and out of her slick opening and she shattered almost immediately, her body shuddering with her release.

"Kaelen!! Yes, that, there, god, so good."

"Now, my little Luna," I told her, "we are definitely not done."

I picked her up, wrapped her in a fluffy towel, and carried her to our bed, setting her down gently.

"Wait right there."

I set the bed up the way I wanted it then; I positioned her over a stack of pillows, her ass presented high in the air. "Godsdamnit, Luna, your ass is exquisite. Are you comfortable?"

"Yes, Alpha," she answered, her head turned to the side on her crossed arms.

I rubbed my hands down her back a few times, loving the way I raised gooseflesh with each stroke. Reaching down between her legs, I found the wetness I knew would be waiting for me. Then I slipped my fingers back into her tight entrance and was rewarded with her sweet whimpers and moans.

"You make the prettiest sounds, Maya. Never hold them back."

"Mmmm hmmm."

Goddess, she made me happy.

In one motion, I entered her.

"ALPHA!" she gasped.

I rocked in and out of her. "Are you good, Luna?"

"Mmm. Perfect."

That was all I needed to hear.

Goddess help me, there was no going slow or easy with this woman. I gave her as good as she took. Reaching around, I rubbed her clit, slick with her own arousal. It didn't take long until she cried out with another release, her movements causing her beautiful ass to move in a way that felt like heaven. My knot expanded as I got closer to my release. The larger my knot, the louder Amaya's moans.

"I'm going to come again, Alpha!" Her body writhed with her release, and the feeling was too incredible for words.

I wanted to make the feeling last, but even I was not man enough to hold back, as my own release soon followed. I grunted as I moved as much as my knot allowed. I swear I saw the moon and stars.

"Luna! You undo me." I managed between breaths before I crashed down beside her, pulling her to my side, still connected. I lay there for a few minutes until I noticed her breaths were slow and rhythmic. As my knot subsided, I rose, grabbed a warm cloth from the washroom, and gently cleaned her before holding her close to me. She looked up at me with such adoration and love.

"Alpha, you are everything to me."

I took a moment to admire the ethereal beauty before me. Her golden hair fanned out like spun silk, her skin glowing in the soft light of the morning sun. "I will spend every day of my life showing you how much I love you."

Amaya's eyes shone with a love so profound it stole the very breath from my lungs. "And I will spend every day loving you, my fierce Alpha, my soulmate," she whispered, her voice steady and filled with conviction.

I brushed a strand of her golden hair away from her face, letting my fingers linger against her soft skin. The way she looked at me, like I was her entire world, made my chest ache with emotions too big to name.

As we lay there, wrapped in the warmth of each other, the memories of the night before surfaced in my mind—her courage, her determination, her unyielding strength in the transformation's face.

"You were incredible last night," I murmured, my voice thick with awe and pride. "The way you controlled your wolf, the strength and grace you showed... Amaya, you are truly a remarkable woman."

She leaned into my touch, her eyes fluttering closed as a soft sigh escaped her lips. "I couldn't have done it without you, Kaelen," she admitted, her voice tender. "Your love, your support... It gives me the strength to face anything."

Her words filled me with a pride so fierce it felt like it could split me in two. I tilted her chin up gently, forcing her to meet my gaze.

"I meant what I said, Amaya. You are my bad-ass Luna. The Goddess makes no mistakes. You are exactly what our people need at this moment in time. A fighter. Someone brave enough to stand against whatever Magda sends our way." My voice dropped, carrying the full weight of my belief in her. "That fighter is you, Maya. You fight for those you love. That's why our kingdom is the most blessed of all."

Her smile bloomed, radiant and filled with a love so pure it made me believe in the impossible. She reached up, tracing the line of my jaw with her fingertips. "Together, we can face anything," she said, her voice steady with quiet determination. Her eyes softened, glistening with unshed tears. "I think it's going to be love that defeats this force of evil, Kaelen. Genuine love. That's the strongest magic of all."

Her words resonated deep in my soul, igniting a fire I'd never known before her. I pulled her close, my lips brushing hers in a kiss that was more promise than passion. Together, we would fight. Together, we would triumph.

And together, we would prove that love was the most unbreakable bond of all.

CHAPTER 26

Olivia

The glass walls of the Crystal Citadel loomed around me as I strode into the council chamber, my heart heavy with the weight of the premonition that had haunted my dreams. The gathered leaders fell silent as I entered, their faces a mix of concern and determination. The air was thick with urgency, a collective awareness that time was running out.

"Thank you all for coming on such short notice," I began, my voice steady despite the fact that I felt like I had a three-ring circus performing in my gut. "As you know, I saw a vision of an impending attack. We're all aware that Magda has been tirelessly working to reopen the rifts since I closed them after the last assault. This dream—vision—or whatever the frick it was, felt like the Goddess warning us that the heifer is close to figuring out a solution to getting the rifts goin' again."

Miranda leaned forward, her dark curls spilling over her shoulders, worry clouding her eyes. "What can we do, Olivia? How do you think we should prepare?"

I drew in a deep breath, my gaze sweeping over the assembled leaders. "We need to strengthen our patrols and heighten our vigilance. Our best defense is having as many varied patrols in as many regions of Eldoria as possible. Grandpapa," I turned toward Farin, "how has the progress on the command center builds been?"

Farin's rugged features softened slightly as he stepped forward, unrolling a large map onto the crystal conference table. The aerial view of Eldoria glimmered in the sunlight streaming through the walls. "We've constructed command centers in all major quadrants of the realm." He gestured to the map, tracing a finger across its corners. "As you can see, we've got centers covering the north, south, east, west, and the central regions. In addition, there are sub-hubs—smaller barracks designed for troops who aren't actively patrolling to rest, eat, and recoup before their rotations."

He paused, his voice steady and confident as he continued. "Each sub-hub houses 100 troops, and they work in eight-hour shifts to ensure everyone remains sharp and alert. Altogether, we've established 200 sub-hubs scattered across the realm, supporting the command posts. When an attack occurs, the command centers can quickly direct sub-hub troops to respond to the locations. This way, we'll be able to handle multiple rift openings simultaneously."

I stood silent for a moment, utterly stunned at the precision and care that had gone into my grandfather's strategy. The enormity of his plan hit me like a wave, each detail meticulously thought out.

"Grandpapa," I said, my voice tinged with awe, "this... this is brilliant."

Farin's lips curved into a faint smile. "We've all been preparing for this, Olivia. And we'll be ready when she makes her move."

Miranda nodded, her worry momentarily giving way to determination. "With this network in place, we stand a real chance of keeping Eldoria safe."

I placed my hands on the edge of the table, leaning forward as resolve filled me. "Then let's make sure every leader, every soldier, and every citizen knows the plan. We're not just going to defend Eldoria—we're going to show Magda that her darkness has no place in our world."

The leaders around the table murmured their agreement, their collective determination palpable. This was our stand, our fight. And we would be ready.

"Grandpapa, you are a miracle. Thank the Goddess for you."

"Child, stop that," Farin said with a dismissive wave of his hand. "I'm just using my base of knowledge to help get things done."

"Alright then," I said with a small grin. "Has everyone gotten their people assigned to these sub-hubs?"

Miranda spoke up, her tone cautious. "Well... *most* of us have."

I blinked, stunned. *"Most?"* My voice rose, sharp with disbelief. "We don't have complete troops of every type of magic in the realm set and ready to fight?"

As my gaze swept across the room, it landed on the one person I suspected was dragging their feet. "Ignis."

The King of Aurelion bristled under my stare, his fiery red hair catching the light as he straightened in his seat. "Now hold on there, Olivia," he huffed, his tone defensive.

"Hold on?" I shot back, my hands planting firmly on the table. "How many troops have you sent to join up with those of other magical orders?"

"Well..." Ignis hesitated, his jaw tightening. "None, at this time."

My mouth fell open in disbelief. "None? Are you kidding me, Ignis? That's a problem. Do you want your people to die? Because trust me on this one, buster—Magda will *kill you.* Then she'll systematically wipe out your entire kingdom. And *why?* Because you don't want to take a chance on your people falling in love with someone who wields a different magic than they do? That is plain horse doo-doo, Ignis. For cryin' out loud! People from a different magical order? Those people have *already* fought and bled for *your* people! You are being a selfish, bigoted piece of—"

"Starlight, my darling," Cade interjected smoothly, placing

a calming hand on my shoulder.

Cade

I needed to step in before Olivia strangled Ignis.

"Ignis," I began, keeping my tone calm but firm, "you understand Olivia has firsthand knowledge about this and is understandably passionate. But is there another reason you've not added your troops to the rest of the realm's joint forces?"

Ignis hesitated, his gaze darting around the room like he was searching for an escape route. After some half-hearted excuses and a bit more hemming and hawing, he finally admitted the truth.

"This is... difficult for my people," he said, his voice strained. "You must understand. We aren't used to co-mingling with other kingdoms. Our traditions have always kept us... separate."

I couldn't believe what I was hearing. Olivia's face was turning redder by the second, and I knew I had little time before her frustration boiled over.

"Well, Ignis," I said, keeping my tone even though my patience was fraying, "you won't *have* a kingdom if you don't compel your people to join forces. We've been providing protection for Aurelion just like every other part of Eldoria, often at significant cost. Many have sacrificed, including myself."

"Now," I continued, leaning forward slightly, "I suggest you immediately speak to your generals, to ready thousands of your troops, and have them stationed at the command centers and sub-hubs by this evening. Otherwise, I'm afraid Olivia might be... *compelled* to visit Aurelion with the Dragonia. And I'm fairly certain they'll have no trouble convincing your troops if you can't."

Ignis paled slightly, his fiery demeanor dampened. "Do not define us by our magical orders today, Ignis," I added, my voice soft but resolute. "We are not separate kingdoms right now.

We are Eldorians. All of us. And we're trying to save our realm."

There was a long pause before Ignis finally nodded, sufficiently chastened. "Cade, you're absolutely right," he admitted, his tone subdued. "I will command our generals to ready our troops immediately. I'll have the list of names sent to Farin by dusk." He turned to Farin, his expression tinged with regret. "Just tell me which quadrant sub-hubs they need to report to and who their commanding officer will be."

"Absolutely, Ignis. And thank you," Farin replied with his usual grace. Ever the diplomat, his kind tone helped smooth the tension in the room.

Ignis straightened, his shoulders squared. "It sounds like we're up against it, based on Olivia's recent vision. I think it's wise to take this seriously."

Olivia stepped forward, her fiery spirit undimmed despite the long battle of words.

"Listen, y'all," she said, her drawl thickening as her passion took over. "Magda's gonna be pissed and meaner than usual. I shut down those rifts for a couple of weeks, and when she finally gets them reopened, she's gonna be loaded for bear. We gotta be ready."

She paced as she spoke, her words hitting like hammer strikes. "Get locked and loaded with every weapon we've got in the arsenal. Heck, create some new ones if we can. She'll want her pound of flesh—*my flesh*, most likely. But she won't stop at me. Unfortunately, she'll go through every one of y'all to get it. So you *must* be ready." Her brow was worried.

"And don't forget," she added, her gaze sweeping the room, "she's still tryin' to get through that barrier herself. I don't know what it's gonna take for her to figure it out, but I'd just about bet the farm she will. So we gotta stay on our toes."

I leaned over and kissed her forehead, hoping to break some of the tension in the room. "If you're like me," I said, addressing the council with a wry smile, "you probably didn't catch half of what she just said. But I *think* to sum it up: Magda is coming. And she won't stop until she has Eldoria in her grasp."

I looked around the table, my voice steady and unyielding. "We will not let that happen."

The room broke out in a chorus of agreement, the collective determination palpable.

"With that," I said, addressing the gathered leaders, "I think we can adjourn this meeting. Let's get back to our kingdoms and make sure our people are prepared to deploy to their assigned locations."

One by one, the leaders rose, nodding their farewells and exchanging last words of encouragement. As we filed out into the forest surrounding the Crystal Citadel, the dappled sunlight filtering through the trees felt like a small blessing from the Goddess, a reminder of what we were fighting to protect.

After bidding our goodbyes, I turned to Olivia, wrapping her in my arms. Her presence, always my calm within the chaos.

"You ready to go home, my love?" I murmured, brushing a strand of dark hair from her face.

"Past ready, Highness," she replied with a soft smile, her eyes sparkling with affection and just a hint of weariness.

My shadows rose around us, dark and comforting, cocooning us in their cool embrace. In the blink of an eye, we were gone, misting back to Vesparra and the sanctuary of our home.

CHAPTER 27

Olivia

The scent of freshly baked bread and sizzling bacon wafted through the air as I stepped into the breakfast hall, my heart swelling with an unexpected sense of peace. After weeks of chaos and uncertainty, the sight before me was like a warm blanket in the chill of uncertainty that had been so constant.

My family sat gathered around the long wooden table, their faces alight with easy laughter and warm conversation. Even Max and Finn were basking in the light of a sunbeam on the floor. For a moment, I could almost forget the weight of our responsibilities and the looming battles that awaited us. Here, in this sunlit room, we were simply a family sharing a meal.

Cade's eyes found mine, and a slow smile tugged at the corners of his mouth. Sliding into the seat beside him, I felt his large hand engulf mine, a shiver of warmth spreading through me. Our bond hummed between us, a quiet reminder of the love we shared, even in the smallest moments.

"Good morning, my queen," he murmured, his deep voice sending a familiar thrill down my spine. "I trust you slept well?"

I nodded, giving his hand a gentle squeeze. "Better than I have in ages," I admitted, my voice soft. "Though I missed you when I woke."

Across the table, Seraphine's silvery laugh rang out. "Oh,

spare us the lovesick glances," she teased, her eyes sparkling with mischief. "Some of us are trying to enjoy breakfast without swooning into our porridge."

Darius, ever the voice of reason, chuckled and shook his head. "Let them have their moment, Sera. Goddess knows they've earned it."

Reaching for a warm roll, I caught Gaylene's eye. Darius's beautiful mate gave me a knowing wink, a smirk tugging at her lips. "Ready for today's training, Olivia? I hear the Dragonia are chomping at the bit to put you through your paces."

My stomach fluttered with excitement. "Lookin' forward to it," I replied, grinning. "Though who knows what those big ol' lizards have planned?"

A laugh rose from the table.

"I'm telling them you said that," Cade threatened.

"You better not!" I giggled right back.

Ilyria, her hands wrapped around a steaming mug of tea, leaned forward. "This, this love that flows through and around this table, *that* is where our greatest strength lies."

A chorus of agreement rose from around the table, and a swell of pride filled my chest. These people, once strangers to me, had become my family. Through fires of adversity and trials none of us had ever anticipated, we'd forged unbreakable bonds. I knew without a doubt that I'd fight to my last breath to keep them safe.

Biting into my roll, I savored the simple pleasure of good food and better company. The contrast to where we'd been only weeks ago struck me like a quiet revelation. Recently, Cade had been fighting for his life, and fear had paralyzed us. Now, here we were, planning our next moves over eggs and bacon. Life, even in a realm filled with magic and monsters, had its moments of grace.

"You're quiet this morning, love," Cade murmured, his thumb tracing slow, soothing circles on the back of my hand. "What's on your mind?"

I met his gaze, catching the concern etched in the faint lines around his piercing blue eyes. "Just... appreciating this moment," I said softly. "It feels almost too good to be true."

Understanding flickered across his face, and he leaned in to press a gentle kiss to my temple. "Then we'll savor every second," he promised, his voice a steady anchor in the sea of emotions swirling within me. "And use it to fuel us in the battles to come."

Around us, the hum of conversation flowed, punctuated by bursts of laughter and the clinking of silverware against plates. I allowed myself to sink into the warmth of it all, the easy camaraderie of family and allies. Whatever trials lay ahead, whatever darkness threatened to consume us, I knew we'd face it together. And that was enough.

A ripple of excitement passed through the room, drawing my attention to the doorway. My heart leaped as Kaelen and Amaya entered, their hands intertwined. There was something magnetic about them—a glow that seemed to radiate from their connection, lighting up the space around them.

"Look at them," I whispered to Cade, unable to keep the smile from my voice. "They're practically glowing."

Kaelen's sharp eyes found mine, and for a brief moment, a rare softness flickered in his expression. He guided Amaya to the table, his protective yet gentle touch unmistakable. They moved in perfect harmony, as if an invisible thread bound them together, allowing them to communicate without a single word.

"Brother," Cade greeted, rising to clasp Kaelen's arm in a firm embrace. The bond of brotherhood between the two kings was clear in the warmth of their smiles and the unspoken respect in their gestures.

"You're looking well-rested," Kaelen remarked, his gaze flickering between Cade and me with a knowing gleam. "I trust you've been taking good care of each other?"

A blush crept up my neck, unbidden, as memories of the previous night surfaced. I cleared my throat, attempting a casual tone. "We manage," I quipped, earning a chuckle from both men.

Cade's grin widened as he wrapped an arm around my shoulders, pulling me closer. "We do more than manage, Starlight."

Kaelen smirked, his gaze twinkling with amusement as he held out a chair for Amaya. "Good to hear. Let's hope the troops take inspiration from your teamwork."

I turned to Amaya, my curiosity bubbling over. "Now, tell me everything. How did it feel? Shifting into your wolf for the first time?"

Her face lit up with excitement, a spark of wonder dancing in her eyes. "It was... incredible. Like nothing I've ever experienced. I felt free, powerful, and... whole."

Amaya launched into a detailed description of her transformation, her fight for dominance over her wolf. Her voice, filled with awe and animation, made me awed at the change in her. Gone was the scared, uncertain girl we'd once rescued. In her place sat a woman, practically vibrating with newfound confidence and power. It was as if she'd finally stepped into her skin—literally and figuratively.

I reached across the table, squeezing her hand. "I'm so proud of you, Itty Bitty," I said, with a teasing smile. "You've come so far in such a short time."

She beamed at me, her cheeks flushing with gratitude. Then her gaze shifted shyly to Kaelen, her fingers brushing his. "I couldn't have done it without help," she admitted softly.

The look that passed between them spoke volumes—a wordless exchange of love, pride, and partnership that tugged at my heart. My little sister had grown up and found her place in this magical world that we'd been thrust into. And while a part of me mourned the loss of her innocence, I couldn't deny the strength and resilience she'd discovered within herself.

As the lively conversation flowed around us, I took in every detail of the moment. The way Amaya's eyes sparkled as she described her wolf form, the gentle pride radiating from Kaelen as he watched her, the steady warmth of Cade's hand in mine. For just a little while, I let myself believe that we could have this—love, family, belonging—despite the shadow of war looming on the horizon.

My gaze shifted to Seraphine, who sat quietly sipping her tea, her silver hair catching the morning light. Her sharp navy-rimmed eyes darted between the lively chatter, her usual composure intact, but I caught a flicker of uncertainty beneath her calm façade.

"Seraphine," I said, leaning forward to catch her attention. "I was thinking you should join us for training today."

Her eyebrows shot up, her expression a mix of surprise and skepticism. "Me? Training? Olivia, I'm not exactly a warrior."

I shook my head, the weight of the Goddess Star resting against my chest bolstering me. "You don't need to be. Your mind is a weapon all its own, Sera. Your strategic insight is just as valuable as any sword or spell." I gestured to the others around the table. "And let's not forget—you wield magic, same as the rest of us."

Her fingers traced the rim of her teacup, her gaze lowering as she considered my words. "I'm not sure... My place has always been in the library, not on the battlefield."

"That's exactly why we need you," I pressed, my voice firm but encouraged. "You see patterns, connections the rest of us might miss. And it'll give you a better understanding of everyone's strengths for future planning."

She bit her lip, hesitating. I could practically see the wheels turning in her mind as she weighed the options, her sharp intellect analyzing every angle.

"Come on, Sera," Cade chimed in, his deep voice tinged with a teasing affection only a brother could muster. "It'll do you good to get out of those dusty stacks for a bit."

Seraphine shot him a glare but couldn't hide the small, amused smile tugging at her lips. "Fine," she said, relenting at last. "But don't expect me to start swinging a sword or anything."

"Wouldn't dream of it," I said with a grin, feeling a rush of satisfaction. Sometimes, all it took was a little push to reveal someone's hidden potential.

As the conversation shifted, my thoughts strayed to Ignis, and the frustration I'd been trying to tamp down began bubbling back to the surface. His arrogance, his maddening refusal to fully commit to our cause... it grated on my nerves like nails on stone. And yet... I understood how difficult change can be when it's engrained so deeply. But a king has to be the master of that change and I expected more.

My emotions warred within me—gratitude clashing against resentment, hope tempered by suspicion. I wanted to trust him, to believe that beneath his prickly exterior lay an ally we could count on when the time came. But the stakes were too high for blind faith.

I sighed and shoved the thoughts aside. For now, we'd work with what we had and hope that Ignis would prove himself worthy of the faith we'd tentatively placed in him.

The scrape of my chair as I pushed back from the table broke through the comfortable chatter. I stood, rolling my shoulders to shake off the lingering tension. "Alright, folks," I said, a thread of excitement creeping into my voice. "Time to work off that breakfast."

Cade rose beside me, his hand finding mine in a familiar gesture that sent a spark of reassurance through me. Around us, our Circle stirred, purpose settling over the group like a tangible force.

Amaya was the first to spring to her feet, her enthusiasm infectious. "I can't wait to try out my new shifting abilities!" she exclaimed, her eyes practically glowing with excitement.

Kaelen chuckled, the deep sound resonating in his chest

as he reached to steady her with a hand on her arm. His eyes softened as they met hers. "Patience, little wolf," he rumbled. "We'll start slow."

"Slow is boring," Amaya shot back with a playful pout. Kaelen just grinned, a rare smile that softened his otherwise commanding presence.

I glanced around at the faces of those who had gathered with us—our family of vampires, shifters, and elemental mages. We were family, forged in the fires of battle and bound by love and loyalty.

As we filed out of the breakfast hall, I felt a swell of pride and determination. Whatever darkness lay ahead, we'd face it together, stronger than ever.

CHAPTER 28

Olivia

We headed to one of the quadrants to train with the Dragonia, and as usual, the logistics of travel brought its own chaos.

"Seraphine, are you good to shadow mist to the location, or do you wanna tandem up on Vaelith with me?" I asked, grinning at her over my shoulder.

The look she gave me was priceless, like I'd just suggested she dine on a plate of live bugs.

"Umm, no, that's okay, Ollie. I'll go ahead and mist on over," she said, her tone as dry as the Aurelion desert.

I couldn't help but laugh as I swung up onto Vaelith's broad silver back. "Okie dokie, Sera. See you there."

Cade let out a booming laugh as he strode toward Eryndor, the emerald-hued dragon already waiting patiently for his rider. "Vaelith, be gentle with her," he teased, shooting me a wink as he mounted his dragon with the ease of long practice.

Zarvyn, the dark-scaled dragon with a molten gold underbelly, had been saddled earlier and was lounging nearby, looking vaguely bored. An idea struck me, and I leaned forward to pat Vaelith's neck. "Hold up a sec, big guy." Turning to Zarvyn, I asked, *"Hey, do you think you could handle Kaelen and Amaya tandem?"*

The dragon's golden eyes narrowed, glinting with mischief. *"Are you trying to insult me, little one? As though I'm not dragon enough to handle two puny humans on my back?"*

I felt Vaelith's chest vibrate beneath me as he let out a deep, rumbling chuckle. *"You know she wasn't insulting you, Zarvyn,"* Vaelith said with a hint of amusement in his voice.

"Of course not," I said aloud, rolling my eyes. "I meant their inexperience as riders, not your ability, you overgrown drama queen."

Zarvyn huffed, a puff of smoke curling from his nostrils. *"Oh, well, in that case, I'll take them. But I'll be careful with the puny humans."*

"Good to hear," I shot back with a grin. Turning, I cupped my hands around my mouth. "Hey, Kaelen!" I hollered, drawing his attention. "You and Amaya wanna ride Zarvyn tandem to the training field? He says he'll take good care of y'all."

Kaelen's eyes lit up like a kid stepping into a candy store, excitement written all over his face. He turned to Amaya, who looked significantly less enthused. Her expression teetered somewhere between cautious curiosity and outright terror, but after a deep breath, she nodded, her shoulders squaring in determination.

"Alright, y'all, mount up!" I called. "You got this, Itty Bitty. You've ridden plenty of horses. Just sit in front of Kaelen, hold on to the pommel, and grip tight with your legs. You'll be fine!"

Kaelen gave Amaya a reassured smile as they approached Zarvyn, who lowered his head and body to let them climb on. Kaelen settled behind Amaya, wrapping a protective arm around her waist while she gripped the pommel as if her life depended on it.

"Comfortable?" I asked as I gave Zarvyn a final once-over to ensure they were secure.

"Define 'comfortable,'" Amaya muttered under her breath, earning a hearty laugh from Kaelen.

"All right, y'all," I said, signaling the start. "Let's fly!"

With a powerful beat of wings, Vaelith launched into the air, the rush of wind whipping through my hair as Zarvyn followed close behind. Cade and Eryndor rose effortlessly into formation, their emerald glow catching the sunlight as the dragons soared toward the training field.

Amaya

Flying on the back of a dragon is not something you can prepare for. It's exhilarating and utterly fear-inducing at the same time. The moment Zarvyn launched into the sky, the earth vanished beneath us, leaving my stomach somewhere far behind. Kaelen's arms tightened securely around me as we banked left, Zarvyn's powerful wings slicing through the air with rhythmic grace.

The world below blurred as the landscape of Eldoria unfolded in breathtaking detail—rolling hills, glittering rivers, and the disappearing peaks of Vesparra's mountains. Despite my initial nerves, the thrill of soaring through the skies took over. The wind tore past us, a whooshing sound that felt like freedom itself.

"This is incredible!" I shouted over the roar of the wind, my voice lost to the skies but my elation unmistakable.

Kaelen chuckled behind me, his grip firm as Zarvyn surged higher. "Told you it would be worth it!"

The journey ended too soon. I'd just started to enjoy the ride when Zarvyn descended in a graceful arc, his massive claws hitting the training grounds with a gentle jolt. His powerful strides slowed until he came to a halt, wings folding neatly against his sides.

Sliding down the rope attached to the saddle, I planted my feet firmly on the ground. The sensation of solid earth beneath me felt strange after the weightless freedom of flight. I reached out and stroked Zarvyn's warm, obsidian scales, marveling at their smooth texture and the subtle golden shimmer beneath the sunlight.

"Thank you, sir," I said with a grin. "That was amazing."

Zarvyn lowered his massive head, his molten gold eyes meeting mine as he gave a small, dignified nod.

The training grounds buzzed with energy, the morning light glinting off the armor and weapons of soldiers from every corner of Eldoria. The air itself seemed alive with magic— fire crackling from Aurelion's warriors, gusts of wind swirling around Ilyndorian elementalists, and shadows creeping and twisting near Vesparran mages. Troops sparred, strategized, and shouted commands, their determination as tangible as the hum of the surrounding forest.

Kaelen stood beside me, his broad shoulders taut with focus as he watched two shifters practice evasive maneuvers. One stumbled over a branch, drawing his immediate attention.

"Stay low to the ground!" Kaelen barked, his Alpha voice cutting through the noise like a whip. "You'll be an easy target if you don't move with the terrain!"

The young shifter nodded quickly, adjusting his stance and trying again with renewed determination.

Nearby, Olivia wasted no time jumping into the thick of things after dismounting from Vaelith. Her sharp voice carried over the chaos, drawing the attention of a group of firecasters who had accidentally set the edge of a training dummy ablaze.

"Y'all think a rift monster's gonna wait while you admire your fireballs?" she shouted, hands on her hips. "Put it out and get back in formation! And for cryin' out loud, don't aim at your allies!"

A laugh bubbled up in my throat, but I quickly stifled it, glancing over at Cade and Seraphine, who stood near the edge of the field beneath a towering tree. Cade was leaning casually against the trunk, arms crossed, watching his wife with open amusement.

"You gonna save them?" I teased, nodding toward the firecasters who were frantically scrambling to douse the flames under Olivia's stern gaze.

He smirked, his shadowy eyes glinting with mischief. "Not a chance. She's terrifying, and I'm smart enough to stay out of the way when she's in 'general' mode."

"What *he* said," Seraphine added, then laughed as she sipped from a silver flask. "She's a force of nature. You don't mess with that."

I grinned, turning my gaze back to Olivia, who was now gesturing wildly at the firecasters as they hurriedly lined up again. Seeing her like this—confident, commanding, and completely in her element—filled me with pride. Whatever challenges we faced, we had each other. And with a team like this, I knew we stood a fighting chance.

All movement on the field ceased as the Dragonia lumbered closer, their massive forms casting long shadows across the training grounds. The soldiers froze, their gazes snapping upward, some in awe, others in palpable intimidation. Vaelith's gleaming silver scales shimmered like molten metal in the sunlight as he towered over the gathered troops, his presence commanding instant silence.

Cade stepped forward, his hand briefly touching Vaelith's flank as though grounding himself. His posture straightened, and his voice rang out with authority. "Listen up! I'll be relaying instructions from the dragons, so pay close attention."

Vaelith's deep, resonant voice must have been rumbling in Cade's mind, and with each word Cade repeated aloud, the soldiers leaned closer, hanging on every syllable.

"You fight with determination," Cade began, his tone steady, "but determination alone will not save you. Strategy. Unity. These are your greatest weapons."

"Unity," Olivia repeated, her hands on her hips as she scanned the crowd. Her piercing gaze landed squarely on King Ignis, who stood near the Aurelion troops. "That means knowing your allies' strengths and leaning on them when you need to. You hear that, Ignis?"

From across the field, Ignis scowled, his fiery red hair catching the sunlight like a living flame. He muttered something inaudible to his second-in-command, his broad shoulders stiff with annoyance.

"Did you just sass the fire king?" I whispered to Olivia, wide-eyed. Memories of his imposing presence at the mating ceremony flashed through my mind.

Olivia smirked, her eyes twinkling with mischief. "He deserves it." She clapped her hands. "Now, back to work, people!"

Vaelith shifted his attention to a group of elementalists who were attempting to shield a line of Vesparran shadow mages from a barrage of projectiles conjured by Aurelion firecasters. The shimmering shield the elementalists had created flickered under the onslaught, leaving the Vesparrans vulnerable.

Olivia turned to relay Vaelith's booming observations. "Y'all, listen up—Vaelith is making some freakin' good observations here." She gestured emphatically toward the struggling group.

"Again, you falter because you act as individuals," Cade conveyed from Vaelith, his voice a commanding echo of the dragon's. "An army that does not move as one is an army that falls. Blend your magic. Trust in each other's abilities. Watch."

Vaelith spread his enormous wings, and with one powerful movement, he conjured a gust of wind that sent the Vesparran shadows surging forward. The inky tendrils merged with the elemental shield, transforming it into a swirling barrier that both protected and attacked, deflecting the fiery projectiles while striking back with tendrils of darkness.

Amaya stepped closer to the elementalists, her tone encouraging but firm. "Do you see how it works together? Don't hold your magic so tightly—it's not meant to be forced. It wants to flow, to merge. Trust it, and trust each other."

The group nodded, determination etched on their faces as they adjusted their approach.

Meanwhile, Eryndor, the emerald-scaled healer, hovered near a group of soldiers tending to minor injuries from the day's sparring. His calm presence was a stark contrast to the intensity of the field. Cade approached, sensing the wisdom the dragon was imparting.

"He wants you to understand this," Cade relayed, his voice quieter but no less commanding. "Do not underestimate the importance of recovery. A warrior who fights recklessly is a warrior who falls. Endurance will be our greatest asset when Magda strikes. Pace yourselves. The battle she brings will test not just your strength, but your resilience."

Seraphine stood nearby, her sharp eyes darting from group to group. She observed the strategies, the successes, and the weaknesses with the precision of a scholar cataloging invaluable data. Her fingers twitched, itching to jot down notes, but her mental map of the training exercises would be more than sufficient.

"She's plotting something," Cade murmured, leaning closer to me with a knowing smirk.

I laughed softly. "Oh, you know she is. And it'll be brilliant. She doesn't give herself enough credit."

Across the field, Zarvyn's molten gold eyes gleamed as he scanned the soldiers. His voice must have filled Cade's mind, and he repeated his words aloud.

"Zarvyn wanted me to tell you, and I repeat, verbatim, do not think me unimpressed by your progress," Cade translated. "But if any of you think you can challenge me in combat, know this—I will end you before your heart finishes its next beat."

The soldiers burst into nervous laughter, a tension-breaking sound that rippled across the field.

"Real motivational speaker, that one," Olivia muttered, shaking her head, though a small smile played at the corner of her lips.

Vaelith huffed, a sound that was unmistakably a Draconic chuckle. "Motivation comes in many forms, little one," Cade relayed with a grin.

As the training continued, the dragons, the leaders, and the soldiers worked together seamlessly, their movements growing sharper and more unified with each passing moment. In the distance, the sun climbed higher into the sky, its golden light reflecting off the determined faces of those preparing for the fight of their lives.

Watching them, I felt a surge of hope and pride. We weren't just training for a battle. We were forging something stronger —an unbreakable bond that would carry us through whatever darkness lay ahead.

Kaelen stepped into the sparring ring, his dire wolf aura radiating a commanding intensity that made even the seasoned soldiers step back. His silver eyes locked onto a young Vesparran shadow mage, who fidgeted nervously under the weight of the Alpha's presence.

"Attack me," Kaelen said, his voice low and even, carrying an edge that promised no room for hesitation.

The mage faltered for a moment before summoning his courage. With a sharp motion, he lashed out, shadows slicing through the air in a deadly arc. Kaelen moved like lightning, dodging with practiced ease and closing the distance in a single heartbeat. In one fluid motion, he had the mage pinned to the ground, his hand pressed firmly against the young man's chest.

"Too slow," Kaelen growled, his tone as cutting as the shadows the mage had conjured. "Again."

The mage scrambled to his feet, brushing off his cloak as determination replaced his earlier apprehension. This time, he feinted left, sending a rapid succession of shadow strikes in Kaelen's direction. Kaelen deflected the blows, his movements precise and economical, but a flicker of approval softened his stern expression.

"That's better," he said. "Use your surroundings. Think ahead. Don't fight me where I am—fight me where I'm going to be."

Nearby, Olivia was putting her own group through their paces. She paced between a cluster of firecasters and wind mages, her sharp gaze scrutinizing their every move. "Alright, y'all," she barked, clapping her hands to get their attention. "Pair up—fire and wind together. One of you brings the power; the other directs it. And for the love of the Goddess, try not to burn the whole dadgum forest down!"

Thyra trotted over, her silver-gray coat gleaming in the fading light. Her lavender eyes sparkled with amusement as she chimed in, *"Are you sure you can trust them not to set the forest ablaze, Olivia?"*

Olivia threw her hands up in exasperation. "Not helping, horse."

Cade, lounging nearby with shadows curling lazily around his fingers, chuckled. "You could always call in the water mages as backup. Just in case."

Before Olivia could retort, Zarvyn landed with a resounding thud, the ground trembling under the weight of his massive form. He tilted his molten gold head, his voice rumbling in Cade's mind, and he quickly relayed it to the group. *"Or perhaps you should let them burn the forest. A scorched battlefield favors the firecasters, after all."*

Olivia whirled on him, her glare as sharp as a blade. "Why do I even try?"

Kaelen, having dismissed his sparring partner, strode over with a satisfied smirk. "You do it because you love us," he quipped, dodging the playful swat Olivia aimed in his direction.

As the sun dipped below the horizon, bathing the training grounds in hues of amber and violet, the soldiers gathered for a final debrief. Their faces, streaked with sweat and dirt, were lit with a blend of exhaustion and determination. The air crackled with the remnants of magic, the day's efforts leaving a tangible energy in its wake.

Vaelith stepped forward, his silver scales catching the twilight like liquid moonlight. His deep, resonant voice filled Olivia's mind, and she relayed his words with unwavering confidence. "Here's Vaelith's ultimate wisdom for the day:"

"You are not yet ready. But you are stronger than you were this morning. And tomorrow, you will be stronger still. The Goddess watches over you all. Stand united, and you will not fall."

Olivia squared her shoulders, her eyes sweeping across the gathered troops. Her voice rang out with the clarity and conviction of a genuine leader. "And now, y'all get to hear my take. We've got this. Magda may have her monsters, but we've got somethin' she doesn't—each other. Keep fighting, keep pushing, and keep makin' each other better. That's how we're gonna win!"

The soldiers erupted into cheers, their voices blending with the mighty roars of the Dragonia. The sound rippled through the training grounds, defiant and triumphant, a rallying cry against the looming darkness.

As the troops dispersed, Olivia turned back to the group, her tone more subdued but no less resolute. "Now," she said, her hands resting on her hips, "we just have to repeat that training about a bajillion more times and pray we're ready before Magda starts openin' those rifts again."

Kaelen clapped a hand on Cade's shoulder, his eyes gleaming with determination. "We'll be ready," he said firmly. "We have to be."

CHAPTER 29

Callie

The oppressive darkness of the Underworld clung to me like a second skin, its weight seeping into my bones with every passing moment. I stood in the dimly lit chamber, my heart hammering against my ribs as I fought to keep the rising tide of panic at bay. The air was thick with the fetid scent of decay and ancient magic, each breath scraping against my lungs like sandpaper.

I clenched my fists until my nails bit into my palms, grounding myself in the sharp sting of pain. "Stay strong, Callie," I murmured under my breath, the words more plea than command. "For Olivia. For Eldoria. You've survived worse."

But as the heavy stone doors groaned open, their sound reverberating through the cavernous space, my resolve faltered. Magda swept into the chamber with the precision of a predator. Her stilettos clicked against the worn stone, the rhythm a chilling counterpoint to the malevolent energy rolling off her in waves.

"Ah, there she is," Magda purred, her blood-red lips curving into a smile that held no trace of warmth. "The lost little royal, playing at bravery. How quaint." Her dark, gleaming eyes appraised me like a cat sizing up a mouse, and I had to fight the urge to shrink under her gaze.

I straightened my spine, forcing myself to meet her eyes despite the cold knot of fear twisting in my gut. "I won't let you use me to hurt Olivia or Eldoria," I said, my voice firmer than I'd expected.

Magda's laughter rang out, a sound that was both beautiful and grotesque, reverberating through the chamber like shattered glass. She glided closer, her presence as suffocating as the shadows that clung to the walls. "Oh, sweet child," she crooned, trailing a single sharp nail along the line of my jaw. I flinched, the icy prick of her touch leaving my skin crawling. "We've been over this. You don't have a choice in the matter."

Her words dripped with mockery, and I felt the weight of her power pressing down on me, a force that threatened to crush what was left of my courage. Still, I held my ground, my teeth clenched as I glared up at her. "I'll never let you win."

Magda's smile widened, a predator delighting in the defiance of her prey. "My darling," she murmured, her voice silky and venomous. "We'll see about that."

She spun, her form-fitting black dress swirling around her legs like liquid shadow. "Eldric!" she barked, her voice sharp enough to cut stone. "Prepare the amulet. It's time we showed this insolent girl her place."

From the shadows, Eldric emerged, his chiseled features carved into a mask of cold indifference. In his hands, he held an ornate amulet, its surface flickering with dark, pulsating energy. My breath caught in my throat as I stared at it, every fiber of my being screaming at the malevolent power it exuded.

"No," I whispered, taking an instinctive step back. "Please, don't do this."

Magda's eyes glinted with cruel delight, her crimson lips curling into a smile. "Oh, yes, Callie," she breathed, each word laced with venom. "Your power will be mine, and with it, I will crush my sister's precious kingdom. And you, my dear, will have the honor of being the instrument of Eldoria's destruction."

Eldric approached with measured steps, the amulet glowing brighter as he drew nearer. My knees threatened to buckle beneath me, and I stumbled back, my thoughts racing for an escape. But there was none—not here, not in this cursed realm where the walls seemed to close in with every breath. Helplessness crushed me, its weight as suffocating as the oppressive darkness around us.

"I won't let you win," I said, the defiance in my voice trembling like a fragile thread. Yet even as the words left my lips, doubt crept in. How could I fight a goddess? What hope did I have?

Magda's laughter echoed through the chamber, cold and mocking, sending shivers racing down my spine. "Oh, Callie," she drawled, taking a step closer. "Your spirit is delicious. Let's see how long it takes before I break it."

As the amulet drew nearer, its dark energy coiling like a living thing, I closed my eyes, a silent prayer forming on my lips. *Please, give me strength. For Olivia, for Eldoria, for everyone I love... I have to endure this. I must fight.*

Eldric's approach was deliberate, his boots clicking against the stone floor, each step reverberating in the cavernous space. His piercing green eyes locked onto mine, an unreadable mix of determination and... something else. Concern? Was I imagining it?

When he reached me, his towering frame cast a shadow that swallowed what little light remained. He leaned closer, his expression impassive as he raised the amulet.

"Hold still," he commanded, his tone cold and clipped. But then, his lips barely moved as he whispered, "When the ritual begins, be ready. We'll make our escape."

My heart stuttered in my chest. Was this a trick? Another layer of Magda's cruel manipulation? I searched Eldric's face for answers, but his expression remained carved from stone, his voice steady, as if he had said nothing at all.

"What are you whispering about?" Magda's sharp voice cut

through the air, each syllable slicing like a blade.

Eldric turned smoothly, his face a mask of subservience. "Nothing, my queen," he replied, his voice calm and deferential. "I was merely instructing the girl on how to conduct herself during the ritual."

Magda's eyes narrowed, suspicion glinting like a predator's gaze. "Good. Make sure she doesn't ruin this with her pathetic trembling."

I fought to suppress a shiver as Magda turned away, her focus now on the preparations for the ritual. Eldric's whispered words echoed in my mind, a fragile thread of hope that I clung to desperately.

Could I trust him? Did I even have a choice?

As Magda's attention shifted, the weight of the amulet settled against my skin like a chain of ice. It pulsed faintly, a sinister heartbeat that seemed to sync with my own racing pulse.

"Good," Magda purred, her blood-red lips curving into a wicked smile. "Now, let us begin."

The air thickened with oppressive energy, dark tendrils of magic swirling and writhing like angry serpents. The ancient stones of the temple groaned, their protest echoing in the cavernous space as if aware of the desecration about to unfold. Magda's voice rose, a guttural chant in a language older than time, scraping against my ears and clawing at my very soul.

I squeezed my eyes shut, focusing on Eldric's whispered words: *"Be ready."* It was a fragile thread of hope, but it was all I had. The suffocating energy pressed down on me, seeping into every pore, and I couldn't help but wonder if any escape was even possible.

Magda's power lashed out, a tendril of darkness snaking toward me like a predator. My body stiffened, every muscle locking in resistance. The weight of the amulet grew heavier, pulsing in time with the magic surrounding us.

"You can't resist me, little one," Magda's voice slithered into my mind, her tone dripping with malice and mockery.

I bit my lip hard enough to draw blood, tasting the sharp tang as I forced my trembling voice to steady. "Watch me," I spat, defiance sparking through my terror.

The amulet throbbed, its cold tendrils weaving into my skin, seeping into my veins. Magda's laughter echoed, a chilling sound devoid of humor.

"Your power will be mine," she hissed, her voice vibrating with certainty. "With it, I will break the rift wide open, and nothing will stand in my way."

A surge of fury rose in me, defiance blazing through the fog of despair. "Never," I growled, channeling every ounce of strength into resisting her pull. My vision blurred, the oppressive energy pressing in harder.

Magda's face twisted into something monstrous, her beauty corrupted by fury. "You dare defy me?" she shrieked, the sound reverberating off the shuddering walls.

Tendrils of shadow surged forward, writhing and clawing at the edges of my mind. The temple trembled, the groaning stones reverberating with the force of her rage. The shadows danced across the walls, growing thicker, darker, more alive with each passing second.

"What's happening?" I gasped, my voice barely audible as the weight of the amulet threatened to crush me. My eyes darted to Eldric, searching for answers in his impenetrable expression.

His emerald eyes flickered with an emotion I couldn't place —regret, perhaps, or determination. "Hold on," he muttered under his breath, his voice so low I almost missed it.

The shadows surged again, coiling tighter around the chamber like living chains. Magda raised her arms high, her chant escalating into a crescendo that sent another wave of oppressive magic crashing over me. My knees buckled, and I hit the stone floor hard, gasping for air.

"You belong to me!" Magda thundered, her voice amplified

by the force of her power.

"No!" I screamed, my voice raw with desperation. Every memory of Olivia, of the life I was fighting for, surged to the forefront of my mind. *You can't have me. I won't let you win.*

Magda's laughter was pure malice. She took a step closer, her black dress sweeping the floor as she loomed over me. "You think you're strong enough to fight me, little revenant?" she sneered. "Let's see how long you last."

The amulet's weight grew unbearable, the magic within it warring against my will. My thoughts fractured, spiraling into chaos. Desperation clawed at my resolve, but I clung to Eldric's words, to the promise of escape.

"I will break you," Magda said, her voice a low, dangerous growl. "And when I do, you'll beg to serve me."

Her chant resumed, the ancient words slicing through the air like daggers. I felt the power of the Underworld tighten its grip, binding me in a prison of darkness. But deep within the storm, a spark of defiance flickered—a light that refused to be extinguished.

Hold on, I told myself, clinging to that spark. *For Olivia. For Eldoria. Hold on.*

Olivia

Suddenly, the world tilted. Vesparra's misty mountains materialized around me, the oppressive weight of the Underworld fading like a nightmare at dawn. I gasped, my body trembling as though I'd been plunged into icy water.

What was happening? How had I...?

The realization hit like a thunderclap, a bone-deep certainty that chilled me to my core. Danger. Impending and terrible.

My gaze swept over Vesparra's craggy peaks and shadowed valleys. Everything looked deceptively peaceful, but I knew better. As The Chosen of the Goddess, I was attuned to

Eldoria's very essence. Right now, every instinct screamed that something was terribly wrong.

"Cade!" I called out, my voice tight with urgency. "We need to gather the others. Now."

He appeared at my side in an instant, his shadows swirling faintly, concern etched into his handsome face. "What is it, Olivia? What did you sense?"

I shook my head, struggling to put the feeling into words. "It's Magda. She's... done something. The balance is shifting, Cade. Something's brewing, and we have to act fast."

Cade nodded grimly, his jaw tightening. I felt his steady presence grounding me, even as my awareness stretched outward. Somewhere out there, darkness was rising. And I knew, with grim certainty, that I would have to face it head-on.

I closed my eyes, reaching out with my mind to the ancient, powerful allies who had guided us through so much already. *"Vaelith,"* I called silently. *"We need you."*

The response was immediate. A warm, comforting presence enveloped me, and I felt my racing heart slow. The Dragonia's voices, a harmonious chorus of wisdom and strength, echoed in my mind.

"What troubles you, StarHeart?" they asked.

Cade's hand found mine, his grip a quiet assurance as I poured out my fears and suspicions to the ancient dragon. *"Something's wrong,"* I explained. *"I can feel it in my bones. Magda's making her move, and I'm afraid we're not ready."*

Vaelith's voice resonated through me like a gentle roar. *"Your instincts are rarely wrong, little one. We, too, sense a disturbance in Eldoria's energy. We are on our way."*

Cade and I moved quickly, dressing in silence before stepping into the early morning sun. Outside the castle walls, the Dragonia descended from their mountain caves, their magnificent forms shimmering in the dawn's light. The rhythmic beat of their wings sent waves of air rippling through the trees.

Ariaxom and Thyra, the Pegasi, their luminous forms a welcome sight, landed gracefully near us.

"We're here, darling," Thyra whispered into my mind, her soothing tone steadying my nerves.

Even Skorn, usually the most playful of the wyverns, was uncharacteristically serious. His sparkling gray eyes locked onto mine. *"Your feelings align with ours, Chosen One. The balance has shifted."*

"What can we do?" Cade asked, his voice tight with determination.

Eryndor, his emerald scales catching the morning light, responded, *"We must prepare not only for battle, but for protection. Magda's power grows, but so does yours, Olivia. The Goddess does not abandon her Chosen."*

I squared my shoulders, letting their confidence bolster my resolve. "I'm up for the challenge. Eldoria will not fall as long as we stand together."

Vaelith stepped forward, his silver form radiating strength and wisdom. *"You will never stand alone."*

Cade moved closer, his steady presence at my side, my Iron Heart steadfast and sure. I glanced at each of the dragons, wyverns, and Pegasi surrounding us, their forms gleaming with quiet power, and felt a surge of confidence. Together, we were a force of nature.

"We'll face this fight," I said, my voice steady and sure. "And come hell or high water, we'll win."

A chorus of voices echoed back, harmonized with the roar of the Dragonia and the gentle mental tones of the Pegasi: *"Together."*

In that moment, the word became a shield, a promise, and a battle cry. "Together," I repeated, feeling its power resonate through every fiber of my being. I had never heard a more beautiful word in my life.

***

We mounted up, me on Vaelith and Cade on Eryndor, the other Dragonia flying in tight formation around us. The wind whipped past, carrying the faint scent of pine and the crisp bite of impending frost. The sky stretched endlessly above, but the weight of the realm's danger pressed heavily on my shoulders.

"*We need to consider every possible entry point,*" Cade said, his ice-blue eyes scanning the craggy landscape below. "*Magda's not just powerful; she's cunning.*"

We communicated silently through our bond, our thoughts flowing as naturally as speech.

"*What about the Shadow Shards?*" I suggested, my mind racing. "*Could we use them to set up an invisible perimeter?*"

Cade's eyes lit with approval. "*Brilliant, Starlight. Combined with the Elemental Wards from Ilyndor, we'd have a double-layered defense. If she tries to open a rift, she'll meet resistance before she even steps through.*"

"*And the Mist Orbs,*" I added, my thoughts quickening. "*We can use them to disorient her forces if they make it through. Confusion is just as important as strength.*"

As we soared over the vast expanse of Eldoria, the tension in the air was palpable. Each mile felt heavier than the last, the weight of our responsibility pressing down on me like a tangible force. But no matter how hard I tried, I couldn't shake the gnawing feeling that we were missing something crucial.

Suddenly, a sharp jolt of urgency tore through me, making me gasp. My body tensed, every nerve on edge.

"*Do you feel that?*" Cade's voice cut through the bond, sharp with alarm.

I struggled to put the sensation into words; it was overwhelming, like standing in the middle of a storm's eye. "*Something's wrong,*" I finally managed, my voice tight. "*I can feel it. It's like... like the realm itself is groaning in pain.*"

"*Vaelith,*" I called out, my mental voice steady despite my racing heart. "*What are you feeling?*"

The silver dragon's deep, resonant voice answered in my mind, a comforting anchor in the chaos. *"Subtle shifts, StarHeart. It's as though the realm's energy is rippling—disturbed by something vast, something malevolent. The ripples spread outward, originating from a central point."*

"Can you pinpoint the source?" Cade demanded, his voice coiled with tension.

Vaelith paused before responding, his tone grave. *"Not exactly. But I am certain this disturbance is Magda's doing. She's not just preparing for battle—she's almost ready."*

"Then so are we," Cade said, his voice low and resolute. *"We rally our forces. Now."*

A surge of determination filled me, my fear dissolving under the weight of purpose. *"The Shadow Shards,"* I said suddenly, my thoughts crystallizing. *"Your Vesparran warriors need to be equipped with them. If Magda opens the rifts, we'll need their invisibility advantage to outmaneuver her creatures."*

Cade nodded sharply. *"I'll shadow-mist back to Vesparra and see it done. Meanwhile, the Thalassan forces should start deploying their Mist Orbs. It'll keep Magda's monsters off balance if they breach the barriers."*

"Vaelith," I called out, urgency sharpening my tone. *"We need a central rally point. What's your take on the Crystal Citadel? It's the heart of the realm—it makes the most sense."*

Before the wise dragon could respond, Drathom, ever the irreverent wyvern, interjected with his usual sarcasm. *"Well, look at that. Our little StarHeart is taking charge, thinking on her tiny human feet. Don't hurt yourself, darling."*

I rolled my eyes even as a grin tugged at my lips. *"Drathom, remind me to put a boot in your wyvern butt when this is all over."*

Vaelith's chest rumbled beneath me, a low chuckle vibrating through my body. *"He may jest, but your instincts are sound. The Crystal Citadel will serve well as our staging ground. Send word to the other kingdoms immediately."*

"I'll contact the royals through the Crystal Network," I said,

my resolve solidifying. *"Cade, use the Crystal Network as well to relay instructions to the command centers and sub-hubs. Every soldier in the realm needs to be ready to move at a moment's notice."*

Cade's shadows swirled around him as he prepared to mist away. He glanced back at me, his eyes fierce with conviction. *"We'll do this, Olivia. Together."*

I nodded, glancing at the dragons, wyverns, and Pegasi gathered around us, their combined strength a tangible force. *"Together,"* I echoed, the word ringing with determination.

As Cade disappeared into the shadows and the Dragonia roared their assent, I felt a renewed sense of hope. We were running out of time, but we had something Magda didn't—unity, loyalty, and a determination that burned brighter than any darkness she could summon.

As we turned toward the Citadel, a renewed sense of purpose settled over me. These creatures weren't just our fierce defenders; they were my friends, our allies in this fight for survival.

"Y'know," I said, my thoughts light despite the weight of our mission, *"I never thought I'd be grateful to have voices in my head."*

Zarvyn chimed in with his usual dry humor, *"Just so long as you can account for where they're coming from, little one, you'll be alright."*

I snorted, the laugh breaking through the tension gripping me. *"Fair point, Zarvyn. Fair point."*

The levity eased the tight knot in my chest, even as the gravity of the moment pressed down on me. With the Citadel's spires coming into view, anticipation and dread warred within me. This was it—the moment we'd been preparing for, the culmination of countless hours of training and strategizing. The thought was overwhelming, but there was one thing I knew with unshakable certainty—we weren't facing this alone.

Reaching into the pocket of my vest, I retrieved the crystal and began contacting the royals. The magic coursed through the crystal, a low hum resonating as I called each sovereign. *"Inform your commanders. The attack is imminent. This is not a drill. Meet me at the Citadel as soon as possible."*

The crystal grew warm in my palm, its glow pulsing with urgency. Each time a voice answered with a solemn affirmation, I felt a little steadier. They were listening, and they were coming.

As we entered the Citadel's war room, the weight of the moment hit me. The massive crystal table at its center gleamed faintly, casting its light over the grim, determined faces of our most trusted advisors and generals. Maps and diagrams of Eldoria's defenses lay scattered across the table, illuminated by the faint blue glow.

I cleared my throat, forcing my voice to remain steady. "Alright, y'all," I said, letting my drawl slip through just enough to remind everyone of who I was—Olivia, the fighter who wouldn't back down. "We've got a fight comin', and we're gonna be ready for it."

Cade had returned and stood at the far side of the table, his imposing presence my anchor in this storm. He began outlining our defensive strategies, his voice was calm but firm, each word deliberate. The soldiers and advisors leaned in, their focus unwavering.

As Cade spoke, a familiar warmth bloomed in my chest. My hand moved to the Goddess Star at my heart, fingers brushing over its smooth surface. The symbol of my power and destiny pulsed faintly beneath my touch, a reassuring rhythm that steadied my nerves. Across the table, Cade's hand instinctively found the mark of our bond on his chest, his eyes locking on mine. Piercing, filled with both pride and concern.

In my mind, the Dragonia's voices echoed, their harmonious tones enveloping me in reassurance.

"We are with you, Chosen One. Our magic is yours to

command."

Closing my eyes briefly, I sent a wave of gratitude back to them. *"Thank you,"* I thought, my silent words reverberating with sincerity.

When I opened my eyes, Cade was still watching me. His gaze softened, his pride in me clear even amid our preparations. I squared my shoulders, drawing strength from the bond we shared.

"Together," I murmured, loud enough for him alone.

His lips curved into a faint smile. "Always," he replied.

"Olivia," Cade said, his deep voice cutting through the chatter of the room. "What do you sense?"

I closed my eyes, reaching out with the magic that had become as much a part of me as breathing. The energies of Eldoria pulsed and shifted—water, fire, earth, air, blood, and shifter magic—all weaving together in a complex, chaotic rhythm. It was beautiful, but it was also unsettling.

"The balance is... shifting," I said slowly, opening my eyes to meet Cade's steady gaze. "It's like the realm itself is holdin' its breath, waiting for something to break. I don't think this is just another batch of rifts opening. It feels bigger than that —but not quite like Magda crossin' over. Not yet, anyway. It's something in between."

A hush fell over the room. All eyes turned to me, expectant and anxious. Around the crystal table stood my allies—some of whom I'd fought beside for months, others I'd only just begun to trust. But looking at their faces now, a fierce protectiveness surged in me. This was my family, as unconventional as it was, and I would do everything in my power to keep them safe.

"Listen up," I said, my voice carrying an authority I didn't know I possessed. "We're facin' a darkness that wants to tear our world apart. But we've got somethin' Magda doesn't—each other."

Cade moved to my side, his presence uplifting me. The bond between us thrummed like a steady drumbeat, a constant source of strength.

"We're gonna protect Eldoria," I continued, letting the fire in my chest grow. "Not just because it's our duty, but because it's our home. All of us—together."

The tension in the room shifted. Shoulders squared, jaws set, eyes steeled with determination. It was like the pulse of the room itself had strengthened, responding to the shared resolve.

"I know I was born in this world," I added, my voice softer now but no less resolute, "but I wasn't raised here. I didn't grow up knowin' magic or the power it gives. But back in the mortal realm, we've got a ton of stories about good versus evil. And you know what? In those stories, it always looks like evil's about to win. Like it's got the whole thing locked down so tight that good doesn't have a chance in hell of winnin'."

I paused, letting my words sink in before continuing, my tone sharpening.

"But y'all, no matter how bad it looked—no matter how dark the night or how hopeless it seemed—good always found a way. And that's what's gonna happen here. Good is gonna find a way to win. Against all odds. Against Magda. Against any evil, she sends our way. Good is gonna triumph."

Cade leaned in, pressing a kiss to my forehead, and the rush of love and pride that flowed through our bond swept over me like a flood. His eyes looked over the room as he addressed the gathered leaders.

"Olivia's right," he began, his voice steady and commanding. "But it's not just about fighting for victory. It's about leading our people—showing them strength when they need it most. When rifts open, and monsters appear, some will lose loved ones—sons, daughters, friends. They'll look to their kings and queens for guidance, for hope. That's our role now. Be there for them. Be the leaders they need."

He paused, letting his words settle like the first stones of a foundation. Then his voice dropped into a deep, resolute tone that resonated with every person in the room.

"So let us depart with one thing in mind: With the blessing of the Goddess, we leave to defend the heart of Eldoria. We fight for unity in the face of division. For hope against despair. For victory over the evil that threatens to overtake us."

The silence that followed was electric. Then, one by one, each royal bowed their head in agreement. The room felt alive with purpose as they began to file out, ready to return to their kingdoms and prepare for the battle to come.

As Cade turned back to me, I saw the fire in his eyes—a reflection of the determination burning in my own heart.

"Together," I said again, my voice firm.

"Always," he replied. And I knew, with him at my side, we would see this fight through.

CHAPTER 30

Cade

The wind rushed past my face, crisp and invigorating, as Eryndor's powerful wings sliced through the air. Each beat surged through me like a drum, syncing with the rapid rhythm of my heart. I glanced left, my gaze drawn to Olivia astride Vaelith. She looked every inch the queen she was born to be—back straight, chin high, fierce and commanding.

Her presence stole my breath. The sight of her, illuminated by the fading light, was a vision that would remain etched in my memory forever.

"We're making good time," I sent the thought to her through our bond, unable to keep the admiration from coloring my mental voice.

Olivia turned, the wind catching strands of her dark hair and sending them flying in wild, beautiful tendrils. That grin of hers—a mix of determination and playfulness—lit up her face. *"These guys are rarin' to go. Can't you feel their excitement?"*

I nodded, my chest swelling as I marveled at her easy connection with the Dragonia. She wasn't just their ally; she was their friend, their leader, their chosen. Watching her command the respect of these ancient, magnificent creatures was like witnessing pure magic. But that was Olivia—effortlessly magnetic, her light drawing every soul, human or otherwise, into her orbit.

As we rode the currents of the sky, my thoughts wandered to her, unbidden but welcome. Our mate bond pulsed with a rhythm all its own, each beat a reminder of the incredible woman who had claimed my heart. The urgency of our connection hummed under my skin, and I longed to reach for her, to feel her warmth against me.

"Cade?" Olivia's voice broke into my thoughts, teased and full of affection. *"You're starin'."*

"Can you blame me?" I shot back, a grin tugging at my lips. *"You're magnificent up there."*

She laughed, a sound as bright and free as the wind itself. *"Save it for later, love. We're with company right now."*

Her words sent a thrill through me, but I forced myself to focus. She was right, as usual. This wasn't the time for distraction, no matter how tempting.

Still, I couldn't stop my amazement at her. The transformation from the shattered girl I had first met to the commanding presence beside me was nothing short of miraculous. She had endured so much, and yet she carried it all with grace, strength, and a determination that burned brighter than the stars.

"What's goin' through that head of yours?" she called over her shoulder, her voice tinged with curiosity.

I smirked, letting my admiration for her spill into our bond. *"Just thinking about how lucky I am to have you as my mate."*

Even though the shadows of dusk had begun to creep across the sky, I knew she was blushing, her cheeks glowing with pleased warmth. *"Flatterer,"* she murmured, though her joy echoed across our connection. *"Now, let's pick up the pace. I want to reach Vesparra before it gets too terribly late."*

With a thought, Olivia urged the dragons faster. I felt Eryndor's powerful muscles bunch beneath me as he surged forward, the rush of speed exhilarating. But even that thrill paled in comparison to the woman flying beside me.

Suddenly, a deep, rumbling voice echoed in my mind. *"If you two don't stop making goo-goo eyes at each other, I might just barrel roll and dump you both off."*

I chuckled, recognizing Eryndor's dry humor. *"Jealous, old friend?"*

Vaelith's musical laughter chimed in. *"Oh, please, Eryndor. You're just cranky because it's been a century since you've gotten any action."*

"I'll have you know I'm perfectly content with my solitude," Eryndor grumbled, though I caught the faint edge of indignation in his tone.

Olivia's amused voice joined the exchange. *"Now, now, children. Play nice."*

I glanced her way, catching her teasing grin, and we shared a private smile. The easy banter with the dragons filled my heart with warmth. This wasn't just a kingdom or a mission; this was a family we'd built, with bonds stronger than steel.

"Don't worry," I sent back to them with a smirk. *"We'll behave... for now."*

A chorus of groans echoed in our minds, and I couldn't help but laugh out loud. Olivia's giggles joined mine, the sound like sunlight breaking through the tension that had shadowed us for weeks.

As we approached Vesparra, the towering silhouette of the castle came into view. Its jagged spires rose like protective sentinels from the mountainside, familiar and imposing. The dragons began their descent, wings angling to carry us gracefully into the courtyard below.

Vaelith's voice was thick with teasing mischief as he spoke. *"Try not to tear each other's clothes off before you reach your chambers."*

I laughed, the sound light and genuine. Olivia, ever unbothered, winked at the dragon. *"No promises."*

The moment our feet hit the ground, the courtyard's buzz of activity enveloped us. Servants darted about with purpose, arms laden with weapons, armor, and provisions. The air was thick with tension and resolve, the hum of preparation for the battle we knew was coming.

A breathless messenger approached, bowing quickly before addressing us. "Your Majesties—"

I nodded briskly as Olivia waved off the messenger. "Later," she said, her tone leaving no room for argument. The messenger hesitated, but Olivia's eyes flicked to him, and he scurried off, sensing she meant exactly what she'd said.

We made our way up the familiar stone steps leading to the family wing of the castle. As we climbed, Olivia's hand slipped into mine, her warmth infusing me with calm amidst the storm of emotions brewing in my chest.

"Ready?" she asked softly when we reached our private quarters, her eyes fierce and determined, the fire in them echoing the strength of the woman I loved.

"With you by my side? Always."

I barely registered the heavy oak door slamming shut behind us as we stumbled into our chambers, my hands already working feverishly at the clasps of Olivia's riding leathers. Her fingers tangled in my hair, pulling me down for a searing kiss that ignited my blood.

"Goddess, I need you," I growled against her lips, my fingers deftly peeling away her top. The sight of her breasts, rising and falling with each ragged breath, sent a sharp pulse through me.

Olivia's laughter was breathless as she tugged at my clothing. "Goddess, if you don't take me... We've waited long enough."

I couldn't agree more. With a growl, I lifted her, her legs instinctively wrapping around my waist as I carried her to the adjoining bathing chamber. The ornate shower beckoned with its promise of privacy and warmth, and I wasted no time in activating the knobs. Steaming water cascaded over us, enveloping us in a mist of heat.

"Ohh!" Olivia gasped, arching into me as the warm streams

caressed her curves. I pressed her against the cool tile wall, the contrast of sensations—her heated skin under my palms, the rising steam, the water's rhythm matching the frantic beat of my heart—was intoxicating.

My lips found the curve of her neck, tasting the water mingled with the salt of her skin. "You're magnificent," I murmured, letting my hands explore the contours of her body. "So strong, so fierce…"

Olivia's fingers dug into my shoulders as she ground against me, her voice teasing yet laced with urgency. "Less talkin', more action, Highness."

I chuckled, nipping at her collarbone. "As my lady commands."

I ran my hands down her water-slicked body as her feet hit the floor, my hand reaching between her legs. My mouth was still on hers.

"Always so fucking wet for me, aren't you, Starlight? If I could have misted over onto Vaelith's back and reached into your leathers, I'd have found this pussy dripping for me, wouldn't I?" I asked as my fingers entered her, feeling her tight heat.

"Ahh, yes, you would have! Of course, you… ahh… would have with… oh yes, right there… all the dirty feelings you kept sendin'… mmm, through the… ahh… bond!"

I licked along her neck while I replaced my fingers with my impossibly hard erection. I moved in and out of her, slowly at first until my thrusts became demanding.

"Cade, you feel so good."

"I'm going to bite you, my love."

"I wish you would."

"You are such a dirty girl, aren't you, Starlight? So fucking dirty, and so very fucking mine."

My fangs elongated, and I bit down, drinking deeply while injecting her with venom at the same time.

"OH GODDESS! Highness, yes, yes, I love that so much. Love

you, so much."

Her body quaked and shuddered with her beautiful release, and I found my own immediately after. I eased my fangs from her neck, sealing the bite marks with a gentle lick.

"Starlight, you are exquisite. You're always beautiful, but never more so than when you come."

As I lost myself in Olivia's embrace, a part of me awestruck at the vulnerability she allowed me to see. This woman who commanded dragons, who had faced down monsters and tyrants, trembled in my arms with need and trust. It humbled me, even as it stoked the fire of my desire to protect her, to cherish her, to give her everything she deserved.

I wrapped Olivia in a plush towel, my touch gentle as I patted her skin dry. The urgency of our lovemaking had faded, replaced by a tender reverence that made my chest ache. I traced the scars on her back, a testament to her past battles and her enduring strength.

"You're staring," Olivia murmured, a shy smile playing on her lips.

I met her gaze in the mirror, drinking in the sight of her damp hair curling around her face, her eyes soft with contentment. "Can you blame me? You're breathtaking."

She leaned back against my chest, and I enfolded her in my arms. "I never thought I'd have this," she whispered, vulnerability lacing her words. "Someone who sees me—all of me—and still wants to stay."

I pressed a kiss to her temple. "I'm not going anywhere, my love. You're stuck with me."

Olivia turned in my arms, her expression suddenly serious. "Promise me something, Cade."

"Anything."

"When we face Magda... don't let your guard down. I couldn't bear to lose you."

I cupped her face, my thumb tracing her cheekbone. "We'll face her together. And we'll win."

As Olivia nodded, determination replacing the fear in her eyes, I sent up a silent prayer to the Goddess Vesperia. Let me be worthy of this woman's love. Let me have the strength to protect her, to stand by her side as she faces whatever comes.

CHAPTER 31

Callie

Tired. So Tired. How much pain can a person endure? Apparently a lot. And the darkness, it's almost as bad. Now I know how Olivia must have felt being thrown in that hole when she was a little girl. Poor Olivia. Poor Callie. I slumped against the jagged obsidian wall of my prison, my muscles burned with exhaustion and pain. Every breath was a struggle, the air thick with decay and the nauseating stench of dark magic. I felt like I was reaching the end of my resolve, but I'd fight on.

"Poor little Callie," Magda's voice sliced through the silence, dripping with mockery and venom. "Are you ready to give in yet?"

I forced my head up, meeting her gaze with every ounce of defiance I could muster. "Never," I rasped, though the word barely made it past my cracked lips.

Her blood-red lips curled into a cruel smile as she stepped closer. I really hated the sound of her stupid shoes clicking against the black stone floor. In an instant, her manicured hand shot out, gripping my chin with a force that belied her flawless appearance.

"Such spirit," she drawled, tilting her head as if examining an exotic specimen. "I'm almost impressed. Watching you resist is... gratifying. Watching you break will be exquisite."

I wrenched my head away, though the effort sent a fresh wave of agony tearing through my body. I bit down on my lip to stifle a scream, tasting blood as Magda's magic coiled around me like barbed wire, digging in with every pulse of her power.

She began circling me, her dark gown trailing behind her like a living shadow. "Why resist?" she mused, her tone almost conversational. "Your precious Olivia isn't coming for you. No one is. You're alone, pathetic girl. But serve me, and I'll make you powerful beyond your wildest dreams. Power like hers—no, greater."

Her words slithered into my mind, a poison designed to corrupt the cracks in my resolve. For one fleeting moment, the temptation flickered—an end to the pain, the promise of strength. But then the image of Olivia filled my thoughts, her laughter, her determination, her light. She hadn't given up on me. She wouldn't.

"I'd rather die," I croaked, my voice trembled with the effort.

Magda's serene façade cracked, a snarl twisting her beautiful face into something monstrous. Her grip on my chin tightened, nails biting into my skin.

"Oh, but you see, Callie girl," she hissed, leaning closer, her breath a chilling whisper against my cheek. "That can't happen. You *can't* die. But you *can* suffer. And suffer you *will* until you beg for mercy I'll never give."

Her words barely registered before another wave of dark magic surged through me, igniting every nerve with white-hot agony. My body arched against the unyielding stone, a scream clawing its way from my throat.

Through the haze of torment, I clung to a single memory—the warmth of sunlight on my face, the laughter of friends, the stubborn spark of hope.

Hold on, I told myself, the thought as fragile as a flickering candle. *For Olivia. For Eldoria. You can endure this. You have to.*

A flicker of movement caught my eye, pulling me away

from the agony of Magda's relentless torment. In the shadows beyond her obsidian throne, I glimpsed Eldric's face. His piercing green eyes found mine, and for a moment, everything else faded. He gave an almost imperceptible nod, a silent promise that sent a spark of hope surging through my chest.

"When the time is right, I'll help you escape. Be ready."

His words echoed in my mind like a lifeline. I swallowed hard, fighting to steady my breathing as a surge of conflicting emotions churned in my gut. Could I trust him? Eldric was as much a prisoner of the Underworld as I was, yet his motives remained cloaked in shadows.

"What are you looking at, little mouse?" Magda's voice sliced through my thoughts, sharp and laced with suspicion. She whirled around, her gown of inky black fabric flowing like liquid night as her gaze raked the darkness.

My heart thundered in my chest. Forcing my focus back to her, I summoned the last dregs of composure. "Nothing," I rasped, the sound brittle against the oppressive silence. "Just... wishing I could see the sun again."

Magda's lips curled into a slow, venomous smile. "Oh, you poor, pathetic thing," she purred, tilting her head as if to mock my pain. "Still dreaming of escape?" Her hand reached for me, icy fingers tracing along my jawline. The sensation burned like frostbite, leaving a trail of sharp, numbing pain. "Give in to me, and I'll show you wonders beyond imagining. Power beyond anything you've ever dared to dream."

I clenched my jaw, forcing myself to meet her gaze even as her magic scraped against my defenses. "Never," I whispered, though my voice trembled under the weight of her power. Deep inside, cracks formed in the fragile armor of my resolve.

Magda's expression twisted, her beautiful features contorting with fury. Her magic surged, a dark tide pressing harder against my mind and body, suffocating and insidious.

Just as my knees threatened to buckle under the onslaught, Eldric's voice rang out, sharp and commanding, cutting through the oppressive haze like a beacon of light.

"Now, Callie!"

Without thinking, I reached deep within myself, grasping at the tattered remnants of my magic. It responded sluggishly at first, weak and fractured, but it was still there—alive and thrumming with desperate determination.

Magda's head snapped toward me, her eyes blazing with fury. "What are you doing?" she shrieked, the power in her voice rattling the very walls of the chamber.

I didn't answer. I couldn't. Every ounce of will I had left was focused on the spell forming in my mind. I felt the magic surge, chaotic and raw, as it twisted through me. The air around us grew thick with energy, crackling like a summer storm about to break. A blinding light erupted between us, sending waves of searing heat rippling outward.

"No!" Magda howled, her voice a mix of rage and disbelief. She lunged forward, dark tendrils of power reaching for me.

But it was too late. With a sound like a thousand mirrors shattering, the rift tore open, a swirling vortex of wild, uncontrollable magic. Through the churning rift, glimpses of another world flashed—sunlit trees swaying in a breeze, a sky painted with gold and lavender, and the distant clash of steel against monstrous roars.

I staggered toward the rift, my legs trembling and my vision swimming. My lungs burned with every breath, but I forced myself forward, the pull of freedom stronger than the agony coursing through me.

Behind me, Magda's scream of rage echoed through the chamber. "You'll regret this, Callie! I'll hunt you to the ends of the realm!"

I didn't look back. I couldn't. Just as I reached the rift's edge, my gaze caught Eldric's across the chaos. His expression was unreadable, a storm of emotions flickering in his green eyes—triumph, fear, and something deeper that made my heart ache.

Creatures poured through the now open rift. I hated we

couldn't stop them. But this was our only chance.

I plunged into the rift, the swirling light and sound swallowing me whole.

The world spun violently as the rift slammed shut behind us; the force sending me sprawling onto hard ground. My ears rang with the deafening clash of steel against fang, monstrous roars blending with the shouts of battle. The acrid stench of blood, sulfur, and magic hung thick in the air.

I tried to push myself up, but my strength failed me. My legs buckled, and I collapsed onto my hands and knees, gasping for air.

"Callie!" Eldric's voice cut through the chaos. In an instant, his powerful arms were around me, lifting me effortlessly from the ground.

"Hold on," he growled, his voice steady and commanding as his gaze scanned the battlefield. The tension in his jaw betrayed his urgency. "We're not safe yet."

He pressed me tightly against his chest, his body a shield between me and the nightmare surrounding us. I clung to him as he ran, his strides unyielding despite the chaos erupting all around.

Creatures born of the Underworld swarmed the field, their twisted forms tearing through soldiers wielding magic of all kinds. Firecasters hurled searing flames at beasts with charred, blackened hides. Swords clanged against talons the size of daggers. The ground itself seemed alive with battle, trembling beneath the weight of war.

I forced my head up, my blurry gaze locking onto the horizon. The sunlight filtering through the trees was dazzling after the suffocating darkness of the Underworld. But even amidst the carnage, it felt like hope.

"Almost there," Eldric muttered, his grip on me tightening. "Just a little longer."

I didn't know where "there" was, but I trusted him. For now, he was the only solid thing in a world of chaos, and I clung to that lifeline with everything I had left.

Almost. The word echoed in my mind as I clung to Eldric, too weak to do anything else. My body ached, my spirit drained from Magda's torment and the magic I'd expended to open the rift. But we weren't safe yet.

A beast lunged at us, a mass of razor-sharp teeth and matted fur, its soulless eyes locked onto me. Eldric pivoted sharply, narrowly avoiding its snapping jaws. The air crackled as he flung out his free hand, a burst of dark energy erupting from his palm. The creature yelped as it was hurled backward, crashing into another monstrosity.

"Dammit," he hissed, his green eyes darting across the chaos. "There are too many."

I forced my eyes open, though my vision blurred at the edges. The battlefield was a nightmare come to life—soldiers of every magical kind clashing with Magda's twisted creations. The golden gleam of armor shone like a beacon against the writhing mass of beasts, a stark reminder of the stakes.

"The gates," I rasped, my voice barely audible. I managed to lift a trembling hand, pointing ahead. "We're close."

Eldric glanced in the direction I showed, nodding tightly. "Just a little further. You did well, cousin. Rest now."

His pace quickened, each stride measured and powerful as we outpaced the creatures, snapping at our heels. My head lolled against his chest, the steady beat of his heart settling me amid the chaos.

"Thank the Goddess," I whispered as the towering city gates loomed before us.

Eldric sprinted the final distance, his dark power flaring as a monstrous shape lunged from the shadows. The gate guards shouted warnings, the massive doors groaning as they began to close behind us. He crossed the threshold just in time, the heavy slam of the gates reverberating through the air as they sealed out the worst of Magda's horde.

The sounds of battle receded, muffled by the walls, though

the tension in the air remained sharp as a blade. Eldric carried me a few more steps before lowering me gently to the cobbled ground just inside the gates. He propped me up against the wall, his hands steadying me as I struggled to keep my eyes open.

"Thank you," I murmured, my voice thin. My fingers found his hand, grasping it weakly. "For keeping your promise."

A flicker of something—regret? guilt?—passed over his face, there and gone in an instant. He kneeled beside me, his piercing green eyes softer than I'd ever seen them. "Rest now, Callie. You're safe. But I must leave. I have to find Olivia and explain why I'm here." He hesitated, his jaw tightening. "And hope she doesn't kill me before I get the chance to say I'm sorry."

My grip on his hand tightened slightly. "She'll listen," I whispered. "She'll understand."

He shook his head, a bitter smile tugging at his lips. "I don't deserve her forgiveness, or yours. But I'll try, anyway." He stood, his broad shoulders silhouetted against the torchlight. "Goddess speed, cousin."

"Goddess speed," I echoed faintly, exhaustion pulling me under as he slipped back through the gates, disappearing into the night.

Ignis

The roar of battle drew closer, a deafening symphony of chaos and destruction, and I knew I couldn't hesitate any longer. My people needed me. My kingdom needed me. I sprinted toward the city gates, the weight of duty pressing against my chest with every step.

As I rounded the corner, a figure on the ground brought me to a sudden, jarring halt. A woman lay crumpled in the dirt, her blonde hair tangled and streaked with blood and grime. Something deep within me—primal and ancient—shifted. It was as though the very core of my being had been struck, and an invisible cord pulled me toward her.

My feet moved without thought, drawing me to her side. I dropped to my knees, my breath catching as I took in her fragile form.

"By the sun's fire," I breathed, reaching out with trembling hands.

The moment my skin touched hers, a jolt of searing heat surged through me. My vision blurred, the world tilting violently before snapping into sharp focus. It was impossible. My chest heaved as I tried to make sense of the impossible truth unraveling before me.

Goddess, help me. This broken, beautiful woman lying in the dirt was my True Fated Mate.

The revelation hit like a thunderclap, shaking the very foundations of my existence. I stared down at her, cradling her face with a reverence I didn't know I possessed. Her features, delicate even in her battered state, stirred something fierce and unrelenting within me.

"Who *are* you?" I whispered, my voice hoarse, raw with disbelief and awe.

Her eyelids fluttered, revealing eyes so green they put the lush vineyards of Aurelion to shame. My breath hitched.

"Callie," she murmured, her voice a fragile thread of sound, barely audible.

Her name settled in my chest like a brand. Callie. The one I'd never expected. The one who would change everything.

The name echoed in my mind, resonating with a truth I couldn't deny. Every fiber of my being screamed to protect her, to shelter her from harm. But as I took in her features—so clearly not Aurelion—an icy dread coiled in my stomach.

"This can't be," I muttered, even as my hands gently probed for injuries. "You're not... you can't be..."

Her eyes fluttered open, unfocused at first, then narrowing on me. A flicker of recognition sparked in their green depths, but before she could speak, a violent cough wracked her body.

"Shh, don't speak," I urged, the protective instincts of the mate bond clashing with the rigid voice of duty in my mind. "You're safe now."

Safe. The word felt hollow as I said it. Was she truly safe? This woman—my mate—was so obviously not of Aurelion. Everything I'd been taught, everything I believed about our kingdom's isolation and superiority, now seemed paper-thin in the face of this undeniable connection.

"I need to get you to the healers," I said firmly, carefully lifting her into my arms.

Her body was impossibly light, and yet, the weight of my choice felt crushing. My people needed me in this battle, their leader, to defend them from the creatures pouring through the rifts. But this woman—Callie—needed me, too.

"What am I going to do with you?" I whispered, more to myself than to her.

Her icy fingers trembled as they clutched weakly at the front of my tunic. "Don't... leave..." she pleaded, her voice barely audible.

My chest tightened, the mate bond roaring its demands, pulling me toward her like a magnetic force I couldn't resist. How could I leave her when every instinct screamed to stay? But how could I stay when my people were fighting for their lives?

I clenched my jaw, burying the rising tide of emotions. "I won't," I murmured, though the promise felt heavier than steel.

Callie's gaze softened briefly before exhaustion claimed her, and her eyes fluttered closed.

I moved quickly, weaving through the narrow, cobbled streets of Aurelion with her cradled against me. The pull of the mate bond hummed insistently, urging me to cherish her, to never let go. And yet, with every step, the weight of my duty as a leader bore down on me.

"Stay with me," I murmured, feeling her grip on

consciousness slipping like sand through my fingers.

"I... don't understand," Callie whispered, her eyes fluttering weakly. "Why do I feel...?"

I swallowed hard, my throat dry. "It's the mate bond. We're... connected."

Her brow furrowed, confusion clouding her gaze. "Who are you?"

"Ignis. The king of Aurelion."

"You're Aurelion." Her words were soft, unsteady, not fully grasping the weight of what she said.

"And you're not," I replied, the admission bitter on my tongue. "Which makes this impossible."

We reached the healers' tent, a chaotic flurry of motion as the wounded poured in, bloodied and broken from the battle beyond the gates. I carefully laid Callie on an empty cot, my hands lingering against her too-cold skin longer than I should have.

"My lord," a healer approached, her gaze darting between us. "Who is this?"

I hesitated, the words catching in my throat, before I straightened and forced an answer. "A refugee. Tend to her wounds."

Callie's eyes widened, a flicker of hurt cutting through the haze of exhaustion. "You're leaving?"

My chest tightened, the weight of her question nearly undoing me. "I must. My people—"

"Need you," she finished for me, her voice trembling as a tear slid down her dirt-streaked cheek. "I understand."

But she didn't. How could she? How could she know the torment ripping through me, the impossible choice between duty and the bond that already felt like it had seared itself into my soul?

I turned away, unable to bear the sight of her pain—pain I was causing. "I'm sorry," I whispered, my words barely audible, and strode out of the tent.

The sounds of battle swallowed me as I approached the gates. Flare arrows streaked across the sky, their fiery arcs illuminating the carnage below. The ground trembled with the detonation of Runestones of Resonance, and the air crackled with the electric hum of magic. My people fought valiantly, their shouts of defiance rising above the monstrous roars of Magda's horde.

But for how long could they hold the line?

I summoned my fire, feeling its heat roar to life within me, wild and powerful, matching the rhythm of my conflicted heart. As flames danced along my hands, Callie's face burned in my mind. Her emerald eyes, her whispered plea, the spark of the bond I was denying.

I'd turned my back on her. On us.

But how could I embrace a future that defied everything I'd been taught, every belief woven into the fabric of my life, of my peoples' lives?

The gates swung open with a groan of iron, revealing the chaos beyond. I stepped forward, into duty.

Into fire.

Into an uncertain future, where the flames of war and the embers of forbidden love threatened to consume us all.

THANK YOU

From the bottom of my heart, thank you for reading Starlight & Luna Rising. I know there's an endless number of fantasy worlds and countless authors you could have chosen, and yet, you chose to continue on this journey with me. That means more than I can possibly put into words.

Being a brand-new author, with this being only my second book, every bit of support matters. Your decision to spend your time in Eldoria, to follow these characters through their struggles and triumphs, means everything to me. Your encouragement fuels the magic that keeps these worlds alive.

If you enjoyed this story, I have a small favor to ask. Reviews are absolutely vital for new authors like me. Your thoughts whether it's a few simple words or a more in-depth review, can help this book reach new readers and keep these adventures going strong.

Every page, every twist, and every battle was written with you in mind. Thank you for choosing to walk this path with me. I hope to see you back in Eldoria some time after the first of the year for Book 3!

With all my gratitude and love,

Dex

About The Author

I'm Dex Haven, a romance author nestled in a small town in central Texas—where my dreams take flight. I'm living my own insta-love story (and have for several decades after saying "yes" to my true mate after knowing him for only 2 weeks). I create fantasy stories that brim with love, adventure, and a good amount of spice. I believe a good romance novel can reignite that essential spark, rekindle passion and remind you to cherish your own desires. Through my stories, I hope to take you away on an expedition, leaving you enchanted—and maybe even a little fired up along the way.

Whether you're here for the adventure, the love story, or the heat, I hope my books offer you a place to escape, dream, and rediscover the magic within yourself.

Follow me on Facebook - Dex Haven Author for a look at character images, news and some fun stuff that's on the horizon. This also is where you'll get the first looks at Book 3 also.

KINGDOMS OF ELDORIA

Born in the mortal realm with no memory of her past, Olivia thought she was ordinary—until her 25th birthday shattered that illusion. Her dormant magic awakened, her fate was revealed, and she was pulled into the realm of Eldoria, a world she belonged to but never knew.

There, she discovered she is more than mortal. More than an heir to a lost kingdom. And according to an ancient prophecy, she is the key to saving her world.

But darkness has risen. Magda, the Goddess of the Underworld, seeks claim Eldoria for herself. To stop her, the five kingdoms —Fire and Sun, Water and Ice, Earth and Wind, Shifters, and Blood and Shadows—must work together, combining their magic to have any chance to stop her.

But unity is easier said than done. Prejudices run deep. Betrayals cut deeper. And not every kingdom has the will to join the fight.

At the heart of it all is Olivia, who must come to terms with her true identity, her growing powers, and her connection to King Cadeence of Vesparra, her Fated Mate. Their love will strengthen her—but love alone may not be enough to win this war. Legends will awaken. Armies will rise. And before it's over, Olivia's ability to control the ancient dragons, wyverns, and Pegasi of Eldoria will take her on a journey she never imagined. Will she find the strength to be the Chosen One she was born to be?

ach book in the trilogy follows Olivia's journey along with the journeys of her sister Amaya, her best friend Callie, and other family and friends she comes to know and love.

Love will be tested. Bonds will be broken. Legends will be reborn.
Will they rise together—or fall divided?

For fans of epic fantasy romance, fated mates, found family, and unforgettable battles, the Kingdoms of Eldoria Trilogy is an adventure of love, power, and destiny.

Claiming Starlight: Book 1

Her birthright stolen, her heart torn—Olivia never knew she was destined to change the fate of a realm she didn't even know existed.

When Olivia's world shatters after discovering her true heritage, she finds herself thrust into a kingdom teetering on the brink of war. Eldric, a power-hungry sorcerer, demands her submission, believing her magic will make him unstoppable. But Olivia has chosen her own path—and the dangerously captivating vampire king, Cadence Vesparra, stands at its center.

As dark forces close in and her own power threatens to consume her, Olivia must choose: embrace her destiny, or risk losing everything—including her chance at a love powerful enough to shake realms.

Made in the USA
Coppell, TX
16 February 2025

46031632R00184